A
Step
Beyond

A
Step
Beyond

C. K. Anderson

iPUBLISH.com
at Time Warner Books

For information address iPublish.com, 135 West 50th Street, New York, NY
10020.

An AOL Time Warner Company

ISBN 0-7595-5031-X

First edition: October 2001

Visit our website at www.iPublish.com

Contents

Contents

Acknowledgments

I am deeply indebted to George Herbert, Frank Crary, Ralph Lorenz, David Knapp, John Childers, David Palmer, Filip De Vos, and Frank Scrooby for their technical advice. Any errors that the reader may encounter are entirely mine. I'm also indebted to family members and friends for their careful reading and much-appreciated comments. To Paul Witcover, my editor and good friend, for his tireless efforts and invaluable advice. And to Cynthia, my wife, for her support, strength, love, and tolerance.

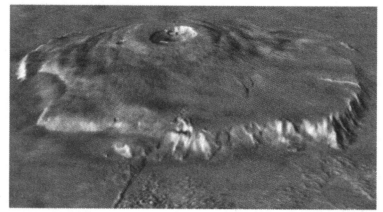

Olympus Mons, at 24 kilometers high and 600 kilometers in diameter, the largest volcano in the Solar System: site of the American landing.

Candor Chasma, part of the Valles Marineris canyon system, which spans over 3000 kilometers of the Martian surface: site of the Russian landing.

Earth is the cradle of mankind,
but one cannot live in the cradle forever.

KONSTANTIN TSIOLKOVSKY

The Russian Attempt

Mission commander Colonel Alexander Titov, strapped loosely to the ceiling, hung suspended inside the billowing fabric of his sleep restraint. Beneath him was a small desk, upon which he had taped a picture of his wife and two children. A faint glow from the computer display provided just enough light for him to see the pale blue sky of Kazakhstan and a silhouette of his family standing hand in hand upon its arid steppes. His gaze remained fixed upon the picture as he reached behind his head to adjust the volume of the communications channel. Cosmonaut Sergei Demin was transmitting the daily report. He could be heard sipping his coffee while he paused every few minutes to review the material he was about to read.

The silhouettes of Titov's children were half the size of his wife, and they were waving at him. His youngest child was only two years old. She would be four when he returned from Mars. The thought pained him, but he told himself—as he had countless times before—that the mission was too important to have passed up. His son had just learned how to ride a bike. He was about to turn five and wanted to be a cosmonaut, just like his father. Although Titov spoke with his family almost every night, the eleven-minute delay made it impossible to interact with them.

A rattling snore came from the adjacent compartment, where research engineer Boris Gorbatko was sound asleep. Commander Titov considered banging on the wall, but he knew from experience that it would do no good. Gorbatko would only stop until he fell back asleep, which never took more than a few minutes.

The habitat module contained six personal compartments identical in size and layout to Titov's, five of which were occupied. It was in the tight confines of these compartments that the cosmonauts enjoyed their only privacy. The module was located at the rear of the spacecraft. Above the hallway that separated the compartments hung the galley. There was no table or chairs, only an oven, a water dispenser, and several drawers of prepackaged food. At the back of the module was the personal-hygiene facility. At the other end was a portal. It was secured. Beyond it lay the health and science module. Through a view panel in the upper quadrant of the portal, assorted equipment could be seen protruding from the walls. At the far end another portal, also secured, led to the flight deck, the foremost cabin of the ship.

At 3:43 A.M. Moscow time a meteoroid less than one inch in diameter, traveling at a speed of thirteen miles per second, pierced the hull of the flight deck and struck a liquid-oxygen tank. The tank exploded.

The blast ripped through the side of the hull and into the flight deck. Cosmonaut Demin had just finished his third cup of coffee and was reaching for his laptop, which was somersaulting at arm's length from his nose, when he saw the flash. The explosion picked his body up and slammed it against the portal. His head struck the metallic rim of the view panel. He died instantly.

The environmental-control sensors detected a drop in the oxygen level and opened the valve controlling the remaining tank several nanoseconds before the heat and smoke detectors alerted the main processor to the presence of fire. Before instructions to shut down the oxygen supply could arrive, a stream of pure oxygen had entered the cabin. Fueled by the fresh supply of gas, the fire raced voraciously toward the source. There was a second explosion. A swirling fireball engulfed the flight deck. The flight-control panel burst apart, sending shrapnel into the surrounding walls and Demin's dead body. A closed-circuit monitor and two computer screens exploded. The circuitry for the main processor melted under the intense heat. A chair went up in flames. Wires stretched out from the naked consoles and shot sparks as they collided. Another chair caught fire. The entire compartment was in flames, then suddenly the fire was drawn by the vacuum through the rupture in the side of the hull. The room went dark.

The trajectory of the *Volnost* was altered by the explosion, causing it to veer away from the unmanned supply ship. Both ships had been in space for six months. The date was October 11, 2017, and the Russians were attempting the first manned trip to Mars. They were better than halfway to their destination.

Commander Alexander Titov rose to his elbows at the sound of the first explosion. As he twisted his head to check the monitors above him, he was thrown suddenly against the compartment walls, bashing his head and nearly breaking his nose. A rush of adrenaline drowned the pain. The general alarm sounded.

Dazed, Titov checked the monitors, where the messages FLIGHT DECK—O PRESSURE and FLIGHT DECK—FIRE were flashing red. He coughed to clear his throat as he extracted himself from his sleep restraint. Before releasing the safety latch of his compartment, he verified that the pressure in the habitat module was one hundred kilopascals, standard sea level. It appeared that only the flight deck had been affected.

Colonel Titov was the first to emerge into the open space of the habitat module. The yellow lights of the emergency system cast ghostly shadows about the room. Pushing with his legs, he propelled himself toward the control panel, where he switched to the emergency oxygen supply and strapped a portable oxygen mask to his head. Just then, Mikhail Chertok, the ship's pilot, sprang half-dressed from his compartment. "What the hell's going on?"

Titov pointed toward the oxygen masks, then flipped the switch to the electrical backup system. The shadows faded as white light filled the cabin.

Chertok watched as his commander threw several more switches. He was activating emergency backup systems that had not come automatically on-line. The computer monitor blinked brightly. Within seconds, the local processor had booted and prompted for instructions. Titov attempted to access the main processor but failed as the message SYSTEM UNAVAILABLE flashed on the screen.

"Check the portal," directed Titov, his eyes fixed on the monitor while he tapped at the keyboard.

As Chertok pushed his way toward the portal, the other three cosmonauts tumbled from their sleeping compartments, disheveled and confused. Squinting from the sudden change in light, the cosmonauts surveyed their surroundings. They were relieved to find the cabin intact, but they were still fearful. Titov turned to address them.

The sight of the oxygen mask, attached like a spidery creature to Titov's face, heightened their fears. The commander motioned for the others to don their masks.

"There has been an explosion on the flight deck," began Titov. "The extent of the damage is unknown. I am unable to access the primary computer. The emergency warning system indicates there is a fire in the forward cabin, and the pressure is zero kp's. I cannot verify this." He pointed at the console behind him. "Boris, I want the main processor back on-line."

"Commander," Mikhail Chertok said as he peered through the portal, "the laboratory does not appear to be damaged. I can't see beyond the second portal—everything is dark. I should be able to see some light."

"Not necessarily," Titov replied. "The emergency lights may be too dim to see from here."

Chertok and the others knew this to be false, but said nothing. It was unlike Titov to be less than truthful. A terrible silence followed as they slowly realized that something else was wrong.

"Where is Sergei?" Boris Gorbatko asked finally.

Surprised, they all looked around to verify that Sergei was indeed not with them. All except for Colonel Titov, who stood perfectly still as he observed and noted each reaction.

"He was on the flight deck," said Titov, when their gazes eventually returned to him.

———————

Eleven minutes after the explosion, Cosmonaut Sergei Demin disappeared from the screen that dominated the front wall of the Russian Space Agency's control room. The sudden shift in brightness was enough to divert Yuri Tretyak's attention from the environmental data on his monitor. FLIGHT DECK—0 PRESSURE flashed across the main screen. Moments later an alarm sounded as the second message FLIGHT DECK—FIRE appeared. Tretyak did not immediately grasp the meaning of the messages. He stood up. His throat went dry, and he was unable to swallow. He looked down at the controls on his panel and keyed in the instructions to bring up the flight deck transmission. Nothing happened. He read the messages again, and as he read, it occurred to him that perhaps Demin was dead. He had been on the flight deck. It occurred to Tretyak that the others might also be dead. He was growing frightened. The main screen went blank. Several of the smaller screens were flashing red.

A numbness enveloped his body as he realized they had lost contact with the *Volnost*. He looked to his colleagues for an explanation. They had risen to their feet and were staring dumbfounded at the blank screen. It was the rising pitch of the alarm that finally startled Tretyak into action.

"Oleg, try to contact the cosmonauts," he said to the communications engineer. "I must call Schebalin."

"What does it mean?" asked one of the scientists.

As Tretyak dialed the operations director, his mind raced with possibilities. He knew that even a small mishap could be fatal, and with the craft several million kilometers from Earth there was little hope of rescue. If they were not already dead, they would almost certainly soon be. But he mustn't jump to conclusions. He was overreacting, he told himself. He must be. But what if he weren't? This was to be Russia's greatest technological and political triumph, the crowning glory of the New Republic. Details of the mission were being publicized worldwide. A disaster now would be a major political embarrassment. Tretyak felt ashamed. The political consequences should be secondary.

The phone rang several times before Colonel Leonid Schebalin answered. Schebalin was the operations director for the Mars mission and the second Russian to walk on the moon; difficulties with his inner ear as a result of a cold contracted during his last flight in space had scrubbed him permanently from the program. Until then, he had been the primary candidate for mission commander of the Mars flight.

"Yes," he said, tired and disoriented.

"Sir," began Tretyak, "we have a problem here."

"Who is this?" Schebalin asked drowsily.

"Yuri Tretyak at mission control."

"Yes, Yuri, what is it?"

"Sir, something has gone wrong. We received a telemetry from *Volnost* several minutes ago indicating a fire and loss of pressure on the flight deck. Then all transmissions ceased. I called you immediately." Tretyak struggled to maintain a professional tone. The other scientists were crowding around him. He closed his eyes and waited for Schebalin to speak.

"Who knows about this?"

Tretyak was momentarily taken aback by the coldness in the colonel's voice. "Just the men on duty. You were the first person we called."

"Good. It would be unfortunate if this matter reached the press before we were able to determine the extent of the damage; if indeed there is a problem and this is not simply a computer malfunction. We must determine the facts before we release them. It is imperative that you alert no one else. Do you understand?"

"Yes, sir," Tretyak replied automatically.

"Good. I will notify the appropriate people from here. Have you attempted to contact the cosmonauts?"

"Yes, sir. We're still waiting for their reply."

"Very well. I will be there within thirty minutes." Schebalin disconnected the line with a sharp tap. He could sense his pulse quickening. He had spent the last eight years working directly with the cosmonauts, and he counted them among his closest friends. But, he knew, his first responsibility was to the Republic.

Boris Gorbatko, his hair disarrayed like a mad scientist's (a comparison he would find flattering), viewed the screen with his head slightly cocked. The keys clicked rapidly under his long fingers as he grumbled at the data that scrolled before him. His attempts to access the main processor had failed.

"The main computer is most likely down," he said while typing, "although I can't be certain. Whenever I attempt to access it, the comm line returns a disconnected status. The fiber optics may have been severed. The only way to find out is physically to trace the wire. The closed-circuit cameras in the forward cabin are out." He motioned upward with his eyebrows. "On monitors three and four is the external view, nothing unusual there, but then the cameras were not designed to scan that sector of the hull. The environmental monitors are dead. I am unable to verify the zero-kp reading or the fire. There was definitely an explosion, however. We are several degrees off course."

"Comm status?" asked Titov.

"I have built a circuit that bypasses the main processor and feeds directly to the high-gain antenna. We are receiving the signal from the tracking satellite. Kaliningrad should know about the explosion by now, but it is still too soon to receive their response," he said, looking up from his watch. "We should be able to transmit."

"Patch me in for a downlink." Titov pushed himself toward a free terminal. Eleven minutes before Earth would receive this transmission, he thought, and another eleven minutes before he would receive a reply—a total of twenty-two minutes, plus the time it would take for ground control to assess the situation and decide upon a course of action. The last environmental telemetry might have alerted them to the problem, hopefully reducing their reaction time. That would be helpful, but he doubted it would be enough. Time was short. He looked into the small lens of the camera above the monitor and cleared his throat.

"There has been an explosion on the flight deck," he said. "The module lost pressure and might be on fire. The midcabin and aft cabin appear undamaged. The main computer is down. We are still in the process of determining the extent of the damage. Lieutenant Colonel Demin was on the flight deck at the time of the explosion. It is unlikely that he survived. Please advise."

Titov shut down the link and turned to Chertok, the ship's pilot. "We shall commence our investigation while we wait for their response. The first step will be to enter the midcabin. Since the risks are unknown, only one person will go. I want that person to be you. Any objections?"

"I will go."

"Good," replied Titov. "Take the hardsuit. Once you're inside the midcabin, you will perform a visual check of the flight deck. If it looks safe, reduce the pressure of the cabin to zero. You are to record the entire deck with the video camera. Miss nothing. Above all, proceed with caution. Questions?"

Chertok shook his head to indicate that he had none. "I'll need some help with the suit."

"Of course."

The hardsuit was constructed of metallic tubes and weighed 215 pounds on Earth. The tubes were joined by constant volume joints, which maintained a steady air pressure of 62 kp's, eliminating the need for prebreathing pure oxygen. Prebreathing was necessary when using a softsuit and was normally started two hours prior to extravehicular activity in order to purge nitrogen from the blood. Without this precaution, the nitrogen would bubble out and collect in the joints of the body. This condition was known as dysbarism, or the bends. Severe cases could be fatal.

As Titov assisted Chertok with the suit, he wondered if they would survive. He assumed their chances to be slim but was determined to pursue every possible course before admitting defeat. If the damage to the forward cabin was minimal, they should be able to correct the *Volnost*'s trajectory and continue to Mars. Upon their arrival they could dock with the sister ship, refuel, and conduct repairs. They would then return to Earth as soon as the launch window opened. But for that to happen, the damage had to be minimal, and given what they already knew, that did not seem likely.

"Everybody make sure your oxygen masks are secure," Titov said once he was certain the fittings of the hardsuit were properly fastened. He held Chertok by the shoulders. "Are you ready?"

"Yes," Chertok replied.

Titov opened the portal separating the aft cabin and mid-cabin, allowing Chertok to step through. Upon entering the cabin, Chertok stopped to survey his surroundings as the door closed behind him. By the dim light of the emergency lamps, he could make out the microscope on the laboratory bench to his left, and directly above him a stationary bike; the control console was to his left on the forward wall. The room was compact and for that reason had always seemed disorganized, but as far as he could tell everything was in its proper place.

He carefully made his way toward the control console. Upon reaching the console he engaged the emergency power and switched on the lights. The sound of his breathing, amplified by the silence, reverberated through his helmet as he rotated slowly. The room was hauntingly still. He spoke into his microphone.

"Everything appears to be in order, nothing damaged or disturbed. I will proceed to the forward portal."

"Be careful."

Chertok obtained a high-powered flashlight from a supply

cabinet and propelled himself in the direction of the flight deck. Although he had expected some damage, he was not at all prepared for the devastation he saw. For nearly a minute he stared in disbelief, without speaking, without hearing Titov's voice demanding a response. There was a blackened body, arms extended, floating in the middle of the room. Chertok felt a surge of nausea. He started gasping for air—and as the initial symptoms of hyperventilation seized him, he regained his senses enough to decrease the oxygen flow through his suit. He became aware of Titov's anxious voice ordering him to report.

"Sergei . . ." He swallowed and began again. "Sergei is dead. I can see his body. The flight deck console is destroyed."

"Clarify 'destroyed,' Mikhail."

"It is not there. Gone. Torn from the wall. Just a bunch of dangling wires. Hold on . . . There is a hole."

"How wide is the breach?"

"Approximately twenty centimeters in diameter."

Twenty centimeters, thought Titov. What in the world could blow a hole in the side of his hull twenty centimeters wide? A meteoroid possibly. The *Volnost* was constantly being bombarded by micrometeoroids; in fact, Russian scientists had estimated the ship would be struck over two billion times in the course of its journey by particles less than one-ten-thousandth of a gram. But the *Volnost* had an outer shell that protected it against such collisions. He estimated the object would have had to be at least a gram in size to pierce the shell. The odds were less than one in ten thousand that they would be struck by a particle that large.

It was more likely that the breach had been caused by an internal explosion, he thought. Considering the amount of time and effort expended to ensure the safety of the ship, such an explosion seemed unlikely. But not as unlikely as being struck by a meteoroid large enough to wreak this degree of havoc. The

Russian engineers had not provided him with the probability of such an occurrence, just their assurance it would not happen. It was a recognized danger, and contingency plans had been prepared, but their effectiveness depended upon the extent of the damage.

"Any indication of what may have created the hole?" Titov asked.

"It is too dark to make out much detail."

"Is the metal at the edge of the opening bent inward or outward?" Gorbatko asked. His thoughts regarding possible causes had paralleled Titov's.

"I cannot tell from here," Chertok responded.

"Commence depressurization of the cabin," Titov said.

They had the equipment and materials to patch a breach. It was a standard drill, and they had practiced it several times underwater. Titov was more disturbed by the damage to the flight-deck console. Without the console they would be unable to alter the course of the *Volnost*. He wondered how Gorbatko was progressing. Pushing against the wall, Titov propelled himself toward the engineer.

"Appears we're going to have to do without the main processor," Gorbatko said.

Titov nodded that he understood. He sat down and brought up the directory for the habitat computer. It contained many of the same files as the main processor, but was not powerful enough to perform some of the more complex functions. He was studying a schematic of the ship when an image of the forward cabin appeared on monitor one. Chertok had entered the flight deck and was scanning his surroundings with the remote video camera. The burned shell of the cabin swung back and forth on the monitor. Pieces of the console floated within a maze of twisted metal and loose wires. The camera lingered on Demin's charred remains for a moment, then turned away. Chertok located the breach. It enlarged and filled the screen as the camera zoomed in. Titov could see stars through the hole. Although he had anticipated the damage, he had not expected it to be so bad.

"Looks like the explosion was caused by an external force," Gorbatko said. "The metal of the opening is definitely bent inward."

The camera made several slow circles outside the hole, revealing sheets of twisted metal blackened by the explosion. Titov grew pale as he studied the monitor.

"I think it is the remnants of the main oxygen tank," he said. "Mikhail, if you could scan to the left. Back a little. It looks as if both tanks are gone. Boris, check the reserve tanks."

"One second," Gorbatko replied. His throat went dry. The two reserve tanks were located in the aft cabin and contained a forty-eight-hour supply of oxygen for six men. Titov had already switched over to the reserve tanks.

"Ninety-five percent full," Gorbatko replied. They were six months from Earth with less than two days' worth of air. A long minute passed in uneasy silence. Titov could see the fear building in the eyes of his men. A thought occurred to him, but in the back of his mind he wasn't sure if it would work.

"We still have a chance," he said. "It may be possible to dock with the supply ship."

He had their attention. They all knew that the supply ship had been designed to accommodate the crew in the event the *Volnost* experienced catastrophic failure.

"Without a flight deck we are unable to control the *Volnost*, but Kaliningrad can still control the supply ship. If they can bring her in close enough to dock, we could transfer over. I will contact ground control and consult with them regarding the rendezvous. They can perform the calculations to determine the feasibility. Meanwhile, we need to proceed with our investigation of the damage." He switched on his microphone. "Mikhail?"

"Yes, Colonel."

"We have less than forty-eight hours of oxygen. It is imperative that we act quickly. We need to salvage what we can, as quickly as we can. I want you to gather the necessary gear to patch the breach so that we can restore pressure to the flight deck."

"Affirmative."

Titov turned to face his crew, and said firmly, "I would appreciate any other suggestions that you may have."

Colonel Leonid Schebalin stood in the main hall of mission control with his hands clasped behind his back. He appeared to be unaware of the noise and commotion that surrounded him. His uniform was sharply pressed and crisp, his boots recently polished; despite his haste to reach mission control that morning, he had taken extra care to make himself presentable. He knew that before the day was out he would be delivering a statement to the press.

"Play back the video," ordered Schebalin. There was no need to review the video again; the first time he saw it, he knew the deck was beyond repair. But it seemed so unreal, the charred cabin with floating wires and the blackened body and a breach in the hull the size of a man's head. He watched it as he had watched tapes of the *Challenger* explosion, over and over again, his thoughts shifting between disbelief and curiosity. Perhaps there was something he could spot that might make a difference; that was his hope and the hope of the people who occasionally glanced up at him. Forty-seven hours, he thought, might very well turn out to be a blessing.

He checked the clock on the wall. It was five o'clock; most of Russia was still in bed. Sipping from his coffee cup, he peered over the rim at Emil Levchenko.

The disheveled scientist shuffled from one terminal to the next, shaking his head, obviously not pleased with the information his colleagues were providing him. He picked up a printout from one desk and, after a quick glance, threw it back down. He spoke with the scientist at the desk and could be heard throughout the control room as he raised his voice to instruct him to redo his calculations.

Schebalin went to his office and closed the door. On his desk were several contingency plans. He sat down to review them, and was soon interrupted by a knock on his door. It was a propulsion specialist with an update. After several hours of reviewing contingency plans and listening to progress reports, he had learned nothing to give him hope. With a growing sense of defeat, he closed his eyes and prayed. It was an unusual act for him, for he didn't believe in God. Then he wondered how Levchenko was coming along. If there was a solution, he felt certain that Levchenko would find it. The young scientist was the architect of the Mars mission, the driving force behind the reinvigorated Russian space program. Schebalin picked up the phone and called him to his office.

When Levchenko appeared several minutes later, Schebalin motioned for him to take a seat on the other side of the desk. The scientist's shirt was partially untucked and looked as if it had been slept in. He sat down and began bouncing the eraser of his pencil against his right knee. He smiled nervously at Schebalin.

"Well?" Schebalin asked impatiently.

"It can't be done. The supply ship will never make it to them in time," responded Levchenko.

"Why not? The ships are supposed to be within two days of each other at all times."

"They are, assuming the *Volnost* can maneuver. But it can't. Their current trajectories make it impossible for the supply ship to reach the *Volnost* in two days. We have run several simulations, and even with best-case coefficients it would take approximately four weeks to complete the rendezvous. Basically, the two-day dock required the *Volnost* to be maneuverable, not the supply ship. Additional time was also required to compensate for the deviation in course caused by the explosion. Twenty-seven days is the best I can do."

Schebalin had suspected the damage would be too great, but all the same he was taken aback by the number of days required to complete a rendezvous. The supply ship was to be no more than two days away. How could two days possibly stretch to twenty-seven? As though he could read Schebalin's thoughts, Levchenko shoved his paperwork across the desk.

"A contingency for this sort of accident was never developed. It was considered fatal. Frankly, they are lucky to be alive."

"I'm not so sure of that."

"You know what I mean," Levchenko responded, hurt by Schebalin's tone.

"Sorry." Schebalin took a deep breath, pushed his chair back, and looked up at the ceiling. "Well, then, we need a miracle."

"A miracle would be helpful," responded Levchenko. "The damage could be superficial. In which case, they could repair the flight deck enough to maneuver the ship. However, the video gives us good reason to believe the damage was anything but superficial."

"Could they build a bypass?"

"They have lost critical circuitry."

Schebalin had to agree about the damage.

"Any other miracles?" he asked.

"None come to mind."

"If their only chance is to repair the *Volnost*, then we will concentrate our efforts on that objective."

"Why give them false hope?"

Schebalin paused at this. "Would you rather give up?"

"No," Levchenko replied meekly. He suddenly felt very

uncomfortable; although he sympathized with Schebalin's desire, he did not share his optimism and felt guilty because of it. He didn't want to appear uncaring, but he had to be realistic.

"I just—" began Levchenko, attempting to explain.

They were interrupted by the buzz of Schebalin's intercom. "Yes."

"Sir, the general is here."

"Send him in." Schebalin smiled awkwardly at Levchenko. "I need to speak to the general alone."

Behind a glass panel overlooking the control room sat the wives and a few of the older children. They watched a timer, a computer image in the lower corner of the main monitor, which tracked the remaining minutes of the emergency oxygen supply. Ten hours, forty-three minutes, and fifty-two seconds flashed across the screen, and with each second that appeared and disappeared they knew there was one less breath of oxygen for their husbands, their fathers, to breathe. The cosmonauts had been informed that morning, thirty hours after the explosion, that a rescue attempt would not be possible.

Each family was waiting its turn to send a final transmission. They were allotted fifteen minutes apiece, and had to wait nearly thirty minutes for the response. Katrina, Gorbatko's wife, was the first to return. She was smiling, her makeup streaked with tears, and although she walked with her head held high, she had to be guided by two cadets. She did not see the floor before her; her eyes were blank, her thoughts consumed by images from the transmission. As they entered the waiting room, Valentina Titov went over to Katrina and assisted her to a chair. They sat and hugged each other. Katrina cried softly as her eldest son handed her another tissue. Valentina thought of her children, who were home at her husband's request. He wanted to spare them the ordeal. He would send them a special transmission that they could view at home. Several minutes passed before Valentina realized the two young cadets were still there, standing at attention only a few feet away. She looked up, puzzled.

"Mrs. Titov, whenever you are ready."

Colonel Schebalin would occasionally look up and over his shoulder at the wives behind the glass window, but never for more than a few seconds. He felt guilty, as if he were to blame. Though he told himself that he was no more responsible than anyone else in the room, somehow that didn't help. He felt the resentment of the wives and children. They did not display it in their faces or in their manner. It was not outwardly evident at all. But it was there. Whenever he looked up at them, they would smile sadly and politely nod, and he felt more uncomfortable than he would have had they been pointing accusing fingers at him. He was certain they blamed him.

As Valentina Titov was led away to say her final good-bye to her husband, Schebalin looked down at his watch—it was five minutes until the press conference. He headed straight for the bathroom, where he splashed cold water on his face, then grabbed a towel to stop the water from running down onto his shirt. He studied his face in the mirror. His eyes were encircled by dark rings. His lips were pale. He ran a comb through his hair and patted his face dry. It seemed to help. He took several deep breaths, straightened his back, and made for the conference room.

The room burst into blinding flashes of light as he entered. With his arms waving like a blind man's, he felt his way to the podium. The flashes subsided, and his eyes slowly adjusted. He recognized several of the reporters; many of them were regulars, assigned exclusively to the Russian space program. He also recognized reporters he had not expected to see, famous television personalities from the United States, Japan, and the European Community. They must have flown in last night, thought

Schebalin, shortly after the story broke. The Russian press occupied the first several rows. Schebalin felt perspiration roll down his back; the room was unusually warm.

"Gentlemen and ladies, I have a short opening statement, after which I will answer any questions you may have."

With unusual quickness the conversations stopped, and after a brief rustling of papers and shifting of chairs the room went quiet.

"At 10:00 A.M. this morning we reached the unfortunate conclusion that a rescue attempt would not be possible. Without the ability to maneuver the *Volnost*, a rendezvous with the supply ship would take a minimum of twenty-seven days. As you know, the reserve tanks held only forty-eight hours of oxygen. The details are outlined in the press kits, which will be distributed at the doors when you exit. The cosmonauts were informed at 10:05. They decided to continue their investigation of the explosion. We have reason to believe the ship was struck by a meteoroid."

Several of the reporters started shouting questions, but Schebalin motioned them to remain quiet.

"The press kits contain everything we know at this point." He looked back down at the prepared text. "As I stand here talking to you, the cosmonauts and their families are exchanging final farewells. President Kerimov will be speaking with them after the families. At 4:12 A.M., five minutes before their oxygen supply is scheduled to run out, the cosmonauts will confine themselves to their individual sleeping compartments, where they will take a pill that will painlessly end their lives. The Russian Space Agency deeply regrets the lost of these fine cosmonauts. We are conducting an exhaustive investigation and analysis. With the help of the data Commander Titov and his crew are providing us, our intent is to design ships that will reduce the risk associated with this type of collision and ensure that these brave heroes did not give their lives in vain."

When Schebalin finished he looked out at the reporters, his eyes moist and slightly pink. He smiled sadly.

"They were great men," he said. "I was privileged to call them my friends." He paused, not sure what to say next. He wanted to express his feelings. There was an awkward silence; for once, the reporters seemed at a loss for words. Schebalin cleared his throat. "Any questions?"

T itov was floating in midair, his eyes shut, his legs and arms extended. He had just said good-bye to his wife, who, by now, was listening to the first part of his transmission. He had tried to picture her in his mind, her firm, elegant features, the concern in her eyes, her hands and how they would be cupped properly in her lap. He had told her about his fears of what their failure would do to the space program. This troubled him deeply. He did not want to be responsible for the delay their failure would undoubtedly bring. The Russian Space Agency should have waited for the Americans. Combining the efforts of more than one nation could only result in a safer, more reliable mission. Redundancies were not as cost-prohibitive. He had dwelled on these concerns far longer than he had intended, and suddenly only a few minutes were remaining to him. He'd quickly told her to find someone else. Now he imagined her shaking her head, telling his delayed image that it was foolish even to suggest such a thing, while his image continued to talk, ignoring her objections, telling her how much it loved her.

He had been fine until he had talked to her. He was not concerned about himself; he had accepted his death. He knew there was nothing he could do to prevent it. Nor was he overly concerned about her. She was a strong woman. She would marry again and probably sooner than either one of them would feel comfortable predicting. But she had a way of stirring his emotions in unpredictable ways. He felt that all he had worked for, his high hopes of a grand and historic contribution, would now end in an unavoidable setback to the program. He thought of his children and wondered how they would handle his death. His son possessed an understanding of death, and this troubled Titov greatly because he knew his son would suffer. But he also knew that in a few years his youngest child wouldn't even remember him. And that pained Titov even more. He opened his eyes. To his surprise, he saw tiny droplets of water floating before him. Titov had never seen tears in zero gravity before. They looked tranquil and pure.

With a swift swipe of his hand the tears broke into a thousand smaller tears and scattered across the room. It would not do for his men to see him like this.

The Brick Moon

Mission specialist Dr. Carl Endicott, the Canadian member of the American-led crew, twisted his face into an exaggerated grimace as he brought up the day's menu on the high-definition screen along the galley wall. Thermostabilized, irradiated corned beef with rehydratable asparagus, two slices of irradiated, natural-form bread, intermediate moisture-dried peaches, powdered lemonade, and peanuts. Endicott, who enjoyed fine cuisine, found his appetite considerably diminished. The dehydrated food they served on the International Space Station *Unity* was a far cry from the thin slices of chateaubriand with béarnaise that had been his last, now deeply savored, meal on Earth.

He pulled six trays from a lower cabinet and attached them vertically to the magnetic strips on the doors of the galley. He opened the drawer marked DAY 1 MEAL A THRU DAY 5 MEAL C. Tightly packed side by side and arranged by day, each meal was wrapped in a prunelike plastic bag. He selected the bag marked DAY 3 MEAL B. It was not much larger than a book, but it contained enough food for six astronauts. Examining the bag, he sighed. The rehydratable food expanded and slowly assumed a more reasonable size as he injected water into the individual packages. He turned on the small oven and placed the plastic bags and aluminum pouches inside.

Lieutenant Colonel Al Carter propelled himself from the far wall and floated eagerly toward Endicott. He was amused by the doctor's dislike of space food, and goaded him by sniffing the air suspiciously.

"I believe it is the rehydratable asparagus that you detect," Endicott said. He considered Carter's behavior childish, but he kept that thought to himself, for he knew that he would have to spend the next two years in close quarters with Carter, and it was best that they got along. With his thin lips pressed tightly together, he returned his attention to the preparation of the food.

Al Carter was the pilot for the American-led team. He had taken the experimental X-51 on its first flight into space six years earlier, an accomplishment that would almost certainly guarantee him a place in aviation history alongside Yeager. He had been president of his class at the Air Force Academy and had graduated with a degree in aeronautical engineering. He understood the complex propulsion systems that powered the crafts he flew better than most auto mechanics understood a simple four-cylinder engine.

But he did not fit the clean-cut image NASA liked to project. He was known for his reckless behavior, and though such behavior was not unusual for test pilots, Carter was more reckless than most. One antic had nearly gotten him fired. Late at night, after he had drunk a few at the local bar, he would take his car, a black Porsche, and head for the nearest highway. He would don a pair of night-vision goggles a few miles after the entrance ramp, turn the car lights off, and floor the accelerator. The police had clocked his car at speeds upward of 160 miles per hour. They did not bother chasing him. It would have been futile. But after a few months, they noticed a pattern and shortly afterward enlisted the assistance of a helicopter. Carter pulled over as soon as the beams from the powerful searchlight struck his car. When the ground police finally arrived, they found him sitting on the grass, smoking a cigarette. He was still wearing the goggles. The incident had been the reason the selection board had first passed him over for the Mars mission. It was rumored the president had secretly intervened in his favor.

"You may wish to inform the others that lunch is being served," Endicott said.

Still sniffing the air, Carter pushed his way through the galley and through the docking adaptor to the utilities module. Carter found Colonel Tom Nelson in the forward habitability module. He was above Carter, strapped to a multipurpose exercise bench pulling against a three-inch-wide strip of rubber. There was barely enough room for his long legs to fit between the machine and the wall. Drops of sweat were floating in the air around him. He was the oldest member of both crews, and the most fit.

"C'mon, you ol' warhorse, chow time," Carter announced.

"It'll take a few minutes for me to clean up," Nelson responded.

"Where's Jean Paul?"

"In the GP lab."

Carter made his way to the general purpose laboratory, where he found Jean Paul Brunnet, a doctor of planetary science and biology, wearing a pair of virtual goggles and moving his hands in midair as if they held something. The blue veins in the back of his hands were visible.

"Chow time," Carter announced.

"Shhh . . ." Brunnet waved his arm behind his back for Carter to be quiet and did not notice him leaving. He was examining particles, less than two-thousandths of an inch in diameter, from a Martian rock that contained possible evidence of fossilized cells. The rocks had been brought back by a Japanese robotic mission. They weren't much different from the rocks returned by an earlier American mission. Like the American samples, the evidence was inconclusive. The formations resembled a variety of bacteria found on Earth, but were much smaller, so small, in fact, most scientists doubted that they could be fossilized cells. Brunnet disagreed. The sample currently under his scope was several billion years old.

He took a slide of a more recent sample and examined it closely. Nothing. Not even evidence of organic material. It was as if life and any trace of it had completely ceased to exist, for none of the younger rocks contained the controversial fossils. But Brunnet did not accept this conclusion. He knew that life evolved to meet the changing conditions of its environment, particularly the lower life-forms such as bacteria. It seemed the surface of Mars was too much for it now. Mars's thin atmosphere did not filter out the ultraviolet rays of the sun. The combination of the rays with a highly oxidizing soil created an environment that was destructive to organic material. But still there could be pockets of life, perhaps deep below the surface. Small oases protected from the deadly radiation. He pulled up another slide. Again nothing. He had spent the entire morning preparing the rack of slides in front of him.

With a sigh, he carefully removed the slide and filed it with the others he had examined. He vaguely recalled that Carter had said something about lunch, then realized he was hungry.

He was the last to enter the galley. There were five men altogether, the four astronauts chosen to go to Mars and Jack Robbins, a space-station specialist, who had been aboard the *Unity* several months prior to the astronauts' arrival. His primary responsibility was to oversee preparations for the Mars trip.

Having pulled up the daily assignments on the main screen, Nelson commenced his review of the morning's activities while they ate. His voice was sharp and clear, and sounded as if he were giving commands. He listened to Endicott's report on the medical facility and Brunnet's account of the Martian rocks, then looked at Carter and pointed with his free hand at the final item on the screen.

Carter responded to the look. "Performed an exterior check of the propulsion stage this morning. The propellant lines outside the truss and both the propellant and the oxidizer manifolds checked out. I still want to take a closer look at the main pump assembly; otherwise, everything appears to be in order."

"Any questions about the afternoon assignments?" Nelson asked as he pulled up the next screen.

Carter cleared his throat. "Says here, you and I are to run out to the co-orbital platform to complete the electrical maintenance check on the Liberty. It also says fully suited. Why the formality?"

"A routine computer check detected a possible pressure leak. We suspect it's just a bug in the software. Jack here is checking on it. If our hunch is correct, we should be able to do shirtsleeves by tomorrow afternoon."

Carter grimaced at the prospect of a fully suited maintenance check, then tossed back his head and gobbled down a naked slice of corned beef. When the meal was done, conversation turned to the Russians.

"They should be arriving at thirteen hundred hours Tuesday," Nelson confirmed.

"Been a while since I've seen that ol' son of a bitch Dmitri," Carter said with a smile that revealed his friendship for his ex-rival. Colonel Dmitri "Dima" Fyodorovich Komarov was the mission commander for the Russian-led team. Prior to becoming a cosmonaut, he had been, like Carter, a test pilot and had gone head-to-head with Carter in establishing many of his records. He had attended the Furuze Military Academy, where, again like Carter, he had graduated with an engineering degree in aeronautics. "He didn't want this to be a joint mission, you know. He was hoping, like President Kerimov, to do it alone."

"Yes," Nelson confirmed. "I've heard that the backroom politics at the Kremlin got quite ugly. Kerimov was threatening to fire the entire Russian Space Agency. At first, he wouldn't even consider a joint mission. He still wanted to demonstrate the greatness of the New Republic by reaching Mars first. But he had lost a lot of credibility with the *Volnost* disaster. Then there was the tape of the late Commander Titov telling his wife that a joint mission was the safest way to proceed."

"Did they ever learn how the press got the tape?" Brunnet asked.

"Not that I know of. Some say that Valentina, his wife, sneaked it out. Others say it was Colonel Schebalin's doing— that he didn't want another disaster on his hands. Kerimov had a more serious problem though. The New Republic simply didn't have the means to put together another mission in time to beat us. Kerimov's only viable option was to accept our offer of a joint mission. He was lucky to score a draw."

"I hear Dmitri's cheating on his wife," Carter said, returning to his original subject. "Why she puts up with the son of a bitch is beyond me."

"I suspect that Tatiana will present an interesting challenge," Endicott said.

Major Tatiana Sergeievna Pavlova was the only female selected to go to Mars. She was attractive and full-figured, and she would be aboard the *Unity* within three days' time. Despite her outstanding scientific qualifications, it was rumored that the Russians had selected her so they could say they had put the first woman on another planet. She was married to Vladimir Pavlov, who would pilot the Russian-led ship, the *Druzhba*, to Mars. They had met during a training exercise and had married shortly afterward. The marriage had made her the obvious choice for the female slot of the Mars mission, and some people suspected it was the reason she had married Vladimir.

"They should have never included a woman," Endicott said. "The potential complications introduced by sexual relationships between crew members could prove detrimental."

"She is married," Nelson said.

"That only makes it worse." Carter was chewing a dried peach. "The *Druzhba* is only so big. By the end of two years the men will be at each other's throats trying to get into her pants. Except for her husband. He'll be at their throats trying to keep them out."

Nelson interrupted the discussion by glancing at his watch and declaring in a loud voice that lunch was over.

"*Sokop*, this is *Unity*, initiate roll maneuver," Carter instructed. "Twenty-five meters and closing."

"Initiating fourteen-point-two-degree roll," came the response over the intercom in a thick Russian accent. It belonged to the pilot of the Russian Space Shuttle *Sokop*. The *Sokop* was making its approach for a soft dock with the space station.

"*Sokop*, you're coming in high. Correct pitch by zero-point-three degrees."

"Correcting pitch."

"*Sokop*, hold your position at seventeen meters," Carter said.

"Holding position."

"Extending the MSC arm," Carter announced. "Prepare for soft dock."

A long, robotic manipulator arm slowly unfolded from the Mobile Service Center of the space station and reached out to snag the Russian shuttle. The metallic appendage was capable of handling a two-hundred-thousand-pound load. Television cameras served as the eyes for the arm and were located at the elbow and wrist joints. At the far end of the arm was the capture mechanism, a hollow tube that resembled a fingerless stump, inside of which were three wires that crossed to form a triangle. When a grapple was placed inside the stump, a ring attached to the wires would rotate, shrinking the triangle until the wires were tightly wrapped around the grapple.

Carter maneuvered the arm with a joysticklike control. The control was connected to a panel cluttered with an assortment of dials and switches. When turned, the dial marked JOINT would activate a different section of the arm, which could then be manipulated through the joystick. Carter viewed the two monitors to his right as he carefully extended the mechanical arm toward the Russian craft. He had practiced the soft-docking maneuvers in the simulator the day before. This was his first actual docking, and, as far as he could determine, there was no detectable difference from the simulator.

When the robotic arm was within two meters of the Russian shuttle, Carter stopped its forward motion. He activated the wrist joint. The capture mechanism swung back and forth, allowing the camera mounted on the mechanism to scan the hull. Carter located the grapple and slowly moved the arm forward. He stopped chewing his gum as the two came in contact. Because of the enormous mass involved, the slightest miscalculation could severely damage the robotic arm.

"The grapple is secured," Carter said. "Commencing approach."

He adjusted the sensitivity of the joystick and slowly pulled it back. At first the movement was imperceptible. But then, after a few seconds, the two ships began to visibly close. The robotic arm brought the Russian shuttle to within a meter of the space station.

"Prepare for docking," Carter said, and resumed chewing his gum.

The Russians extended the cylindrical docking adaptor, through which the cosmonauts would crawl to reach the space station, and mated it to the adaptor on the *Unity*. Neither adaptor was male or female. The sexless coupling had evolved from the universal docking mechanism introduced in the mid-seventies during a joint mission between the Soviet Union and the United States, when both nations mutually realized that neither wanted to be identified with the receiving end. The delicate issue was skirted as the obvious benefits of a universal mechanism became apparent. Any ship could dock with any other ship without the complications of various adaptors.

Colonel Tom Nelson was standing at the portal waiting to greet the first cosmonaut through. The other astronauts were floating behind him, peering over his shoulder. The large smile of Colonel Dmitri Fyodorovich Komarov and his extended hand appeared at the portal.

"Good to see you again, my friends," Komarov said, grinning, as he pulled his large frame through the adaptor.

"Greetings, Colonel Komarov," Nelson said. "I believe you have met everyone, except perhaps Jack Robbins here."

"It is good to meet you in person," Komarov said, and then took Jack's hand and shook it heartily.

"Indeed an honor," Jack replied.

Komarov released the hand, then walked past Robbins and wrapped his arms around Carter in a large bear hug.

"How's my old comrade doing?" Komarov asked in a loud and booming voice.

"It's been a while, Dmitri."

"We must talk later," Komarov said, holding Carter at arm's length. "I am much interested in hearing of the X-51."

"It would be my pleasure," Carter responded, masking his uneasiness at being approached so suddenly and so forwardly on such a sensitive matter. Much of the information he could relate regarding the plane was still classified. But this was Komarov, his Russian counterpart, one of the few men Carter truly admired. He would talk with him, but he would be cautious. "We have much to talk about."

Major Vladimir Mikelovich Pavlov was the next to emerge; his smile reserved, almost strained. He was noticeably younger and much more fit than Komarov. Unlike his commander, he had not taken to drinking vodka or smoking cigars on a regular basis. After nodding politely, he turned to lend his wife a hand. Major Tatiana Sergeievna Pavlova—Tanya—was even more beautiful than Carter recalled. She wore no makeup. Her dark hair was straight, with a slight inward curl at the ends. Her eyes, sharp and businesslike, possessed a disconcerting quality, as if she knew the sort of thoughts a man was contemplating as he gazed upon her. With a slight, almost mysterious smile, she nodded gracefully as she entered the room.

Close behind and in sharp contrast was the fourth and final member of the Russian-led crew: Dr. Takashi Satomura. The Japanese had paid the Russians a considerable sum to have him placed on the roster. There had been some controversy over his selection within the Japanese Space Agency because he was not universally liked. But no one had quarreled over his qualifications or abilities. They were exceptional. He possessed doctorates in planetary geology and medicine, master's degrees in physics, chemistry, and literature, and several bachelor degrees. He had been among the crew of the first Japanese-manned spacecraft and had logged the second highest number of hours in space for a Japanese astronaut. And although there were other men just as qualified in their own way, the quarrels over Satomura stemmed mostly from bad feelings. He was ruthless in backroom politics, and several good men had been pushed aside and even ruined for having been in his way.

The Japanese astronaut was neither young nor physically

attractive. His face was streaked with lines caused by years of cigarettes, which he smoked surreptitiously and perpetually gave up
cold turkey months prior to the qualifying physical of a mission.
As a result of cigarettes and perhaps even more so because of coffee, which he drank by the pot, his teeth were noticeably stained.
He told the doctors it was the coffee, and the concentrated
amounts of caffeine they found in his blood seem to corroborate
his story. When he had fully emerged from the portal, he dipped
his head slightly, a compromise to the traditional Japanese bow,
and shook the hands of the men present with a formality and precision that induced immediate but guarded respect.

Robbins, with the video camera fixed to his eye, floated off
to the side and slightly above the others. The docking module
was not designed to hold so many human bodies at one time,
complicating Robbins's ability to maneuver to a good vantage
point.

"Welcome to Space Station *Unity*," Nelson said. "I am
Colonel Tom Nelson, and these are my colleagues. . . ."

As soon as the camera was turned off, Komarov looked
around the room, and declared: "There have been some addi-
tions since I was here last."

"Yes, there have," Nelson responded. "The MSC was modified to accommodate the new arm. And the German GEM II
module was installed last month. I will be taking you there
shortly."

"Your fondness for acronyms will be your undoing,"
Satomura remarked.

Nelson smiled politely. There was something about Satomura
that he didn't like. "The new arm can handle fifty percent more
mass. One hundred and fifty thousand kilograms total."

"Yes," Komarov said, touching his surroundings. "The simulator was accurate. And beyond this module lies the life-
sciences research laboratory."

"Quite correct," Endicott responded. "I spend a large portion of my time there. We are about midway through an embryogenesis study. The Chiroptera order has yielded some interesting results."

"Chiroptera?" Tanya asked.

"Bats," Endicott responded politely.

"We, too, have had some interesting results with the Chiroptera," Satomura said. "The experiments were conducted during our last mission."

"I have read the preliminary reports," Endicott replied and was on the verge of giving his opinion of the reports when Nelson interrupted and invited the others to follow him through the portal. They formed a semicircle around Nelson at the far end.

"Has anyone heard of Edward E. Hale?" Nelson did not wait for a response. "In the late eighteen hundreds he described a space station two hundred feet in diameter. The station was made of brick. He called it the brick moon. The inhabitants, he speculated, would communicate with Earth by jumping up and down on the surface of the moon to produce Morse code signals. As you can see, we have come a long way since then."

"Our Konstantin Tsiolkovsky was, how do you say, more real," Vladimir said.

"Yes," Nelson responded. "He also appeared on the scene half a century later. By that time bricks had been determined to be aerodynamically unsound." They all chuckled at this.

"Very amusing," Colonel Dmitri Komarov said. "I am pleased to see we have progressed beyond their early designs."

"I agree wholeheartedly," Nelson replied with a short laugh. "Although, I suspect a hundred years from now this station will seem as primitive as a brick moon."

"A hundred years from now," Komarov said in a thick Russian accent, "our great-grandchildren will read about us in history books. We are the pioneers of the solar system. Our names will live forever."

They knew what he said was true. Decades would pass, centuries, even millennia, and their names would survive. In a couple of hundred years the discovery of America would dwindle in comparison to their feat. And though they felt proud of this, it did not seem entirely justified to them. Their role was fundamentally different from that of many of the earlier explorers. Christopher Columbus was the driving force behind his mission; they were not. Their part did not go too far beyond that of passengers. The American engineers had chosen a monkey to be the very first astronaut, and the monkey had performed admirably. The engineers preferred to consider the astronaut as a redundant component, a backup in case the automated systems failed. But it would not go down in history that way.

"This is the life-sciences research lab," Nelson said.

"What have you done?" Tanya asked, pointing to a battered hummingbird with its wings tied back.

"Ah," Dr. Endicott said, "most unfortunate. In the middle of our first night, the poor creature managed to free herself of her restraint straps. She thrashed about uncontrollably in her cage until she knocked herself senseless. No gravity, you see. I found her unconscious the next morning. Feathers are still popping up. We were going to see if it was possible to train her to fly in space."

"How horrible," Tanya said as she moved closer to examine the wounded bird.

"Impossible," Satomura barked. "A bird's wing is structured to counter gravity. One flap of her wings and this bird would have gone straight up and slammed against the ceiling."

"I am inclined to agree with you," Endicott said. "The bird's trainer, however, felt she might adapt. It would have been a most interesting experiment."

Tanya turned away in disgust. She stopped at the sight of a small aquarium filled with goldfish. As she moved closer, she noticed there was something very odd about the way they were swimming. Some were upside down, some were right side up, and some were sideways. She watched one goldfish swim belly-up toward her. The fish stopped within centimeters of the glass and for a brief second appeared to study her face, then turned and headed sideways to the center of the aquarium, where it pushed its nose against a large air bubble. At the bottom, a school of fish was floating horizontally to the surface, but as they swam upward and separated from each other they quickly lost their orientation.

"The next module is GEM II—the German Experimental Module," Nelson said.

Colonel Komarov had coaxed Carter into the Russian shuttle on the third evening of their stay with the promise of vodka. Carter knew that if NASA found out he had imbibed alcohol, there was a chance he would be scrubbed from the mission, even at this late date. NASA regulations on the consumption of alcohol in space called for the immediate and permanent dismissal of an astronaut. All the same, Carter was not overly concerned—like all the other times he had violated a regulation, he had no intention of being caught.

Dmitri squeezed the plastic container until two ounces of the Russian vodka passed his lips. His eyes brightened as the chilled liquid burned its way through his body. He smiled and handed the vodka to Carter. Without hesitation, Carter put the container to his lips and squeezed. He welcomed the taste like a long-lost friend, and fought the desire to drink more.

"Good," he whispered, his voice stolen by the fumes of the alcohol. He handed the container back to the Russian. "You'll need to come to the States and try some of our sour mash."

"Sour mash?" Dmitri asked, puzzled.

"Bourbon," Carter replied.

"Ah, no thank you. I have tried. It tastes like bad scotch." Dmitri grinned broadly and took a drink from the container. "Another?"

"I must be careful," Carter said. "Regulations."

"I understand. Your country, with all its talk about freedom, still has its restrictions. Does it not? No matter. Politics are not why we are here. Let us talk flying. Tell me about the X-51."

"Much of what I could say about the X-51 is classified," Carter replied.

"I would not want you to reveal classified information, of course. Tell me what you can. No more."

"I'll have that drink after all," Carter said, partly to reassure Dmitri that he trusted him and partly because it had occurred to him suddenly that he was acting like a prude. He took a large swig and felt the familiar warmth of the liquor entering his system. "I'm a stick and rudder man," he said, sinking into a deep Southern drawl. "The X-51 flies too much like the shuttle for my liking. Almost everything is controlled by computers. If today's engineers had their way, they would eliminate us pilots altogether. Reduces the number of parameters they have to concern themselves with. She sure is one helluva ride though. One minute you're under a blue sky, the next the sky is black as night." He took another drink, this time unconsciously, as he recalled how the blue sky had disappeared. Komarov took the vodka from Carter.

"Not too much," Komarov said. "Regulations, remember?"

"And I thought you were trying to get me drunk," Carter said, grinning.

"No, if I were trying to get you drunk, I would have brought bourbon." They laughed at this.

"The plane is little more than one giant fuel tank," Carter continued after he had regained his breath. "There's fuel in the wings, the hull, the nose, you name it. And as if that wasn't enough, the scramjets are sucking up the atmosphere for more.

Shit, they'd harness my farts if they could figure a way."
Komarov slapped his legs and laughed, and Carter waited until
he was finished. "I heard someone once compare the space
shuttle to a fish in the ocean carrying along a bag of water to
breathe. Well, they finally figured out how to dispense with the
bag."

"Very good," Komarov roared.

"Tell me about your plane," Carter said.

"That is where you have finally surpassed us. Our country
still hasn't flown the plane into space with a man aboard, as you
know. Our automated flights are proceeding as planned. Our
engineers are apparently afflicted with the same fear as yours.
They don't trust pilots."

"It must be something they teach them at school. Any idea
when they're going to let a man take it up?"

"They say ten months. Maybe nine." Komarov's thoughts
slipped inward as he stared unfocused at the vodka container.
Streaks of gray and silver dominated the thick eyebrows of the
Russian. Several creases lined his forehead. Even though he had
the most coveted of all assignments, leading the Russian team
to Mars, a part of him regretted more than anything that
Vladimir would be in the pilot's seat.

At that moment Tanya Pavlova burst into the cabin and
began speaking rapidly in Russian. Carter made out the name of
her husband, Vladimir. There was a reddish mark on her cheek.

She noticed Carter then and stepped away from Komarov as
though she had mistaken him for someone else. She looked
Carter in the eye. "I am so sorry. Please don't be alarmed. It is
nothing."

Carter mumbled a few unintelligible words in reply,
attempting to impart his understanding and disguise his curiosity. He knew that she was lying, that she had been in a fight with
her husband, and that he had struck her.

"If you could excuse us," Komarov said.

"Certainly," Carter replied, and turned to leave. He was dumbfounded. He wondered what had happened. The red mark on Tatiana's face had to have been inflicted by Vladimir. Unless Dr. Satomura had slapped her, and that did not seem likely. No, it was Vladimir, no doubt. One week prior to their departure, and Tatiana and Vladimir were having marital problems. But was there more to it than that? Carter thought he had detected a sort of intimacy between her and Komarov. But he couldn't be sure. Komarov's wife, Vyera, was a member of the Russian jet set whose father had been a distinguished and wealthy member of the Russian Duma. She had kissed him good-bye on the launchpad in front of millions, perhaps billions, of people. Komarov had once told Carter that he loved his wife deeply, but also that he was occasionally unfaithful to her and did not feel the two were at odds.

As he floated toward the docking adaptor, Carter felt a little giddy and disoriented, which was unusual for the small amount of alcohol he had drunk. Because of the absence of gravity, the stabilizing liquids in his inner ear, whose purpose was to maintain a sense of balance, sloshed unrestrained and erratic. He started to feel an uneasiness in the bottom of his stomach, and pushed his way quickly through the corridor toward the waste-management facility at the other end.

———

The voices ceased and eyes looked up as Carter entered the galley the following day. Tatiana Pavlova had been talking. Her husband, Vladimir, was seated next to her, and Colonel Komarov was in the far corner with Nelson, eating breakfast. Vladimir's hand rested on his wife's knee. A layer of makeup had been carefully applied to her cheeks. Only someone who had seen her face the previous evening would know she had been struck. For a brief moment she stared nervously at Carter, then continued talking.

"The estimated speed of the meteoroid was twenty-one kilometers a second. It was no larger than four millimeters in diameter. With our current technologies it would have been impossible to detect."

"But it could have been prevented," Satomura said.

"Yes," Tatiana replied. "An exterior shell to absorb the impact could have prevented the accident."

"The additional weight would have been excessive," Nelson interjected. It was an issue that had been heatedly debated after the Russian tragedy, and one which he felt would do little good to discuss further. "The odds of a similar incident are remote."

"One in ten thousand, to be precise," Satomura said. "It is much more likely that we shall all die of old age."

Carter watched Tanya and her husband closely. They gave no indication of having been in a fight. In fact, they were holding hands. Carter was not familiar enough with Russian customs to know whether or not hand-holding was appropriate for a married couple in a professional setting, but that made little difference. It was obvious the two were going out of their way to appear happily married—most likely for his benefit. He looked directly at Tatiana until he caught her attention, then looked inquisitively at the joined hands. Her eyes shot him a warning glance. He noticed that her hand tightened slightly around Vladimir's. Pleased at having obtained a reaction, he turned his attention to the rehydrated eggs on his plate.

"A joint review of the flight plan is scheduled for this morning," Nelson said, after everyone had finished their breakfasts. The review was primarily for the public, who would be watching it live. "Robbins, are you ready?"

Robbins gave the camera lens one final wipe, then nodded as he brought the viewfinder to his right eye. A light on top of the camera flashed on to indicate the event was being televised.

"The charts, Jean Paul."

Brunnet typed in a quick command at the keyboard, and a

chart marked OPPOSITION CLASS—OUTBOUND VENUS SWINGBY appeared on a large screen against the wall. The chart was of the inner solar system, and a pair of dotted lines intersected the elliptical orbits of Venus, Earth, and Mars. The lines represented the trajectories of the American spaceship *Liberty* and the Russian ship *Druzhba*. In the event of an emergency, their flight paths were close enough for one ship to serve as a backup to the other. A box in the bottom right-hand corner of the screen contained dates.

2021 OPPOSITION CLASS

1. Earth departure, October 27, 2021
2. Venus passage, April 9, 2022
3. Mars arrival, October 16, 2022
4. Mars departure, December 17, 2022
5. Earth arrival, August 18, 2023

"Good morning, Colonel Nelson," said Dr. James D. Cain, his broad smile appearing on the high-definition monitor above their heads. Cain was the assistant administrator for the NASA Office of Planetary Exploration. He wiped some sleep from his eyes and acknowledged the others. Moments later the screen split in two, and Colonel Leonid Schebalin appeared on the other half. He spoke a few brief words in Russian to his crew, and when he was finished, he said in English: "Colonel Nelson, you are first on the agenda."

"Thank you, Colonel. The purpose of this discussion is to review the mission flight plan. The supply ship initiated trans-Mars injection five days ago. The ship is unmanned and contains scientific experiments, emergency cargo, and the backup lander. Three days from today, the two crews will board their respective crafts. Final preflight preparations and maintenance checks will commence upon their arrival." He approached the screen and pointed at the blue-green planet everyone knew to be Earth. "Two days later, trans-Mars injection will commence with the ignition of the main engines. The burn will establish a trajectory that will take the ships around the sun and past Venus. Shortly after the first stage has been jettisoned, the ships will extend their habitat and lab modules and begin a point-four-g spin."

Nelson placed his finger on a red-dotted line at a spot near the sun. "As we pass by the sun, our primary concern will be solar flares. The storm shelter will automatically be inflated with water by the computer when it has determined with eighty-five percent certainty a solar flare will occur. An alarm, similar to *Unity's*, will sound. Jean Paul."

A high-pitched siren rang through the air, causing everyone to wince. It continued for five seconds, then mercifully stopped. "My apologies," said Nelson. "The Russian alarm, I understand, is not quite as loud—partly owing to the fact that your habitat module is adjacent to the shelter."

"If our alarm fails," said Satomura, "I am certain we will hear yours."

"The solar radiation will be one of many concerns," Colonel Schebalin said, his stern voice bringing a quick end to their laughter.

"Our next encounter will be Venus," Nelson said, pointing at a rotating gold sphere. The sphere increased in size. "The gravitational field of Venus will accelerate the spaceship in relation to the sun. At Venus, the *Liberty* will release the probe, *Greenhouse*. The probe will land on the planet and deploy a robotic rover. We will control the rover from the *Liberty* as we pass over. This will eliminate the long delay associated with an Earth-based system. The surface will be photographed, and soil samples will be collected and analyzed. We will be looking for clues as to what might have triggered the greenhouse effect on a planet so similar to Earth. Surface temperatures on Venus can reach as high as nine hundred degrees Fahrenheit, mostly because of its thick carbon dioxide atmosphere. We will also be looking for evidence of life."

"We should not underestimate the importance of this project," said Satomura. He was disappointed by how little press the *Greenhouse* probe had received. In his mind, they treated it as they would a sideshow at a circus. Endicott signaled his agreement and was about to launch into an explanation of how Earth could very easily meet with the same fate when Nelson, perceiving Endicott's intent, pressed on with the flight plan.

"The passage from Venus to Mars will take six months," he said. He touched the red planet, and it increased in size until it filled the entire screen. The room assumed a pink glow.

"The god of war," said Schebalin to himself, but his voice was picked up and amplified by a sensitive microphone connected to the communications console. He smiled awkwardly.

"Both ships will use the Martian atmosphere to aerobrake. They will strike the atmosphere at thirty-thousand kilometers per hour. The rapid deceleration will produce a force of five-point-five g's. This is essentially the same maneuver that caused the aerobraking accident seven years ago. We lost three of our best astronauts then. They were good friends of mine. The problem was an unpredicted atmospheric disturbance that shifted the angle of entry. The onboard computer failed to compensate correctly for the change. We have since updated the program and are highly confident the aerobrake will be successful."

The next chart showed two dotted lines circling the planet Mars.

"Once the maneuver is completed," Nelson continued, "both ships will assume a twenty-four-hour elliptical orbit with an inclination angle of approximately thirty degrees. After several days in orbit, we will initiate descent operations. My landing crew will consist of Lieutenant Carter, Major Brunnet, and me. Dr. Endicott is to remain aboard the *Liberty*."

"Our crew," Schebalin said, "will be Colonel Dmitri

Komarov, Major Tatiana Pavlova, and Dr. Takashi Satomura." Unlike the others, Satomura did not acknowledge his name with a nod or a smile. His expression remained unchanged, oddly impatient.

"The Mars Excursion Modules will separate from the main vehicles and descend to the planet's surface," Nelson continued. "We will land at the base of Olympus Mons, approximately two klicks above mean planetary level." The planet grew several times in size, and Nelson pointed at a spot at the base of a volcano with his pen. "Major Brunnet."

"Olympus Mons is the largest known volcano in the solar system," Brunnet said. A large photograph of the volcano appeared on the screen. "It towers twenty-seven kilometers above the surface—three times higher than Mount Everest. The caldera is eighty-one kilometers across. The base of the volcano spans nearly six hundred kilometers. It also contains some of the youngest lava flows on the planet's surface. The age of these flows is determined by crater density. This site will answer one very important geological question: When did volcanism cease on Mars? Rock samples from this region will be varied in age and chemical composition. They should provide a good cross section of Martian geological history."

"The decision to land on Olympus Mons was not without controversy," Nelson said. "The elevation was thought by some to be too great to provide sufficient aerobraking, and the site too rocky for a safe landing. But geologically Olympus Mons holds considerable promise, and a majority of our scientists were determined not to pass it up. They chose a site lower than originally considered and reworked the landing strategy to compensate for the elevation. They also redesigned the landing gear to be able to handle less than perfect conditions." Nelson scrolled the screen eastward and pointed to a spot inside a large, jagged canyon. "The team led by the Russians will land here. Commander Komarov."

"Like you," Komarov said, "we were lured to a spot that holds great potential. Candor Chasma. Six degrees south, seventy-three degrees west. We are to land on a small mesa, one-point-three kilometers high. Candor Chasma belongs to the Valles Marineris canyon system. The system stretches nearly four thousand kilometers in length. To give you a better sense of the size, the Grand Canyon in America is only four hundred and fifty kilometers long. Valles Marineris would stretch the entire length of the United States. It is as much as seven kilometers deep, which is three times deeper than the Grand Canyon. We'll be using an airship to explore the chasm. A dirigible, I believe you call it. But I will let Dr. Satomura describe the scientific value of this site."

"This region is interesting for many reasons," said Takashi Satomura, stepping forward with a laser pen. "The walls of the canyon are layered. We believe the layers are from different periods of Mars's geological past. They contain the history of Mars. And to some degree our solar system. To give an example, samples taken from the layers could be used to determine the climatic cycles of Mars. If these cycles correspond with those on Earth, such as the great ice ages, we can assume they were due to variations in the sun's output."

"Or it could lend further credence to Milankovitch's theory regarding the influence of planetary rotation upon climate," Endicott remarked.

"Of course," Satomura said. "All depends on what we find." He traced the outer perimeter of the canyon with his laser beam. "There are those who believe that the canyon could have been an ancient lake. We know that life on Earth began in the oceans approximately three and a half billion years ago. We suspect that conditions on Mars at that time were similar to those on Earth, and that Martian life may have lived in the waters that once filled this canyon."

Carter listened with amusement as the two nations rationalized their respective landing sites. There was another reason, more genuine, yet unspoken. Neither nation wanted to be outdone by the other. As agreed by both beforehand, their ships would touch the ground simultaneously, or as simultaneously as conditions would allow. The Russian and American commanders were going to emerge from their landers, descend their respective ladders, and diplomatically hop onto the Martian soil at precisely the same time. A symbolic gesture of unity. Man, not a Russian, not an American, but man, an Earthling, would land on Mars.

Despite this gesture, politicians soon came to the realization that one landing site could be superior to another. The Russians, who realized it first, announced they would land at Candor Chasma, perhaps the most promising site with respect to geology and the search for life. The Americans, not wanting to be outdone, retorted by announcing they would land at Olympus Mons, the highest and most spectacular mountain in the solar system. The site for the failed *Volnost* mission had been the ancient channels of Mangala Vallis—an equatorial site, relatively safe, but geologically dull in comparison to Olympus Mons or Candor Chasma. The glory had been in being first. The challenge posed by the two sites had the unexpected result of reinvigorating the space program. As Carter smiled inwardly at the thought, a change in Komarov's tone drew his attention back to the discussion.

"While we are on the planet's surface, Vladimir will conduct an investigation of the supply ship for the *Volnost*. The ship, which is configured similarly to the supply ship for this mission, with its cargo hold and backup lander, has lost power, and we want to find out why.

"The two landing crews will remain on the surface for two months. Their duties will be many. They will spend much of their time exploring the surrounding terrain and conducting surface experiments. They will depart the planet in the excursion modules. Trans-Earth injection will occur on December 17, 2022. This time," Komarov said, tracing the dotted line with his finger, "rather than swinging by Venus, we will set a course directly for Earth. We are scheduled to arrive eight months later. The ships will aerobrake into the Earth's atmosphere, where they will be picked up by orbital-transfer vehicles and tugged back down to low-Earth orbit and the newly constructed Orbital Quarantine Vehicle. The facility will be separate but adjacent to this space station. We are to remain in quarantine for two weeks."

"And if we are found to be contaminated?" Tanya asked.

"Then we stay quarantined until it is determined the contamination does not pose a threat or until it is neutralized. We don't anticipate any complications."

Tanya Pavlova watched Colonel Komarov as he checked his console and verbally relayed the settings back to Kaliningrad. His voice was mature and confident. Not like her husband's, which would on occasion crack as though he had not entirely grown up. She loved her husband, but at times he could be so childish, and his suspicious nature was a constant annoyance. Komarov was different. He was older than Vladimir, more fatherly. His military stature and large body, almost too large to fit in the cockpit of the jets he flew, commanded respect. There were rumors that he had been unfaithful to his wife, but that did not disturb Tatiana. With such a man the problem had to be with the woman. Not that it was any concern of hers.

Vladimir's jealousy annoyed Tanya. He had struck her the other night because he thought she was getting too friendly with Komarov. Of course, he had overreacted. Komarov had placed his hand on her shoulder, that was all. She thought that perhaps it was guilt that made Vladimir act so. She suspected him of having an affair just a few months earlier during a training exercise in Japan. She hadn't confronted him yet, because she still wasn't sure. A friend of hers was checking into it. Or, she thought, perhaps his jealousy stemmed from suspicions that she had married him to secure a spot on the mission. There was some truth to that, but not to the extent imagined. She had fallen in love with Vladimir and would have married him anyway—just not so quickly.

She had to admit, though, that she was attracted to Dmitri and felt a certain warmth when she was near him. The gray streaks in his hair gave him an air of distinction.

She remembered an incident back on Earth when all four of them had been submerged underwater in the immersion facility. The facility was used to approximate weightlessness. During the two-hour session, she, at first unconsciously, had stayed close to Komarov through the training maneuvers. As Vladimir grew visibly irritated, Tanya became angered by his distrust and paid less attention to him. That, of course, only aggravated the situation. The tension increased until everyone in the tank felt it. When they finally emerged, she and Vladimir exchanged a few sharp words before charging off in separate directions; under any other circumstance no one would have noticed, but they were training for a two-year stay in space, and their trainers were instructed to notice such things. The trainers filed their report that evening.

The next morning the couple was called before a special review board, which included several mission psychiatrists. It was just a marital spat, they explained to the board. A perfectly normal thing. These were not perfectly normal circumstances, they were informed by one of the psychiatrists. Confinement of the sort they were about to endure could place unusual demands on the human psyche. Even a spat had the potential to blossom into something of graver consequence. It was their responsibility to select cosmonauts who could control their emotions. If a repeat of such behavior occurred, the board might be forced to reconsider its selection. It was the first and last public outburst between the two. But in private . . . Tatiana didn't want to think about that.

"Prepare for separation, over," announced a voice over the intercom.

Komarov turned toward Vladimir. Vladimir, without looking up from his console, nodded to confirm they were ready.

"The *Druzhba* is set for separation," Komarov announced. "*Sokop?*"

"The shuttle is set."

"Initiate separation."

Vladimir flipped the switch that instructed the computer to initiate the separation sequence. A message appeared on the main console that the grapples had been released; moments later, he noticed that the stars outside his portal had shifted as a spring pushed the two ships apart. Several tiny rockets, each with 870 pounds of thrust powered by a mixture of monomethyl hydrazine and nitrogen tetroxide, fired on the shuttle when it was a safe distance away.

"Separation complete," Komarov announced. His voice was cold, professional, without emotion. It was Vladimir's duty to announce the separation. But Komarov had noticed Vladimir's mind had drifted, and this was his way of getting Vladimir's thoughts back on track.

"Your orbit looks good."

Vladimir glanced over at Komarov. He had a great deal of respect for his commander. Ever since Vladimir's days in the Furuze Military Academy, Komarov had been a hero of his. Dmitri Fyodorovich Komarov was spoken of with godlike reverence by the young cadets. He was the great Russian test pilot, running neck and neck with his famous American counterpart, Al Carter. Everyone knew that he would have beaten Carter in the race to put the space plane into orbit had it not been for budget constraints. It was not Komarov's fault he had lost that race. The previous century's rash of programs to reform the Russian economy, each more chaotic and corrupt than its predecessor, was to blame. Vladimir's respect for his commander did not, however, alleviate his suspicions.

He had no proof. He had never caught them in the act. There was no hard evidence he could point to. Just suspicions. The way she acted around Komarov. Hands sliding by each other and hesitating before continuing, the tone of her voice when she talked to him, or a smile when there was no reason for a smile. When he confronted her she would become angry and deny it was anything more than his overactive imagination. The more suspicious he became the more angered she would become and the more it would seem, as a result of her anger and a desire to strike back, that her attentions were diverted to Komarov.

Vladimir did not want to believe that his wife could be unfaithful. There were periods when she would act as if no other man could possibly interest her, and she would love him and caress him and speak softly to him, and he would forget his suspicions. But he had no way of knowing for certain whether or not she was having an affair. It angered him not to know, and it angered him even more that he did not know whether his anger, which she resented, was justified.

Komarov, he knew, was not to be trusted. He did not know if he could trust his wife. He did not know if he were distorting innocent gestures into something secretive and lustful. It might be, as she said, nothing more than his imagination. There was only one way to know for sure, and that was to catch them in the act. His thoughts were disrupted by a distant voice that he recognized as Colonel Schebalin's. The colonel was reviewing the scheduled activities with the crew.

They would spend the next three days in geosynchronous orbit, running through a seemingly endless checklist to verify that the system components functioned according to specifications. The components and their redundant counterparts had been checked and rechecked a multitude of times, at the manufacturers', prior to assembly at the RSA plant, after assembly, prior to launch, after launch while in low-Earth orbit, and now in geosynchronous orbit, before the final burn that would send the ship and its crew on their way toward Mars.

Queen's Gambit Declined

"*Liberty*, this is control. You are go for burn, over."
The crew aboard the *Liberty* were making final preparations for
trans-Mars injection, a maneuver which would free their ship
from the gravitational pull of the Earth and establish a trajectory for Mars. Carter checked his flight-deck console and,
pleased with what he found, gave Tom Nelson a thumbs-up.

"Roger, we are go for burn. Out."

Carter could feel his heart beating. He watched his hand as
it moved in slow motion through the weightless environment of
the spacecraft. His finger trembled as it pulled down on the
metallic gray switch to ignite the main engines of the spacecraft's Trans-Mars Injection stage. The TMI stage held
450,000 kilograms of propellant. Within the next few minutes,
the entire 450,000 kilograms would explode in the rocket combustion chambers beneath them. The force of the explosions
would accelerate the ship to a velocity of 26,000 kilometers per
hour. Carter heard a voice counting backwards.

"... four ... three ... two ... one. We have first-stage ignition."

A stream of supercold liquid hydrogen flowed into preburners, where it combined with liquid oxygen to produce hydrogen-laden steam. The steam drove the turbopumps, which fed the fuel and oxidizer into the main injectors. The *Liberty* was fitted with two engines; each engine had four turbopumps and one main injector. The injectors sprayed a mixture of hydrogen and oxygen into the combustion chambers. The entire fuel supply for the first stage was forced through the system within a matter of minutes. If an injector failed to maintain a critical pressure within a combustion chamber, then the chamber would become unstable and explode. The ship would be destroyed. Despite the danger, the risk was relatively low. The basic design of the engine had been in use for many years in the space shuttle. The thrust from the engines pushed the crew back into their seats and propelled the ship to a speed twenty-two times that of sound.

"Control, this is *Liberty*," Nelson said. "The first-stage engines are at seventy percent, over."

"We confirm, over."

As the ship accelerated, the g forces increased. After several weeks of weightlessness, the astronauts could feel their bodies regain their normal weight. Then they grew heavier, several times heavier than they would have felt on Earth, and since they had begun to adapt to the weightless environment of the space station, the effect was intensified. Carter lifted his arm from his seat and placed his hand several inches in front of his face. As he struggled to hold it steady, the g forces caused it to shake. He occupied his mind with the struggle and found a certain pleasure in it. And then suddenly his hand became very light and flew away from his face. He was able to stop it within inches of the flight-deck panel.

"Control, this is *Liberty*. We have first-stage burnout, over." When the first-stage rocket had consumed its fuel, the ship stopped accelerating, and the g forces created by the acceleration vanished. Once again the crew was weightless.

"Roger, *Liberty*, prepare for separation."

The computer began the countdown to jettison the large TMI stage, which would reduce the spacecraft to less than one-half its original size and weight. Bright green numbers flashed across the screen. The astronauts felt a slight jolt as the TMI stage separated from the spacecraft.

"We have first-stage separation," Nelson announced. "Trans-Mars injection burn complete. Do you copy? Over."

"Roger, TMI burn complete. Out."

"Module extension to commence in ninety minutes," Nelson said as he released his safety straps.

Dr. Endicott experienced a momentary uneasiness at the mention of the maneuver. It involved the extraction of the habitat and lab modules from behind the aeroshields, where they were safely tucked at the front of the ship, and their extension outward on a pair of trusses eighteen meters in length. The ship's final configuration would look something like a crucifix, with the lab module at one end and the habitat module at the other. The two modules were connected to the main vehicle by a collapsible tunnel. Once extended, the modules would begin to spin to produce a gravitational effect four-tenths that of Earth's.

Ninety minutes later both Endicott and Brunnet were pressed against a portal watching the long trusses slowly extricate themselves from the inner structure of the space vehicle.

"Does not exactly fill one with confidence, does it?" Endicott whispered to Brunnet.

Brunnet, who had been admiring the mechanical aspect of the maneuver, realized with some reluctance that Endicott's doubts were not completely unfounded. He did not want to express his opinion, particularly in the presence of Nelson and Carter, and merely shrugged. The structure is perfectly safe, he told himself. It only appears unsafe.

But Brunnet could not rid his mind of the knowledge that

the engineers had argued strenuously against the trusses, that they had agreed to their implementation only after it could not be determined how to maintain the necessary levels of calcium in the bones of an astronaut without the constant stress imposed by gravity. The bones would become so brittle after two years in a weightless environment, the length of the Martian voyage, that the g forces of reentry would snap them like dried-up twigs. The ill-fated *Volnost* had not been equipped with artificial gravity. The expense had been too great. The Russian scientists had opted for a constant regimen of exercise and calcium supplements. But the cosmonauts had complained continuously about the exercise and had often been too exhausted to do much else. Once it was agreed that gravity was necessary, the debate shifted to the amount required. The physiologists pushed for one g, which called for trusses over sixty-one meters in length, three times longer than the .4 configuration. The engineers refused to compromise the structural integrity of their ship any further and .4 was finally adopted.

The flight deck console blinked blue at Carter.

"Fully extended," he responded.

"We have full extension." Nelson turned to Carter. The next step was to spin the trusses using the Reaction Control System. "Proceed with spin."

"Initiating RCS burn," Carter announced as he punched the instructions on the keyboard to activate the miniature hydrazine-powered rockets located at the ends of the extensions.

The ship remained stationary as the two eighteen-meter extensions gradually achieved a speed of two revolutions per minute. The Russian craft possessed similar extensions, but was different in one notable respect. The entire ship spun, not just the extensions. Although the design was simpler to engineer, it had its own complications. Certain navigational and astronomical devices, such as telescopes, had to be spun in the opposite direction to avoid a constantly spinning image.

"Two rpms," Carter announced.

"Houston, gravitational spin achieved, over."

"Roger, *Liberty*. Congratulations, gentlemen. Godspeed and have a safe trip."

————————

D r. Takashi Satomura was seated on the floor with his legs crossed beneath him. He was studying a holographic chessboard that floated several centimeters from the ground. Miniature Russian soldiers, dressed in winter rags, stomped their boots to keep their feet warm as they glared across the board at their adversary, the French. Behind a line of foot soldiers, adorned in full military regalia with one hand tucked conspicuously inside his jacket, stood Napoleon and, beside him, his lovely wife Josephine. A royal purple evening gown flowed from her shoulders and fluttered delicately in the wind. She acknowledged Satomura's gaze with an elegant curtsy. The French foot soldier several squares in front of her shook his bayonet at his opponents and spat in their direction to register his disgust. A Russian soldier yelled back profanities and soon the entire board was engaged in a violent shouting match.

"Quiet," ordered Satomura.

The pieces stopped immediately and froze into tiny statues. Eventually, a few of the soldiers began to shuffle their feet impatiently. A restless knight reared back on his horse. The Czar carefully pulled out a gold watch connected to a fourteen-karat chain and held it at arm's length. He motioned to Satomura to check the time.

"I know. I know," Satomura replied. He looked up and down the board. He pulled on the stubbly hairs of his chin. He closed his eyes to concentrate. When they opened several minutes later they were bright and alive. He announced his move in a slow and deliberate voice.

"Queen to bishop two."

"Ah," Napoleon said. He pulled a map from his vest and rolled it out on the snow-covered ground in front of him. He studied the map carefully. It was a two-dimensional representation of the chessboard upon which he stood. Josephine bent over and whispered something in his ear. He waved her away. If he had wanted her advice, he would have asked. Moments later, he looked up at Satomura and smiled.

"Pawn takes pawn," he ordered. He wiped the snow from a pair of leather binoculars, then peered through them to watch the ninth move.

The soldier in question unslung his rifle and readied his bayonet. He pointed it directly at the Russian soldier standing on the white square diagonal from him. The queen's bishop's pawn dropped to one knee and readied his gun. He aimed carefully and pulled the trigger as the French soldier charged. The rifle exploded violently in his hands, leaving a pair of bloodied stumps. He was blinded by the hot powder of the blast, and it was not until he attempted to rub his eyes that he realized he had lost his hands. He never saw the bayonet that pierced his heart. He screamed, then slowly faded away. The snow upon which he had stood was sprinkled with brilliant red droplets. The French soldier reslung his rifle, fresh blood dripping down the wooden stock. Napoleon clapped his hands and looked up at Satomura triumphantly.

"Bishop takes knight," Satomura replied without the slightest hesitation.

"*Merde,*" Bonaparte responded, as he swung to his left to watch the battle. There was no need to use his binoculars, the fight would take place only a few squares away.

The bishop, who had been standing perfectly still and perfectly straight, threw back his cape and, with a majestic flourish, produced a long staff. The knight, heavily armored and mounted high on his horse, laughed loudly. Surely, a bishop, a Russian bishop at that, wearing a robe and armed with nothing but a staff, was a poor match against a trained soldier. He turned to his beloved emperor to assure him the battle would be short. And it was. His emperor's eyes opened wide, and he began to shout something, but the knight never heard the words. With a broad sweep of his staff the bishop swiftly decapitated his opponent. The knight's head, mouth still laughing, tumbled lifeless to the ground, and his horse reared back in protest. The bishop stepped forward.

Satomura giggled with pleasure.

"Napoleon," he said, "the defense you've chosen was demonstrated to be unsound in the second game of last year's championship. You don't stand a chance, my friend."

The French emperor responded with a grunt and was about to announce his next move when he was interrupted by Vladimir Pavlov entering the room.

"Pause," ordered Satomura. Napoleon placed his map back inside his vest and commenced to tap his foot impatiently.

"What do we have here?" Vladimir asked.

"A friendly game of chess," Takashi replied.

"Queen's gambit declined."

"Quite correct."

"A little gruesome, the head rolling across the board like that."

"I modified the program. A personal touch. Do you like it?"

Vladimir watched the head as it rolled off the chessboard and fell to the ground, where it bounced once, then faded away. He appeared unaffected. The remaining French knight caught his attention, and he bent down to scrutinize the piece closer.

"He is wearing armor," Vladimir remarked. The tone in his voice expected an explanation.

"Another personal touch," Satomura responded. It was obvi-

ous he was proud of his personal touches. "To me a knight without armor is like a Russian without vodka. Wouldn't you agree?"
He laughed sharply at his own wit.

"Well, yes, I suppose," Vladimir responded, uncertain
whether he should consider the remark an insult. He did not
dwell on the matter long. He was wrestling with something that
meant far more to him, and he had come to Satomura to find
out what he might know.

His suspicions had grown worse, but he was afraid to confront
Tanya. He was afraid an accusation, even the slightest hint of an
accusation, would infuriate her. She would deny everything of
course. She would become angered by his lack of trust. He had to
be certain before he spoke to her. Which was why he was standing
in front of Satomura looking intently at the oddly dressed soldier,
wondering how he should begin or if he should begin at all. He
considered how much easier it would be simply to walk out.

"Can I speak to you in confidence?" he began cautiously.

"You can trust me," replied Satomura. He had anticipated
the role of confidant, and he relished it in a perverse sort of way.
He was older, an impartial bystander, outside the triangle; it was
natural they would come to him. So Vladimir was the first.
Well, that was to be expected. He was the one being cheated on.

"What do you think of Dmitri?"

"How do you mean?" Satomura replied.

"What sort of man would you say he is?"

"He is a fine commander."

"Yes, he is," Vladimir agreed with a pained smile. He paused
and thought to himself that he often wanted to be like
Komarov. To accomplish the deeds and to earn the respect of
others like Komarov had. To be a national hero. Even to have
guiltless love affairs. He was not ready to admit that to Takashi,
however. "What else?"

"Perhaps if you were more specific, I could be more helpful?"

Vladimir thought for a moment and decided it was best to

be indirect. What if his suspicions were ill founded? He did not want to raise unnecessary concerns in Takashi's mind. He realized how foolish he had been in thinking Takashi would simply volunteer what he wanted to hear. It appeared Takashi did not even know what he was alluding to. He had not formed a plan beyond simply asking what Takashi thought of Dmitri. For nearly a minute he stood staring at the glistening soldier, wondering how best to proceed.

"I see that something is troubling you," Satomura said.

"It is probably nothing," Vladimir said. "It's just that sometimes I feel he is hiding something from me."

"Ah," Satomura replied as if he finally understood. "I would not trouble myself too greatly."

"Why is that?" Vladimir asked, relieved.

"How long do you suppose he could hide something in a ship this small?"

"Very true," Vladimir replied. He did not have the courage to speak of his problem any more directly, although he sensed that Takashi fully understood it. He convinced himself that for the time being he would learn little else from Takashi. But what Takashi had said about the ship being small was true, and that now dominated his thinking. He realized with sudden clarity that he would eventually find them out. It was absurd to think they could carry on an affair in such small confines. He was beginning to think of ways he could spy on them, something he had always before considered undignified. Each room had its own microphone. He could reprogram the circuits, but decided the move could be too easily detected by Tatiana. She was responsible for maintaining the ship's software. As he contemplated the various ways he might be able to find them out, he became increasingly conscious of Satomura's presence. A sense of guilt overcame him. He wanted to be alone so that he could think. He complained of the schedule and said it was time he got back to work.

"You know where to find me," Satomura said.

The aging scientist watched Vladimir's back as he departed through the portal. He attempted to recall what it had been like when he had been in love. The recollection was overwhelmed by all the troubled emotions that had ensued, and produced a knowing smile, for Vladimir was apparently experiencing many of the same emotions. Satomura's wife was dead. She had died of a sexually transmitted disease, a disease from which he had not suffered. The nature of her death, which Satomura had managed to keep secret even from her family, had left Satomura with a contempt for women. Even that he managed to conceal, but not quite as well.

"Proceed," he ordered the board.

"Knight takes bishop," Napoleon responded.

"Of course," Satomura replied with a sharp bark of a laugh.

"They could be some sort of crystophages," Brunnet said.

"Creatures that consume ice," Endicott replied doubtfully. He pressed his thin lips tightly together. He was not opposed to the idea that life could exist on Mars; what he objected to were the forms that life took when Brunnet began to speculate out loud.

"Precisely," Brunnet confirmed. "But they need not eat the ice directly. They could melt it through some sort of metabolic process."

"I suppose it is an improvement upon the creatures you were advocating yesterday. A chemical catalyst to suck water from a rock is a bit extreme."

Brunnet chuckled as he pulled down on eighty-five pounds of resistance. Sweat dripped off his brow and dropped in slow motion to the metallic ground. Grimacing, he crunched his stomach until he achieved a fetal position. He detested exercise.

Endicott, on the other hand, happily watched the green hills of Montreal float by on the high-definition as he pedaled vigorously on top of his stationary bike. He imagined the smell of the clean country air as it passed through his nostrils to fill his lungs with oxygen. His conversations with Brunnet were a source of mental stimulation for him.

"I haven't given up on them entirely," Brunnet replied in between gasps for air. "It's just that I don't believe a Martian life-form needs to resort to such desperate measures."

"If your hypothesis regarding underground rivers is correct, you may not need to resort to crystophages."

"That's right. I was just considering various possibilities." Brunnet was resting against the rubber straps of the exercise machine, collecting his thoughts. "Sometimes I'm convinced Mars must be teeming with life below its surface. That is, if the rivers do exist."

"I'm not so sure I would go that far. The absence of sunlight must be an inhibitor."

"Nonsense. There are all sorts of creatures that can survive without sunlight. Earth's oceans are filled with them. I can name several dozen species that live quite happily in absolute darkness."

"Still, I think I would stop somewhat short of 'teeming.' You must admit that certain environments are more hostile to life than others."

"Yes, but we are talking about water. And water is the friendliest of all."

Brunnet's triumphant smile lasted only a few seconds. His facial muscles tightened. A low and painful moan slipped through his lips. He doubled over, grabbing his abdomen with both hands.

Endicott, who was absorbed with the green hills of Montreal, reluctantly tore his eyes from the screen to investigate the source of the moan. Because of the maze of metal and rubber that surrounded Brunnet, he was unable to see him clearly. The second moan, much louder and more drawn-out than the first, left little doubt in Endicott's mind that Brunnet was suffering from severe pain.

"What is it?" he asked. He stopped pedaling.

"I thought it might have been space sickness." The voice that responded was weak and shaky.

"What might have been space sickness?"

"I was feeling nauseous earlier this morning."

"Vomiting?" Endicott asked.

"At the very beginning. But it subsided."

"Where is the pain?"

"My stomach." He was gasping for air.

Endicott climbed off the stationary bike and hurried over to Brunnet.

"Where exactly?" he asked.

Brunnet, his eyes closed now, pointed at the lower right side of his abdomen.

"Can you climb out of that contraption?"

Brunnet nodded, then unstrapped and carefully extracted himself from the resistance machine. He attempted to stand up straight, but upon reaching midway stopped and smiled awkwardly in defeat.

"Have you experienced the pain before?"

"No."

"Temperature?" he said, placing his hand on Jean Paul's forehead, not waiting for a response.

"Maybe, I'm not sure," Brunnet responded, shuddering as a wave of nausea swept through his body.

"You're hot. Take your shirt off and lie down on the table."

Brunnet fumbled with the buttons of his shirt. They were too small for his trembling fingers. Endicott came to his assistance. Several minutes later Brunnet was flat on his back, looking up at Endicott with considerable concern. He was now certain in his own mind that something was seriously wrong with him.

"OK, does this hurt?" Endicott asked, tapping sharply the lower right side of his abdomen.

"*Merde,*" shrieked Brunnet.

"I'll assume that means yes," Endicott said. "And how about here?"

Endicott carefully tapped his way around Brunnet's stomach. The pain diminished the farther he tapped from the lower right quadrant.

"Did the pain originate from the back and move forward?"

"I don't think so. It was more like a stomachache. Mild nausea at first. Like I said, I thought it was space sickness."

"Constipation or diarrhea?"

"I did not have a bowel movement this morning, but I wouldn't go so far as to say that I am suffering from constipation."

"Let me see your eyes."

Brunnet opened his eyes wide. Endicott was visibly relieved: the eyes were clear, not the pale yellow that would suggest cirrhosis of the liver.

"What do you think it is?"

"Could be a kidney infection, acute pyelonephritis, or even kidney stones, but I doubt it. The symptoms are textbook. I believe you are suffering from an inflamed appendix."

"Appendicitis?"

"We will need to consult with Earth and perform some tests to confirm the diagnosis. If my suspicions are correct, your appendix will have to be removed."

"When?"

"As soon as we are sure of the diagnosis. Time is of the essence. A burst appendix can be fatal."

"Do you have the proper equipment?"

"Of course," Endicott replied with a false smile. He was

wondering how he would conduct the diagnosis without an X-ray or an ultrasound machine.

Endicott and Nelson were standing in front of the high-definition waiting for Dr. Cain to silence the men surrounding him. When he finally succeeded, he smiled briefly at the camera.

"Good morning," he said. "You may already know some of the doctors here."

The camera swiveled past Cain's silver curls and focused upon a panel of doctors. Seated at the center, an elderly man lifted his graying head and, with his index finger, pushed back on a pair of wire-framed glasses until they settled into the red indentations that marked each side of his nose. Cain introduced him as Dr. Lear.

"Good morning, Dr. Endicott. I had hoped our next meeting would have been under more pleasant circumstances," Dr. Lear said, articulating each word with crisp precision. "In order to minimize the delay, I will pause between questions to allow you to respond. Of course, we will be unable to respond to any questions you may have until several minutes later. They tell me the delay is nearly twelve minutes. I understand you are used to this sort of disorientating dialogue, but I assure you my colleagues and I are not, so please bear with us." He paused to look down at a sheet of paper. "The white blood-cell count was slightly higher than I would have expected. Over eighteen thousand."

"Eighteen thousand, five hundred, and sixty-two," Endicott clarified.

"The elevated count and the shift to the left could indicate a perforated appendix. Under the circumstance we must assume the worst. Commence intravenous hydration and start the patient on Mefoxin immediately. Any evidence of albuminuria in the urine?" He paused.

"None."

"Did you check for Rovsing's sign?" He paused again.

"I'm sorry. I'm not familiar with the technique."

"The level of amylase in the urine was normal, which rules out acute pancreatitis," piped in a younger doctor, seated to the left of center. Dr. Lear peered over the top of his glasses, his eyebrows lowered in disapproval. After several uncomfortable seconds he continued.

"Appendicitis can be easily confused with several other disorders, and without a barium enema or ultrasonography the diagnosis can be tricky. Do you feel confident he is not suffering from a severe case of gastroenteritis?" He paused, and while he waited he arranged the lab results on the table in front of him.

"As you have said, without the appropriate equipment it is difficult to make an accurate diagnosis," Endicott replied. "I am as certain as I can be."

Lear went on to discuss many of the complications that could arise and had just finished describing the procedures for a perforated appendix when Endicott could hear his own voice over the high-definition saying, "Yes, I am."

He watched the doctors as they listened to him respond to their questions. Intermixed with his replies a tape of the Earthside dialogue was being played quietly in the background so that the physicians were able to associate the answer with the question.

Dr. Lear turned to the camera. "Rovsing's sign occurs when pressure is applied to the lower left side of the abdomen and pain is felt on the lower right. The symptom does not always present itself, but when it does there is a high probability the cause is appendicitis."

"There was no indication of pain," Endicott responded.

"As I was saying," Lear continued, "it will be impossible for us to assist you directly with the operation owing to the time delay; however, the medical assistance program should be able to guide you through any complications that might arise." He glanced at a paper that had been passed to him. "I have just been informed that if you have any further questions, you must ask them now."

"What should I look for if it turns out not to be the appendix?" Endicott asked.

Slides of an appendectomy appeared on the high-definition while Endicott and Nelson waited restlessly for a response. As the slides advanced in slow motion, the recorded voice of an elderly woman explained the various aspects of the operation. Thin layers of oblique muscles, crisscrossing, were being pulled back with curved, spoonlike utensils. Behind the muscles was a confusion of organs, dominated by a reddish mass the voice of the elderly woman referred to as the cecum. The bloody organ was being pulled up and out of the wound when suddenly it disappeared and was replaced by the crisp image of Dr. Lear.

"In the event the appendix does not appear to be infected, examine the small bowel for enteritis or Meckel's diverticulitis. The lymph nodes should also be examined for mesenteric adenitis. The simulation will explore each of these possibilities. If indeed nothing is found to be wrong, the appendectomy should still be conducted."

There was a pause.

"Good luck." Dr. Lear's warm smile had been digitized and torn apart bit by bit, then mathematically reconstructed after oscillating, single file, through space. The smile conveyed confidence in Endicott or was at least meant to convey confidence. Endicott could not be certain. The camera swiveled and focused on Cain. His smile seemed forced, which for Cain was unusual.

"Best of luck, gentlemen," he said.

Endicott wondered just how much luck he would require. As part of his training for the mission he had performed several surgical procedures, including an appendectomy, but he was not a surgeon. His understanding of medical matters was mostly academic. He glanced at Nelson and saw that he appeared to be waiting for instructions. Normally, Nelson would be giving orders in a crisis of this magnitude. He seemed uncomfortable, or perhaps he was just nervous. Endicott glanced at his watch in order to collect his thoughts.

"We should get him started on the antibiotics," he said upon looking up.

———

The compartment was too small to be a proper operating room. There was barely enough space for the EKG machine or for Lieutenant Colonel Carter, who was standing nervously in front of the machine with his back to the patient. His responsibilities were to monitor the life-support readouts and enter information dictated by Endicott into the computer. He purposely did not turn around. His skin was still damp with cold sweat and his stomach tight. He had seen the scalpel make a vertical slice across Brunnet's bare abdomen, leaving a trail of red dots that grew into pools of blood until a sponge swept them away. That was all he could bear to watch. In an attempt to force the image from his mind, he concentrated on the steady pulse of the EKG. He was beginning to think of other things when he heard, or thought he heard, the sound of flesh pulling apart. He closed his eyes and swallowed hard. He wanted to close his ears to stop the sound, and desperately fought the urge to clasp his hands over them. He heard Endicott say something, but his voice was distant. Then silently and without warning came the smell. At first he was uncertain. So he sniffed a little bit deeper. The odor was sweet and slightly pungent. As it slowly expanded into his lungs, he realized that it was intestinal gases. The gases had grown foul inside the wound. He began to gag.

Endicott looked up to see Carter's back hastily retreat through the portal. He then looked across the table at Nelson, who with a blood-soaked sponge in hand was about to go after him.

"It's not unusual. Some fresh air and he'll be all right," Endicott said. Tom Nelson looked uncertainly at the portal.

"I need you here," Endicott said. As their eyes met, they heard the sound of Carter vomiting in the next room.

They quickly returned their attention to the body on the table. Towels were draped over the abdomen to form the boundaries of a rectangle outside the wound. The skin was pulled back, revealing a thin layer of red oblique muscles. The lower portion of the opening was filling with blood.

"Sponge," Endicott said.

Nelson carefully pressed a sponge against the blood.

"Hemostat," Endicott said.

Wiping the perspiration from his brow as he placed the sponge in the sink, Nelson hesitated at the sight of several clamps of various sizes. He chose a medium-sized one and handed it to Endicott.

"Sponge."

Nelson wiped the blood clear.

"Don't wipe. Press," Endicott instructed. "Wiping the sponge across the vessel may increase the hemorrhaging."

Endicott located the severed vessel and quickly clamped it shut.

"Hold this," Endicott said, presenting the end of the hemostat to Nelson. They heard Carter quietly enter the room to resume his vigilance at the life-support monitors.

"Ligature."

"What?" Nelson asked, his voice strained.

"The thread."

"Thread," Nelson repeated as he placed it in Endicott's hand.

"We are going to tie off the vessel to stop the bleeding. Listen carefully; although the simulation made this look easy, it can be somewhat tricky the first time you try it. I want you to hold the hemostat straight up while I pass the ligature around behind it. You will then lower the handle and raise the tip so that I can tie a knot around the vessel. When I say 'off,' remove the hemostat. With the scissors cut the thread at the points I indicate. Take care not to cut or touch anything other than the thread. Are you ready?"

"Ready," Nelson replied, attempting to sound more confident than he actually felt.

"OK, lift the hemostat."

Nelson obeyed and held the clamp perpendicular to the body, allowing Endicott to pass the thread behind it.

"Pull up slightly so that I can get the thread around the vessel."

As Nelson pulled, the clamp slipped off the vessel and blood spurted from the severed tip.

"Damn," Nelson said.

"Sponge," Endicott ordered. "Quick."

Endicott took the sponge and dipped it into the wound. "Blood pressure."

"One-thirty over eighty," responded Carter.

"Good," Endicott replied. "Let's try it again. Hemostat."

Nelson handed the hemostat over and watched as Endicott clamped the vessel shut at a spot slightly farther back than he had the first time.

"OK, hold this here," Endicott said, offering the clamp. "Do not put too much tension on the blood vessel. Pull back gently. That's good."

Endicott tightened the thread around the vessel. He looked up and smiled triumphantly. "Off."

Nelson released the clamp and, when he was sure the knot would hold, breathed a sigh of relief.

"Cut the ends with the scissors." Endicott held the two ends of the ligature apart. They formed a giant V. "Not so close."

"Where then?" Nelson asked.

"A centimeter up from the knot. It may come undone if you cut too close, and the ends may get in the way of the scalpel if you cut too far."

Nelson, taking a deep breath, bent over the body and clipped the thread.

"And now," Endicott said, "the external obliques."

Without turning around, Carter spoke. "The computer says to split the external oblique muscle in the direction of its fibers, then split the internal obliques, and then split the transversus abdominis. What the hell is that?"

"Another muscle group."

Carter returned his attention to the EKG. He was thankful that he did not have to look at the open wound and decided the cartoonlike depiction on the screen before him was not so bad. It was the smell that troubled him the most.

Endicott separated the internal obliques with the retractors and saw that his hands were shaking. He paused to breathe deeply.

"Everything OK?" Nelson asked.

"Everything is fine." Endicott looked at his hands. They were steady now. He waited a few more seconds before proceeding.

"When will we be done here?" Nelson asked.

"Fifteen minutes, maybe longer."

"How much longer?"

"Depends upon what we find behind the cecum. If the appendix is not the culprit, then we'll have to search elsewhere. It is difficult to estimate the unknown."

Endicott split the transversus abdominis; he instructed Nelson on how to secure the muscle group; then he delicately lifted the cecum out of the wound, revealing the appendix. The inflamed protrusion was immersed in a turbid pool of white pus, leaving little doubt in the minds of the two men hovering above the tiny organ that it was responsible for Brunnet's condition. Endicott slowly extracted the pus with the hand-operated suction. Once he had the immediate area cleared, he lifted the appendix to examine it. The flesh on the underside near the tip was shredded.

"Not good," he said. "It's perforated. Hemostat."

Endicott lifted the burst appendix from the abdomen and clamped it shut at its base. The organ turned pale. He inserted the suction into the cavity and sucked the remaining pus into the clear device. After irrigating the wound, he cleansed the surrounding area with a sponge treated with a topical antibiotic. He severed the appendix, handed it to Nelson, and motioned for him to enclose it within the sterile container on the counter.

Nelson wasn't sure what Endicott meant, so he stood there without moving, the bloody specimen in the palm of his hand.

"Place it in that container there," Endicott said.

"You plan to keep it?"

"They want to examine it back on Earth."

Endicott bent down near the open cavity and sewed the stump closed. He handed Nelson the needle. With the appendix successfully removed and tied off, Endicott was beginning to relax. "Ease up slowly on the retractor." He gently pushed the abdominal contents into the cavity. The muscles fell neatly into place. He left an opening in the skin so that the wound could be easily drained if an infection developed.

"That should be it for now," Endicott said, suppressing his relief. "I'll remain with him for a while. There's no reason for you two to stay."

"Congratulations," Nelson said, and extended his hand.

Carter had already left the room.

———

Nelson was reviewing the daily activity sheet as he sipped his morning coffee. The workload had been reduced to compensate for Brunnet's absence during his recovery, but to a much greater degree than Nelson had expected. It was obvious that the mission planners didn't want to tax them. But it was also obvious that the planners didn't want them idle either. Nelson considered this and decided to approve the activities.

He didn't want to give his men time to worry about Brunnet's condition. The wound had become infected overnight. Endicott had assured them that this was not unusual for a perforated appendix, and with proper treatment the infection did not pose a danger. He had drained the wound earlier that morning and increased the antibiotics.

Carter was seated next to Nelson in the command module and was watching with intense interest as numbers scrolled up the screen of the main console. He tapped at the keyboard. The numbers switched from yellow to a light shade of red as a new series of calculations appeared. He stared at the screen for several minutes, lost in thought.

"I'm not so sure about this," he said.

"What is it?" Nelson asked.

"The computer has detected a rise in solar activity."

Nelson looked over at the computer console and saw that the screen was pink, and without having to see the numbers he knew there was cause for concern. "How bad?"

"The spectrometer readings have been higher than usual. The computer estimates a ten percent increase in solar activity. New polarized regions are beginning to appear on the radio map, and the magnetic field has undergone some mild disturbances. There's a seventy-three percent chance of a solar flare." Carter paused for all this to sink in. "It gets worse."

"Let's hear it."

"The sort of preflare activity we're detecting is typical of the more powerful flares. It may even be a plus three." A plus-three solar flare could spew forth the equivalent of ten million hydrogen bombs in the first few minutes of its existence, releasing a barrage of radiation that would be fatal outside the ship's shelter.

"We should move Jean Paul to the shelter as a precaution. I'll alert Carl." Nelson recalled that Endicott was exercising and typed the commands to direct the intercom to the habitat module. "Carl, you there?"

There was silence.

"Carl?" he repeated.

Still, silence.

"Where do you suppose he can be?" Nelson asked.

"One moment," Carter responded. He pulled up the status report for the ship's life-support system and quickly confirmed what he suspected. The system was supplying water to the habitat module. "He's probably in the shower."

"I guess we can give him—" Nelson was interrupted by the loud blare of the ship's siren. The sound caused both Nelson and Carter to jump. "Turn that damn thing off."

Carter hastily typed in the instructions to abort the alarm sequence. "We've got our plus three. Looks like it erupted only a few minutes after the computer had detected preflare activity."

"How long till impact?" Nelson asked.

"Sixteen minutes." Carter shoved a piece of gum into his mouth.

"That doesn't give us much time." He switched the intercom back on. "Carl, you there?"

Carter saw that the demand for water from the habitat module had stopped.

"What was that racket all about?" Endicott replied, sounding out of breath.

"A plus-three solar flare just erupted. We've got sixteen minutes till impact."

There was a tense moment of silence as Endicott considered this. "We have to move Jean Paul. But first, I'll need to close the wound. He'll never make it through the despin platform in his condition."

"Can't you just tape it shut?"

"Too risky. Besides, we wouldn't save that much time. It'll take ten minutes to close the wound. I'll need your help though."

"Of course. But keep in mind that it'll take at least five minutes to get him to the shelter. That doesn't leave us with much time to spare." Nelson switched the intercom off and turned to Carter. "I want you in the shelter."

Carter began to protest, but Nelson abruptly interrupted and ordered him to leave. As Carter departed through the portal, Nelson glanced at the monitor, which now prominently displayed the time remaining before impact. Fifteen minutes. A minute had already passed. Without further delay, he made for the habitat module, running as quickly as the tight confines of the ship permitted.

When he arrived, he found Endicott tugging at a pair of surgical gloves. Brunnet was in bed, his eyes struggling to stay open. They closed moments later.

"I gave him enough to keep him out for at least an hour," Endicott said. "Let's get him on the table. I'll take the feet."

Nelson grabbed Brunnet under the arms, and at the count of three they picked him up. Because of the reduced gravity, the body did not weigh much more than that of a child's. They placed him carefully on the table and opened his shirt. Endicott shook his head with concern as he removed the dressing.

"I should drain it," he said.

"How long will that take?"

"Four, five minutes."

Nelson glanced over at the main monitor in the habitat module. It was flashing eleven minutes. He realized that if they took the time to drain the wound, the flare would reach the ship before they could make it to the shelter. "Are you sure?"

"The radiation shouldn't reach hazardous levels until approximately twenty minutes after impact," Endicott said. His voice was strained.

"Perhaps we should check with the computer."

Endicott turned his back without responding and silently entered the relevant data. Activated by his strokes, a stream of stop-start bits pulsed down the fiber-optic cable to the central processing unit, where they initiated a series of parallel operations. An artificial-intelligence-based algorithm evaluated the various options. The resulting bit streams converged upon the output channel and emerged in yellow upon the screen.

"It concurs," Endicott said, secretly relieved the decision had been made for him. He opened a drawer that contained his medical instruments and pulled out a closed-suction catheter. "I need to sterilize this."

Nelson bit his lip as he glanced at the clock. Nine minutes. He placed his hand on Brunnet's forehead. It felt warm.

"I think he's got a fever."

"Low-grade," Endicott confirmed, without turning around. "Brought about by the infection. Nothing to worry about. It's a common reaction."

The remark did little to comfort Nelson.

Endicott returned to the body and inserted the catheter into the wound. A sickly reddish yellow substance crawled up the tube. "There we go," Endicott said, holding the tube out at eye level so that he could examine the contents. He saw that his hand was shaking and quickly placed it at his side so that Nelson wouldn't notice.

But Nelson did notice. "You all right?"

"I'll be fine," Endicott replied. He was angry with himself, and it showed in his voice. Their eyes met in hard silence. Endicott was only able to maintain the contact for a few seconds before he tore his eyes away. He looked back down at the open wound. Nelson was justified in his concern, and they both knew it. He had to concentrate. The next step was to cleanse the wound and treat it with an antiseptic.

Carter's voice sounded over the intercom. "The shelter is fully deployed. Only seven minutes remaining until impact."

Nelson looked questioningly at Endicott.

"It'll take at least ten." He irrigated the wound with saline solution. He poured a small amount, then removed it, repeating the process until the effluent solution was clear. As he applied the antiseptic, he could feel his heart beating inside his chest. He bit down hard and started to breathe through his nose. When he was satisfied the entire area had been treated, he put aside the antiseptic and prepared the needle. It was shaking in his hand. He was horrified to see that it struck a spot nearly half an inch from the wound. He pulled the needle back out and tried again. This time it pierced the flesh very close to the intended target. "Hold the skin firmly together while I sew. Not too hard. Make certain the edges are not inverted."

Carter's voice came booming over the intercom. "The hull sensor detects a ten percent increase in electromagnetic radiation. It's starting. I'm listening to the particle detector. Sounds like goddamn rifle shots. Estimated ninety rads in the first half hour, three hundred and fifty in the first hour, and nearly one thousand in the second. Jesus, you guys better get moving."

"Over two hundred can be lethal. Anything under forty is relatively safe. We should be all right if we get out of here in the next few minutes," Endicott said.

"You've got one," Nelson said.

"I need three."

"Carter," Nelson said, speaking into the intercom, "I want you to arrange a space for Jean Paul's stretcher. His back is to face the sun. We'll be out of here in three minutes."

"Roger," Carter responded.

"We're almost done."

Nelson looked back over his shoulder at the console. "Estimated exposure, two-point-seven-six rems," he said.

Endicott wondered how much radiation Brunnet could bear

as he swiftly wove the curved needle in and out of the skin. He used a square knot to tie off the suture.

"Dressing," he said.

Nelson handed over an iodine-soaked gauze. Endicott placed it over the suture and taped it down. He dabbed alcohol at the outer edges of the dressing to remove the excess iodine.

"I'm done," he said, backing away from the body.

"Let's get the hell out of here," Nelson said.

"I'll need a few things for postoperative care."

"You've got exactly ten seconds."

Endicott could still feel his heart beating against his chest. He threw an assortment of vials and hypodermics onto the stretcher. "Ready."

"Carter, we're on our way," Nelson announced into the intercom.

"I'll warm the coffee," the intercom returned with a Southern drawl.

Nelson grabbed the front of the stretcher and Endicott the back. As they plunged through the portal, they both looked up to check the console. ESTIMATED EXPOSURE: 13 REMS.

Their jog quickly turned into a walk as they approached the center of the ship and were forced to correct for the shifting gravities of the extension. When they reached the hub, the transition between the rotating and stationary modules proved to be a challenge for the stretcher. Endicott went first. He stepped inside the despin platform, where he allowed the centrifugal force to push him up against the outer wall. He reached back for the stretcher. He could see Nelson hoisting the body over his head. He grabbed the stretcher with one arm and after some difficulty placed it vertically alongside him. Nelson soon followed. Once Endicott was certain they were all safely in place, he punched the switch to stop the rotation of the platform. As it slowed down their bodies became lighter, and they floated into the center of the chamber. They were breathing hard.

Nearly five minutes had passed since they had left the habitat module.

They looked overhead and saw Carter waiting at the portal of the shelter. The console behind his head displayed an estimated exposure of thirty-six rems.

A Solar Flare

At the sun's surface, twisting ribbons of electrical current and solar gas swirled into an emerging flux of magnetic tension and exploded. Streams of ultrafast electrons streaked outward from the explosion, accelerated by plasma waves cresting at speeds approaching that of light. Those particles that headed back toward the sun collided with the chromosphere and produced an even greater explosion. The resulting mixture of electromagnetic waves and ionized particles burned a deadly path through space.

Both the American and Russian spacecraft were traveling directly through that path. Even in their storm shelters the crew members were not entirely safe. A few radioactive particles still made their way through the protective structure. Of the three thousand rads bombarding the ships in the first two hours, only fifty would make it through the American storm shelter, thirty through the Russians'. The surgical team, who had not been sheltered for the beginning of the flare, would absorb approximately one hundred rems. Although not lethal, one hundred rems was a substantial amount of radiation to absorb in such a short period of time. The astronauts would most likely suffer from radiation sickness.

Major Vladimir Pavlov's eyes were fixed on the radiation count. The estimated exposure was displayed for each cosmonaut. Every few minutes a counter would increase. His count was twenty-two. Although his wife's count read the same, they both knew it should have probably been slightly less, since he was holding her in such a way that his body formed a shield against the radiation. She felt warm in his arms. There was nothing for them to do but watch and wait.

"I wonder how Jean Paul is doing," Tanya said. No one replied. Their thoughts focused hazily upon Brunnet as they watched the rem counter silently increase. They knew that each ionized particle that passed through their bodies left a wake of altered cells.

"I wonder how Jean Paul is doing," she persisted.

Vladimir squeezed her hand, and she returned the warmth. His suspicions had nearly disappeared under the tender influence of her affection. The danger had brought them together. He did not fully understand why, but then he did not really care. All that mattered was that they were happy again.

"I suppose we could contact them," he offered.

"No," said Komarov.

"Why not?"

"It would not be appropriate."

"Why would it not be appropriate?"

"If they need our assistance, they will contact us."

Vladimir thought about his commander's response and decided not to pursue the point further even though he disagreed. Tanya, on the other hand, would not be put off so easily.

"I think we should radio them," she said.

Dr. Takashi Satomura, who had nearly fallen asleep, perked up at the sound of the challenge. Without opening his eyes, he raised his head so that he might be able to hear better. He was seated next to Komarov.

"No," Komarov said in a low, firm voice.

"What harm could it do?" she replied softly.

Komarov looked up at the ceiling. "They will contact us when they are able." He glanced at her hand clasped within Vladimir's.

Suddenly Tatiana understood. Dmitri was jealous, and he was trying to anger her. She started to speak, but checked herself. She did not want the others to hear what she had to say. After a moment of indecision, she stood up and walked over to the communications console.

"I shall contact them myself," she said.

Komarov started to get up, but Satomura stopped him by placing a hand on his shoulder.

"It's not worth it," he said softly into his Komarov's ear. "Let her be."

Dmitri Komarov knew he had gone too far. Lowering his head, he rubbed hard on the creases above his brow. He did not know why he had insisted upon waiting for the *Liberty* to contact them. He was angry with Tatiana, and he wanted to upset her. But he had allowed his anger to interfere with his judgment. He had given them reason to question his authority, and this now angered him even more. He closed his eyes so that the sight of Tatiana would not anger him further. He concentrated upon regaining his composure.

"*Druzhba* to *Liberty*." She spoke louder than usual.

"This is *Liberty*, over," Carter responded.

"How is your patient?"

"He's sleepin' like a baby. They got him to the shelter just in time. Although Doc here looks like he's starting to glow. How's the weather over there?"

"Weather?"

"Radiation count."

"We're averaging about twenty-five rems."

"That's better than us. I'm sitting at forty. The other guys are close to ninety."

"That's high. Is there anything we can do?"

"Negative. Looks like we're just going to have to ride this one out."

"Good luck then."

She turned around to face the others. All eyes were upturned and looking at her.

"He is doing fine," she said. An ionized particle passed through her body.

Endicott was beginning to feel nauseous, but he felt certain it was his nerves. It was still too soon to experience the effects of the radiation. He was checking the pulse of Brunnet, whose head was rolling back and forth on his shoulders as if the muscles in his neck had been severed. Brunnet's eyes were open but blank. The drugs they had administered for the surgery were beginning to wear off.

"Did you see that?" Carter asked excitedly.

"See what?" Nelson asked.

"There was a streak of light that just flashed across the room."

"Where?" Nelson asked, searching back and forth.

"Right there. In the center. Right there," Carter said, and pointed emphatically at the center of the shelter.

Endicott held up his hand to stop the conversation.

"That was radiation striking your retina," he said wearily.

Carter stood up and walked over to area where he saw the flash. Crouching down on his knees, he waved his hand cautiously through the air. He hesitated. He touched his eye, and then his chin, and then his eye again. He swiveled around slowly until he was facing the other astronauts, his left hand rubbing his eyes. With his free hand he reached into his pocket and pulled out another piece of gum. He added the gum to the growing collection in his mouth. He chewed for nearly a minute while he pondered the situation.

"You're shittin' me," he said.

"I assure you, it is a common phenomenon," Endicott replied, slightly annoyed that the American would doubt him.

"Will it damage my eye?" Carter said with a halfhearted laugh.

"Only time will tell."

"Carter," Nelson said, "get back against the wall. Under the circumstances, we must observe every precaution."

Nelson's commanding tone had a sobering effect on Carter. He obeyed immediately, pushing himself away from where he thought he had seen the flash of light. He returned to his designated position and placed his back against the shelter wall, where the muscles in his back provided protection to his internal organs. He turned his undivided attention to the rems displayed on the console above him.

The next fifteen minutes passed in silence. The room filled with a stillness that settled into dark puddles around the astronauts. Their thoughts focused upon the rem counter, which rippled orange against its black display. There were four names on the display, and under each name was a number. Every few minutes one of the four numbers would increase. And as it increased, each astronaut wondered what subtle changes had taken place in the cells of the body through which the ionized particles had just passed. They knew that many of the cells would die. And that others would be damaged. That some could grow several hundred times their normal size, while others could multiply uncontrollably and form cancerous growths. Some could mutate. Their chromosomes could break apart and fuse into genetically unsound structures, the effect of which would not be known until their children were born. They knew that many of the injured cells would release toxic substances into their bodies. Nausea, fits of vomiting, and diarrhea could result from the sudden influx of toxins. They knew that after several days their white blood cells could reduce drastically in number and that their immune system could collapse. Or that their blood could fail to clot and they could bleed to death from a paper slice. They knew that internal organs, such as the liver, could begin to function abnormally, setting off a series of near-fatal complications. And they knew if their exposure was high enough they would die.

All of this could happen, and yet the radiation passed through their bodies without sensation. There was no physical discomfort. No piercing pain. No pins or needles. No hotness. No coldness. Not even the slightest of prickles. They felt nothing.

Commander Nelson emerged from the silence with a fabricated smile. It was his duty to maintain the spirits of his men, and it was not until he had caught Endicott's dejected look that he realized there was a need to do so.

"Congratulations are in order," he began. "Carl, you conducted yourself admirably. I will see that you receive due recognition for your actions."

"Well, thank you, but I really don't . . ."

"Nonsense, what you did back there was heroic. Most men would have fallen apart under the pressure."

"Sometimes one, willingly or not, has little choice but to rise to the occasion." His tone was flat, without emotion. "I only hope that fewer occasions present themselves."

Brunnet, still under the influence of the sedation, mumbled a few unintelligible words. He took several deep breaths in an attempt to clear his mind of the lingering effects of his medication. He motioned for Endicott to come closer and waited until Endicott's ear was only inches away before whispering into it. The two words barely made it past his lips.

"He told me thank you," Endicott said. He was still worried over Brunnet's condition, but for the first time since the operation he actually felt proud of what he had done. He attempted to contain the smile that emerged.

———

"Vladimir suspects," Tanya Pavlova said.

"Suspects what?" her commander asked. They were in the command module, alone, their faces dimly lit by the multicolored lights of the navigation panel.

"Us."

"Nonsense, there is nothing to suspect."

"He suspects us, nonetheless."

"If he suspects, then we should oblige and provide him with something to suspect. I am tired of waiting. Why do you tease me so?"

"Come now." Tanya laughed. "You are beginning to sound like Vladimir. Perhaps I like to tease you. Perhaps it gives me pleasure."

"You are cruel."

"I have never heard anything so ridiculous. He suspects; therefore, you must not be so open with your advances."

"Ah-ha, so you don't mind?"

"Mind what?" she replied, feigning confusion.

"You don't actually mind my advances." As he spoke, he moved a few inches closer to Tanya. "You just mind their openness." She responded by moving the same distance backward, which without the benefit of full-Earth gravity she did awkwardly, and was forced to grab Komarov's sleeve to steady herself. He offered his hand to help, but she withdrew hers the moment he touched it.

"Of course I mind. I am a married woman, and you are a married man, and neither one of us is married to each other. It would be wrong of me not to mind. I warn you, Dima, keep your distance. Vladimir is a sensitive person; I cannot bear to hurt him."

"There is no need for him to know," her commander persisted.

"I said no."

"Yesterday you didn't say no."

"Yesterday was another day, and I did say no."

"You said, 'Perhaps later.' That is not no."

"Well now is later, and I say no."

Realizing it was time to change his approach, Komarov backed away. Almost immediately, his stern countenance melted into a forlorn pout. He turned his palms outward as if to ask the gods what he had done to deserve such harsh treatment.

"Do you find me disagreeable?" he asked.

"Save your theatrics for sixteen-year-old girls who don't know any better." Tanya paused, placed her hands on her hips, and looked him up and down. "No, I don't find you disagreeable, Dmitri Fyodorovich, but I am not interested. I already have one man to tend to. I don't need another."

"A hypothetical question then. If you were not married, would you be interested?"

"I refuse to answer your hypothetical question."

"You are an impossible woman."

"So I have been told."

"You will change your mind. Not today, but eventually."

"Maybe," she said. "Maybe not."

"You will," he repeated, with a knowing smirk.

"You are incorrigible, Dmitri," she said with a smile.

"It is one of my better traits."

Tanya suddenly leaned over and kissed her commander hard on the lips. For a brief moment her tongue slipped from her mouth into his, then darted quickly back. She pulled away before he could respond.

"Just something for you to think about," she said. She turned her back and left the room without another word.

———

Al Carter was in the lab module, leaning back on a chair, his feet plopped upon a stack of books placed between two makeshift beds. A stethoscope dangled from his neck, and a thermometer poked out from his shirt pocket. He flipped an aluminum coin in the air. It spun in slow motion as it climbed to the top of its arc, where it hung suspended for a second, then lazily fell into his outstretched hand. He flipped the coin again. The difference in its motion because of the reduced gravity intrigued him.

"Why don't you get some sleep." The voice came from one of the two beds. It belonged to Endicott. "We'll be all right. You can't do anything for us right now."

"It's no bother," Al replied.

"Seriously," Endicott insisted. "The best thing for all of us is some rest. You received a relatively high dosage yourself."

"How do you feel?" Al asked.

"Slightly nauseous," Endicott admitted. "Although the diarrhea appears to have ceased."

"How about you, Jean Paul?"

"I've felt better." At the blurred edge of Jean Paul's vision, a coin flashed brightly as it twirled through the air.

"It's time to take some blood," Carter said.

"Didn't you take some just a few hours ago?" Brunnet protested. "I'm weak enough as it is. Carl, are you going to let this man stick another hypodermic into me?"

"I assume you have checked with the med-assist," Endicott offered weakly.

"I am to take samples every twelve hours. I can bring it up on the screen if you like."

"No need." Endicott allowed his head to roll to one side until one eye was buried in the white clouds of his pillow. The other peered over at his fellow patient. "He needs the blood to assess your condition. I would do the same."

Brunnet sighed and withdrew into silent reflection. He wasn't feeling well enough to offer resistance. He stared blankly at the ceiling. Carter's hand appeared above him and descended, growing larger as it got nearer, until it touched his forehead. It was uncomfortably cold.

"Jesus, you're burning up," Carter exclaimed.

"Am I?" Brunnet replied meekly. "I feel cold."

"The med-assist should have detected the rise in temperature. What the hell is going on?" He turned to the computer and requested a temperature check. The reading remained at 98.7.

"Are you certain?" Endicott asked.

"He's burnin' up, I tell you."

"Might be a malfunction in the sensor," Endicott said, propping himself up by his elbows. "Check it manually."

Carter retrieved the thermometer from his pocket and cleaned it with a tissue soaked with disinfectant prior to placing it inside Brunnet's mouth. The digital readout climbed quickly: 98 . . . 99 . . . 100 . . . 101 . . . 102 . . . 102.5 . . . 103.

Carter shook the electronic thermometer as if it were broken, as if the sudden motion would fix it, or at least lower the reading. The number did not change.

"One hundred and three," he said. "Doc, what should I do?"

"The very first thing we've got to do is bring his temperature down. Could you pass the keyboard over here." Endicott scanned the distant screen then typed several instructions. "That should take care of the medication. I want you to take several towels and wet them down with cool water. We're going to lower his temperature by covering his body with the towels. I'll remove his clothing."

"Right," Carter said.

With some effort, Endicott managed to sit upright and drop his legs over the edge of his bed. He shook his head to clear it and, after pausing to gather his strength, jumped the few inches to the floor. The sudden shift in blood from his head to his lower extremities caused him to sway and buckle at the knees. He grabbed his bedsheet for support, but the sheet gave away and he fell to the deck.

Carter turned around in time to witness the white sheet settle gently on top of Endicott. It formed a large, white lump on the floor, and looked similar to a shroud placed by the police upon a dead body at the scene of a crime. The body underneath the shroud was still.

He hesitated, wondering if he should alert Nelson, but decided against it. He bent down next to the doctor and cautiously pulled back the sheet. Endicott's face was pale. The lips were white. Carter placed his hand next to the mouth. He did not feel anything. He checked Endicott's wrist for a pulse. The wrist was warm. He thought he could detect a pulse but was unsure. He checked his own wrist to make certain he was applying the right amount of pressure, then he rechecked the doctor's. He felt a slight pulse. He grabbed one of the towels he had just dampened and placed it on the doctor's forehead.

Sluggishly, Endicott opened his eyes.

"What happened?" he asked, slurring his words.

"You tell me. One moment you're sitting up telling me to soak some towels, the next I find you passed out on the floor. You tell me what happened."

"I must have fainted."

"You're damn right you must have fainted. Jesus, Doc, just stay in bed. I'll take care of Jean Paul."

The room swirled by in blurred shadows as Endicott shook his head. Carter grabbed him under his arms and helped him to the makeshift bed. The reduced gravity made it seem like he was picking up an old man. Brunnet was watching from the corner of his eye.

"Feeling any better?" Carter asked.

"I must have fainted," Endicott repeated.

"Just stay where you are." Carter tucked in the bedsheet to prevent the doctor from getting up. He turned to face Brunnet, then looked down at the wet towels he had dropped on the floor. Without saying a word, he picked up the towels and tossed them on the bed beside Brunnet. With the tips of his fingers he gently touched the scientist's forehead. He shook his head in disbelief, wondering how his temperature could have risen so quickly and without warning. He untied the cotton gown that was wrapped loosely around Brunnet's body, and carefully removed it. The sight of the inflamed wound caused him to step back. It was red and purple and a sickly yellow, and it was bulging outward against the stitches. He was unable to take his eyes away. The infected area absorbed him and filled him with revulsion. He started to feel the same nausea he had felt in the operating room. He closed his eyes and took a deep breath, then concentrated on blocking the feeling from his mind. He grew angry. A man's life was in his hands. After several more deep breaths he regained his composure.

"Doc, you'd better see this," he said.

"I don't think I should get up," Endicott replied. "I'm still feeling a bit light-headed. Why don't you describe it to me."

"How about I show you." He went over to a cabinet and unclipped a mirror attached inside. He held the mirror with both hands above the two beds and attempted to angle it so that Endicott could see the wound. The doctor turned his head until the pillow blocked his view and motioned with his index finger for Carter to move the mirror slightly. He cringed as the reflection of the wound came into full view.

"You need to increase the antibiotics," he said weakly. "Double the dosage."

"You sure?"

"Do it," Endicott replied.

Carter typed in the command to adjust the amount of medication administered by the IV. The med-assist challenged the request.

"What do I tell it?" Carter asked.

"Tell it severe infection in the lower right quadrant of the abdomen accompanied by a fever of one hundred and three."

At the sound of the last key the med-assist turned a brilliant red and reported a conflict in the temperature reading. It requested verification. Carter explained the discrepancy as a sensor malfunction. The med-assist accepted the explanation, but made an alternate recommendation.

Carter looked over his shoulder at Endicott. The doctor's pupils were broken into jagged dots, obscured by the tiny slits his wrinkled eyelids had formed.

"I can barely make it out," he said, squinting.

Carter enlarged the print.

"Increase the clindamycin by one-third," Endicott said.

The med-assist analyzed but did not question the adjustment, and moments later the medication flowed into Brunnet's veins. "I want you to wrap him in the towels," Endicott said. He was becoming more alert. "His temperature is dangerously high. I suspect the radiation might have reduced his white blood-cell count, in which case he would be more susceptible to infection. I may need to go back in. Do a blood analysis as soon as you've wrapped him. An accurate white count is critical. Also, see if you can determine what is wrong with the sensor. The med-assist should have detected the rise in temperature."

"Do you think it is serious?" Brunnet asked, his voice shaking.

Endicott hesitated for a second before responding. He knew that under the circumstances Brunnet's condition could be fatal. The radiation could have complicated his recovery. If the antibiotics did not take effect, he would have to open him and clean out the wound. He did not have the strength to perform any more surgery.

"An infection is not an uncommon development after an appendectomy," he said. He tried to sound optimistic. "The antibiotics should clear it up."

"Just how bad is it?" Brunnet asked, as damp towels were being draped over his body.

"We don't know yet," Endicott replied. "The diagnosis depends largely upon the results of the blood analysis. We should have . . ."

Nelson's voice trumpeted from the ceiling. The startled occupants of the lab module looked up at the plastic webbing that covered the intercom. "The main console is showing a condition red medical emergency. What's going on in there?"

"The sensor that was monitoring Brunnet has malfunctioned," Al replied. "He's got a temperature of one hundred and three, and his gut appears to be infected. The doc says he may have to go back in."

"I'll be right there."

Carter placed the last of the wet towels over Brunnet's feet. He then went to the drawer that contained the hypodermics and selected the needle he had sterilized earlier. Needles had bothered him ever since he was a young child. He could recall a white office that smelled like rubbing alcohol and a man with a long needle that looked like it would go all the way through his arm. He had swung his arm back as the needle entered it. The needle broke. He remembered the pain and his fear that there would be even more pain because the needle had broken. The doctor removed the needle with a pliers.

The doctor said he would have to try again, and they strapped him down to a table. He had nightmares for months afterward.

Carter jabbed the needle into Brunnet's arm.

"You're perspiring," Brunnet said.

"I'll be damned," Carter said, wiping his forehead with the back of his sleeve. He watched as the blood filled the syringe. "Must be all that heat you're puttin' out."

Colonel Nelson entered the room and stopped. The lines around his mouth could have been chiseled in rock. He displayed no emotion. He scanned the faces and the eyes of his men. Without a word he went to Brunnet and placed his hand on his forehead.

"How long has he been like this?" he demanded.

There was an awkward pause as both Carter and Endicott wondered who should respond. Carter placed an antiseptic strip on the puncture. The strip turned red.

"Well?" he prompted.

"I don't rightly know," Carter replied. "The damn sensor . . ."

"Endicott, diagnosis."

"The wound is infected. We'll need to perform a rectal examination to determine if there is an intra-abdominal abscess."

"Give it to me in layman's terms."

"Pus near the inflamed tissue. It can be drained through the rectum if necessary. His condition is not uncommon, and under normal circumstances can be safely treated. I am concerned about the amount of radiation he absorbed. Excessive radiation can induce leukopenia."

Nelson raised his eyebrows.

"A decreased production of white blood cells," Endicott explained. "The very same cells that neutralize infection. His immune system could be impaired. I may need to go back in to clean the wound. Al is about to run a blood analysis. Hopefully, the additional antibiotics will clear the infection."

"You don't look so good. You up to this?"

"I can do it."

"Has anybody notified Earth?"

"Not directly," Carter replied. "They should have received the information I fed into the med-assist. That was about half an hour ago." He paused to read the flashing contents of a window that had opened on the console. "The results of the blood test just came up. Appears the white count is low."

"That's not good." Endicott had managed to free himself from his sheets and was once again sitting at the edge of his bed. "We should proceed with the rectal examination immediately."

"Concur," Nelson said. He looked at his watch, which was set for Greenwich Mean Time, and calculated the time would be 3 A.M. in Houston. Doctors Lear and Cain would have to be awakened.

Carter pulled the thermometer out of Brunnet's mouth and held it at arm's length to examine it.

"One hundred and two," he said. "It's gone down."

"I certainly hope so," Brunnet said. "It's cold under these towels. Can they be removed now?"

Carter looked over at Endicott, who shook his head.

"Sorry, pal," Carter said. "No can do."

Moments later the communications window announced over the intercom that a message had been received from Earth. The window automatically expanded to fill the entire screen, and the familiar, somewhat pale face of the night operations manager appeared.

"The med-assist telemetry indicates a sudden increase in Major Brunnet's temperature with possible infection. Medical condition red. Please confirm."

"Condition confirmed," Endicott replied weakly. "Transmitting medical data now. I will be conducting a rectal examination to determine the extent of the infection. Please alert the appropriate medical personnel."

"**I** have just received a communication from Colonel Nelson indicating that Brunnet's condition is critical," Colonel Dmitri Komarov said to his three crew members. "They will be performing emergency surgery within the hour. His chances of survival are at best fifty-fifty."

"Fifty-fifty," Vladimir repeated unbelievingly. His hands were entwined with Tanya's. "How can that be?"

"There were complications owing to the radiation. His immune system is failing him."

"What if he dies?" Tanya asked. "How would that affect the mission?"

"They can get by without him. The American lander does not require a full crew to land. There will be some differences, of course."

"He is a brilliant man," Satomura said. "It would be a great loss."

"He won't die," Tanya said. "We must pray that he doesn't."

Satomura frowned at Tatiana's suggestion. For them to pray would not help Brunnet survive. He looked at Tatiana and Vladimir, fingers interlocked, and could see that they were scared. They were too young, he thought, to be aboard a mission like this. They should be back on Earth raising children. Satomura's attempt to smile produced awkward breaks in the lines that creased his face and revealed two crooked rows of dull white teeth. His intention was to reassure the couple that everything would be all right. But a smile was so foreign to his face, it had the opposite effect.

"Are you feeling well?" Tanya asked.

"Yes," Satomura scowled, "I am feeling well. If you'll excuse me, I have work to do."

Before Komarov could say otherwise, the aging scientist disappeared abruptly through the portal.

"What was that all about?" Vladimir asked.

"I've never seen him so concerned," Tanya remarked. "He's always so analytical. I had almost forgotten he was human."

"Comrades," Komarov said in a tone that marked his disapproval.

"Well, it is true," he said. "Sometimes he is like a robot. All logic, no emotion. Scientists can be that way."

"Perhaps death frightens him," Vladimir said. "He might be thinking of his wife. I understand he was never quite the same after she passed away."

Within the small confines of the cabin, the several meters that separated the couple from Komarov were uncomfortably short. Eyes were focused on the floor and the ceiling. Although Vladimir could sense the tension, he attributed it largely to Brunnet's situation and thought it unlikely it had anything to do with his wife and Dmitri. To reassure himself, he hugged Tanya warmly. She returned his warmth with a gentle kiss. Komarov saw all of this and decided it would be best to leave.

"I'll leave you two alone," he said. "I will notify you as soon as I hear something."

The couple nodded in silence as they watched Komarov disappear through the portal. Vladimir was the first to speak.

"I apologize," he said.

"And for what are you apologizing?"

"For last night. For accusing you of sleeping with Komarov. I don't know what could have gotten into me. Sometimes my mind gets so filled with crazy thoughts I just can't think."

"I don't think this is the time to discuss such things."

"You're right. But I want you to know I am sorry."

"There is nothing to be sorry about."

"I'm still sorry."

"Consider yourself forgiven," she said, and gently placed a finger on his lips to silence him. He kissed her finger. "Do you think he'll survive?"

"I don't know."

"Why does it take death to remind us how precious life is?"

Vladimir did not answer the question. It was not meant to be answered. All he could do in response was hold his wife tighter. He could sense her sadness and wanted very much to remove it but knew the only thing that would change her mood would be word from the American ship. He closed his eyes and prayed that Brunnet would survive.

They received the communication three hours later. Jean Paul Brunnet had died during the operation.

———

The NASA contingency plan for a funeral in space took into consideration the minutest of details, including the specific articles of clothing the deceased was to wear, the color of his socks, his underwear, and the medals, if any, to be pinned on his chest. The necessary passages from the Bible were included, along with suggested sentiments that could be expressed. How the body was to be prepared and what samples, hair, skin, fingernails, blood, urine, et cetera, had to be preserved for analysis on Earth were described with meticulous care. What combination of chemicals could be used to form a makeup base filled several screens. The arms were to be folded over the chest. The hair was to be sprayed in place. The eyes closed. Once the deceased was prepared and the final words spoken, the body was to be ejected into space. As Colonel Nelson read through the screens he began to think the level of detail was excessive. It was typical NASA. They possessed an insatiable need for detail. He was disgusted by it.

He turned the monitor off and watched the screen fade slowly into black. That was how Brunnet had died. The light had just faded from his eyes. Nelson did not feel well. He was suffering from mild symptoms of radiation sickness. Resting his elbows on his knees, he lowered his head and cradled it between his two large hands.

There was a United Nations flag aboard the ship. It was to be planted by Nelson into the red Martian soil. He wondered what NASA would have to say if the flag never made it to Mars. They would not be pleased. The flag was politically significant. It was to stand as a symbol of their achievement. He walked over to the drawer that contained the flag, pulled it out, unfolded it, and held it at arm's length. He watched it ripple and thought of the men who had been buried with a flag over the centuries. It was an honor they had earned. He decided Major Jean Paul Brunnet would not be denied that honor.

He carefully folded the flag into a small triangle and placed it under his arm. His decision made him feel better. He knew that he was doing the right thing. He slapped his hand down on the button that activated the intercom.

"Carter."

"Yes," came the digitized response.

"I'm on my way."

It was an odd feeling. He did not know whether it was his imagination or if it was real. As he walked through the cylindrical passageway that joined the modules, he could sense Brunnet's presence, as if he were floating above, slightly behind, watching. He told himself that it was his imagination, that it was nothing, but he could not shrug off the sensation. He stopped, looked up at the ceiling behind him, and held out the folded flag.

"You deserve it," he said. Somewhere in the back of his mind he was glad no one was watching.

The passageway remained absolutely silent. Had there been

the tiniest disturbance, he would have interpreted it as a sign that Brunnet was there.

"Are you there?" Although he did not expect to hear or see anything, he felt compelled to ask. "If you are, I want you to know the mission will continue as planned. I assume that is what you would have wanted. I suppose you would have also wanted to see the flag planted on Mars. I'm sorry, but I can't accommodate you on that one."

He studied the blank ceiling and wondered if Brunnet was actually present. The ceiling did not look any different. After some thought, he decided against saying anything else and proceeded down the corridor and into the lab module.

Endicott was hovering over the body. He was checking the space suit, making sure the fittings were properly fastened. His face was ghostly white. Nearly as white as that of the body within the suit. His eyes were tired, with big, dark rings that hung like iron weights beneath the lids. In zero gravity a face is normally bloated from the collection of body fluids that would otherwise gather in the lower extremities. But Endicott's face was drawn tight, partly due to stress and partly due to his inability to keep his food down for the past several days. His double chin, which had grown more prominent since leaving Earth, had nearly disappeared. He did not acknowledge Nelson as the latter entered the room.

Carter was seated in the far corner, his hands cradled in his lap. He stood up immediately when he saw the commander and pushed his way over to him. Upon seeing the flag he stopped dead in his tracks. Their eyes met and after several seconds, during which neither said a word, smiles appeared on both their lips.

"To hell with 'em," Carter said.

The unusual remark was enough to divert Endicott's attention from the body he was preparing. Not seeing the flag, he was unable to determine the intent behind the remark and grew visibly angered at the sight of Carter's smile. His pale face regained some of its color.

"Do you mind," he said. It was a demand rather than a question.

Carter appeared somewhat apologetic as he pointed at the flag. The doctor understood immediately and signaled his concurrence with a nod.

They unfolded the flag in silence. They lifted Brunnet several feet off the table and allowed him to float there while they wrapped the flag around his body. Some things were easier in zero gravity, and they were grateful that this was one of them. There wasn't enough material to cover his entire body, so after a few moments of quiet discussion they decided to leave his helmet uncovered. It seemed more appropriate than his feet.

They stepped back from the floating body. It was time. Carter activated the television downlink. A green light above the camera indicated they were being recorded.

Nelson unfolded a sheet of paper that he had retrieved from his pants pocket. He briefly looked up at the camera and then down at the body, which, suspended above the table, took on a ghostly quality. It suddenly seemed terribly inappropriate to have the body floating, but it was too late to do anything, the digitized image was already on its way to Earth. He began to read from the paper in his hands, his voice a low monotone. The room was bright with light for the camera.

He could barely hear his own words as they emerged through his lips. And he could barely understand them. He had written the parting words earlier that morning. There was a great noise inside his head, like the sound of the sea inside a seashell. He wondered if he was saying everything correctly. At the edges of his vision he could see that Carter's head was bent low and that his hands were clasped in prayer. Endicott's eyes were moist. He was looking at the body. His knees appeared unsteady. He was not standing straight. Nelson wondered if

Endicott were going to faint. He watched Endicott as he read. The rushing sound gradually subsided and was gone when he reached the end of the eulogy.

As he lowered his head in prayer, the moisture that had collected on his eyelid formed a small tear that broke away and floated gently into the center of the room.

Venus

The Russians had deliberately designed Tatiana's clothing to obscure the curves underneath. They were plain, loose-fitting, baggy, and tailored for utility. Not so much that it was obvious, but enough, they hoped, to dampen any wayward thoughts that the male members of the crew might develop. Two years without female companionship was a long time. The mission psychologists had decided it would be best for all parties involved to deemphasize Tatiana's sex. The task was not easy. Her breasts and well-rounded hips presented curves that were apparent in even the baggiest of garments. And it was those curves that turned Komarov's head as she exited through the hatch of the transfer tunnel.

She knew that he was watching, but she had other things on her mind. The day had been long and tedious, and she was tired. They had assisted the Americans with preparations for the launch of the Venus probe *Greenhouse*. There had been a lot to do, and she had found it difficult to concentrate. She had gotten into an argument with Vladimir that morning when he had attempted to assist her in rerouting some of the circuitry in the command station. His large hands had made it impossible for her to see what she was doing. She snapped at him, and when he doltishly persisted she lost her temper. The brief fight that ensued ended with Vladimir accusing her of being self-centered. She began to feel guilty several hours later and now, by the end of day, she very much wanted to make it up to him.

She could sense the steam as she entered the hygiene module. The room was warm and humid, and there was the sound of water. She saw Vladimir's wrinkled shirt on the sink next to the shower.

"Is that you, Vladimir?" she asked, removing her clothing and dropping the articles onto the floor one by one.

The sound of water stopped.

"What?" came the muffled reply from inside the collapsible shower. It was made of nylon and entirely watertight.

"Is that you?" she repeated.

"Tanya?" Vladimir said. "What is it?"

"Open up," she said. She was completely naked, her clothes strewn about her in a haphazard circle. "I want in."

"You can't . . ." he began to say as he unzipped the shower door far enough to allow his head to peer through. Regulation required the shower to remain closed until all of the stray water had been removed with the suction hose. But the sight of her standing there, without clothing, her breasts soft and pearl white, persuaded him to reconsider. He opened the door the remainder of the way and stood there, speechless, as though it were the first time he had ever seen her naked.

"Hello, my love," she said seductively, and stepped into the shower.

He didn't know what to say, so he guided her in, wrapped his arms around her waist, and kissed her. She responded by pressing her body closer to his, slowly running her fingernails down his back, and passionately licking the inside of his ear. Her heart was beating hard and fast. The shower was barely large enough for one person.

"Turn the water on," she whispered.

He motioned behind her at the open door. She turned to zip the door shut and as she did he brought his hands around her waist to caress the inside of her thighs. A moan of pleasure slipped through her lips. Vladimir reached up and turned the valve to start the shower. A blast of warm water directed by jets of warm air blew down on top of them, and with the air and water striking sensuously against their skin they made love.

The hygiene module, programmed to conserve water, turned the shower off several times before they were finished. Vladimir was the first to emerge from the collapsible tube, with Tatiana immediately behind. Grabbing a towel, he sat down and patted himself dry. Tatiana did the same.

"What brought that on?" he asked after some time. It was the first words spoken since they had turned on the shower, and he realized he shouldn't have asked the question—the words sounded harsh and sarcastic—but they hadn't made love in nearly two weeks, and he wanted to know what had triggered her sudden interest. He was no longer angry about the morning.

"Follow me," she said softly. "I'll show you."

After they had put the remainder of their clothes on, she took him by his hand and led him through the portal. He felt like a child being led by his mother. They walked in silence, through the transfer tunnel to the end of the module where the observation port was located. They sat down and she pressed the button to withdraw the shields that protected the glass from micrometeoroids.

The observation window filled with stars and a brilliant white band he knew to be the Milky Way. In the center of the band shone a luminous sphere of alabaster and gold. The colors swirled and faded gently into each other. It was the planet Venus. A thin halo of light flowed outward from its clouds.

Vladimir was moved by the planet's beauty. He knew that underneath the veil of clouds the surface resembled a hellish inferno. He tried not to think about the surface.

After a while he closed the door to the observation port and took Tatiana into his arms. They removed each other's clothing. The sight of their bodies illuminated by the light of Venus excited them. He touched her gently at first, exploring her outer contours with the tips of his fingers. Moments later they were passionately entwined.

"Ten minutes till separation," Carter announced.

"Ten minutes and counting," Dr. Endicott repeated for the benefit of the Russians.

Carter tapped a key that popped open the event window on their monitors.

"Check probe power."

"Probe power checks."

"Check thermal control."

"Thermal control good."

"Verify *Liberty* deployment angle."

"Tilt table twenty-nine degrees."

"Hydraulics."

"Hydraulics check."

At T minus twenty seconds the three metallic arms that held the probe against the hull withdrew into the ship.

"Grapples released. Five seconds and counting."

"OK boys, here goes nothing."

"Spring activated." Three springs gently pushed the probe into space. "*Greenhouse* has been deployed. Rate of separation is point-five meters per second."

"*Greenhouse* has been deployed," Endicott announced through the comm link.

"We verify proper separation," Vladimir responded over the intercom.

"Prepare to fire aft thrusters at T plus one minute," Nelson said while watching the event timer. At one minute past deployment the probe would be approximately nine meters from the *Liberty*, a distance safe enough to fire the thrusters. The aft thrusters were a series of small rocket engines, located at the rear of the ship, which made up part of the reaction-control system. The maneuver would increase the rate of separation between the probe and the *Liberty*.

"Fire aft thrusters."

"Eight-second burn on afts."

They watched the probe diminish in size, then disappear altogether. At T plus five minutes, Carter instructed *Greenhouse* to initiate a slow spin. The rotation of the probe distributed the heat from the sun evenly over its surface. The astronauts checked the various subsystems of *Greenhouse* as they waited for the distance between the two craft to increase. Attached to *Greenhouse* was a small single-stage engine that would propel it toward Venus.

"T plus twenty-one minutes," Carter announced.

"Activate avionics for single-stage ignition."

"Avionics activated."

"HYPACE firing attitude-control thrusters. Point-three-second burn. All three axes are stabilized."

"T plus twenty-three minutes. We are set for ignition. Ten seconds and counting. Seven . . . six . . . five . . . four . . . three . . . two . . . ignition."

"We have ignition," Endicott announced.

Through the view port, they were able to see a brief flash of light. The probe was nearly three kilometers distant, and the flash from the single-stage engine appeared smaller than the flame from a match. There was no sound.

"She's on her way," Nelson said. It would be three days before *Greenhouse* reached Venus.

"Single-stage separation." The booster engine fell away from *Greenhouse* and tumbled toward Venus along a slightly different trajectory.

Nelson was about to thank his men for their hard work when he noticed that Carter was no longer grinning. He followed Carter's gaze. Endicott's back was slightly slumped and turned away from them.

"What did you think?" he asked as he placed his hand on the doctor's shoulder.

The doctor stood up straight and rigid. Nelson's hand fell away.

"Flawlessly executed," he said without turning around. "I'll be in the lab if you need me."

Endicott moved sideways to avoid facing the astronauts and left the control module. The dark contrast of his back against the antiseptically white corridors remained imprinted on their retinas for several long seconds. It followed the movement of their eyes. There was a long silence.

"Brunnet," Nelson ventured.

Carter, having already guessed the cause of the peculiar behavior, somberly nodded in agreement.

———————

D r. Takashi Satomura was monitoring three screens, situated side by side, each divided into multiple windows. His head barely moved, but his eyes were constantly scanning back and forth between the screens. He was humming the final movement of Beethoven's Ninth. The screens contained data from the *Greenhouse* probe, which was scheduled to impact with the Venusian atmosphere in six minutes and twenty-three seconds. The sensors aboard the probe had been activated fourteen minutes earlier. Every few minutes he would type in a command to alter the presentation of the output.

As a result of Brunnet's death, Satomura was to take a more active role in the *Greenhouse* mission. He was to monitor the data as it poured from the probe's high-gain antenna onto his screen. To Satomura it was like riding the probe itself. He would be the first to see the data. And when the probe landed he was to direct Nelson where to steer the rover, which had been Brunnet's role. Other probes had landed on Venus, but this was the first one with a rover.

"Five minutes until impact," Vladimir announced.

Satomura's nose drew closer to the center screen. The data he had been receiving up to that point was of little significance. There was not that much the probe's instruments could detect outside the Venusian atmosphere. It was mostly a vacuum. As signs of positively charged ions began to appear on the center monitor, his humming grew noticeably louder.

"Thirty seconds until impact."

Sweat began to gather at Satomura's brow. He paused to listen as Vladimir counted the final seconds.

"Impact."

The data on all three screens froze and remained frozen for several minutes. A ball of fire had engulfed the probe as it passed through the upper layers of the stratosphere, producing a barrier of ionized particles through which the high-gain telemetry was unable to pass. The probe was protected by an aeroshell of aluminum and ceramic. Suddenly the screens turned white with data. Several of the windows were a blur. Satomura focused on the slower windows, those that contained the high-level analysis. He was pleased to see that every window was active, which meant all of the probe's sensors had survived the four-hundred-g impact.

"How does it look?" Komarov asked, peering over the scientist's shoulder. The screens were meaningless to him.

Satomura did not respond. He did not hear the question. The monitors had his entire attention. He flinched as the numbers from the accelerometer jumped erratically, and his fingers tightened around the ends of the keyboard almost as if he were bracing himself. The change in acceleration had not been unexpected. The probe was passing through a thermal layer in the atmosphere.

"How does it look?" Komarov repeated.

"All instruments functioning," Satomura responded.

The probe was seventy kilometers above the surface when it struck the first layer of clouds. It was traveling much slower now, the friction and heat were much less, and the fire that had surrounded *Greenhouse* was gone. The probe fell another twenty kilometers before the parachutes opened.

"Parachute deployment at fifty kilometers," Vladimir said.

The opening of the parachute was confirmed by the sudden change in velocity reported by the accelerometer. Moments later the high-definition camera attached to the side of the probe began filming. All eyes, including Satomura's, turned to the monitor with the images. The screen was mostly white with streaks of yellow and lemon. They were looking at the inside of a cloud.

"Sulfuric acid, eighty percent," Satomura read automatically, almost mechanically. "Acid droplet diameters ranging from zero-point-zero-zero-five to zero-point-zero-zero-nine millimeters. Crystal particles with a diameter of zero-point-zero-three millimeters composed of iron chloride. Good. Very good."

"How frightening," Tanya whispered.

The whiteness that filled the screen suddenly vanished and was replaced by a yellowish orange sky accentuated by a jagged horizon composed of volcanoes and mountains that curved inward and bounced awkwardly with the camera. The surface, obscured by a hot steam bath of haze, was reddish orange and dark.

"Welcome to hell," Vladimir said.

"Temperatures increasing," Satomura announced. "Three hundred and fifty K."

"Beginning to detect some water vapor," Satomura continued. "Zero-point-zero-two percent. Carbon dioxide, ninety-six percent. Nitrogen, three-point-five percent."

"The probe appears to be shaking more than during the simulation," Tanya commented.

"It is passing through a strong westerly wind," Satomura responded. "Nearly ninety-eight meters per second. The winds will decrease as the probe descends." He paused for a moment, then assaulted the keyboard with his long fingers. He anxiously watched the monitor on his right for the results. "The probe has entered a convective layer."

"Convective layer?" Tanya asked.

"A section of the atmosphere where hot air rises and cold air descends." He stopped abruptly. "That's peculiar. The water vapor has increased to one-tenth of a percent. That's considerably higher than anything measured before. I did not expect this at all. The temperature reading is four hundred K. If only I had the proper instruments."

"Instruments for what?" Komarov asked.

"There is some speculation that if life were to exist on Venus, it would exist as microbes floating in the atmosphere in a region such as this. It's not likely. But with the proper sensors we would know for certain one way or another."

"From what I see they would have to be very hearty microbes."

"It certainly doesn't look like a friendly place," Vladimir said. Tatiana and Vladimir approached the monitor until they were only inches away. The bleak and unforgiving horizon it portrayed filled them with a sense of how tenuous their hold on the universe actually was.

"Two and a half kilometers," Satomura announced.

"To what?" Vladimir asked, looking at the event timer and finding nothing scheduled to happen.

"The convective layer was two and a half kilometers deep. The turbulence should ease up now."

And as the last word left his lips, the surface of the planet stopped bouncing. Although the probe was still being buffeted by high winds, winds greater than seventy meters per second, the program that processed the images was able to stabilize the picture. The planet did not look any friendlier. They watched in silence as *Greenhouse* slowly descended.

"Forty kilometers," Satomura said. "The temperature is steadily increasing."

The surface was obscured by a misty haze of aerosols and dust. Through the haze they were able to make out impact craters and long rift-valleys. The probe was descending just south of a mountainous region known as Aphrodite. The highest peak was five and a half kilometers high and was contrasted by a jagged gash in the ground that dominated the landscape. The gash was a twenty-three-hundred-meter deep chasm.

"The parachute has been released," Tanya said, "and retro-rockets have ignited."

The ground began to enlarge very quickly. The impact craters grew in size, and the circular rims that formed their boundaries broke apart into large arcs composed of scattered rocks that grew into misshapen boulders. Many of the boulders glowed from the intense heat at the planet's surface.

"One kilometer," Satomura announced. He felt as though it was all happening too quickly, that there was not enough time to absorb the data. Forty-seven minutes had passed since the probe first struck the atmosphere. Only seven remained until it landed.

"Point-five kilometers."

They watched as Nelson steered the lander away from a region strewn with boulders. Due to the limited capability of the retro-rockets, he could only alter the probe's course within a radius of a hundred meters of the original landing site. A cloud of dust sprang up and engulfed the ship, blocking their view of the surface.

"Impact," Tanya announced. "The probe has landed."

"*Greenhouse* has landed," Vladimir repeated into his microphone for his colleagues back on Earth.

"Checking instrumentation," Satomura said excitedly. "The nephelometer is down, all other instrumentation checks."

"Received confirmation on instrumentation check from the Americans," Vladimir said. "They are preparing to deploy the rover."

"Temperature is seven hundred and thirty-seven Kelvin." Satomura was running the fingers of his left hand across the screen and tapping at the keyboard with his right as he read the information out loud. "Surface pressure is ninety-four atmospheres. Wind velocity is one-point-two meters per second."

Greenhouse was expected to function three hours and thirty minutes, after which time the electronic components that made up the scientific instruments would melt. The rover was designed to survive twenty-eight minutes before it would suffer a similar fate. Time was critical. Satomura glanced over at the event timer and waited impatiently for Nelson to deploy the rover.

The rover was a small remote-control vehicle, seventy-five centimeters long, thirty-three centimeters wide. Its tires were made of wire mesh and were disproportionately large with respect to the body of the vehicle. Two cameras were perched above the tires in front. They provided the controller with a three-dimensional view of the planet. At the rear a straight-wire antenna relayed data to and from *Greenhouse*. Adjacent to the antenna was a battery pack the size of a soup can. It was heavily encased in order to protect it from the planet's intense heat. A vertical pole, fifty-one centimeters high, protruded from the center of the vehicle. The pole was a drill designed to extract a single core sample thirty centimeters in length. Surface soil was to be gathered by a strong arm, a multijointed rod with a serrated scoop at the end.

Satomura placed a pair of goggles over his eyes. Two spheres of light illuminated the interior of the probe. The bay door was directly in front of him. He switched on his microphone.

"Satomura, here," he said.

"This is Nelson," a voice responded. "Deployment in thirty seconds. Over."

At two seconds and counting the bay door of the probe slid open, revealing a reddish orange surface of sand and rocks and a dark, yellow sky. The rover leapt out and the bay door slammed shut behind it. Nelson rotated the rover a full 360 degrees. As the cameras swung by *Greenhouse*, Satomura noticed dark streaks on its surface and immediately recognized them as burn marks caused by atmospheric entry.

"Where to?" Nelson asked.

The horizon glowed orange and curved upward. The rover appeared to be in a valley, but Satomura knew that to be an illusion. It was actually on flat terrain. The extreme surface pressure caused light to refract; as a result, the edges of the horizon rose into the sky like distant mountains.

"Proceed northeast twenty degrees for ten meters," Satomura instructed.

"Roger. Twenty degrees northeast. Ten meters. Over."

The rocks appeared to pass underneath him. Satomura felt as if he were actually on the surface. The sensation was exhilarating, and despite his desire to remain composed, he could feel his hands trembling with excitement. Superimposed on the surrounding terrain was the time remaining before the rover had to return and the distance in centimeters from the probe. At 1,237 centimeters with twenty-four minutes remaining, the rover stopped on top of a slight mound.

"Rotate right," Satomura said.

"Roger."

As far as the eye could see, broken, flat rocks were strewn haphazardly across the planet's surface. Some of the rocks glowed from the heat. The land was barren. There were no signs of life. No thorns, no dry grass, no ragged claws. Nothing scuttling across the orange sand. Satomura wondered if Earth would meet a similar fate. If left unchecked, he felt certain it would. The wheels had already been set in motion. As he looked around, he felt a strange sort of joy. The surroundings were oppressive, stark, and hellish, yet he felt like a child stepping outside for the first time. The goggles blinked twenty-three minutes.

His first task was to find a suitable site to extract the core sample. He required soft ground, soil the drill could easily penetrate, preferably loose dirt or sand.

"Seven meters at twenty-two degrees," he said.

"Roger," Nelson responded. "Seven meters at twenty-two degrees."

The rover crept slowly around the larger rocks, many of which were porous. They were fragmented chunks of hardened lava.

"Check soil resistance," Satomura said.

"Checking resistance," Nelson said.

He used the strong arm to dig into the top layers of the soil. The serrated scoop at the end of the arm cut deeply into the dirt.

"Minimal resistance," Nelson noted.

Satomura had him check two other locations, each seven meters apart, before he settled upon the first.

"Activate drill," Satomura announced, and suddenly he felt very tense.

"Activating drill."

They watched and waited as the drill worked its way through the soil. Their attention was focused on two numbers, both of which were slowly increasing, the depth in centimeters the drill had achieved and the level of resistance it had encountered. If the resistance became too great, the computer would stop the drill, preventing it from being damaged. They breathed a little bit easier as each centimeter appeared on the screen, and they clapped in relief when the drill had reached its desired depth.

"Open block windows," Satomura said, after checking his monitors.

Block windows were small apertures around the sides of the drill that allowed dirt to tumble inside when opened. The soil had to be loose, noncohesive, or it would not fall through the windows. Their breathing was delayed and intermittent as they waited. After several seconds, a sensor inside the drill was tripped and a flashing green light indicated the soil had been collected.

"Close block windows."

"Closing block windows."

"Withdraw drill."

Satomura watched the seconds disappear as the rover pulled the drill out of the ground. The vehicle was four minutes from *Greenhouse*, which gave Satomura eleven minutes unless he chose to travel farther from the probe. He was starting to consider his options when he noticed that the temperature of the rover was increasing faster than had been anticipated.

"Tanya, can you run an analysis on the temperature?" he asked.

"Holy shit." The exclamation came over the intercom. They recognized the voice as Carter's.

Satomura focused on a number that was blinking red. It was the time remaining before the rover had to be back inside the probe, and within a few seconds it had dropped from fifteen to seven minutes. The temperature of the rover jumped forty degrees. Satomura considered the possibility of a malfunction in the sensors, but the risk was too great to continue as planned. Reluctantly, he concluded they would have to abandon the collecting of surface materials with the strong arm. He only had one option, and there was little time to lose.

"Return to *Greenhouse*," he said into his microphone as calmly as he could manage.

Nelson had anticipated the request and already had the rover heading full throttle toward the probe.

"Roger," he replied. They had three minutes to spare, less if the temperature of the probe increased again unexpectedly.

"Tanya," Satomura said, "the analysis."

"Nothing yet, Takashi," Tanya answered.

Another forty-five seconds disappeared from the time remaining.

"Prepare to open probe door," Nelson instructed Carter.

Satomura watched the temperature of the rover climb rapidly. The timer dropped to sixty seconds remaining. The rover was two minutes from the probe. They watched the screen in tense silence as Nelson steered it through the maze of rocks. The ground rolled slowly underneath as *Greenhouse* grew larger. At five seconds remaining, the screen went blank.

"We've lost the cameras," Nelson said calmly. "The comm link is active."

Satomura ripped the goggles off his eyes. He looked up at the monitor that contained images of the Venusian horizon transmitted by the camera mounted on *Greenhouse*. The rover was nowhere to be seen.

"Where is it?" he asked, his voice nearly a whisper.

"It went behind that boulder," Tanya said, standing up to point out a rock.

"I'm going to bring her in," Nelson said over the intercom. "It was approximately a meter in front of that rock before we lost the cameras. I'll take her around the east side."

Satomura scrunched his eyelids tight as though it would help him to see through the planet's yellow haze. He stared at the orange dirt to the east.

"There it is!" Tanya said, pointing.

The rover emerged from behind the rock. It crept over the rough terrain like a toy tank.

"Twenty seconds." They could faintly hear Carter's voice through Nelson's microphone.

The rover disappeared under the view of the camera.

―――――――

"Open the probe door," Nelson ordered.

"Probe door open."

"Ten seconds."

Nelson had nothing but memory to guide him now. He knew that the aperture was slightly below and several centimeters to the right of the camera and that there would be only a centimeter of clearance on either side of the rover. He closed his eyes and imagined the brightly lit opening and steered the rover toward it.

"Five seconds."

He visualized the rover climbing into Greenhouse and faintly considered the possibility that the rover was banging against the metallic exterior of the probe.

"Three . . . two . . . one."

Nelson hit the switch to stop the vehicle. If it went too far, it would damage the scientific instruments inside Greenhouse. If it did not go far enough, it would be mangled by the probe doors as they closed. His eyes were still shut. He imagined the rover sitting on a platform in the center of the probe.

"Close probe door."

"Probe door closed."

The closing of the doors would activate a sensor indicating whether the rover was in position for soil transfer. They waited for the signal, but nothing happened.

"I'm going to nudge her forward another centimeter," Nelson said, his voice was flat, without emotion.

They waited again and after a few seconds the message INI-
TIATE SOIL TRANSFER appeared quietly on their screens; the
appearance of the message implied the rover was properly
docked. Nelson breathed a sigh of relief that was audible over
the intercom. He closed his eyes and listened to the others
speak excitedly about the events that had just taken place.

———

Satomura watched a replay of the rover's short trek across
the planet's surface as he waited impatiently for the results of
the soil analysis. He could detect the telltale signs of a lava bed.
The rocks were porous and when viewed through a filter that
blocked out the reddish tints of the atmosphere they were dark
brown and black. Many of the rocks showed signs of erosion.
Data from the mass spectrometer finally appeared on the
screen. It confirmed his observations. The rocks were basaltic.
This was in line with findings from earlier missions. The entire
length of the sample proved to be similar in composition. And
since it was a lava bed, they would probably find similar soil several meters deep. He smirked at the thought of this. What
would one expect so near a volcano.

The probe continued to transmit data for nearly an hour
beyond its expected life span. Satomura jumped from one
analysis to the next. He uttered odd and, to Tatiana's mind,
unseemly sounds whenever he found something unexpected.
After some time he turned his attention to the biological
analysis of the core sample. Temperatures at the surface were
too high to support organic molecules. They would denature in
a matter of seconds. But if there were life in the clouds, some
evidence of that life would eventually fall to the ground.
Satomura was studying the spectrograph for elements that
might make up the decomposed remains of a life-form. Many
of the elements were present, but not in the mixtures he would

have expected. Still, he told himself after several hours of
scrutiny, the hypothesis had not been disproved. They were
simply looking in the wrong place. As he stretched he noticed
that he was alone in the room. He could not remember the
others leaving. A glance at the clock revealed that he had been
working for nearly thirteen hours since the probe had landed.
The others must have left hours ago. He did not feel tired, but
decided it would be best to retire, since his crew mates would
be waking shortly, and he did not want them to think that he
had been up all night.

Reluctantly, he shut down the terminals and made for his
quarters. He fell onto his bed fully clothed. His thoughts were
racing with possible interpretations of the data. He looked up at
the ceiling and, after some time had passed, focused on a tiny
green light and began to meditate.

——————

Unaware that Carter was watching him from the edge of
the portal, Endicott injected premeasured amounts of nutrient
into the hydroponic containers. The gentle sounds of a piano
filled the garden. His movement was automatic and seemed to
be guided more by the music than by his own will. The high-
pressure sodium lamps above him glowed faintly. Normally the
room would have been more brightly lit, but he had turned the
lights down. The dim light helped him relax. He was thinking of
Brunnet. He told himself that there was really nothing he could
have done differently. Had he known there was going to be a
flare, he could have set up in the shelter; but the flare hadn't
been detected until it was too late. No one actually blamed him.
The radiation had caused Brunnet's death. He couldn't have left
the wound open; although he knew that if he had, Brunnet
might still be alive.

Endicott re-created the events in his mind in search of

alternatives that he might have overlooked. If only the appendix had not been perforated. He knew it was best to put such thoughts to rest. But the manner of Brunnet's death and his own role in it was not the only thing that troubled him. He had lost a companion. Nelson and Carter were not Brunnet's equal. He found it difficult to talk with them. And now more so than ever. Because he couldn't help thinking that perhaps they blamed him in some way. It was best not to think about it, he reminded himself. He focused on the solitary tomato plant in the garden. The stem was supported by an intricate cage of wire that Endicott had constructed himself.

"It's gettin' late," Carter said.

Startled by the sound, Endicott jumped and felt his hand strike the wire cage as he turned around to confront the intruder. He turned back in time to see the cage hit the deck. Two of the tomatoes broke open and splattered red juice across the floor. It looked like blood. He knelt on one knee to inspect the damage.

"I'm sorry," Carter said as he approached to assist.

"Please," Endicott said. "I can handle this."

"Of course," Carter replied.

Endicott looked around for a towel, but there weren't any in sight. He thought about asking Carter to fetch a towel, but that meant Carter would return, and he would rather that he just left. For a moment he was at a loss as to what he should do. Carter was between him and any towel that was to be had, and he did not want to seem rude. Carter might report the incident. The medical consultants back on Earth were considering a psychiatric evaluation, and an outburst would probably be enough to convince them to proceed. He did not see the need for the evaluation. His reaction to Brunnet's death was not abnormal. He simply wanted some time to himself. If an evaluation was conducted, he feared that others might find out. He did not want that on his record, and he certainly did not want it to become public knowledge. He decided he would have to make a greater effort to interact with Carter and Nelson. He was guilty of avoiding them, even more so than before.

"If you could find a towel . . ." Endicott said.

"Right," Carter replied, and disappeared through the portal.

He carefully undid the wire that held the plant to the cage and removed the plant as if he were removing a stillborn from its mother's womb. It was fragile. Far more fragile than its Earth counterpart. He was examining the end of the broken stem when Carter entered the room with a white towel.

"What are you looking at?" Carter asked.

"The stem," Endicott replied simply. Then added in way of explanation: "The lignin and cellulose content is considerably less than that of the same plant grown on Earth."

"So it is," Carter replied. "Here's the towel."

"Thank you," Endicott said. He took the towel and wiped the floor with it. The towel turned red, and he thought of Brunnet. He paused in thought.

"What is it?" Carter inquired.

"Nothing," Endicott replied.

"It's Jean Paul, isn't it?"

Endicott was startled by the suggestion, and at first did not know what to say. "Why do you think that?"

"I've seen it before. My line of business has a high casualty rate. I'd say you're handling it pretty well. Most people don't. Those were the ones I took out and got drunk." He grinned as if it were a joke, but they both knew it to be true. "Anyway, you don't need to worry about the shrinks. I've taken care of them. Told 'em you were doing fine. That you just needed some time to yourself. Tom did the same."

Endicott was at a loss as to what to say. He wanted to express his appreciation, but at the same time he did not want to admit anything. He was genuinely surprised at Carter's support.

"It was nothing," Carter said, stepping back to leave. "You would have done the same for us."

"Yes, of course," Endicott replied.

"If you ever want to talk about it, you know where to find me. Guess I'll be going now."

Endicott wanted to stop him, but he did not have the nerve. It was what Carter had said about doing the same for them. He realized that it was probably not true. He probably would have insisted upon psychiatric examination if it had not been himself, and he would have been confident that he was taking the correct course. But would it have been? Now he wasn't so certain. He sat down on the floor with his legs crossed and closed his eyes and smiled as he considered what Carter had done for him.

Tatiana tiptoed into a dark room. She turned and locked the door behind her.

"Are you there, Dima?" she whispered over her shoulder.

"Yes, I am here," a deep guttural voice replied.

She cautiously took one step forward, her arms outstretched. Several meters in front of her was a panel of tiny lights she recognized as indicators for the environmental-control system. They illuminated only a small corner of the room. Her heart was beating fast. She wondered if he would be waiting in the bunk. She could have turned on the light, but she did not want to be seen. Nor did she really want to see him. It would make it too real. She hesitated for a moment. As she stood there, peering into the dark, she wondered if she was doing the right thing. She pushed the concern from her mind. The thought of Dmitri nearby excited her.

"Where?" she asked to be certain.

"Over here," he said.

She turned to her left at the sound of his voice. Within arm's length there was an unmistakable masculine form, a V-shaped torso and long muscular legs, stepping forward. The sharp, defined lines meant only one thing. He was not wearing any clothing. She took a deep breath and held it. She stood rigid, frozen in place, as his arms surrounded her. She could feel his warm, hard skin through her clothing.

"I'm glad you came," he whispered into her ear.

"I told you I would," she said.

"I thought you might have changed your mind," he said, kissing her behind the ear. "It is late."

She pushed back gently and shook her head. "Not so fast."

"It has been seven months," he offered apologetically.

"Yes, so it has. A few more minutes should not matter then. Should it?"

"Where is Vladimir?"

"I took care of him," she replied. She had left Vladimir curled in a ball at the edge of the bed with the covers wrapped tightly around him. "He will sleep soundly."

"You are wicked," he whispered. "Perhaps that is why I like you so."

"You like me so," she said, pressing her body against his, "because I am the only female aboard this ship, and you can't wait another year and a half for your wife."

"She is taking advantage of my absence." He could feel her nipples harden against his chest. "So why should I not take advantage of hers?"

"I wouldn't want to say anything that might change your mind."

"I'm sure you wouldn't," he said, pressing his mouth hard against hers as he pushed her back against the door.

He grabbed her shirt and ripped it open. As she struggled to pull the shirt off, he took her breasts into his hands and kissed them. With trembling fingers she reached down and unbuttoned her pants and pushed them down below her knees, where they fell to the floor. She could feel the cold door against her back.

"I want you," she said.

Mars Orbit Injection

Colonel Tom Nelson pulled tightly on the restraint straps that held him secure in the contoured chair designed to protect him against high g forces. The *Liberty* was about to pierce the upper layers of Mars's thin atmosphere, a maneuver that would reduce its approach speed. He checked the command console to make certain the ship's trajectory did not require a correction. From the portal it looked as if they were going to crash into the very edge of the planet. The console contained a graphic that displayed the *Liberty*'s position with respect to its desired flight path. Two lines indicted upper and lower safe limits. Nelson verified that the oblong symbol, which represented the *Liberty*, was between the two lines. He scanned the vertical and horizontal position displays and lingered upon the attitude-direction indictor, which gave the pitch and yaw of the ship. His eyes dropped to the scale that indicated their current velocity. They were traveling at 26,332 kilometers per hour. The event timer clicked five seconds. Nelson gripped the arms of his chair to brace himself.

The sudden roar was deafening. He was thrown back hard against his seat. The g force plastered his body into the contours of his chair. His face became a distorted rubber mask that vibrated uncontrollably, and his lips turned white and peeled back, baring his teeth and gums. Unable to move, he could feel the ship shake and tremble. It felt as though it were coming apart. He could hear the metal screech as the hull bent under the impact. The sound was loud and sudden. Air rushing past the umbrella-like aeroshield burst into flames and engulfed the ship in fire. He could see the flames through the portal.

He attempted to read the numbers on the center screen, but they jumped and vibrated so fiercely they had disassembled into jagged lines. It did not really matter. There was very little he could do. He simply wanted to reassure himself that the ship was still on course. He started to keep track of the time by counting the seconds. One one thousand, he said to himself. Two one thousand . . .

Then suddenly a great weight was lifted from his chest, the ship stopped shaking, and the howling ceased. Nelson looked down at the event timer. Six minutes and twenty-three seconds had passed. They were still alive. The *Liberty* had plunged into the Martian atmosphere and emerged intact. They had come within forty-five kilometers of the planet's surface. He scanned the flight deck to make certain that all systems were functioning properly. The screens were clear of warning messages, and the ship appeared to be on course.

"Abort check," Nelson said.

"All systems check," Carter responded.

The *Liberty* was in a highly elliptical orbit that would, if left unaltered, pull the craft back into the atmosphere. A main engine burn was necessary to raise its perigee to 480 kilometers. Its apogee would remain at 32,000. They felt a gentle push as the reaction-control system fired jets of hydrazine to align the *Liberty* for the burn. As the ship rotated, the Martian surface rolled by on the monitors. The ground was reddish orange and cratered. They could make out mountain ranges and canyons and what looked like dried-up riverbeds. The sight filled them with awe. Carter pointed at a volcano and attempted to lean forward to get a better look but was pulled back by his safety straps.

"Engine ignition armed."

"Roger. All systems go," Carter replied.

"We are go for burn."

"Ten seconds to ignition."

Nelson could feel his heart beating as he waited and watched the final seconds tick away. If the main engines failed to fire, they would fall back into the Martian atmosphere, but this time they would not emerge. The ship wouldn't have the necessary velocity to escape the planet's gravitational pull. It would crash into the surface. They felt a slight jolt as the engines fired. Moments later the computer indicated the *Liberty* had achieved its parking orbit.

Carter whistled loudly as he unstrapped himself from the pilot's chair. His eyes were wild with excitement. He was looking for signs that the others shared his enthusiasm when his attention was diverted by a low-to-high whistle originating from the communications window. Carter opened the channel.

"Comrades, we have arrived," Komarov said in a booming voice. "Our ship is intact. All systems operational. How did the *Liberty* handle the aerobrake?"

"Everything appears to be in order," Nelson replied. "Won't know for sure until we run a full diagnostic. It was a little bumpy there at the end."

"That was to be expected," Komarov said, as if he had done it a thousand times before. They could hear the others talking excitedly in the background. "We, too, will have to run diagnostics. And afterward we will celebrate. We are only a few days away from being the first men to set foot on another planet."

"Go easy on the vodka," Nelson said. "I wouldn't want you to find pink elephants on Mars."

"Pink elephants?"

"Just an expression," Nelson said, deciding an explanation would take too long. Besides, he wasn't certain if Komarov would take it as an insult. Nelson watched the window disappear into an icon, then turned to face his men, his pulse still beating hard. "Gentlemen, we've got work to do."

———

"Augustus, you chose your guardian well," Satomura said, looking down through the portal at the dusty red planet, with a plastic container of warm sake dangling from his tired hand. It was Augustus who had made the Roman deity Mars the personal protector of the emperor.

Satomura pressed his nose up against the glass and pulled back when his breath began to condense and obscure his view. He wiped the portal with his sleeve, then shook his head and scrunched his eyes together to steady the planet. It was scarred with deep, long gashes that stretched for thousands of kilometers across the surface. The gashes were the dried-up remains of dead rivers. He could see Valles Marineris, an intricate labyrinth of canyons that carved a bent path along the equator. "Noctis Labyrinthus," he mumbled, "Tithonium Chasma, Coprates Chasma, and Candor Chasma." He pointed with his long fingers at Candor Chasma. It was there they would land. He could see the V-shaped tributaries and layered rock that suggested the canyon had once housed an ancient lake. He knew the area well. After the others had retired for the night he would pour himself another coffee and peruse the maps of Mars, filling his computer screen with shaded reliefs and photo mosaics. And when he had finally decided upon a site he would don his goggles. Footprints would appear behind him as if he were actually on the surface. He took another drink from the container.

He was tired and drunk, but his mind was racing. His thoughts became more vivid when he closed his eyes, which was why he could not fall asleep. Just northwest of the canyons were three prominent volcanoes standing like giants side by side. They were perched on top of the Tharsis bulge, a large swelling in the Martian surface. "Ascraeus Mons, Pavonis Mons, and Arsia Mons." His speech was slurred. He looked down at the calderas and wondered what the volcanoes might have looked liked when they were active. He could visualize fire spewing from the vents and dark smoke twirling high in the air and glowing red lava flowing slowly down the sides. They were dead now, but remnants of their past glory scarred the surrounding land. The ground was rippled, with snakelike extensions where the lava had stopped and hardened. Portions of the volcanoes were buried in their own lava, from fissures along their flanks that had erupted.

His eyes were drawn to a single volcano northwest of the others. Surrounded by low-level plains stood the largest known volcano in the solar system. Olympus Mons. Home of the Greek gods. It was where the American-led crew would land, approximately thirty-five hundred kilometers northwest of Candor Chasma, well outside the range of the manned rovers, but within the range of the Russian airship. He studied the peculiar land formation encircling the volcano. The geologists referred to it as the aureole because it looked like a radiant halo. Its origin was a mystery. Some speculated it was the collapsed remains of an even larger volcano. Others believed it was formed by massive landslides. Satomura favored the first explanation.

He focused on the very top of the volcano. Despite the small aperture, he knew it to be a mammoth caldera over eighty kilometers in diameter. It had, at one time in its past, contained a sea of bubbling magma. He was envious of the Americans, who would be sending rocket-driven probes into the caldera.

With the aid of a computer simulation, he had stood at the very edge of Olympus Mons, but all he had been able to see was

a wall of rock. The base was a sheer cliff that stretched six kilometers into the sky. No matter how far back he moved he was
unable to make out that Olympus Mons was a volcano. Above
the cliff the upward slope was gradual, almost imperceptible.

He took another drink from the container and allowed his
eyes to wander. The planet was barren. Other than the whisper-
thin clouds of water and carbon dioxide that floated in the
upper atmosphere, there was no movement. The surface
beneath the clouds was motionless. It was heavily cratered and
covered with rock. Water did not flow through the riverbeds,
and smoke did not vent from the volcanoes. Unlike Earth, it
was not painted in pleasant colors: it was murky shades of gold
and maroon and dark crimson, except for the north and south
poles, which were ashen white.

Satomura grunted as he stretched, and having forgotten he
was in a weightless environment soon found himself floating
backwards. There was little he could do but wait until he
reached the far wall.

"Oh well," he said, and took the last sip from the container.
"Close portal."

The metallic shutters that protected the portal glass from
micrometeoroids closed shut and replaced Mars with a white panel.

"I must go to sleep," he said to the empty container of sake,
and shook it to mimic agreement.

"W e are go for separation," Carter said. He was seated next
to Nelson inside the lander. The seat behind them was empty.

"All systems check," Endicott said over the intercom.

"Roger," Nelson replied. "Ten seconds to separation."

The first few seconds passed in silence, then Endicott
started the countdown.

"Docking latches have been released," Carter announced.

The Mars excursion module was pushed outside the *Liberty* by a spring inside the docking bay. A television camera transmitted the event back to Earth. Several billion people, crowded around high-definitions, would be watching the images twenty-one minutes and thirty-three seconds later, the time it took for the transmission to reach Earth. Carter, who had maintained a perpetual five o'clock shadow for the past several months, was clean-shaven in honor of the occasion.

"The *Shepard* has just come into view," Endicott said. The lander was named after Alan Shepard, the first American astronaut to fly in space. The Soviet cosmonaut Yuri Gagarin had orbited the Earth twenty-three days earlier. Endicott was watching the craft through the *Liberty*'s forward portal.

There were two red buttons, both marked ABORT, that Carter would have to push simultaneously to terminate the landing. The computer would recommend an abort if something went wrong, but it would be up to him to activate the sequence. He would have to decide whether the computer had advised him correctly or whether a glitch in the software or a malfunction in the hardware had resulted in a false warning. If the hazard was real, he would have to decide whether he could pull them out of the danger by taking manual control. They only had one chance to land. It was his opinion that the abort thresholds were set too low. He was determined not to abort unless he had absolutely no other choice.

"Burn attitude obtained," Endicott said. "Fifteen minutes to deorbit burn."

They were going to fire the braking engines of the *Shepard* to lower its orbit. If it were to make a direct descent from its current orbit, the deceleration would be too great for the astronauts to withstand without risk of injury. At the time the mission was being planned it was not known exactly how much calcium their bones would lose. And although they were in much better shape than they would have been without the artificial gravity on the

Liberty, their bones were still more fragile than they had been on Earth. The four-point-nine g's they would have undergone was considered unacceptable. By lowering their orbit they would reduce the deceleration to two-point-two g's.

"Engines have been armed," Carter announced. "Forty-five seconds to burn."

"Roger, you are go for deorbit burn."

"Countdown to burn: seven . . . six . . . five . . . four . . . three . . . two . . . one . . . ignition."

"I have visual confirmation, over."

They were pushed back as the braking engine fired. The ship started to slow down and descend. The burn lasted forty-eight seconds.

"Burn complete," Carter announced, as the lander began to drop. "Deorbit engine shutdown. E minus fifty-seven minutes."

Carter allowed his head to fall back on his shoulders and roll to one side as he savored the taste of the gum he had placed in his mouth prior to locking down his helmet. He was in his element. The *Shepard* was his baby. He would take over the controls from the computer when they were close enough to pick out a landing site visually. He wanted to take over now, but knew he had to wait. The entry was too complex for a human to handle. From the corner of his eye, he peeked up at the high-definition to see how Endicott was holding up. He was alone now and would be for the next three months. Well, that's what he said he wanted. Endicott smiled back awkwardly.

T atiana watched her husband on the high-definition monitor as he counted the seconds to impact with the Martian atmosphere. His face was expressionless, his voice disciplined and military. It was what the Russian people expected from their cosmonauts, but for Vladimir it was too perfect. His voice should have cracked or there should have been a smile or a grimace or a nervous twitch or something. To anybody but Tatiana he would have seemed perfectly normal; to her he was *too* normal. His cold professionalism reminded her of Komarov; the similarity was unnerving.

They would be apart for the next three months. He was to remain aboard the *Druzhba*, while she was on the planet's surface with Komarov and Satomura. She knew their upcoming separation bothered him. She knew that he still suspected her of being unfaithful even though he had not said anything for some time, and knew that he did not trust her alone with Komarov. The next three months would be difficult. Perhaps it would be better that way. Perhaps he would become less dependent upon her. That would be nice, she thought. But as she watched him, an uncomfortable notion that there would be trouble ahead swelled inside her. His face was a mask of sculpted iron, the muscles beneath the skin taut and rigid. There was no emotion in his voice, just the flat sound of the countdown.

"E minus one minute," he said. "Atmospheric spectrometer activated."

"Activation confirmed," Komarov replied as he glanced at a stream of data flooding the lower half of Satomura's monitor.

Tatiana looked quickly out the portal and saw that outside was still black. Sprinkled with stars. She looked back at Vladimir.

"E minus zero seconds. The *Gagarin* has just entered the Martian atmosphere," Vladimir said. "Entry angle is fourteen-point-twelve degrees."

She did not feel anything at first. The computer flashed 0.05 g. They were 240 kilometers from the surface and eight minutes and forty-seven seconds from touchdown. She looked over at the portal and still no change. Her heart was pounding quickly in her chest, and Vladimir and his troubles were slipping from her mind as she began to sense the weight of her body.

"L minus seven minutes."

"Spectrometer deactivated."

She scanned the control panel and focused on the event timer, where the seconds appeared to be ticking at an accelerated pace.

"L minus five minutes," Vladimir said.

His face began to bounce and break apart into a haze of white snow. They were losing contact with the *Druzhba*. Tatiana felt heavier as the g forces gained intensity. The display indicated 2.2 g's. Turning her head to look out the corner of her eye at the portal, she saw the red-and-orange flickering of flames.

The lander was shaking from the turbulence. Her muscles tightened. She tried to relax, telling herself it was not as bad as what they had endured a couple of days earlier. She looked up to see if Vladimir had reappeared, even though she knew it was too soon. The high-definition monitor was filled with snow that crackled like tiny firecrackers. For the next few minutes they would be entirely on their own. All communications had been severed by the ionized gases that surrounded the lander.

As she watched the instruments on the control panel, the altitude decreasing, the velocity increasing, she visualized the red Martian surface growing larger as their capsule plunged toward it. A wondrous feeling chilled her body. She was about to land on a strange planet.

She felt a sudden jolt.

"Main parachute deployed," Komarov announced. "L minus one minute and thirty-three seconds. Five-point-nine kilometers."

The flames disappeared, to be replaced by a pink sky. The high-definition monitors displayed a rocky, red surface that swayed back and forth with the motion of the craft. The surface was chopped into an intricate network of canyons. Valles Marineris. Although she had flown the landing simulator many times before, the sheer size of the gorges startled her. They were growing in size with each second. The edges of Valles Marineris disappeared over the horizons, and all she could see were canyons. It was an imposing sight.

"L minus sixty seconds," Vladimir said, as his image reappeared on the monitor.

"Five seconds to descent-engine ignition," Komarov said. "Four, three, two . . ."

Tatiana was pushed back into her chair by a second jolt.

"We have descent-engine ignition. Parachutes have been jettisoned. Deploying landing gear."

She heard the sound of the landing gear extract itself.

"Righting maneuver complete," Komarov said. The ship, which had been coming in at an angle, was now heading straight for the surface.

Tatiana could see the sides of the canyon as they descended into it. She felt as if she were being swallowed up by the planet. The opening was gigantic. The canyon wall outside her portal was nearly one hundred kilometers distant. She magnified the image on the monitor and could see thick layers of rock sandwiched one on top of the other. Each layer was from a different period in the planet's evolution. At the rim the stone was much darker and appeared to be basalt, a dense rock formed by molten lava. As they descended, the tiers became thinner, compressed together by the rocks above them. The tiers near the bottom were from earlier periods in Martian history.

They were headed for a mesa in the center of Candor Chasma. It rose a little more than a kilometer above the canyon floor, but was still a kilometer beneath the surface. The satellite photographs of the landing site showed the surface to be relatively flat and free from boulders. They were expecting mostly sand. But the monitor was cluttered with rocks.

"Surface is rough," Komarov said calmly. "Assuming control. Prepare for manual landing."

"Recommend alternate landing site," Vladimir said. "Proceed to seven degrees south, seventy-seven degrees west."

"Negative," Komarov responded. "We're going to take her down here."

They were only fifty meters above the surface, and the thrust from their engines was beginning to kick up sand. Tatiana pressed forward as far as the restraint straps would allow to get a better look at the monitor. There was no place to land. The ground was covered with rocks, some of which were large enough to pierce the hull. The dust was beginning to swirl and obscure their view.

"I'm taking her up ten meters," Komarov said. As the ship climbed, the dust cleared and fell back onto the rocks.

"You have nine minutes and twenty seconds of fuel before descent abort," Vladimir warned.

"I'll have her down long before then," Komarov replied. He looked over at Satomura and raised his eyebrows. "Where to?"

"Let's try north," Satomura said.

Carter was looking down inside the ancient vent of Olympus Mons. The giant rim encircled the vent like a castle wall that had been ravished by violent bombardments. Portions had collapsed and crumbled into the caldera, leaving large gaps. Through the gaps, molten lava had spilled and flowed down the sides, forming long, spidery trails of hardened magma that seemed to stretch forever. Inside the volcano were several vast craters, broken circles, overlapping each other. Each crater was formidable in itself. The largest was over forty-two kilometers in diameter.

"Parachutes have been released," Nelson announced, as the ship jumped forward.

Carter returned his attention to the job of piloting the lander. They were heading for the base of the volcano on the southeast side. The site was about five kilometers above mean planetary level. As a result they had less room to brake. The *Shepard* was still traveling fast enough to come in at an angle. It was heading straight for the side of the volcano, a vertical wall of rock towering four kilometers above the surface. Just like the simulation, Carter thought to himself. The wall of rock completely filled both monitors.

"Five seconds to retro-rocket ignition," Endicott announced over the intercom.

The rocks grew larger, and it looked as if they were going to crash into the side of the volcano. Carter caught Nelson glancing over at the override switch that fired the retro-rockets. He looked back at monitor and thought the cliff did look close, but he did not let it bother him.

There was a deafening roar as the restraint straps pressed deeply into their flesh. A mixture of fluorine/oxygen and methane combusted and burst through the plug nozzle of the descent engine with 140,000 pounds of thrust. Long, hot flames shot out of the bottom of the *Shepard*. The red cliffs disappeared behind the bellowing exhaust.

Carter glanced at the event timer. The ship initiated the maneuver to right itself and start its vertical descent. He looked out the side portal, and the wall of rock seemed no more than two hundred meters away.

"Close," he said, chewing his gum. "Going to have to back her up some. Appears we overshot the landing site. Receiving transponder signal loud and clear."

"A few more seconds and we would have been a permanent fixture on that cliff," Nelson said as he looked out the portal.

"Optical illusion. Just seemed closer than it really was because it's so large."

"You gentlemen all right?" Endicott asked.

"Never better," Carter replied. Nelson gave a thumbs-up to the camera and a forced smile.

"You are point-six kilometers northwest of Landing Site Alpha," Endicott said.

"Roger," Carter replied, directing the craft away from the volcanic wall.

"I have visual contact on Monitor B," Nelson said. "Looks clean."

"Landing Site Alpha is a go," Carter said.

"Take her down easy," Endicott said.

"Fifty meters," Carter said. "Forward five."

"Fuel looking good," Nelson said. "We can be selective with our real estate."

"Forty-five meters."

"Starting to kick up some sand."

"Forty meters. Northeast two. Looks like we could land just about anywhere. I'm going to take her down."

"You are within fifteen meters of the transponder."

"Some rocks coming into view. They're directly below," Nelson said. "Take her forward ten."

"Appears I spoke too soon," Carter replied with a Southern drawl. "Forward ten. Twenty-five meters."

"Fuel pressure good. All systems check," Nelson said.

"Fifteen meters."

A cloud of fine red dust engulfed the lander.

"We have lost visuals. Radar shows flat ground."

"Five meters," Carter said. With a slight bump the *Shepard* settled onto the Martian surface. "The *Shepard* has landed."

"Abort status?" Endicott asked.

"All systems green," Carter replied as he flipped several switches above his head. "We are stable. Proceeding with shut-down of descent engines."

"Checking ascent engines," Nelson said. The monitor in front of him filled with a schematic of the engines and a diagnostic readout. Segments of the schematic turned from blue to green as the computer ran through the check. They were preparing the ship for an immediate liftoff in the event they determined it was unsafe to stay. The last blue line disappeared, and the words READY FOR LAUNCH flashed on the screen. "Engines have passed emergency diagnostics."

"Stay no stay?" Endicott asked.

"We're here to stay," Nelson replied, checking the monitors.

"Congratulations, gentlemen," Endicott said. "How does it feel to be the first humans to land on another planet?"

"Glorious," Carter said, ridding himself of his helmet. He smiled up at the camera with white shiny teeth and placed a folded stick of gum between the brilliant rows. "Most glorious indeed."

——————

"The Americans have landed," Vladimir announced.

"Fuel?" Komarov demanded, unwilling to detach his eyes from the monitor that displayed the Martian surface beneath him.

"Two minutes and seventeen seconds remaining."

"Over there," Satomura exclaimed, pointing to the west. "A clearing about fifty meters due west."

Komarov glanced out the portal, then returned his attention to the instrument panel. His face was expressionless. The muscles in his neck stuck out like rigid bands of steel. He would not get a second chance. If he wasn't on the ground within less than two minutes and seventeen seconds, he would have to abort the landing. He could see Carter, with his large country-bumpkin grin stretched ear to ear, planting the U.N. flag in the Martian soil.

"Rotating ninety west," he said. "Forward fifty. Descending five."

"Two minutes," Vladimir said. "Estimated landing time: fifty-seven seconds. You have one minute to spare."

They arrived at the location Satomura had indicated. The high-definition that displayed the ground directly underneath was littered with scattered rocks. The rocks were smaller but packed together tightly. He scanned the surface for something less treacherous.

"We can't land here," Tatiana said.

"One minute thirty seconds."

"Going north twenty."

"Forty-five seconds," Vladimir said. His tone struck Tatiana as odd. He sounded slightly pleased. This surprised her. She didn't know what to make of it at first. The bastard, she thought. He's actually hoping we're going to abort. She looked at Satomura and could see concern in his eyes. She then looked at Komarov. He appeared unusually grave. The unthinkable was closing in on them. It did not seem possible. She pressed hard against her restraint straps as she searched the monitors for a place to land.

"Forty seconds."

"Arm ascent engines," Vladimir said. "Prepare to abort."

"Over there!" Tatiana shouted, pointing.

"Thirty seconds."

"Where?" Komarov demanded.

"Fifty meters northeast," she said, jabbing her finger at the spot.

"Fifteen seconds," Vladimir said. "You'll never make it. Initiate abort sequence."

"Like hell," Komarov growled. "We're going down."

The lander was not an airplane, it did not have wings or ailerons or rudders or a tail. It did not float or glide. It was an elongated capsule, shaped vaguely like a missile, and was designed to go two directions: straight up and straight down. The descent engines allowed lateral movement, but the movement was limited. The aerodynamics were simple. When the mixture of fluorine/oxygen and methane ran out, 140,000 pounds of thrust would dissipate, gravity would take over, and the craft would drop out of the sky like a lead weight. He was only going as far as the fuel would take him. There was nothing he could do to change that. But he could push the machine. As a test pilot, that had been his job. No pilot worth his salt would do less. He didn't get to be the best by backing off. There really had never been any doubt in his mind. He was not going to give up until the last drop of fuel was spent.

"Forward twenty, down ten." He was surprised at how calm and confident he sounded.

"Ten seconds."

The computer displayed a recommendation to abort.

"Forward twenty, down ten."

"Five."

They had another ten meters to go, Komarov calculated. The remaining five seconds would get them there, but they still would be twenty meters above the surface. A fall from that distance would crumple the landing gear like toothpicks. The rocket nozzles would be crushed, and the lander would probably tip over onto its side. There was a chance the engines would explode. Whatever happened, it was unlikely the lander would be able to take off again. The first of the two plans developed for such a contingency was to fly the dirigible to the American site. The second was to return by the emergency lander docked in the supply ship. He glanced down at the fuel gauge and felt like tapping it, but his hands were full. Experience had taught him there was always more fuel than the gauge indicated.

The screens started flashing red.

"Three," Vladimir counted, unable to disguise the doubt in his voice.

The sand on the surface kicked up and mushroomed into a red maelstrom that engulfed the craft. The landing site disappeared behind the rising cloud of dust. There had been a few rocks, but they were small and far apart. They could land here as long as they had enough fuel. The gauge read empty.

"I want you to hit the abort switch on my command," Komarov ordered Satomura. The computer was constantly calculating escape velocities and escape trajectories, allowing for an abort at any moment in the descent, even at the final moment when the lander was within centimeters of the ground.

"One."

The engines continued to roar defiantly. The distant bashing of drums in the final crescendo of a symphony. Komarov knew as long as he heard that sound the lander still had power.

"OK," Komarov said, "we need to make every second count. Down ten."

"Twenty meters from the surface," Satomura said.

"Down ten."

"Ten meters from the surface."

A violent storm of red dust was beating at the lander's portals.

"We're almost there."

The first eight meters was a textbook descent. The engines blared gloriously. They were beginning to think they would make it. Then there was silence. They were two meters above the ground. An eerie stillness swept through the ship. The last drops of fluorine/oxygen and methane had combined and combusted. For a brief moment the lander hung suspended. Then it fell.

"Hold on." Komarov fingers tightened on the controls.

"Abort!" Vladimir shouted.

"No!" Komarov shouted.

Satomura reached out toward the abort switch but Komarov knocked his hand away.

"*G*agarin, this is *Shepard*, do you copy? Over." Carter waited a few seconds, then repeated the query. He released a deep breath. "We're not picking them up."

"I fear the worst," Vladimir said from the monitor. He was running his hand through his hair.

"You say they ran out of fuel and did not abort?" Nelson asked with disbelief.

"They were two meters from the ground."

"Only Komarov," Carter said.

"They may be alive," Nelson said. "Are you certain they did not abort? Perhaps the ascent engines misfired."

"They did not abort, I tell you. I will send you the transmission. There is much I must do. I must go now."

"How can we help?"

"Keep on trying to raise them. I will contact you as soon as I have something."

"Roger," Nelson replied. "Over and out."

"I'll say one thing for Dmitri, he's one determined son of a bitch," Carter said. "I suspect they're OK. The *Gagarin* must have been damn close to the ground for him not to have aborted."

"What do you think happened?" Nelson asked.

"The way I see it, Dmitri was running her on vapors. The gauge read empty but there was still some fuel in the tanks. So he wagers he can put her down before she runs out of gas. He knows he can abort even within centimeters of the ground. So there's really no danger. He can hit the abort switch the second the engines cut out. But he doesn't. Why? Because he feels he's a safe distance from the ground. Chances are they're all right. Just a bit shaken up."

"He was rushed," Nelson said. "He may not have had time to pick out a level site. He could have struck a boulder or landed in a ditch."

"And pierced the hull?"

"Perhaps."

"I don't buy it. Dmitri's too good for that." His eye was caught by a blinking message indicating a download from the *Druzhba* was completed. "Maybe the tape will tell us something."

The screen filled with the helmets of two of the crew. Glare from the visors made it difficult to discern the faces behind them, but as the one of the helmets turned they were able to make out the deep pits and wrinkled lines of Satomura's face. Another helmet was jerking erratically back and forth behind the first two. It had to be Tatiana's. She seemed to be pointing at something and was speaking rapidly in Russian, almost shouting.

"Computer translate," Nelson ordered.

"Fifteen seconds." They recognized the voice as Vladimir's. The program that translated Russian into English was not sophisticated enough to capture the emotion in a voice, so Vladimir's "fifteen seconds" sounded as if it were being read from a dictionary. Which in fact it was. "You'll never make it. Initiate abort sequence."

"Like Hades." The voice belonged to Komarov. "We're going down."

Nelson and Carter took time to look at each other to register the other's reaction. Both were openmouthed with amazement, with a hint of amusement at the awkward translation. Their eyes shot back at the screen.

"Jesus," Carter said, "that man has balls."

"He had no other choice," Endicott said.

"How's that?" Carter asked.

"The Russian government places a great deal of significance on this mission. It reaffirms their status as a superpower. He had to do it for the New Republic."

"Not Dmitri," Carter said. "He wasn't thinking about Russia when he landed that bird, he was thinking about himself. The son of a bitch has an ego the size of Siberia."

"Quiet," Nelson interrupted.

". . . hit the abort switch on my command." It was Komarov.

"One."

They could hear the descent engines roaring in the background. They seemed louder now.

". . . we need to make every second count." The voice belonged to Komarov.

"That's a fuckin' understatement," said Carter as he reached in his shirt pocket for more gum. The package was empty.

"Ten meters from the surface." It sounded like Satomura.

"We're almost there." Komarov again.

"He's run out of time," Carter said.

The constant noise that had been rumbling in the background stopped. The screen froze like a snapshot. They heard someone yell "abort" and someone else yell "no." Seconds later the monitor went blank.

"Holy shit," Carter said.

———

Komarov could feel the craft falling. His chair dropped away, and his restraint straps tugged at his shoulders. He felt lighter as blood rushed to his head. He was floating. There was a loud crashing noise, and his chair came charging up and slammed hard against his lower back. His head snapped forward. His arms flew past his eyes. The restraint straps pulled him back into his chair. Something fell from the ceiling. He shook his head to clear his vision and thought he could see smoke. The power went out. The only light came from the pink-tinted rays that passed through the portal.

He heard metal screeching and a long drawn-out howl as the lander swayed to one side. It felt as though it was going to tip over. After what seemed an unnaturally long time it rocked back and settled on its landing gear. The overhead emergency lights turned on. The flight panel remained dark.

"Emergency power activated," Komarov said, shaking his head to clear the fuzziness.

"Do we stay?" Satomura shouted, his hand hovering over the abort switch.

"We have no choice," Komarov responded. "We must first determine the extent of the damage."

"Communications link is down," Tatiana said. She, too, was shouting. "We've lost the main power supply. Emergency power to the computer has been severed. The computer is down."

"Probably a short in the electrical subsystem," Komarov said. He was not ready to admit that he had made the wrong decision by landing. No one had said anything yet, but he knew it must have been on their minds. It certainly was on his. "Everybody keep their suits on. We must first restore power. Tatiana, I want you to go below and check the generator. See if it's still running. Take a laptop for diagnostics. Takashi, come with me. We need to find the source of that smoke. Let's move."

He released his restraint straps and stood up. His knees felt weak. He held on to his chair to steady himself. He looked over at Satomura and saw that he was bent over and moving slowly.

"You all right?" Komarov asked.

"Nothing fatal." Satomura was unable to stand perfectly straight. "Must have sprained something."

The emergency lighting cast murky shadows through which they walked with their hands extended. He couldn't be sure, but he thought the smoke was getting thicker. They must be heading in the right direction. He pulled a fire extinguisher from the wall. The smoke started to raise doubts. Two meters was a long drop. They were lucky the craft was standing upright. Why had he slapped Satomura's hand away? The gravitational pull was one-third that of Earth's. So two meters was actually less than one meter. Two-thirds of a meter or sixty-six centimeters. He placed his hand approximately two-thirds of a meter from the floor and stopped to consider the distance. It did not seem that far. The drop was well within the tolerance of the landing gear. He could visualize the black-and-white diagram of the shock-absorption system. The manual was on-line. He would bring it up as soon as he had the chance.

Satomura tapped his shoulder from behind and pointed to his left. Wisps of smoke were slipping through the edges of a panel. Four screws held it in place, one in each corner. Komarov took a deep breath. He was still shaken from the landing. Handing the fire extinguisher to Satomura, he went down on all fours. His eyes were level with the panel.

"Screwdriver," he said. He watched over his shoulder as Satomura placed the fire extinguisher on the floor and departed through the corridor with his hand pressed against his lower back. Komarov took another deep breath. There would be an inquiry. They would demand an explanation. The computer had recommended an abort with ten seconds of fuel remaining. He had ignored the recommendation and continued with the descent. He continued when the fuel gauge read empty. He continued after the fuel had run out and after Vladimir had yelled abort. He continued until the *Gagarin* crashed into the ground. He certainly could not claim it was a miscalculation on his part. He had acted deliberately. He countermanded Vladimir. He struck Satomura's hand away. He had endangered his life and those of his crew. He closed his eyes to clear his mind and felt as if he were about to fall. Darkness was swirling around him. He opened his eyes. Shades of white and gray burst into view. He took several deep breaths. He decided it would be best to keep his eyes open. He looked up at a clock. Less than three minutes had passed since they had landed. He focused on the smoke. It was dissipating. That was hopeful. If the damage was minimal, he could justify his actions. He would actually become something of a hero. But if the damage was so great the *Gagarin* would be unable to lift off, he would have to fly the dirigible to the American site. He did not relish the thought. He took another deep breath. The air in his suit was getting thin. Where the hell was Satomura?

A screwdriver appeared over his shoulder. A bead of perspiration slipped into the corner of his eye, and the salt started to sting. The visor on his helmet prevented him from rubbing his eye. He tapped the visor with his fist. The screwdriver disappeared behind a haze of water. He shook his head back and forth.

"A little warm," he said as he adjusted the valve that controlled the temperature of the coolant circulating through his suit. With his vision still misty, he inserted the power tool into the screw and pressed the switch that sent the Phillips head twirling. The mechanical whir was muffled by his helmet. Within seconds the screw was dangling, magnetically, at the end of the screwdriver. He removed it and proceeded with the next one. All four screws were rolling in blurred semicircles on the floor as he took one last deep breath and pried the panel from the wall. Satomura was standing behind him with the fire extinguisher readied. A puff of smoke emerged and floated over their heads. He waved his hand to clear the remaining smoke. The circuitry was discolored. Several of the wires had been severed by a sheet of metal. He could feel Satomura pressing down on him and waved him away with the back of his hand. There was no need for the fire extinguisher.

"RTG checks out." Tatiana's voice startled him. The speaker in his helmet made it sound as if she were standing next to him. "The power grid indicates a break in the line somewhere between the lower and upper decks."

"I'm looking right at it," Komarov responded. "A piece of sheet metal has sliced through several of the wires. We might want to shut off the power feeding into these lines. They look like they're live. Come on up."

"I'll be there in a second."

"What do you think?" Komarov asked as he stood up to face Satomura.

"Superficial."

Komarov was relieved, but noticed that Satomura still held on to the extinguisher. The damage did appear to be superficial.

A couple of severed wires should be simple enough to fix. He could have them spliced back together within seconds. Of course, it might not be as easy as that. There could be additional damage. They would have to spend the first several days, perhaps weeks, checking and rechecking the various subsystems. The ascent engine would be their primary concern. Without it, the lander would not leave Mars. The engine would be difficult to inspect. Many of the parts were inaccessible. There were only a few tests they could perform, and none of them guaranteed that the engine would fire properly when they threw the switch.

"You did the right thing," Satomura said, having read the doubt in his commander's mind. He attempted to smile. The grim lines that etched his face were unable to settle into a pleasing pattern. But it was the best he could manage. Komarov's grin was large and broad and fell naturally into place.

"Little light on the oxygen?" Tatiana asked as she walked in. She crouched and examined the dark gap in the wall. Her hands were on her hips. "We'll need to shut down the power feeding into these wires."

Komarov did not like the tone of her voice. He noticed that Satomura had retreated behind the fire extinguisher.

"Well . . ." she said.

Her fierce glare was sobering. The electrical subsystem was the ship's central nervous system. Komarov wondered if he had underestimated the danger. He turned to Satomura.

"Shut down the power that feeds into this panel." He moved in closer and crouched to a level just above her shoulders so he could see what she was doing. Her glove-encased index finger was poking at the wires inside the gap.

"How long will it take?" he asked.

She answered without turning around. "Ten minutes maximum."

He looked down at his watch.

"I'll be on the flight deck," he said.

"I may need you." The forced tones of her anger vibrated through the tiny speakers in his helmet. He was beginning to resent her attitude. But she was the ship's technician, and during emergencies of this sort he had to rely upon her.

"Of course," he said. He still felt disoriented from the landing.

"The power to the panel has been turned off," Satomura announced.

"Thank you," Tatiana said icily. "You could help by holding this cable steady here."

Komarov went down on one knee and took the cable. To his astonishment the wire began to shake. He looked at his hand in horror, as if the appendage belonged to someone else. He concentrated on holding the wire steady, but it continued to shake. He took a deep breath and held it. No effect. He could tell that she noticed. He bit his lip until he drew blood; he could taste the blood as it slid down his tongue and into his throat. The pain concentrated his thoughts on the flesh clamped between his teeth. The wire finally stopped shaking. He swallowed the blood and smiled.

"Almost done," she said.

"Takashi," he said, "prepare to restore power."

He was looking at his hand. He had been in situations as dangerous, and it had never trembled before. Perhaps it was the fall. He wondered if Tatiana would think less of him.

"Done," she said, and stood up.

"Restore power," he said.

The lights came on all at once. He swiveled toward the flight deck and, in the distance, could see the computer screens blink on. The panels above and below the monitors were popping to life with tiny bright colors. He felt a great sense of relief and felt like hugging Tatiana, but instead he patted her on the back, and said simply, "Nice job."

"You're damn right," she replied, and stormed off toward the flight deck.

He stood bewildered and said nothing, and after a few seconds he followed her into the cabin. On the screen, with hair pointing every which way and shirt stained with great circles of sweat, Vladimir was beaming down at Tatiana, and Tatiana, Komarov could tell from the tone in her voice, was beaming back up at him. For the moment he was too tired to care, and, actually, to some degree, he was happy for them. He walked over to the portal and looked out and saw canyon walls that dwarfed anything he had ever seen before and a wave of adrenaline-charged elation swept through him.

"I want a preliminary damage report within the hour," he said, as his eyes wandered over the majestic sight.

Mars

Her mouth opened and closed with words, but he wasn't listening to the words, he was listening to the sounds and watching the expressions that framed the sounds. The words didn't mean anything. The words could form the truth or they could form lies. She could mold words into anything she desired, and she would, without the slightest twinge of remorse, if it served her purpose. He watched her eyes to see if they would betray her, but they were looking into a camera lens, which was not the same as looking into his eyes. She could pretend the lens was someone else or no one at all. And although he was there on the screen before her, he was still several hundred kilometers away. He could hear his own voice, and as he listened he cursed himself for playing her game. He was telling her how much he missed her and how much he wanted her, and he remembered vaguely that was how he felt at the time, but now he wasn't so sure. He stopped the tape and rewound it to the beginning of the transmission.

Vladimir was floating naked in the flight deck. Without the

other cosmonauts aboard the ship there didn't seem to be as much a reason to wear clothing. He could regulate the temperature aboard the *Druzhba* to whatever he desired. Many nights he pranced naked from one module to the next and danced and twirled and sang at the top of his lungs, making up the words as they occurred to him, the lewder the better.

Her mouth was moving again. This time he decided to concentrate on her lips. The slightest tremble, and he would have the evidence he sought. He increased the magnification until her lips filled the entire screen. Her lips were wet with moisture. He caught a glimpse of her tongue slipping out between her teeth. It sent warm shivers through his body. He wondered if she were deliberately trying to tease him. He reduced the magnification, and after several minutes of silent deliberation decided the effect had been invoked by the magnification.

She sounded and acted normal. He was unable to detect any clear evidence that she was lying. But he knew she was. He rewound the tape and played it in slow motion. It mutated her words into a painful, slurring moan. He listened until he couldn't stand it anymore. He sped the tape up, and that made her sound like a chipmunk. He rewound the tape again.

He played it at normal speed, and this time he closed his eyes and just listened. Her voice had a soothing influence, and he found himself believing her, falling under her spell. It angered him to think she could have such an effect on him. Despite his nagging suspicions, he realized he was still very much in love with her. He opened his eyes and studied the digital image. He froze the frame.

He moved in close until he was able to distinguish the individual dots of light that made up her face. Thousands of tiny little pixels all blurred into circles the color of her skin. He touched the circles with his lips and wondered what it would be like to touch her skin. The glass was frigid. He pulled back. The dots converged back into her face.

He started the tape again, and the words began pouring from her mouth, cascading into sentences that didn't seem to make any sense. She was saying how she missed him. He tried to concentrate on the words, but he started to think about her and Dmitri.

The son of a bitch had her all to himself. He could caress her warm skin whenever he wanted. He wondered if they had made love. He was certain they had. And then he wondered how often they made love and where and if they had enough decency to do it while Satomura was asleep. That would be almost too much to bear—the old man listening while Dmitri poured himself into her, grunting with each thrust. Tatiana would come in short staccato bursts as she ripped at the sheets with her long fingernails. He could hear the sound in his mind. The first couple of times quietly, and then, as the moment approached, louder and louder.

"The goddamn whore," he shouted.

His face went red with rage. He slammed his fist into the monitor. There was a loud explosion. The glass shattered and tiny projectiles flew outward, striking his face and body. Splintered glass and droplets of blood were floating in the air. He heard a crackling noise and saw several sparks of light from inside the monitor. To his horror there were tiny streams of blood flowing like confetti from his wrist. He moved his hand, and the streams of blood grew longer. He was surprised that he couldn't feel any pain.

"Damn," he said, looking at his hand quizzically. "What have I done?"

Without bothering to stop the flow of blood, he looked back at the monitor and saw that Tatiana had disappeared. He stared at the circuitry inside the tube, wondering why he had reacted so violently. He felt like crying. It was not until his hand started to throb with pain that he looked at his wrist again. It was surrounded by a floating puddle of blood. He shivered and started to feel nauseous as he extracted his bleeding hand, but managed to take his other hand and press down on the cut.

He looked around the room for something to wrap the wound with. The cut grew more painful, and his eyes began to water. He cursed out loud. With his hand pressed firmly on his wrist, he made for the infirmary. He left floating droplets of blood behind him.

————

T he three crew members sat in silence as they waited for the transmission from Earth to commence. They had sent the damage report several hours earlier and were waiting for the Russian Space Agency's recommendation. Their bodies felt strange from lack of sleep and the multiple cups of black coffee. The problems they had found were minor. A sieve charcoal canister was spent and had to be replaced. Several batteries had to be recharged. The gas-coolant separator required a minor repair. Other than the severed power lines, which they had fixed, they were unable to find any damage they could directly attribute to the landing.

The Americans had agreed to delay the first EVA until the internal inspection of the *Gagarin* was completed. Komarov was annoyed at the length of the delay. He felt that Emil Levchenko was being overly cautious, and the more he thought about it the more difficult it was for him to contain his anger. He was trying to imagine what additional inspections Levchenko might require. They needed someone who was more decisive. If Levchenko had his way, he would have them disassembling and reassembling the *Gagarin* the entire three months they were on the surface.

Komarov disliked the attention the delay focused on him. Ordinarily, he thrived on attention. His decision to land was being scrutinized by the media to a degree he had never thought possible. He might as well have been on trial. They were questioning his character and publishing things about his past that were entirely irrelevant. But he was convinced he would be vindicated and all would be forgotten once he set foot on Martian soil.

"Democracy has made everyone too fearful of failure," he had told Satomura while under the command console. His frustration had grown too great to contain. "Communism bred scientists who were not fearful of failure. They had balls. They could afford to have balls. They knew the government controlled the press. If something went wrong, it could be suppressed. No one would know. The people were only informed of the successes. Under such a system we made great strides."

Satomura pointed out that the Americans, who were burdened with democracy from the start, were able to make even greater strides. This annoyed Komarov—but he knew better than to engage in a political discussion with Satomura.

"Finally," Tatiana said.

The mission insignia at the center of the screen was replaced by a white conference room filled with men and women. Plastic badges that contained pictures of much younger people dangled from their shirt pockets. The camera zoomed in on Colonel Leonid Schebalin. He was the only man in the room wearing a military uniform. The creases in his pants were as sharp as razor blades. His shoes were bright black and clicked like tap shoes as he marched across the marble floor. The camera followed him as he walked, back upright, to the center chair at the conference table. He sat down. On either side of him, the scientists were talking in hushed tones. Schebalin cleared his throat.

"We have reviewed your damage reports . . ." Schebalin began. His voice was firm and steady. ". . . and have determined that you should proceed with the external inspection."

Komarov closed his eyes and silently thanked Levchenko.

Perhaps he had been too harsh on the scientist. He would send him an e-mail as soon as he had the time.

"External inspection will commence tomorrow morning immediately after the joint excursion with the U.S. The EVA is scheduled for eleven hundred hours. An updated event schedule has been uploaded to your computer. Review the schedule and make the appropriate preparations." Schebalin paused for a second, then his lips turned upward into a broad smile. "Congratulations, comrades, tomorrow you will set foot on Mars."

Colonel Schebalin stood up, signaling the end of the transmission. The camera pulled backed until the entire conference room filled the screen. Emil Levchenko continued to bounce the eraser of his pencil against the table while everyone else stood up. The conference room faded out, and the mission insignia appeared in red and black on the screen. The cosmonauts watched the insignia in silence, knowing it would disappear in a few seconds. Vladimir appeared in its place.

"We did it," Komarov said, striking his fist against the armrest of his chair. He stood up and opened his arms as if inviting someone to jump into them. Satomura shook his hand. He was smiling that awkward smile of his. Tatiana kissed both of them on the cheek. In their excitement they had forgotten about Vladimir, and when Tatiana finally looked up at the screen she saw that he appeared distracted.

"We are to be here for a while," she said.

"I am happy for you," he said. "I am happy for all of you. Dmitri, it is fortunate that you did not listen to me. Your courage is to be commended."

"I'm ready to go," Colonel Nelson said from inside the airlock of the *Shepard*.

"Just a few more seconds," Carter said. He was responsible for

coordinating Nelson's first steps so that they occurred simultaneously with the Russian's. It was to be a symbolic act. Mankind
united in its effort to explore the universe. Carter felt the official
line was a bunch of crap. The only reason the two men were setting
foot upon the surface at the same time was that neither nation
wanted to be second. He looked up at the monitor at Satomura.

"Well, ol' chap," he said, "are you ready?"

"Commander Komarov is ready."

"OK, Tom, go for it."

"Opening portal," Nelson said. He turned his back to the
monitor and punched in the code to unlock the portal. A green
light appeared. He pushed the portal back upon its hinge. The
ground was rusty red, strewn with rocks and boulders that
extended to the edge of the horizon. The sky overhead was a
delicate pink. There was a maroon sand dune in the distance.
He could see the cliffs of Olympus Mons. The bare red rock
that formed the nearest precipice stretched majestically upward.
He stepped to the edge of the portal and took a deep breath.

"Extending ladder," he said.

"Roger."

Nelson pulled the latch that released the ladder. He watched
as it unfolded toward the ground. It consisted of thirty-seven
rungs. Taking a deep breath, he turned his back to the portal
and lowered his foot behind him.

"I am on the ladder." He had to announce his position so he
didn't get too far ahead or behind the Russian.

"Colonel Nelson is on the ladder," Carter repeated.

"Colonel Komarov has stepped on the ladder," Satomura
responded.

Nelson placed his left foot on the next rung. The space suit
made the simple movement seem awkward. Tightening his grip
on the edge of the door, he looked down to make sure his foot
was planted solidly. The sound of his breathing was amplified by
his helmet.

"I have you on the forward camera," Carter said.

Nelson heard the words as distant sounds. He was concentrating on lowering his boot onto the next step. When he was halfway down the ladder he paused to look over his shoulder. The landscape looked like a surreal painting. He was about to step onto another world. He loosened his grip on the ladder and continued downward.

"I am on the last step," Nelson said. His heart was pounding wildly.

"Roger," Carter said. "*Gagarin*, we are ready."

"One moment," Satomura replied.

"I am ready," Komarov said in Russian.

"We are ready," Satomura said.

"Roger," Carter said. "Proceed."

Nelson looked down at his foot and watched it as it left the ladder and descended gently into the Martian soil. The ground felt solid. He placed his other foot down next to it. The sand crept up around the edges of his boot. He let go of the ladder. He felt as if he were in a dream. He turned around away from the lander and took a step. Nothing but a vast wasteland of sand and rock. He could hear Russian in his helmet. He had almost forgotten the words. He was to say them at the same time Komarov said them in Russian.

"From this day forward the people of Earth are one."

A wave of euphoria swept through him. He had just joined the ranks of the great explorers. He thought of Neil Armstrong and how he must have felt when he stepped onto the moon. He looked down at his feet. Grains of sand were resting on the top of his boots. He reached down and dipped his glove into the soil. He picked up a handful and drew it close to his helmet. The grains slipped through his fingers like flakes of gold dust. He watched the dust flicker as it floated to the ground. He raised his arms above his head to greet the strange world. Waves of adrenaline surged through his body. He looked for a spot from which he could survey his surroundings. There was a rock directly in front of him. It stood half a meter high and appeared relatively flat.

He had a few minutes before he was supposed to start gathering samples, so he walked over to the rock and jumped on top of it. The rock had less room than he had first thought. He looked back at the *Shepard* and waved at the dark window. The lander was dwarfed by Olympus Mons. NASA was stenciled in blue along its side. The United Nations flag was located just underneath the window. He wondered what the Martian flag would look like and how many years it would be before a Martian colony designed one. And then a peculiar thought crossed his mind. He wondered if there had ever been a Martian flag. Judging by the barren landscape it did not seem possible.

"How's the view?" Carter's voice startled him.

"Remarkable."

"See anything scurrying about?"

"Negative, but I'll keep my eyes open."

"Your biostats look good."

"Roger. Proceeding with the sample collection."

Nelson took one last look at the Martian landscape, then hopped off the rock. He flew farther and fell more slowly than he would have on Earth. He was familiar with the feeling because his weight was very close to what it had been on the *Liberty*, where the spinning trusses had produced an artificial gravity of .4 g's. The ground kicked up softly in a fine mist of reddish dust.

Once again his eyes were drawn to Olympus Mons. The cliff at the base of the volcano towered five kilometers straight up. In the space suit it was difficult for Nelson to see the top of the cliff. It was composed of wide bands of red-layered rock. Because of its size the cliff appeared to be only a few hundred meters away. He felt as though he could walk over and touch it, but he knew better. It was actually twenty-seven kilometers away. In three weeks he would be scaling the cliff. He looked down at the rocks at his feet.

His first official task was to collect samples and return them to the ship, so that there would be Martian rock aboard in the event they had to leave the planet unexpectedly. He pulled out the field sample bag and dropped to one knee. He picked up a few rocks and studied them. They didn't look particularly interesting. Reddish black with porous holes. He was not a geologist, but he could tell that they were volcanic in origin. He sealed the bag and pulled out another. This one he filled with sand. He got up and moved to a spot farther away from the lander, where the ground appeared to be slightly darker, and filled another bag. He thought of Major Brunnet, whose responsibility it had been to collect the rocks. The thought tempered his elation. He wondered what rocks Brunnet would have selected. They all looked very much the same. His instructions were to select as many different types as possible. It did not take him long to fill the bags. He waved with boyish enthusiasm at the black rectangle in the side of the ship.

"I'm coming in," he said.

"Roger," Carter replied.

He climbed up the ladder and deposited the sample-collection bags inside the pressure chamber. On the floor was a cylindrical tube. Once again he was reminded of Brunnet, but this time his spirits rose with pride for what they had done. It had been the right thing. The original flag was in orbit around the sun, wrapped around Brunnet's body. The flag inside the tube had been patched together by Endicott. He did not tell anyone he was making it, and when he finally presented it they did not know what to say. Endicott spread the flag out on a table and stood back so they could see it better. It was not perfect. Some of the continents were misshapen. Nelson remembered thinking that from a distance no one would be able to tell the difference. He climbed down the ladder with the tube in hand.

"There's a good spot twenty meters southeast," Carter said.

"I see it."

Their primary concern was that the camera have a clear view of the flag. They had rehearsed the event several times back on Earth. He located a spot clear of rock and slightly elevated. He turned to look at the *Shepard*. The black rectangle was dead center of the ship.

"Hold it right there," Carter said. "Give me a second to get both cameras in focus."

"Roger."

"Proceed."

The seal had already been broken. His fingers were trembling. He unrolled the flag and held it out at arm's length so that he could look at it. He thought the imperfections gave it character. He extended the pole and pushed it into the sand, adjusting it so it stood perfectly straight. He stepped beside the flag and turned toward the black rectangle. He was not to say anything, just salute, but when his glove touched his helmet he felt impelled to say something.

"For Major Jean Paul Brunnet."

Carter repeated the words, then Endicott, whose voice cracked like that of an adolescent's. Nelson held the salute for nearly a minute. He picked up the empty tube and the cap and headed back to the ship.

———

Tatiana was beneath the *Gagarin* inspecting the undercarriage for structural damage and had been quiet for quite some time. Komarov asked what was wrong. She ignored him, and he knew better than to ask again. She had been in a foul mood the entire EVA.

The inspection was exhausting work. They had to examine every inch of the outer hull, most of which was difficult to reach because of its sheer size. With the use of ropes and pulleys, Tatiana managed to scale the outside of the ship. She marked each section she had inspected with colored markers so that she would not inspect it twice. She would visually check the section, then rub her hand over it to feel for anomalies. It was the moving about that was the most demanding. Komarov was on the ground taking in or letting out rope while Tatiana pulled herself from one section to the next. It had taken nearly all day to finish the top half, and all she had found wrong were a few small chips in the heat shielding. The chips had been caused by particles striking the hull during atmospheric entry. They had not found any damage to the craft caused by the landing other than some minor buckling in the landing gear itself. She blamed Komarov for the inspections. It was his decision not to abort. A bead of sweat dropped into her eye, blurring her vision. She cursed out loud.

"What is it now?" Komarov asked, regretting the question before he had even finished asking it.

"Damn sweat," she said. She was shaking her helmet back and forth. Silence, Komarov decided, was the safest course. She would find fault with whatever he said, that he was certain of. She was in one of those moods.

"Damn," she repeated. "We don't even have the right equipment." She turned to confront Komarov. "Enough is enough."

Komarov looked down inside his helmet to check the time. A neon green light indicated the portable life-support system had forty-five minutes of normal operations remaining. He wondered why with her he always seemed to be struggling to maintain his authority. He blamed it on the psychology of human relationships. There was something about intimacy that undermined respect. Forty-five minutes. It was hardly worth it. He looked up from the neon numbers and back into her eyes. They were bulging from their sockets, straining against the veinlike muscles that held them back.

"A good time to break," he said.

"You are so right," she said as she stormed past him.

He watched the back of her suit as she climbed up the ladder. She could have been a man in that suit. Each step radiated defiance. He surveyed the sections of the hull that still had to be inspected. It would take at least another thirteen hours. There was no point in continuing by himself.

"To hell with it," he said.

Tatiana was about to shut the exterior portal when he appeared. He smiled. She returned the smile with a triumphant look, then turned her back to him.

"Locking exterior portal," Komarov said, alerting Satomura, who was monitoring the entry programs. "Lock complete."

"Commencing pressurization," Satomura said automatically.

Komarov could hear the hiss of oxygen as it filled the air-lock. Tatiana's back was to him. Her hands were against the wall above her head. He pulled out the vacuum and removed the dust from the back of her suit. When she turned around, he saw that she looked tired. He did not say anything. He was careful not to linger too long in certain areas. She was studying him. He handed the vacuum to her and placed his hands against the wall. He was relieved that she took her time.

Tatiana's hair came tumbling out as she removed her helmet. She tucked the helmet under her arm and waited for the internal door to open. He decided to take a chance.

"My quarters tonight?" he whispered into her ear. He thought he could actually see the hair rise on her neck.

"You do realize there is no guarantee that this thing will take off," she blurted. She charged through the portal without waiting for a reply.

Satomura was standing at the edge of the mesa in the middle of Candor Chasma looking out upon what he felt certain to be the grandest sight any human had ever laid eyes upon. They had gone to the Grand Canyon to train in a similar environment,

and he had been impressed by the Grand Canyon, overwhelm-
ingly so, but the great canyon before him dwarfed anything he
had ever seen. The enormous size and vastness of his surroundings filled him with awe. The mesa seemed to possess a mystical
quality, the way its edges just fell away, as if it were a floating
valley. He stepped a foot closer to the edge and looked down at
the canyon floor. The 1.3-kilometer drop would have caused
most men to step back with vertigo. But Satomura surveyed the
chasm with the unrestrained delight of a child.

He was to locate a suitable spot to scale. He noted that the
strata were thicker at top, their coloring consistent with volcanic deposits. They could probably descend the first several
hundred meters without their climbing gear. He scanned the
wall for an area that contained tightly packed layers of rock. It
did not take him long to find what he was looking for. Pleased,
he took the binoculars and examined the canyon more closely.
The walls did not look like they had been formed by water erosion. They were much too chaotic and irregular. The rocks were
jagged, as if they had been ripped apart, not smooth like those
of the Grand Canyon. They resembled the rocks they had found
in the faults of Antarctica. Sharp and pointed. The Antarctic
canyons had been formed by the rock collapsing under its own
weight. But this looked slightly different. It looked almost as
though the planet had started to split apart. They were at the
very edge of a great mound known as the Tharsis Bulge, which
stood nearly nine kilometers high. Three gigantic volcanoes lay
at the center of the bulge. Whatever forces had created Tharsis
were also responsible, at least in part, for the canyon. There
were several theories, but the one Satomura favored was that it
had been created by an asteroid that had struck the opposite
side of the planet. He did not see anything that disproved the
theory.

In the distance there were several stretches where the
canyon wall appeared to have collapsed. They were marked by

vertical streaks that looked like long, flat brushstrokes. The strokes faded into the smooth features of a sand dune as they approached the base of the canyon. Piled at the base were layers of debris, remnants of the rocky avalanche that had tumbled down the sides. He knew that by measuring the layers he could calculate the rate at which the material had made its descent. Mentally comparing the debris with measurements he had made of similar phenomena from satellite mosaics, he estimated the rate to have been seventy-five meters per second. He closed his eyes to imagine the event. The rock collapsed like a great waterfall, annihilating everything in its path. The sound was horrendous. Tremors rippled through the ground for several thousand kilometers. A great mushroom cloud rose up and dust darkened the sky, turning day into night.

He clapped his hands at the imagined spectacle. Opening his eyes, he looked down and saw the aftermath. He returned his attention to the matter at hand and took pictures of several possible descent routes. He would examine them more closely later. His time was running out. He was startled to discover that he was to have turned back several minutes before and that he had not noticed the numbers flashing red at the bottom of his visor. Old age must be catching up with me, he thought to himself, then wondered why no one had said anything. He decided that they must be at it again. He would know by the smell when he entered the lander. Smells had a tendency to linger in a closed-loop environment.

He turned his back to the cliff and made for the lander. He wondered where they were doing it. The *Gagarin* was not that large. There were only a few places that lent themselves to love-making. He was certain that Tatiana and Dmitri had found them all. Satomura took a perverse pleasure in the smells and in sniffing out their exact spot. It was the closest he would come to having a woman for quite some time.

It did not bother him that Tatiana was unfaithful to her

husband. He had actually come to expect such behavior. His concern was how Vladimir might react. During his last communication with him, he noticed that he appeared tired and distant. He did not look healthy. He seemed unusually strained. That troubled Satomura because Vladimir was the sole occupant aboard the *Druzhba*. He feared how the emotions building inside Vladimir might be vented.

He decided he would speak to Tatiana about her husband. She must do something to reassure him of her fidelity, at least while they were on the planet.

Komarov was standing inside a hole that came to his shoulders. He planted his shovel squarely before him and leaned against it as he caught his breath. The shovel was dented from the frozen ground. He glanced at his heads-up display to check the time, and his spirits lifted when he saw that they would have to head back soon.

"Half a meter more," Satomura said. He was on his knees, looking down into the hole, and he was eager for Komarov to continue. His bulky suit was blocking much of the light.

Komarov was growing annoyed with Satomura. He waved him back, then took his time as he readied the percussion drill. The vibrations started in his hands and quickly worked their way up his arms and into his shoulders. They felt good at first, but within a few short minutes his body began to tingle with pain. First his hands, then the muscles surrounding them. He gritted his teeth. He continued until the pain in the back of his neck became unbearable.

"Damn," he cursed, and turned the drill off.

"Not much farther," Satomura offered encouragingly.

Komarov rubbed the back of his neck against his helmet. "A moment's rest," he said as he sat down. They were digging down to the ice they had located several days before with their sounding equipment. Its presence supported the hypothesis that the planet still housed much of the water that had cut the channels in its surface. It had been discovered during the robotic mission ten years earlier. A Japanese probe found the water ice under a thin coating of frozen carbon dioxide at the north pole. Satomura was to look for evidence of life in the ice. He could recall the block of ice they had cut from the Antarctic, and the swarm of microbes that came to life when they thawed the ice and placed a sample underneath the microscope. He was told that some of the microbes had been frozen for hundreds of years.

It was Satomura who first noticed the change in the soil. Komarov was in the ditch, head deep, shoveling dirt out over his shoulder and thinking mostly of the effort required to bury and lift his shovel. With the last several shovelfuls white crystal-like particles began to appear.

"Hold it," Satomura shouted.

"What is it?" Komarov replied, startled by the forcefulness of Satomura's command. He sat down to gather his strength.

"Permafrost," Satomura announced.

Komarov looked down between his knees and saw that the ground was spotted white and pink. He gathered some ice that had been broken loose by his shovel and studied it. There was a considerable amount of dirt mixed in with the ice.

"It should turn to liquid farther down," Satomura said. "A kilometer or so. Liquid water is not stable above the two-hundred-and-seventy-three-degree isotherm."

A cloud of vapors, similar to that which sublimes from dry ice on Earth, lifted from Komarov's hand. He was watching the ice evaporate when he noticed the cloud that had formed around his feet. The sight made him anxious to climb out of the hole. He extended his hand for assistance.

"We need to collect some samples first," Satomura said as he handed him several collection bags. "Be sure to seal them tight or else all we'll have to show for our day's work will be a pile of dirt."

Komarov knew that the ice was important. But he was tired, and his thoughts had already turned to Tatiana several times in the past hour. He looked at the event timer on his heads-up display.

"We have less than five minutes," he said.

"This should not take long."

As each bag was handed to him, Satomura held it up to the sun to scrutinize its contents. He wondered what he would find and grew anxious to return to the lander so that he could commence his examination of the samples.

Satomura surfaced from the eyepiece of the microscope to glance at the time. In one hour he was to wake. There was little point, he rationalized, in going to sleep now. It would do more harm than good, so he might as well carry on. He half believed the logic. The truth of the matter was that he knew if he lay down, he would get back up within seconds. He did not feel the least bit tired.

The samples of ice sparkled behind the glass pane of the containment case. He wondered which one he should select. The rubber gloves that dangled against the inside of the case sprang to life as he slid his hands into them. He had already examined several samples and verified they were mostly water ice. Two molecules of hydrogen combined with one of oxygen, frozen. He had found traces of carbon dioxide and volcanic ash, but more importantly he had found hydrogen peroxide, a compound that destroyed organic material upon contact. Although he had given up hope of finding life among the samples, he had not given up on finding fossilized remains. He selected a sample the size of an acorn. It resembled a light ruby. He twirled the ice between his fingers as he examined the particles suspended inside.

His hand froze. One of the particles was green. At first he thought that it might just be a trick of the light or that he was tired and that he was seeing things that were not there. But he took several deep breaths and shook his head to clear his thoughts. He closed his eyes. When he reopened them the particle was still there. He turned the ice slightly, and it disappeared. This did not surprise him. He turned the ice back, and it reappeared. "Well," he said, "at least it is not a figment of my imagination."

It appeared to be translucent. Since it was so small he could not be sure. Chlorophyll came to mind. Chlorophyll meant photosynthesis. But he knew that was impossible. For the past several weeks he had spent much of his time examining the samples they had gathered, and not once had he found any evidence of organic compounds. Without the compounds there couldn't be chlorophyll. Besides, chlorophyll could never form in the presence of hydrogen peroxide, nor could it form so far beneath the surface under such cold conditions. But the tiny speck still fascinated him. He sensed he was overreacting and attempted to contain his excitement. After several minutes of examining the particle, he entered his impressions into the computer.

Before proceeding he stole a quick look at the clock. They would awake in forty-five minutes. That meant he had thirty-five minutes, at best, before he had to return to his sleeping bag and feign sleep. He had reprogrammed the computer to think he went to bed at the scheduled time. The deception was to keep the Russian Space Agency off his back.

If not chlorophyll, then what did he have before him? It had to be a mineral, a rock of some sort. If that were the case, he could melt the ice and easily separate the green particle from the water. But if it were not a mineral, if it were something that would melt with the ice, it might be difficult to isolate. No, he would not melt the ice. He would leave the sample frozen and slice away the ice until he was left with a thin extract that he could place under the microscope.

He fixed the sample between the two ends of a vise. He then removed his hands from the rubber gloves and stood up. The laser was manipulated from the top of the containment case. It would take, he calculated, seven to eight cuts. Each cut would be more difficult as the sample became thinner and more delicate.

A thin ray of light shot toward the ice. Hastily, he brushed the shaved portions aside. It was when he was aligning the laser for the seventh and final cut that he realized he was not alone in the room. His initial reaction was not to look up, to continue with the cut until he was finished, but he found it nearly impossible to concentrate. He was afraid that he might make a mistake. Reluctantly, he released the controls of the laser and turned around.

"Up early this morning," Komarov said with a slight grin.

Satomura wasn't certain whether it was a statement or a question. He responded after a noticeable pause. "I was unable to sleep, so I thought I'd spend the time constructively."

"I see," Komarov replied.

Satomura turned his attention back to the sample. He hoped Komarov would lose interest and walk away. This did not happen. Satomura found himself counting each step as his commander approached the containment case. It would not do to antagonize him, he warned himself. So with a concentrated effort to block out distractions he focused on his next cut.

He could hear the sound of Komarov's voice. It possessed the distinct guttural quality of vocal cords that had been scarred by several decades of drink and late nights. Satomura knew if he tried, he could make sense of the sounds, but he did not wish to divert his attention from the sample, which had now become quite delicate. It was thinner than paper, and the green speck had grown more prominent. With care, he removed the sample from the vise and placed it under the lens of the microscope.

The gloves fell limp against the container wall. Komarov's voice was much louder now and carried a sense of urgency.

"Yes?" Satomura said, without turning around.

"The computer seems to be a bit confused," Komarov said, and then waited for Satomura to break down and ask for an explanation.

"How so?" Satomura finally replied.

"It seems to think you're asleep." Komarov was obviously enjoying himself.

Satomura turned to face his commander. He tipped his head slightly to one side and, with considerable effort, grinned. "I didn't want to alarm anybody. You remember the inquisition they subjected us to last time."

"I'd prefer that you didn't tamper with the bio programs."

"As you wish," Satomura replied curtly.

"So what has kept you up all night?"

"The samples. I have been examining them. Just before you came in, I found something unusual. A green particle. I was just about to take a closer look."

"Green?" Komarov said. "You don't think it is some sort of plant life?"

"Not likely. If you don't mind."

Satomura took his commander's silence to mean that he didn't. At first the image was fuzzy. He adjusted the focus. The green speck emerged from the blurred background. Satomura knew at once that it was not organic. It was crystalline. He studied the magnified image for several minutes. With a deep breath, he straightened and took a step back.

"Well?" Komarov asked.

"Take a look," Satomura offered.

Peering down the tube of the microscope, Komarov saw what he later described as a broken piece of glass that could have come from an ordinary beer bottle. It certainly wasn't moving. Not lifting his head, he asked, "What is it?"

"My guess would be beryl," Satomura replied excitedly. He no longer minded Komarov's intrusion. "I won't know for sure until I conduct further analysis. But if it is, then we have found something that should be quite rare on Mars." He could tell by Komarov's dull expression that he did not understand. "Beryl is a mineral made up of beryllium aluminum silicate and is found primarily in limestone and mica schist; neither of which is overly abundant on Mars."

Komarov was becoming convinced that this one of those discoveries that might be a great revelation to the scientific community but had little meaning to the common man. As a result, he was rapidly losing interest. He listened as Satomura described a surface abundant in magnesium and iron, and was just about to make his excuses when he caught the word emeralds.

"What was that?" he asked.

"I said, beryl is the stuff that emeralds are made of. Not enough on the planet to make anyone rich, however."

Komarov was quiet for a moment. "We gear up in two hours. You'd better get some rest."

"Perhaps you're right," Satomura replied. Suddenly, he was feeling very tired. He summoned his last reserve of energy to store the sample away safely, then headed straight for his cot to claim what little sleep he could before the day commenced. The beryl was not a significant find, but interesting enough to dominate his thoughts as he pulled the covers over his head. The computer program that kept track of the crew and their daily activities branched to a routine that reported back to the Russian Space Agency that Satomura had just awakened and was taking a shower.

———————

Nelson took several steps back from the miniature launchpad and placed his arms akimbo. The rocket was to enter the caldera of Olympus Mons. It was an awkward-looking contraption. Standard rocket fuels did not burn well in an atmosphere of carbon dioxide, so the rocket had to carry its own oxidizers. The oxygen was contained in two tanks that appeared as if they had been added as an afterthought. They were machine-metal gray, unpainted, and were bound to the rocket by a metal strap. It never did fly well on Earth. But then, the engineers asserted it was not designed for Earth-like conditions. Earth's gravity was, of course, much greater and its atmosphere much thicker. The rocket was intended for Mars. The engineers pointed to a computer simulation of a near-perfect parabola over Olympus Mons.

Nelson walked to a ridge that was approximately eighty meters from the rocket. He raised his thumb. "She's ready for launch."

Carter, who was watching through a pair of high-powered binoculars from inside the lander, typed in the instructions that informed the computer to commence the countdown. The sun was directly overhead. The cameras mounted on the nose of the rocket would require the light of the sun as the rocket descended into the volcano. He watched as Nelson sat down upon the ridge, legs crossed. He was to remain there in the event something went wrong.

"Eight minutes to launch," the computer announced.

"Here we go," Carter said. He had the full attention of both crews. Vladimir was watching a wide-screen monitor aboard the *Druzhba*. Unknown to all but himself he was not wearing any clothing. Sipping hot cups of coffee, Dmitri, Tatiana, and Takashi were gathered around a much smaller monitor aboard the *Gagarin*. Dmitri had actually made a bet with Takashi that the rocket would not make it, and Tatiana was furious the two men had reduced the launch to a wager. The winner would receive six ounces of vodka, which was a great prize since vodka was a precious commodity on the planet's surface. Dr. Endicott was watching from *Liberty*'s galley as he picked at a plate of rehydrated eggs.

"T minus three minutes and counting," announced the computer.

Carter pulled his goggles down over his eyes. The world around him was black. He flipped the switch to activate the goggles. He was lying on his back looking up at the pink Martian sky. It seemed unusually bright, but then he was looking straight into the sun. He instructed the computer to filter out thirty percent of the light. At his fingertips were the controls for the rocket. In the lower right-hand corner of his goggles, a digitized launch clock was flashing green.

"T minus one minute."

Although he was fully aware that he was physically removed from the launch, Carter tightened his grip upon the controls. The goggles placed him on top of the rocket, not inside it. His first experience with the simulation had left him exhilarated; his measured physiological response had been much higher than expected. He had roared enthusiastically as the technicians removed the probes from his body. He'd told them that it felt like the rocket had been strapped to his ass. They were startled by his reaction and offered to rewrite the virtual interface, to place him inside the rocket, but he wouldn't hear of it.

"Ten, nine, eight . . ."

He took a deep breath. The Martian sky was deceptively still.

"Liftoff."

For the first few seconds the sky seemed to shake slightly. And then, without warning, it split apart and flew past him, dissolving into a black void. Stars sprang into view. A light pink vapor was all that remained of the Martian atmosphere. He held on to the control panel as if it were the only thing that kept him from being torn from the rocket. He kept reminding himself that he was on the lander, which was on the planet's surface, and neither he nor the lander had moved an inch. He could sense the rocket starting to tip. Then, with a great swing, as if someone had lassoed his feet and lifted him off the ground, he was looking straight down into the heart of the volcano. He had the sudden sensation he was about to fall, but when the ground started to rock back and forth, he knew the parachutes had successfully opened.

He adjusted the filter to allow for maximum visibility. At the upper edge of his peripheral vision he could make out the booster stage just before it dwindled into nothingness. The entire rim of the caldera was visible beneath him, and he knew that it would begin to slip out of view in the next thirty seconds. He was descending fast. At a height of twenty-nine kilometers there was not much air for the parachutes. He had to work quickly. He instructed the computer to display his coordinates—the numbers flashed yellow. To his surprise the ship was several hundred meters south of its planned trajectory. He ordered the computer to overlay the navigational grid and project the rocket's entry point, taking into account wind speed and direction. Thin lines of Martian longitude and latitude appeared superimposed over the mouth of the volcano. A dotted line, originating at his current position, which was represented by a bright yellow circle, curved inward toward the middle of the volcano and terminated dead center of the targeted entry point.

"I'll be damned," he said. Some people, as Carter later enlightened reporters, peed in their pants when they got excited; he cursed. The computer had taken into account a shift in winds. He released his grip on the controls. There was nothing for him to do. He rested his head back against the seat cushion and enjoyed the remaining twenty-three seconds of free fall.

The rim of the volcano disappeared around him. He took a deep breath as he reminded himself that he was not actually in the rocket. The interior of the volcano was cluttered with collapsed craters and long, twisting ridges that looked like veins inside a dissected body. The largest crater, which was also the deepest, was forty-two kilometers across and the one into which he was to drop the glider. The computer highlighted its rim with blue targeting lines. The walls of the volcano had disappeared completely.

The scientific instruments aboard the rocket had already begun their sensing of the volcano's internal conditions. A gas chromatograph/mass spectrometer was separating elements in the atmosphere and reporting their quantity and type to the satellite overhead. Temperature, air pressure, and humidity data were also being transmitted. Satomura was watching the data intently and was pleased with what he saw.

"Wing extraction initiated," announced the computer. A pair of wings extended outward from the body of the rocket. The control panel in front of Carter transformed into the instrument panel of a glider. "Parachutes disengaged."

Carter grinned as the glider plunged downward into the volcano. The first few seconds were the most critical. He had to be careful the glider did not tumble into a spin. He stopped chewing as he pulled back on the yoke. The ground swept out from beneath him, and he was looking at the volcano walls, then the sky. He took the glider as high as it would go. He pushed forward on the yoke and headed for the nearest wall. The upper rim of the volcano was indented by a series of flutes. They blended into a smooth, flat cliff, which descended uninterrupted to the volcano floor.

Carter dipped the glider's nose to get a better look. The solidified field of volcanic rock that he saw left little doubt in his mind the volcano was extinct. Several days earlier they had performed an analysis of the pumice outside the volcano and had determined it was over two hundred million years old. He picked the glider's nose back up and attempted to reclaim some of the height he had lost.

The volcano wall was now only a couple of kilometers away. He was beginning to wonder why he hadn't heard anything from Satomura when the gruff voice of the Japanese scientist burst through the intercom.

"Northeast fifteen degrees," directed Satomura.

"Roger," Carter responded as he checked the altimeter. He had descended several hundred meters since the parachutes had been disengaged. The negligible air currents within the volcano did not provide enough lift to maintain a constant altitude.

Individual rocks in the cliff were becoming visible. He checked his radar. He was forty-seven meters from the volcano wall. He decided to continue for another twenty meters before turning. Even with a stereoscopic view, it was difficult to judge the distance to the wall accurately. He ordered the computer to place the radar readout on his heads-up display so that he would not have to keep glancing down at the instrument panel.

"Turn," Satomura cried out.

Carter chuckled at Satomura's alarm. A two-dimensional monitor, like the one Satomura was watching, made it difficult to judge distances, and although Satomura did have a separate monitor which displayed the simulated instrument panel, he did not have the benefit of a heads-up display. Under the circumstances, the urgency in his voice was more than understandable. To him it must have appeared as if the glider were only centimeters from crashing into the cliff.

"She's got plenty of elbow room," Carter drawled. He fought the urge to demonstrate what a real flesh-and-blood pilot could do. He banked the glider thirty meters from the volcano wall. As the cliff flashed past him, he wondered what had piqued Satomura's interest. This particular section did not look any different from the others, at least as far as he could tell. But then he knew he did not have an eye for such things. He was heading toward the center of the volcano, searching out the winds, when Satomura instructed him to turn back.

Carter brought the glider around in a wide arc and approached the volcano wall several hundred meters lower than before. The flutes had dissolved into the cliff. The wall could have been a dark sheet of glass. It was cracked and scarred with deep pits. A dark, almost eerie wonder filled Carter. He felt as though he were looking at the ancient remnants of a monument beginning to crumble under its own weight. The wall sloped perceptibly outward from the accumulated debris that had fallen from the cliff overhead. The great volcano was in ruins. He flew in toward the wall to the point indicated by Satomura, then back out again in search of an updraft. He lost altitude with each pass. The craft was too heavy, and its wingspan too short to make a good glider. He managed to fly for nearly two hours before he was forced to enter the crater at the volcano floor. The diameter of the crater was more than half that of the caldera. He could see where the nearest wall had collapsed and lava had flowed down the rim. Satomura instructed him to fly toward the breach. The lava must have come from a vent some-where outside the crater. He struggled to keep the craft aloft as he made his oblong passes, but there was even less wind here.

"Need to take her down," he said.

"Five more minutes," Satomura demanded.

"Not possible."

The ground was moving quickly now. A glance at the altimeter revealed that he was eleven meters above the surface. He knew there was a clearing to the east, but the boulder he had seen from overhead was now much larger and blocked his view of the site he had selected. He searched for another clearing. There was none close enough. The boulder was too high for him to fly over, and he wasn't certain he could fly around it. But then he had no other choice. He banked the glider hard. Looking over his shoulder, he saw the ground was only centime-ters from his wingtip. He pulled out of the turn. As the glider leveled out, the outer edge of the clearing came into view. He banked toward the clearing. The touchdown was perfect. His first reaction was to pull off his helmet and open the cockpit to breathe the fresh air. But he knew that was impossible. He could remove his goggles, but he did not want to. He wanted to remain inside Olympus Mons. He wanted to stride majestically across the surface and leave the first man-made footprints in the sand. In the background voices were talking to him, congratulating him. Reluctantly, he pulled off his goggles. The dark red volcanic rocks were instantaneously replaced with sterile white paneling and multicolored computer screens.

Olympus Mons

"Ten minutes remaining," Carter said as he adjusted Nelson's life-support pack. They were both fully suited. The computer screen was flashing the checklist items one by one, pausing at each item until Nelson ordered it to proceed. The astronauts had been prebreathing pure oxygen for the past two hours. The gas had the unintended side effect of a mild stimulant; it intensified their thoughts and actions and infused them with a sense of well-being. The purge of nitrogen molecules from their bloodstream was nearly complete.

Endicott was looking down from a screen above.

"Seismic amplifier," Nelson sounded. His voice could have been computer-generated.

"Check," Carter replied.

"Mass spectrometer."

"Check."

"Heat-flow probe."

"Check."

"Time-base generator."

"Check."

"Data recorder."

"Check."

"UV spectrometer."

"Check."

"Core sampler."

"Check."

"Food supply," Nelson said.

"Containers A and B, NAS-SPEC 5601 and 5607, attached."

"Air pressure."

"Looking good," Carter said. He was savoring a stick of gum as he scanned the gauges. He would have to swallow the gum before the day was out. They were about to undertake a two-day EVA to Olympus Mons and would not be able to remove their helmets until they pressurized the life-support tent.

A message indicating that the prebreathing was completed flashed across the monitor. They made a final check of their space suits. Satisfied, Nelson instructed the computer to open the outside portal. Light from the morning sun poured in. They shaded their eyes with their hands as they stood at the edge of the portal, admiring the salmon pink horizon. It was a perfect day for an expedition.

Using a rope and pulley to control the descent, Nelson lowered a supply chest to the ground within a container that slid down the parallel sidepieces of the ladder. Carter unloaded the container and carried the chest to the rover. It took half an hour to lower four chests. The rover was an open-air vehicle that looked like the lunar buggy of the Apollo days, but was considerably larger. It had six titanium wire-mesh wheels, two in front, four in back. The wheels were coated with silicon rubber for traction. The seats resembled lawn chairs, and situated between them, accessible to either astronaut, was a joysticklike hand controller that served as a steering device. An assortment of scientific devices protruded from the frame. There was a high-definition camera situated above the communication relay unit at the front of the rover, which transmitted real-time images to the other astronauts and to the television networks on Earth. Above the halogen headlights were two digital cameras used for stereoscopic imaging. The rover had two antennae. The high-gain employed a directional beam that had to be pointed at a satellite to be effective, and was usually used only when the rover was parked. Its sixty-six-centimeter parabolic reflector looked like an inverted umbrella. The low-gain, which looked like a tin can on a stick, provided blanket coverage of the sky, and could be used at any time. A radar dome was perched on top of the two oxygen tanks at the rear of the vehicle.

Carter climbed aboard as Nelson circled the vehicle, his eyes passing from the neon checklist to the vehicle and back. He moved in closer and got down on his knees to check the under-carriage. Everything appeared to be in order.

"*Liberty*," he said as he sat down next to Carter, "Olympus Mission Alpha is under way."

"Best of luck," Endicott replied.

Nelson slapped his hand on Carter's knee. "You know what to do," he said.

Carter had the vehicle up to its cruising velocity of thirty-two kilometers per hour within seconds of starting. The rocks were everywhere. They spread out before him like tombstones, and, much to his annoyance, he often had to slow down just to avoid them. The tortuous path he was forced to take would more than triple the distance to the cliff. He relied on Nelson to keep him on course. At the center of the control panel was a computer screen that presented a variety of navigational data. Nelson had his choice of radar images, two- and three-dimensional topographical maps, geological maps, and photo-graphic overheads. The position of the rover was marked by an X, with a black solid line winding back to the *Shepard* and a green dotted line stopping at the base of the volcano. Their longitude and latitude, within thirty-eight centimeters of their actual position, was displayed at the bottom of the screen along with a recommended heading. A geostationary satellite, which had arrived two years earlier, updated their coordinates. In the event the communications link was lost, the onboard computer kept track of their location by dead reckoning. The computer was also capable of directing the rover without the aid of a human driver. The digital cameras just above the halogen headlights were used to locate and determine the size of obstacles. A safe course would then be calculated. Carter took solace in the knowledge that the rover's speed was drastically reduced without a human at the helm.

At a distance of twenty-seven kilometers the base of Olympus Mons dominated the horizon. It stood five and one-half kilometers high and blocked from view the peak of the volcano that lay behind it, and with each kilometer that bounced underneath them it grew even larger. Bit by bit the sky was disappearing. They knew, when they reached the volcano, they would have to look straight up to see the sky.

"Bear due north for the next one-point-seven klicks," Nelson said. "The detour will take us about five and a half klicks out of our way. The ground is broken up pretty bad. Several lava tubes have collapsed in this region." He was pointing at a spot on the screen. Carter did not take the time to look. He had spotted a large rock in the horizon that was due north and was doing his best to head toward it. For the moment it was somewhere off his left shoulder.

While training in Hawaii, Nelson had stood inside a lava tube that was nearly ten meters wide; it was, the instructor had told him, one of the largest on Earth. He was impressed until the instructor had also told him that it was a dwarf compared to the tubes of Olympus Mons, which were over two hundred meters wide. He was tempted to direct Carter toward the tubes, but their schedule was tight. They were to be at the first collection point in less than twenty minutes.

Upon examining the topographical on the screen, Nelson searched his surroundings in an attempt to confirm his position. With the exception of the volcano, there were very few distinguishing landmarks. He was looking for boulders positioned in recognizable patterns. But the patterns he viewed on the screen were from a top-down perspective, and he was among the rocks, not above them, so the patterns took on a different aspect. He wasn't that concerned. There was really little need to identify the boulders—it was highly unlikely that the coordinates displayed by the navigational subsystem were incorrect.

The twenty minutes passed quickly. Nelson motioned to a spot thirty meters up ahead, an opening among several larger rocks, two of which were almost half the size of the rover. He signaled for Carter to stop when they arrived.

"*Liberty*, Collection Point Alpha has been achieved. It is twenty-three hundred hours GMT and . . ." he added, looking up at the sun, ". . . just about high noon here. Over."

"One hour is scheduled for this collection point," Endicott replied.

The surface drill resembled a thin jackhammer. It was powered by the silver-zinc batteries on the rover, and was capable of digging through dirt and sand, but not through dense rock. Nelson was growing frustrated as he bore down on the drill. It was not going anywhere. He carefully removed it from the soil. He was surrounded by holes of failed attempts. His space suit was beginning to bother him.

He looked at his watch to check the time. Fifteen minutes left, and he had only extracted two of the desired eight core samples. He walked over to a rock and sat down. He held the drill up at eye level to inspect it closely, as if the drill were at fault and not the ground. He rotated it slowly. The shiny metallic surface glowed pink from the reflection of the horizon and the sand. He didn't really expect to find anything wrong with it; it just gave him something to do while he rested. Carter came sauntering over.

"Something wrong with the drill?" Carter drawled.

"It's not the drill," Nelson said. "It's the ground."

"Maybe you'll have better luck down the road." Carter chose a rock next to his commander. "You hungry?"

"Depends on what you packed," Nelson replied.

"NAS-SPEC 5601."

"Which is?"

"Don't rightly recall. Rather keep it a mystery personally."

Carter pressed a small button on the chest panel of his soft-suit. He watched with crisscrossed eyes as a clear tube slowly made its way to his mouth from somewhere inside his space suit. At the far end of the tube was an aluminum canister containing a plastic bag packed with NAS-SPEC 5601. As he sucked, a mushy substance crept up the tube and into his mouth. It was slightly cold and lumpy and tasted something like tuna fish.

"It's all in the mind," he said, pointing at his head.

They drove for an hour before they reached the next collection point. The ground was softer, and Nelson was able to extract all ten samples without too much difficulty. They rested and had their snacks and stared at the red wall of stone that dominated the sky. They could barely make out the twin towers through the high-powered binoculars. The towers appeared to be of a darker shade than the cliff behind them. They could not see the top of the cliff without leaning back on the rock they were sitting upon.

"We're not even going to scratch the surface," Carter said after a while.

Nelson looked at the volcano and wondered if anyone would ever climb to the top. It did not seem possible. But he knew that someone would eventually try. He would have liked to give it a try himself. They were to ascend a ridge along the side of the cliff for nearly six hundred meters before it broke off. The steepest grade would be approximately thirty degrees. The cliff itself was a sheer drop.

"How much farther?" Carter asked.

"Five klicks without detours, fifteen with. It shouldn't take much longer than an hour."

The cliff was composed of horizontal bands, which grew more distinct and intricate as they approached. Nelson was fascinated by the different shades that emerged. There was no longer any need to give directions—their destination was in sight. At five hundred meters the twin towers started to stand out. They stopped the rover once to look and take pictures. It was an unscheduled stop, but they were ahead of schedule, and Carter insisted. Seven minutes passed, and they were on their way again. The twin towers appeared man-made, or at least built by some form of intelligent life. Their shapes appeared too symmetrical to be created by the whims of nature. But neither Carter nor Nelson thought the towers were created by anything other than nature. The other possibilities were far too speculative to warrant much consideration. Through the binoculars, Nelson was able to make out irregularities in the formations. The two rocks stood alone. Nelson scanned the surface with the binoculars and was unable to locate any other formation vaguely similar to the towers. At one hundred meters, Nelson put the binoculars down. The two towers were approximately ten meters apart and stood twenty meters high. They were almost identical in height and approximately two and one-half meters in diameter, slightly wider at the bottom. They looked very much like columns from ancient Rome. The sight sent a shiver down Nelson's spine. There was something very eerie about two rock formations that looked like Roman columns at the base of a volcano on a planet other than Earth. But as they got closer the columns looked more like something carved by water. They tapered in the direction of what might have been the flow of a river. Carter stopped the rover a respectful twenty meters from the formation.

"How do you suppose it came about?" he asked.

"Some sort of natural formation," Nelson replied. "The rock is much darker, almost black. Takashi, would you care to speculate?"

"They appear to be basaltic," Satomura said. He was studying the images from the *Gagarin*. With Brunnet gone, Satomura was the only geologist among the two crews. "There is some speculation that Olympus Mons was once even larger than it is today. I suspect you are looking at the remnants of a collapsed volcano. The cliff before you tends to support this. The rock was probably carved into columns by lava."

"Which explains why they taper away from the volcano," Nelson said.

"Yes, the shape is much like we would have expected. It also explains why there are so few rocks about. They've been washed away by lava. A core sample of the column should settle the issue."

"All in good time, Doctor," Carter interrupted. "Right now we need to set up camp."

"Yes, of course," Satomura replied.

Nelson was staring at the triangular patterns stitched in the fabric of the tent. Two hours had passed since he had crawled inside his sleeping bag, and he had not yet fallen asleep. His excitement for the climb had kept him awake. The temperature outside the tent was seventy degrees centigrade below zero. The fabric of the tent crackled like paper. He was fine inside his sleeping bag. Carter was snoring. He had fallen asleep within seconds of lying down.

Nelson's thoughts turned to the debate about whether they should climb the ridge. Those opposed said it was too dangerous, while those in favor fervently disagreed. No one had known about the ridge prior to their arrival. Scientists on Earth had discovered it while examining photographs of the landing. It presented a valuable opportunity to collect samples from different strata. There was a lot of speculation as to its origin. Most of it unscientific. Twin Roman towers at the base of a ridge that looked convincingly like an ancient roadway could only have been constructed by an intelligent race, or so the tabloids went. The scientists were able to demonstrate it had been caused by nothing more than a fault in the regolith. It was finally agreed that the first six hundred meters of the ridge were wide enough not to pose a risk. Nelson was thrilled with the decision. To climb Olympus Mons was something he had wanted to do from the very first day the landing site was selected, but had not even dared to suggest. But now, because of the ridge, he would be able to make the climb. He glanced at his watch. If he were to be well rested, he would have to go to sleep soon. He pulled the sleeping bag over his head and thought of the twin towers. The core samples they had taken supported Satomura's belief that the towers were the remnants of a larger volcano. Recalling the sheer height of the cliff, which formed only the base of Olympus Mons, he found it difficult to imagine the volcano having been much larger.

The day was nearly half-spent, and the astronauts were growing tired from the climb. Although they had stopped several times to collect samples, they had not taken a break. Their muscles ached, and their life-support packs felt as if they were made of lead. Despite several hours a day on the stationary bike, they still were not in the physical condition required to tackle the thirty-degree slope before them. They were standing on a ridge, approximately six meters wide, that hugged the cliff like a small roadway. Carter approached the edge and looked down. They were two hundred meters from the surface, and the drop was nearly straight down. The top-heaviness of the softsuit made him feel uneasy about his footing. He cautiously stepped away from the edge.

"Another five minutes," Nelson said, "and we should be there."

Carter eyed the heads-up-display clock at the lower right-hand side of his helmet. The numbers flickered green. Another five minutes, he repeated to himself for the benefit of his aching muscles. He trudged forward, his eyes focused several meters in front of his feet. The ground was rocky and porous, and with each step the dust at his feet exploded into mushroom clouds.

"Hold up," Nelson said, probing the ground with a sonar stick. "This must be some sort of overhang. We'd better move closer to the wall."

Carter stopped and looked around. The edge was more than half a meter away, a distance he would have normally considered safe. As he took a step toward the wall, the ground underneath his feet began to crumble. Nelson was in front of him with his back turned. He attempted to throw himself forward onto the ridge, but there was nothing for his feet to push off against. His yell for help came much too late. He was falling backwards—the sky was bright pink. Nelson was shouting something into his helmet. He knew that he was going to die as soon as he hit the ground. But he did not want to die. He tried to think of what he should do. In parachute training they had taught him to roll to break the impact. He slammed against the side of the volcano and started to tumble.

He hit the ledge hard. There was a loud snap like a stick breaking. At first he couldn't breathe. Short, white streaks twirled in front of his eyes. He realized he was about to pass out and struggled to maintain consciousness. His leg was screaming with pain. It felt as though an ice pick were tearing through the flesh. He looked down at the limb. It twisted out from beneath him at a weird angle. A compound fracture, he thought. He attempted to move his leg, but the pain was overwhelming. He lost consciousness.

———

Nelson was crawling slowly toward the edge of the cliff, one end of a rope tied to his utility belt, the other end to a boulder. He moved forward a meter and stopped. Cautiously, he swept the loose rocks away and pressed down on the ground with his elbow to test it for his weight. Once satisfied, he unwound more rope and moved forward. He was a meter from where the edge had broken away.

"I'm only receiving his locator," Endicott said. "He must have damaged his comm equipment in the fall; otherwise, I would at least get some bio. Nothing. He's about eighteen meters below you."

"Keep on trying," Nelson said, and crawled forward another meter. His fingers gripped the edge, loose dirt crumbled between them, and a rock broke away and fell. His hand slipped out from underneath him. His upper body fell against the ledge. More rocks broke away. He could feel the ground crumbling beneath him. "Jesus!"

"What's happening?" Endicott cried.

With nothing to support them his elbows dropped and slammed into the side of the cliff. And then he stopped. Half his body was dangling over the edge. He could feel the rope tugging at his belt.

"What's happening?" Endicott cried again.

"Part of the ledge broke away," Nelson said, the words separated by gasps for air. "Close call."

"Be careful."

"Rest assured, I have every . . ." There was a white spot against the red rock directly beneath him. Nelson recognized it immediately as Carter's space suit. It was crumpled together like a broken doll, parts poking out at awkward angles.

"I see him," Nelson whispered.

"Could you repeat that. Did not copy."

"I said, I see him."

"Any movement?"

There was a pause.

"Negative."

"How is he?"

"Too far to tell, but it doesn't look good. I see no movement. Repeat, no movement."

"Use the binoculars."

"Right," Nelson responded. Carefully, inch by inch, he pushed himself back from the edge. When he felt certain he had reached a safe distance he sat up and brushed the red dust from his suit. He pulled the binoculars from their protective casing and turned them on. A green light indicated that the communications link with the computer aboard the *Liberty* was established. The link enabled enhanced imaging; it also allowed the others to see whatever Nelson focused the binoculars upon. He attached the binoculars to his helmet and crawled back toward the edge.

It took a few seconds to locate Carter. Nelson increased the magnification by a factor of four. The space suit was bent in half, caught between two rocks, with one leg sticking straight up and the other twisted back at an awkward angle. The arms were splayed out to each side. Still no movement. He focused on the helmet and increased the magnification. The safety glass was undamaged. He scanned the space suit, looking for punctures, but did not see any.

"The suit appears intact," he said. "I think his leg is broken." He felt unusually nervous, and his throat was dry and sticky. Unable to produce saliva, he swallowed air, which only made his throat feel worse. He reduced the magnification. "Switching to infrared."

The side of the volcano disappeared into a dark haze, and floating disembodied in the middle of the haze glowed a red form. Numbers flashed in the lower left-hand corner of the lens.

"Suit temperature checks out. Life-support systems are functioning." Which was hopeful, thought Nelson, but did not mean Carter was alive. "Switching to computer-enhanced."

The face behind the glass was a beige blur with two dark streaks slanting upward and a red blotch underneath. It was not recognizable as Carter, nor was it really recognizable as a face.

"Sharpen image based on facial composites," Nelson said.

"I'll need a few seconds," Endicott replied.

With the aid of digitized images, the computer assembled the colors into a face. The dark streaks transformed into eyebrows and the red blotch into a mouth. The eyes were shut. He increased the magnification and focused on the mouth, then the nostrils. Both were still.

"Is he breathing?" Endicott asked.

"I can't tell."

He decreased the magnification until Carter's face filled the lens. The computer-enhanced skin was pale white. Nelson felt as though he were looking into an open casket. The body could have been embalmed. And then, without warning, the eyes blinked open. They were pearls, lifeless and cold. Nelson searched the eyes for signs of life. They remained perfectly still. The magnification made the ghostly countenance seem only a few centimeters away. The eyes closed.

"We've got some movement," Nelson said. "I'm going down."

"Not so quick, Tom," Endicott said. "We can't be positive he's alive. It may have been some sort of postmortem twitch. Or a reflection off his visor may have fooled the computer into thinking that he had opened his eyes. Remember, what you saw was a digitized image of a photograph stored in the database. They weren't his real eyes."

"Something moved. If something moved, then he's alive. That's all I need to know. Look, either you're with me or not."

Endicott hesitated before responding. "I'm with you. How are you going to climb down to him?"

Nelson removed the binoculars from his helmet and surveyed the surrounding area. The prospects did not look promising. The side of the volcano was almost perfectly perpendicular to the ground. Carter had managed to land on a lone ledge that jutted out from the side like an outstretched hand. It was a sheer drop of 180 meters from the ledge to the surface. The only approach was from above.

"Well," he began, "I'm going to rappel down."

"Is that wise?"

"If I don't go, he'll die."

"But if you do go, you both may die. You don't have the proper gear."

"It's a risk I'm willing to take. Are you with me or not?"

"I'm with you." Endicott's reply lacked enthusiasm.

Nelson crawled backwards from the edge until he reached a safe distance, then stood up and walked to the boulder to which he had tied the rope. The boulder seemed large enough. He leaned against the rope and jerked it several times. The boulder did not budge. He returned to a point a couple of meters from the edge of the cliff and tossed the rope over.

"You may want to take the sonar stick with you," Endicott suggested.

"Why?"

"You're going to need more than the shovel to immobilize that leg."

Nelson fastened the stick to his utility belt. He wrapped the rope under his leg and across his shoulder, then turned his back to the edge of the cliff and took a deep breath. He could feel the blood rushing through his veins.

"I'm going over," he said.

He leapt backwards off the ridge. The rope slid rapidly through his hands. He gripped down tightly, and his body, which had been free-falling, came swinging toward the cliff. He kicked his legs out. The impact was lighter than he had expected. He realized it was due to the weaker gravity. He pushed off from the rock and rappelled until he was a meter above the body. He lowered himself onto the ledge. It was barely wide enough to hold both of them.

The leg that was sticking straight up seemed fine, but the other was twisted, and the boot was pointing in an unnatural direction. Nelson closed his eyes and took a deep breath. He bent down next to the body, keeping the rope taut, and verified that the life-support systems were still functioning. He looked into the helmet. Carter's eyes were closed. His mouth gaped open. A thin streak of blood ran from a nostril to the corner of his mouth. Nelson gently shook the helmet—Carter's head rolled back and forth as if it were unattached.

"I'm on the ledge, next to him. Unable to invoke a response. His leg is definitely broken. It's a miracle his suit wasn't punctured."

"Is he breathing?"

"I'm not sure."

"How badly is the leg broken?"

"Compound fracture most likely. Bent backwards at the kneecap."

"Above or below?"

"Below."

"Is he bleeding?"

"There's some blood from his nose, but not much."

"Feel for blood pooling at the bottom of his suit."

Carter was bent at the waist with his rear jammed down between two rocks. Reaching underneath, Nelson grabbed a handful of material and squeezed.

"It seems dry."

"If it is a compound fracture, his liquid cooling garment may have contained the bleeding. We must assume he is alive. You'll want to lay him out on level ground so that you can straighten out that leg and immobilize it. Is there enough room on the ledge?"

Nelson looked down at the ledge and decided if he pushed away some of the rock he could make room. "I'll manage."

"There's a problem though."

"What's that?"

"You don't want to disrupt the circulation of the liquid cooling garment when you wrap the leg. The main coolant tube runs down the outside of the leg. You'll want to position the sonar stick adjacent to the tube so that when you tie it down, the rope does not pinch it shut. Position the handle on the inside of the leg. Tie the two together, firmly, but not too tight, and not directly over the break. Use as much rope as you can spare."

To immobilize the leg he realized he was going to have to pull Carter out from the rocks between which he was wedged. That would require some leverage. He cleared the ledge as best as he could, sweeping the loose rocks over the edge with his boot. Bending over, he grabbed under Carter's armpits and pulled upward. Something dug tightly into Nelson's arms. Surprised, he stopped and saw that Carter's hand had grabbed onto it. He looked into the helmet. Carter's face was twisted into a grimace of excruciating pain.

"He's alive," Nelson said with an overwhelming sense of relief.

"Thank God."

Nelson realized that he was aggravating Carter's pain by holding him in such an awkward position and that he had to act quickly. "Sorry, pal, but I have to get you out of there." He tightened his grip and jerked upward. There was less resistance than he had expected. Carter hung in his arms, limp, the broken leg dangling loosely at the knee. He was unconscious. The sight of the leg caused Nelson to shudder. He took a step backwards, mindful of the drop, and carefully laid Carter on the ledge. He twisted the leg, which felt rubbery, into its normal position. Perspiration was dripping from his eyebrows into his eyes, and the salty sting caused his vision to blur. Because of his helmet, he was unable to wipe the perspiration from his eyes. He pulled up the rope that had been dangling over the edge and cut off a piece from the end.

"I have the rope," he said hoarsely.

"Do you have anything that you can pad the splints with?"

Nelson thought for a moment. "The sample-collection bags might work."

"They should do fine. Wrap the two splints with the bags, then tie the splints to the leg."

As Nelson wrapped the leg, he watched Carter to see if he would come to. His face was pale white. The muscles in his jaw twitched as Nelson lifted the leg to pass the rope underneath. He waited for the muscles to relax before proceeding. Beads of perspiration had formed on Carter's brow. Nelson was careful not to apply too much pressure as he tightened the rope. He checked the splints to make certain they were firmly in place.

"I'm going to tie the rope around his chest, then climb up. I'll pull Al up once I get to the top."

"You sure?"

"You have any better ideas?"

"I wish I did."

Gathering the remainder of the rope, Nelson wrapped it

tightly under Carter's arms and tied a knot in front. He started to feel hot inside his suit. Looking up at the cliff, he wrapped the rope once around his wrist and placed his right boot vertical to the rock wall. He lifted his body upward by pulling down with his arms. The backpack weighed thirty pounds, seventy-nine pounds on Earth, which was thirty pounds of deadweight that shifted his center of gravity away from the cliff. The climb was more difficult than he had anticipated. The side of the volcano seemed like a wall of glass. Unable to locate a foothold, he scaled the first six meters hand over hand. He rested against the rope, which was secured fast to his security belt. His feet were planted firmly against the rock, his body perpendicular to the cliff. Another six meters passed, and his arms were growing tired, and despite his regular workouts he was feeling his age and wondering how much strength he had left. He dug his feet into a small crack. He started to turn his head to look down at Carter but felt himself losing his balance and decided not to. He continued upward and less than three meters from the ridge found a small ledge on which he could stand. He rested for nearly a minute, then climbed the remainder of the distance hand over hand. With one final burst of strength he pulled himself up onto the ridge. He was breathing hard, staring up at the pink sky, wondering how he was going to lift Carter by himself.

He calculated, in his mind, how much Carter weighed. Two-fifths of one-eighty was seventy-one plus thirty pounds for the backpack and ten pounds for the suit was a total of one hundred and eleven pounds. Much less than he would have weighed on Earth, but still a considerable amount of weight to be hauled eighteen meters. He looked down over the edge and saw that Carter had not moved.

Nelson positioned himself a meter from the edge of the cliff. Gathering his strength, he gripped the rope firmly with both hands and pulled. When he had sufficient slack he wrapped the rope around his waist by making a full turn with his body. His arms were growing weak when Carter's helmet finally appeared at the edge of the cliff. He wrapped the rope around his waist one final time. Carter's hand reached up over his head and grabbed the lip of the ledge. Nelson watched with astonishment as Carter completed the final part of the climb by himself. Setting himself down, he smiled at Nelson with a grin that said, now that wasn't so bad, was it?

"Well, I'll be . . ." Nelson said.

"What's going on?" Endicott asked.

"He's conscious."

"Where are you?"

"We're both at the top of the ledge," Nelson replied, not taking his eyes off of Carter's silly grin. His head was rolling back and forth as if he were drunk. Nelson mouthed the words, "Don't worry."

Carter nodded that he understood, then closed his eyes and fell back unconscious.

"Do you have any suggestions on how to get him down to the rover?" Nelson asked.

"The leg should be kept immobile. Ideally, you would bring the rover to him. That, of course, is impossible. He's not in any condition to walk. Nor can you carry him. His space suit is too bulky. . . ."

"How about a stretcher? I could drag it behind me."

"That might work," Endicott replied slowly. "You could scavenge the necessary materials from the tent."

"I can be down and back in thirty minutes."

Nelson decided he should somehow inform Carter that he was going to the rover. He tapped on the glass of his helmet. There was no response. He tapped again. Still none. He grabbed him by the shoulders and shook him; first softly, then harder. Finally, Carter's eyes opened. They were glazed over, almost lifeless. Nelson pointed at himself, then down the volcano wall in the direction of the rover and back again. He pointed at his wrist at an imaginary watch and flashed his fingers to indicate he would be gone for half an hour. Throughout his pantomime, he watched Carter to see if he understood the message. He couldn't be certain. The eyes did not seem to follow his motions. But when he finished, Carter nodded slightly and forced a broken smile, behind which two rows of bloodied teeth emerged. He brought his fist between their two helmets and shook it, his thumb extended, pointing toward the sky. He closed his eyes and moments later his head fell forward, the smile vanishing from his lips. Blood seeped out from the corner of his mouth and down his chin. Nelson could not look any longer. He patted Carter on the shoulder and turned away.

He attempted to run down the ridge, but the grade was too steep for him to go much faster than a brisk walk. He was driven by the fear that Carter might die before he got him back to the lander. His breathing was hard, and he could feel his long legs cramping. He fell down once. He did not bother to check his suit when he stood back up. He kept thinking of the blood dripping from Carter's mouth. The frightful image gave him strength, and he was able to descend the entire distance without stopping to rest. His fear was that Carter had ruptured a vital organ.

Leaning against the rover to catch his breath, he checked the time. Seven minutes had passed since he had left Carter. Still heaving, he walked to the back of the rover and pulled out the tent. He made a stretcher by wrapping the tent fabric around several of the tent poles and tying the poles together at one end. It took nearly fifteen minutes to complete, and he was frustrated that it had taken so long.

He gathered the stretcher under his arm and jogged back up the ridge. It was actually easier to ascend. He did not have to keep slowing down to keep from falling. His lungs began to ache. He took in deeper breaths and continued upward without breaking his pace. Upon reaching Carter he collapsed on the ground next to him. They were both propped against the wall of the cliff. He was afraid to look inside the helmet, which had fallen limply against Carter's chest. After a while, he reached over and turned the faceplate toward him. If it had not been for the slight movement of his head caused by his breathing, Nelson would have taken him for dead.

"He's alive, but unconscious," Nelson said.

"That is just as well. The pain would probably be too much to bear."

Nelson spread the stretcher on the ground before him and gently laid Carter upon it. He then grabbed the poles from behind and held them waist high. The far end of the stretcher was supported by the ground. He attempted to look back to make certain Carter was safely inside the stretcher, but he could not see him. His helmet blocked his view. The grade looked steeper now that he had something pressing against his back. He would have to proceed at a slow pace. The entire descent took nearly an hour, and he was dripping with sweat when the rover finally came into view. His arms were numb.

He propped the stretcher against the rover—to his surprise he discovered that Carter's eyes were not shut, but open. He actually looked better than Nelson remembered, his eyes somewhat more aware, and there was color in his cheeks. He was attempting to grin. Nelson wondered how many bones were broken in his body. Perhaps he was in a state of shock. That he was alive was a miracle in itself. Nelson pointed at the rover, which of course Carter could not see, and made steering motions with his hands to indicate that it was the rover he was pointing at and that they would soon be on their way. At first he did not think that Carter had comprehended his motions. His expression had not changed. He was still grinning, and for a moment Nelson thought he was delirious, in a state of complete shock. But then life came into Carter's eyes, and he gestured upward with his thumb. Nelson forced a smile and patted him on the shoulder. At thirty-two kilometers per hour, it would take nearly three hours to reach the lander. Every second counted. He gently picked up Carter and placed him upon the rack above the oxygen tanks.

Carter was staring straight up, his eyes wide-open. They looked like miniature cue balls. His face was streaked where the tears from the pain had washed through the blood. Nelson smiled and placed his hand on Carter's arm to comfort him. "You'll be all right," he whispered slowly, exaggerating the movement of his lips.

Carter nodded to indicate he understood. He was wondering how much blood he had lost. He could feel the rope tighten across his body. Nelson looked curiously into his eyes, then disappeared out of sight. He was able to move his head slightly, and to one side he could see part of the rover with the volcano wall behind it and to the other side the Martian horizon. The straps around his body tightened as the rover accelerated. His leg erupted with pain. He screamed. The rover was swerving from left to right, and with each turn the agony brought him closer to unconsciousness. He struggled to remain alert, afraid that he might never open his eyes again. He cursed Nelson for driving so recklessly. It then occurred to him that there could only be one reason for Nelson's haste. He had to get him back to the lander as quickly as possible—his condition was critical. This did not surprise him. He felt as if he were holding on by the slimmest of threads.

"Slow down," he yelled, but to no avail. The sky became fuzzy and blurred and swirled as if he had drunk too much. Moments later he lost consciousness.

When he awoke he could not feel his leg. He attempted to sit up but his space suit would not move; he realized he was still tied to the rover. The sky had turned blood red. He attempted to look down his space suit at his leg, but all he could see was the tip of his boot. It was crusted with red dust. The boot itself appeared undamaged, and that comforted him somewhat. He wondered what life would be like if he lost the leg and had to be fitted with an artificial limb. He recalled there had been some recent advances in the field. The limb was attached to the bone at the joints and special plastics were fused to the ligaments and skin. Embedded in the plastic were microsensors that responded to signals from the brain. He would be able to move his leg and toes as if they were real.

After a while he began to wonder if he would live. At least he was still alive, which gave him something of a chance. How far had he fallen? Two hundred meters? That could not be— even at two-fifths gravity, he would never have survived such a fall. He had a vague recollection of being pulled upward by a rope. That could only mean he had not fallen the entire distance—something short of two hundred meters. He could taste blood.

As he ran his tongue along the inside of his mouth in search of the source, half-hoping to find a missing tooth, he noticed the rover had come to a stop. His teeth seemed to be intact. A dark mass blotted out the stars in the sky above, and for a brief moment the only thing he could see was the neon pattern at the bottom of his helmet. And then a bright, blinding light paralyzed his eyes. He shut his eyes and attempted to raise his hands to block the intruding glare, but the rope held them tightly in position. He shook his head back and forth to protest his discomfort. The light blinked off, and a white, reddish spot appeared in its place. It floated to wherever he looked and blocked from view everything but his peripheral vision. He attempted to make out the form moving beyond the spot. The ropes loosened around him and two arms grabbed him from underneath. As he was being lifted into the air, the lander swung briefly into view.

At first it felt like someone was tapping gently on his leg. With each step the tapping became more pronounced, and the nerves in his leg began to tingle with sensation. Once again, he could feel the pain. His muscles contracted tightly. He could feel the world slipping away. His final recollection was of a metallic gray ladder ascending toward the sky. He was being carried upward.

———————

Carter was sprawled semiconscious on the floor of the crew quarters. He had not lost that much blood. The bone had barely broken through the skin, and the liquid cooling garment had contained the bleeding. Still, the sight under the thermal blanket covering his naked body was grotesque. His leg was multiple shades of purple and blue and was nearly twice its normal size. A weak, painful moan passed through his lips.

The sound stopped Nelson midstride. He bent down and examined Carter's eyelids and watched for disturbances in his breathing. When he had removed Carter's helmet, Carter asked if he would lose his leg. The question caught Nelson by surprise, and his somewhat startled reaction undermined the confidence he had attempted to convey as he told Carter not to worry. Carter grinned painfully before slipping back into unconsciousness.

Nelson stuck the ampule containing morphine sulfate in the injection gun and pulled the blanket away from Carter's body. His eyes were drawn to the bloodstained wrapping that held Carter's leg together. The leg felt unusually hot.

"I think he has a fever," Nelson said.

"That is to be expected," Dr. Endicott replied. He was looking down at the two from the screen on the wall.

The muscles in Carter's body visibly relaxed as the morphine entered his bloodstream.

"You'll need to set the leg now," Endicott said.

Nelson paused to gather his strength. The most difficult part was about to begin. He forced himself to look at the leg, and to think of it only in terms of what had to be done. The bone, one end of which he could see pressed against the wrapping, had to be positioned back in place. He recalled how detached Endicott had been during Brunnet's operation. It was then he noticed that Carter's eyes were partially open and that the black balls behind the lids were rolling back and forth as if the muscles that held them steady had been severed.

A sense of well-being came over Carter, and he no longer felt any pain. He was floating in a bed of feathers. His body tingled with pleasure. He could see Nelson in the distance and wondered why he looked so concerned. Oh yes, his leg, it was broken. A compound fracture Endicott had said. It would be better soon. No need to look so concerned, Tom. His mind drifted to more pleasing things, the girl Tatiana and her pointy breasts and how they poked against the thin fabric of her blouse. He descended to the warm wonderful wetness between her legs and lingered. He desired to be next to her, and wondered, half-amused, how she was taking the separation from her husband. A healthy, young woman like that should not be away from her husband for too long, he said to himself. Nature abhors a void, he giggled. His eyes floated over to Nelson, who was in desperate need of humor. He decided to share his insight.

"What?" Nelson asked, gliding forward.

His second attempt to speak met with even less success. He giggled at the sounds that bubbled from his mouth and his own inability to make sense of them.

"He's trying to say something," Nelson said, looking up at Endicott for guidance.

"The morphine has impaired his motor skills. It's a perfectly normal reaction."

Carter listened as the two men talked. He couldn't understand why they didn't talk directly to him. Music would be nice, he thought, and closed his eyes. He was pleasantly surprised by the explosion of colors that greeted him.

Candor Chasma

As Vladimir Mikelovich Pavlov emerged from the airlock, he looked down past his dangling feet and saw floating beneath them a golden red ball. The ball seemed unreal. His eyes focused at the point he knew his crew members to be, the western edge of the canyon Valles Marineris. He thought of Tatiana and wondered what she would think if he simply fell out of the sky and crashed into the ground. But he knew that would be impossible. Even if he could somehow break orbit and swan dive toward the surface, his body would be nothing but ashes by the time it reached the ground. Perhaps a few would blow in her direction. The pain it would bring was tempting. He detached his safety tether and released his hold from the spaceship, but nothing happened—he remained stationary relative to the spaceship. This could go on for some time, he thought with a wry grin as he gazed down at the red ball beneath his feet.

He reattached the tether and twisted around until he was facing the interior of the airlock. With both hands gripped tightly around the metal handholds, he looked up. Fifty meters away, darkened by the fires of aerocapture, the supply ship of the ill-fated *Volnost* hung above him. It looked cold and dead. Vladimir did not believe in ghosts or even in life after death; all the same, the ship loomed overhead as if it might be haunted by the spirits of the dead cosmonauts. He knew this to be irrational. The objective of the EVA was to board the supply ship and photographically record its condition and determine, if possible, why the power supply had died two years earlier.

Hand over hand, Vladimir pulled himself toward the manned maneuvering unit. He had been looking forward to this moment. It would be like entering an abandoned house or a wartime submarine that had been scuttled and forgotten. It rekindled memories of his childhood, when he and his best friend had explored the wreck of an old train. The interior had been a labyrinth of twisted metal and broken glass. He remembered the rusty springs that poked through the fabric of the cushions and how when touched they wobbled back and forth with a low, vibrating tone that sounded like the moans of a dying man. That was how his best friend described the sound. There were decomposed beams that would break apart when kicked, and they made a great show of their karate skills. It wasn't until later in the day—the sun had already started to set and the air was growing cold—that they discovered the old crate with holes drilled into the sides. It did not appear to have ever been opened. They peered into the holes but could not see anything but a musty darkness. They imagined great treasures and told each other what they would purchase first and promised they would never let the other fall upon hard times. They took turns striking the box with a large metal rod, which required most of their strength just to lift. It was Vladimir who delivered the destructive blow. The box crumbled inward with a large roar and produced a mushroom cloud of dust that made them wonder if he had set off a hidden explosive. At first it appeared to be empty, so they kicked the rubble, and to their horror they discovered a skeleton. It was the remnants of a dog and strands of wiry hair still clung to the skull. They ran from the train screaming, but soon lost their breath and collapsed on the ground laughing. The discovery excited them tremendously. They felt they should notify the local authorities or a museum curator, but decided against either because they feared they might get into trouble. Vladimir, who had no religious inclinations but had been to several funerals, decided it would be proper to bury the bones.

Upon reaching the manned maneuvering unit, Vladimir slipped his boots into the foot restraints. The MMU was attached to the wall of the airlock. It stood 123 centimeters high, 82 centimeters wide, and 68 centimeters deep, and looked, with its metallic latches and assortment of interfaces and modules, as if it would be more appropriately worn by a robot. Its total mass with full propellant load was 143 kilograms. An inspection checklist popped onto Vladimir's heads-up display. He flipped the main power switch in the top left-hand corner of the MMU. Several small lights and an active-matrix display flickered on. He verified that the battery was fully charged and the fuel tanks had sufficient nitrogen. He methodically went through the remainder of the list.

"Visual inspection complete," he announced several minutes later.

"Proceed," Komarov replied.

Vladimir extended the arms of the unit by pulling down on them. He removed his boots from the foot restraints and turned around until he was facing away from the MMU. He stepped backwards into the outstretched arms of the unit. A message appeared on his heads-up display indicating the MMU was secured. He undid the safety tether. He walked to the edge of the portal and, looking down at the planet beneath him, jumped out into space. The sensation reminded him of skydiving. He was floating away from the spacecraft and would continue floating until some force intervened. In grade school, Vladimir's teacher had used marbles to demonstrate the Newtonian laws of motion. But the marbles, once launched, would always stop rolling within a few short seconds. He, on the other hand, would fall into orbit and would not stop revolving around the red planet for several years—not until his orbit decayed. He felt cheated that he would only be able to enjoy the first seven hours, the point at which his primary life-support system would fail.

"Pitching upward."

He pushed up on the joysticklike knob that controlled the pitch and yaw of the MMU. His body rotated until it was facing the supply ship. He then pressed the left-hand control, which controlled straight-line motion, and several tiny thrusters at the rear of the MMU fired. He released the control, the thrusters stopped, and his body continued forward at a constant velocity. There was nothing to do but wait and perhaps make an occasional adjustment.

As the supply ship slowly grew larger, he had time to contemplate what he might find inside. It should look much the same as it had when it was launched. The exterior, of course, would be dented with the impact of micrometeoroids, but the inside should not have changed. The food would not be safe to eat because of its long exposure to radiation. He was to bring a few packages back for study by the scientists on Earth. He was also to bring back water and samples of the plants. They wanted him to determine why the power had failed. He was curious himself. The most critical system on a spaceship was its power supply—many of the other systems were dependent upon it.

The supply ship, which required only a fraction of the power necessary to run the *Druzhba*, was powered by photovoltaic blankets mounted on arrays outside the ship. The energy captured by the solar cells in the blankets was stored in series of sodium-sulfur batteries located underneath the flooring. The system was simple—there were no moving parts—and should not have failed. But it had.

As the details of the ship emerged, now twenty meters distant, he searched the hull for damage from micrometeoroids, even though the ship was still smaller than the enlarged image he had viewed through the telescopic systems on the *Druzhba*. At ten meters, he started firing small bursts of nitrogen to send him to the far side. As he circled the dead craft—it had no more life than an asteroid—his breathing grew shallow. He was unable to detect any visible evidence of damage and decided he needed to move in closer.

"Approaching the ship," he announced. He pushed the left-hand control forward, and a burst of nitrogen sent him in the direction of the spacecraft. At three meters from the hull he was able to make out one or two dents that had been inflicted by micrometeoroids, but none so deep they might have damaged the power supply. "Commencing close inspection."

"Very good," Komarov replied.

With his hands, he pushed back from the ship and made his way around it with the MMU, maintaining a range of one to two meters. He inspected the hull for thirty minutes, the time allotted by the mission planners, and found nothing more than a few dents. He was not surprised. The Russian Space Agency scientists had said the answer would most likely lie inside.

"No evidence of external damage," he said.

"Proceed with entry," Komarov instructed.

There was something about Komarov's tone that annoyed Vladimir. It sounded somewhat smug. He wondered how close Tatiana was standing next to him, if she was close enough that her skin touched his. A burst of nitrogen sent him toward the hull. Using the metallic rungs that served as handholds, he worked his way toward the airlock hatch. In a cavity next to the hatch was a long red lever with a warning stenciled beneath it.

"Perhaps you should knock first," Komarov said jokingly.

"I'm afraid someone might answer." Vladimir could distinguish Tatiana's voice from the others as she laughed. He gripped the lever firmly in both hands and pulled down. The hatch moved slightly as the lock disengaged. Pausing to consider what he might find, he recalled the abandoned train and the box with the dog's skeleton. He pushed open the hatch. A cone of light, originating from his left shoulder, revealed a compartment almost identical to the one he had just left.

"Anyone home?" he said. Although they all knew there was no reason to wait for a response, they all did. The compartment seemed remarkably new, as if it had never been used. He turned his back to the mounting frame for the MMU and grabbed the large mushroom knobs on either side of him. He pushed himself backward into the locking mechanism.

A message appeared across his visor indicating the MMU was properly mounted. He threw the latch to unlock the MMU from his space suit. Drifting into the middle of the compartment, he swiveled his upper torso to look back through the portal. There were several stars and a blue dot he knew to be Earth. The blue dot looked a long way away. He closed the hatch and pushed himself toward the other end of the airlock. He would have to raise the pressure in the airlock to match that of the main compartment—the pressurization system was mechanical and did not require electrical power to function. He adjusted the pressure knob to one hundred kilopascals, and thought of Tatiana as he watched the gauge rise. It took about three minutes.

"Opening the hatch to the main compartment," he said as he slipped his boots into the floor restraints.

The compartment beyond the portal was a cylindrical corridor, just large enough to accommodate a man, and ran the length of the ship. It was identical to the full-scale model he had practiced with on Earth. Along the walls of the corridor were rows of white drawers, each neatly labeled in black Cyrillic type.

The type formed long thin lines that stretched the length of the tunnel and converged at the far end. It created an optical illusion that made the corridor seem much longer than it actually was. No end was up, and that was disorienting. To Vladimir the neatness of the compartment seemed out of place. It reminded him of a crematorium.

He was to open only certain drawers. They had been selected by the Russian Space Agency for their scientific value. There was not time to open them all, and for the most part it would have only been redundant. Most of the drawers contained food supplies that did not vary much from one to the next. He was to inspect their condition and bring back samples. The first drawer slid open without resistance. Inside were silver and gold packages immaculately wrapped. They appeared undisturbed. He held a gold package up to his visor and slowly turned it around until the label was facing him. BELUGA CAVIAR. Now that was something he had not eaten in quite some time, and the thought of the Russian delicacy appealed to him. Next to it he found some black bread and pickled mushrooms.

"I could prepare quite a feast with all of this," he said.

"Vladimir," Tatiana said disapprovingly.

At the sound of her voice his mood darkened. They had not talked in several days. He tried to think of what he should say, but he was afraid that whatever he might say would start an argument—so after several seconds of indecision he said nothing at all.

He moved on to the next drawer and pulled out a package that was several times larger than the others. It read REHYDRAT-ABLE TURKEY TETRAZZINI. The label struck him as humorous, but then he recalled Sergei Demin, who had been his friend and who had died aboard the *Volnost*. Demin had an insatiable love for Italian food, and it was likely that the meal had been stored at his request. Vladimir had not thought of his friend in months. He had stood at his widow's side at the funeral while the pallbearers of the empty coffin waded through the morning fog. These are the types of ghosts I will encounter, he told himself.

It was not until he was halfway through the corridor that he remembered the deception he had planned. Noticing that he was within a foot of the proper location, he paused for a moment to gather his wits. He pointed the camera situated on his shoulder at a drawer that was eye level. As he opened the drawer with one hand, he reached down and opened a second drawer with the other. His lower hand encircled a soft bag containing liquid. He knew the liquid to be vodka. Twirling a package of strawberries Romanov in full view of the camera, he slipped two bags of vodka into his pouch.

"Now that looks good," Tatiana said.

Vladimir studied the package curiously.

"Would you like me to bring some down to you?" he asked in a halfhearted attempt at a joke.

"Oh, yes," Tatiana replied. "And some pashka, too, if you don't mind."

She laughed, and upon hearing her laughter he hesitantly joined in. It felt good to be laughing with her. Perhaps, he thought, they would talk tonight. He was conscious that his feelings for her had changed so quickly, but he did not let that trouble him too much. It had always been that way. He was simply pleased that they were getting along again.

"Please," Komarov interrupted. "Time is limited."

The bastard, Vladimir thought to himself. He does not want us to be happy. He is trying to keep us apart so that he can have her all to himself. Vladimir bit down on his lip to keep from cursing—he did not want to behave poorly on camera. The EVA was being broadcast live on Earth.

"Of course," he replied, his voice shaking. The location of the next drawer was flashing with annoying persistence on his heads-up display. He placed a silver package on top of the vodka. He did so for three more drawers and finally froze in place.

"To hell with you," he muttered.

"What's that?" Komarov asked. It was clear by the tone of his voice that he had not made out the words and was only looking for clarification.

"The collection bag is full," he lied. "Recommend proceeding with investigation of the power failure."

There was a pause, in which Vladimir could hear Satomura whispering, followed by a muffled guttural sound that he took to be Komarov's reply. Several seconds passed.

"Proceed," came his commander's voice. By his tone, Vladimir could tell Komarov was not pleased.

The Russian Space Agency scientists felt that the environmental-control system was the most likely point of failure within the ship. It was located in the hydroponic garden at the far end of the corridor. He grasped drawers on either side of him and, with a gentle push, propelled himself toward the garden—the point at which the black Cyrillic type converged. He felt as if he were falling headlong into a hole. Upon reaching the hatch, he pulled himself to the viewing port and looked through. What he saw was not at all what he had expected. Sheets of ice, like a maze of broken mirrors, filled the chamber. He knew at once it would be unsafe to enter.

"I'm going in," he announced, and proceeded to open the hatch without waiting for a response. The sounds of urgent whispering filled his helmet. He had the lock pulled fully back when the response finally came.

"You better hold off until we've had time to assess the risk," Komarov said.

Vladimir pulled the hatch open as if he had not heard anything.

"Repeat, do not proceed until we have had time to assess," Komarov demanded, his voice rising.

A slight grin appeared on Vladimir's lips as he considered how best to proceed. The ice was indeed dangerous. A prick from any one of the broken shards could cut open his space suit and bring about almost certain death. He surveyed the compartment. The ice was thicker near the walls where the hydroponic containers were lined. He requested the computer to superimpose the electrical grid for the compartment upon his heads-up display. An intricate network of green neon lights appeared before him. As he turned his head the grid remained stationary. In the far right-hand corner, through the maze of ice, the neon formed a bright rectangle. It was the primary circuit box for the supply ship. He would begin at the box.

"Vladimir, recommend that you close the hatch until we have had—"

"I believe I have determined the cause of the outage."

"We need time to—"

"Time is limited. Remember? Don't worry, I'll take precautions."

Vladimir looked around for something to clear a path through the ice. He decided if he could remove two of the supply drawers, he could use one as a shield and the other as a battering ram. He pulled back with both hands on the nearest drawer, ripping it from the wall and sending silver and gold packages down each end of the corridor. He placed the empty drawer at his feet and proceeded, with even greater force, to do the same with the adjacent drawer. Packages of food bounced off his space suit and ricocheted from one wall to the next. He held both drawers at arm's length.

"I have shut down the voice link with Earth," Komarov said, making no attempt to hide his anger. "What the hell do you think you're doing?"

"I have just emptied these drawers of their contents," Vladimir replied in a matter-of-fact tone.

"You are to close the hatch, now!"

Vladimir pushed off and went flying toward the garden with an empty drawer in each hand.

"That is a direct order."

"The transmission is breaking up," Vladimir replied calmly. "I'm having difficulties hearing you."

Vladimir raised a drawer high over his head, paused for a second, and then, with a giant swing, brought it crashing down into the ice. The ice exploded violently and hurtled shrapnel-like projectiles at him. He ducked behind the drawers. He felt several shards as they crashed into his makeshift shields. Glancing out, he saw a maelstrom of ice swirling chaotically inside the room. He knew at once he had made a mistake. Komarov was yelling in his ear. He returned to his shelter behind the drawers and turned down the volume to the comm link so that he would not have to listen to Komarov. Nearly ten minutes passed before he felt it was safe to emerge from his cover. He was surprised at what remained. His single blow had destroyed the entire structure. The ice was still moving, but had lost much of its momentum.

With the drawers extended before him, he cleared a three-dimensional path and stepped into it. Shards of ice converged on the opening he had created. He put the drawers down and blocked the ice with his hands and forearms, carefully moving them from one position to the next. He did not want to increase the momentum of the ice particles by striking them. He decided for so much water to be present a pipe must have burst. He instructed the computer to overlay the schematic for the environmental-control system. A maze of lines representing pipes, bleed valves, gas-pressure regulators, heaters, chillers, and various other parts of the system appeared before him. He then requested the computer to highlight the points in the system most likely to break. The schematic transformed from a uniform blue to a kaleidoscope of colors. He focused upon the bright red areas. One area, where the ice appeared to be the thickest, caught his attention. It was immediately adjacent to the main power line. He pivoted and proceeded to clear a path toward the pipe he believed to be the origin of the break. As he made his way, he noticed that the hydroponic containers were still intact and that they contained vegetables suspended in blocks of ice. The vegetables looked remarkably fresh. He reminded himself that the radiation would have rendered any food aboard the supply ship unsafe to eat.

From a hole in the side of one of the containers a fountain of ice blossomed. The hole was as thick as his fist, and the ice looked as if it had sprung from a fire hydrant. He cleared some of the ice floating in front of him to obtain a better view. The fountain extended approximately half a meter before it broke. Vladimir realized that this was the origin of the ice sculpture he had shattered. He stepped around the protruding formation and up to the container.

He looked inside. Frozen within a block of ice he saw some carrots. He then realized that the containers should not have contained so much water . . . the shutoff valve must have failed. The containers had filled with water and the container in front of him had burst from the pressure. He instructed the computer to display the location of the shutoff valve. It was at the far end of the containers, inside a control box. Through the portal near the control box he could see the backup lander. It was an earlier version of the one they had aboard their own supply ship. As he picked a path to the control box, he wondered what they might be thinking. He was pleased that Komarov was angry and that Tatiana seemed to have gotten over their last fight. Opening the control box, he quickly identified the valve and confirmed that it was indeed open.

"It's the shutoff valve," he said, turning on his mike.

"Ah, you can talk," Komarov said.

"Of course I can talk," Vladimir replied smugly. He was feeling somewhat vindicated by his find. "You may want to open the comm link to Earth. I suspect they would very much like to see this."

"You disobeyed a direct order," Komarov said. "I must report this."

"Dima," Tatiana said disapprovingly. "Must we report every little disturbance. Wouldn't it better for all if nothing were said. Really, you must learn to contain your anger."

The camera mounted on Vladimir's suit swung drunkenly from one wall to the next. She was pleading with him as if he were her lover. That tone. He had heard it so many times before. But only after they had been intimate. And besides, she had called him Dima. No one called him Dima. No one except perhaps his wife, but certainly not anyone who dealt with him professionally. Certainly not Tanya. Vladimir reached back against the wall to steady himself. The very thought of her with him made his insides tighten. How could she? All the son of a bitch wanted was sex. He didn't give a damn about her. He didn't give a damn about anyone but himself. In the distance a voice, Komarov's, was saying something. The voice sounded urgent.

Vladimir noticed that he was floating. He was in the middle of the compartment surrounded by swirling pieces of ice. He looked below him and saw the container that held the carrots and the fountain of ice that shot out from its side, frozen in place as if for it time had stopped. He started to flail his arms in the air like a swimmer struggling to keep his head above water.

"What is wrong?" Komarov asked. The very sound of his voice annoyed Vladimir. He was trying to sound sincere, as if he actually cared what might be wrong. Why could she not see through him? Vladimir grabbed the corner of a container and pulled himself to the floor.

"You're fucking my wife," he said, "that's what wrong."

There was a long silence, during which no one dared say anything.

"Vladimir," Tatiana said softly.

He did not reply.

"Vladimir," she repeated.

"Yes?"

"Are you all right?"

If anyone else had asked him, or if she had asked him in a different way, he probably would have erupted with even greater rage than he had the first time. But none of his anger came forth. He felt foolish for his outburst. He actually stammered.

"Yes, I'm all right," he said. "A little tired. I did not sleep well last night."

"You do sound tired," she said, agreeing with him. They had shifted the blame to something they both knew had nothing to do with the problem, and they were grateful to have done so.

"Yes, I am tired," he said, half-hoping he could give the deception some substance by repeating it. He sounded much like a defeated man. "This suit is very heavy. I am going to head back to the ship. The mission here is complete."

———

Colonel Nelson tightened his grip on the steering wheel as the nose of the Mobile Unit for Surface Exploration, or MOUSE, tipped downward into a ditch that had caught him unaware. His foot was pressed against the brake, but it was already too late. He released the brake in an attempt to regain control. The miniature rover slid sideways down the rocky slope and nearly flipped over before he was able to bring it to a stop at the bottom of the slope. He brought up the topographical on the heads-up of his telepresence goggles. The rover was sixty kilometers east of the landing site, and he had to remind himself that he was actually aboard the *Shepard*, not the MOUSE.

The walls of the ditch stretched upward, and from the perspective of the cameras they could have belonged to a great canyon. He knew the MOUSE was incapable of ascending the steep incline, so he pointed the vehicle down the length of the ditch and proceeded to go wherever it might take him.

So much has gone wrong, he thought to himself as he steered around the rocks in the way of the rover. Carter was asleep, drugged, with his leg strapped down to keep it stationary. Without a proper cast it was important to limit his movement. The physicians were concerned about how the bone would mend under the weaker gravity and were recommending that Carter remain immobilized for at least another week. That, of course, interfered with many of the mission objectives. The oxygen-extraction experiment required two people to deploy and had to be scrapped altogether. It was a proof-of-concept experiment designed to extract oxygen from the carbon dioxide in the Martian atmosphere. And until Carter was able to walk and serve as backup, EVAs were restricted to the landing site. Even though Nelson agreed with the decision, he was not pleased with it. He did not like being confined to such a small area. Not when there was an entire world to be explored.

Most rocks in the MOUSE's eye were boulders, and it was such a boulder that now blocked its path. Nelson backed up the rover to obtain a better view. The computer informed him that the rock was several centimeters high and that the MOUSE would not be able to climb over it. The ditch was too narrow to turn around in, so instead he looked for a way past the obstacle. He decided if he were able to pick up enough speed, he might be able to climb the side of the ditch just high enough to pass over the rock.

He slammed down on the accelerator, and the MOUSE achieved its maximum speed of ten kilometers per hour almost immediately. When he was several centimeters from the rock he steered for the wall. He held his breath as the tiny vehicle scaled the side. It started to slip, and he felt as if the MOUSE were about to roll over, so he turned the wheel and headed back down. He was on level ground again, with the rock just behind him. He traveled several more meters when he encountered a fork in the ditch. He had a choice of two directions. Both paths sloped upward. He chose the path that forked right, only because he was right-handed.

He was concerned for the Russians. They did not even know if the *Gagarin* could lift off. The contingency plan called for the backup lander, but then they would have to depend on Vladimir. The psychiatrist said that he might be suicidal. Nelson was inclined to believe it. Vladimir did not seem stable. Particularly after the incident on the old supply ship. He had suggested the Russians make for the American lander in the dirigible, but the Russian Space Agency did not feel that was necessary. The damn fools. Their pride would be their undoing.

To his relief the path that he had chosen led back to the surface. The sky was streaked with dark red tentacles. He thought of Tatiana and wondered if she were the type of woman who would cheat on her husband. She was full-figured, and although she did not flaunt her sexuality, she did not hide it either. He suspected that she enjoyed the effect it had on men. He shut the engine off and watched the sun set as he thought of his wife and of how different she was from Tatiana. His wife was not the type to sleep with another man. She loved him and their children and, besides, was too happy with the life that he provided. She was attractive, though, and two years was a long time. He wondered what he would do if she did have an affair. He knew that in his heart he would forgive her, but he also knew that he would divorce her. The sun was fully set when he pulled off his goggles and went to check on Carter.

Satomura marveled at the vast size of the dirigible, which darkened the sky and towered overhead like one of the great German zeppelins of the early twentieth century. It stretched

153 meters from bow to stern and was filled with hydrogen that had been extracted from the Martian soil. The dirigible, along with the rover, had been transported by the supply ship and had arrived on the surface several days after the *Gagarin*.

He stepped inside the small cabin underneath the balloon and turned around to lend a hand to Tatiana. The cabin was just large enough to fit two people. Tatiana sat down in the uncushioned hard-plastic chair intended for the pilot. They would have to keep their space suits on, since the cabin was not pressurized. The flight was scheduled to last seven hours and thirteen minutes.

The flight-deck console did not possess the sleek and finished appearance of the consoles aboard the *Druzhba*. There was a stick that controlled horizontal movement and another that controlled vertical. The altimeter and other navigational indicators appeared on an active-matrix display above the two control sticks. A second display was situated in front of the observer's seat.

Satomura felt a keen sense of excitement as he sat down. A checklist appeared in the corner of both displays. Tatiana read the list out loud as they checked the equipment. His mind was elsewhere, however. They were to descend into the grand canyons of Valles Marineris and examine the layered deposits within the divide between Ophir and Candor Chasmas. He looked over at Tatiana and could see that she, too, was excited, but he imagined for different reasons. She was not a planetary geologist. She had not spent her life peering through the small end of a telescope or hovering over photographs of dead planets. She was an engineer. Her field of study was aerodynamics, and she had actually participated in the design of the dirigible. This was to be its maiden voyage. They had not flown the dirigible on Earth because it was not built for Earth's gravity and, consequently, would have collapsed under its own weight.

"Ready," she said.

"Everything clear here." Komarov's voice was sharp and distinct inside their helmets.

"Ready," Satomura responded, raising his thumb in a gesture that he had learned from the Americans.

"Releasing anchors," Tatiana said. The cords detached from the five anchors that held the dirigible in place and spun rapidly back into the ship. Satomura watched one cord as it whipped around in circles and disappeared into the small end of a cone. The cabin nodded forward, and Satomura noticed that the bow came dangerously close to the ground. For a brief moment he feared that it might be punctured by a rock. He was about to say something but stopped himself as the ground started to recede.

Satomura felt as if he were upon a cloud floating upward into the heavens. He pressed his helmet against the window and gazed down at the red Martian surface. The *Gagarin* dwindled in size. Soon it became a mere speck, then disappeared altogether, and as far as the eye could see the volcanic plains stretched out beneath him. The sun had just begun its climb and threw long shadows against the rusty surface. He watched the rocks and picked out patterns as Tatiana traced a figure eight in the thin Martian atmosphere. She was testing the operation of the ship. The patterns blurred as his thoughts turned to the composition of the ground below. Smectite clays made up of sulfates and carbonates formed the underlying surface. In his mind, he recalled vividly the strong iron absorption lines that ran vertically across the planet's spectrum. He had confirmed that the sand dunes, as well as the rocks that littered them, were composed of iron oxides. It was the rust in the iron that gave the planet its red color. The dirigible descended toward the ground and rose again as Tatiana tested the blimp's buoyancy.

"Proceeding to the descent site," she said.

"Yes," Satomura responded, "yes, of course."

The descent site was the slope of Candor Mensa, which they were to scale in two weeks. Because of Carter's accident, several officials had questioned the wisdom of another climb and were insisting upon additional photographs. It was the only scheduled stop on the way to the layered deposits.

After taking a few seconds to look over the console, Satomura wrapped his fingers around the hand control for the high-definition cameras mounted outside the cabin. A window in the active-matrix display opened. He pressed the zoom button and watched as the surface came rushing toward him.

"There it is," Tatiana announced.

As the ship turned, the towering wall of the mesa came slowly into view. It stood 1.3 kilometers high. From a distance it would have looked like a gigantic tree stump, neatly severed. The dirigible descended several hundred meters, and the mesa wall filled the entire forward window. Satomura had to look over his shoulder, out the side window, to see the sky. The dirigible, which only minutes earlier had so impressed him with its size, now seemed insignificant against this mammoth backdrop.

From the corner of his eye, he saw Tatiana's finger pointing toward the top of the cliff. The dirigible was not equipped with a heads-up display.

"There," she said, pressing her finger against the glass.

Satomura recognized the site almost immediately. He had spent the previous evening studying photographs taken from a balloon they had launched several weeks earlier. The site occupied a tiny fraction of the cliff, and the vastness of its surrounding, despite his excitement, made him think of how much would go unexplored. Their stay was more than half-over, and five weeks was not nearly enough time to do all the things he wanted to do.

"Do you see it?" Tatiana asked.

"Of course."

He turned the recorder on and zoomed in upon the site. The slope of the path they were to take varied from ten to thirty degrees. Promising was a horizontal strip of land a few meters thick that was darker than the ground above and below it, and, more importantly, much thinner than the other strata of the canyon. A rare smile cracked Satomura's wrinkled skin. At that point in the planet's surface a significant change had taken place in a relatively short period of time. Satomura saw that the path took them down to the stratum. He wondered if Tatiana had noticed his excitement. He glanced over at her. She was looking directly at him.

He put her out of his mind and returned to the active-matrix display. He was supposed to be filming the site, but he could not tear himself from the thin layer of rock. He focused the camera upon the dark red line and tracked its path until it disappeared around the corner of the mesa.

"Five more minutes," Tatiana warned.

"Right, right," he responded.

"Do you think it's too dangerous?" she asked.

Annoyed at being interrupted, Satomura wondered if her concern extended to himself, or whether it was confined to her lover. It certainly wasn't for her own safety, since she wasn't going to participate in the climb. He wanted to talk to her about Komarov, but not now. There was too much to do. He returned the camera to the site, forgetting that she had even asked the question, and took shots to placate the officials who were worried about safety. The path never exceeded thirty degrees. He had negotiated greater slopes during his EVAs, and no one had even raised an eyebrow. It was as if they believed the slope was covered with marblelike rocks—someone had actually raised the possibility—and that the moment he set foot upon the treacherous surface he would be sent rolling down the cliff with his equipment tumbling after him.

"Well?" Tatiana asked.

"Well, what?"

"In your opinion, is it too dangerous?"

Couched in the negative, he thought; how so very much like a woman. "Absolutely not."

"Good then," she replied. "You still have one minute."

"All finished here," he said. "Let's proceed."

She turned the dirigible away from the cliff and pointed the bow northward. The large craft descended into the canyon like a submarine submerging into the depths of the sea. They dipped beneath a light mist. Satomura wondered what might have been left behind when the great sea had evaporated into the atmosphere. He imagined the fossilized remains of giant fish and drew a deep breath of oxygen from the life-support tanks as if it were fresh salt air from the Japanese coast.

The sun had climbed high enough to illuminate the canyon with an orange glow. Most of what he could see lay directly beneath him; the canyon walls were too distant to make out clearly. In the dawn's light, the canyon floor took on a surreal aspect. The depressions were dark gray, outlined in orange. Satomura picked several gorges and traced their snakelike paths through the broken terrain. He wanted to be closer to the surface. The resolution from his current height was little better than that detailed in the satellite mosaics.

"Lower," he requested eagerly.

"We are descending, Takashi," Tatiana responded.

"Indeed," he replied. He was quiet for several minutes as he waited for the dirigible to descend lower. "See how the surface is so rough?"

She nodded without bothering to look down at the surface.

"Great forces were involved here," he said. "The very same forces that spawned the volcanoes Arsia, Pavonis, and Ascraeus Mons. The tectonic upheaval was so great that it almost ripped the planet apart."

He looked briefly at the faint mist above him. A fog appeared in the canyons every morning and hovered there until the midday sun burned it off. He felt certain the source of moisture was an underground river that flowed below the surface. Most of his colleagues believed it was from the permafrost. He imagined their faces when he proved them wrong and broke out with a loud laugh. Tatiana was startled by the outburst.

"What is so amusing?" she asked.

"Maybe later," Satomura replied.

"Keeping secrets, are we?" she said with a mischievous smile. But the smile transformed into a look of misgiving, and she turned her head away.

Satomura deduced immediately that she was thinking of Vladimir and decided that it was best to act as if he had not noticed. He did not want to discuss her problems at that moment, which, he knew from experience with his late wife, could take much more time than he was willing to give. His wife had gone on for hours about concerns she had somehow construed to be monumental. Most often he had considered them mundane at best. And no matter what he said, she could twist it into something he had not at all intended. He returned his attention to the surface below.

The next hour passed quickly. Satomura busied himself filming the terrain before it disappeared behind the blimp. He frequently instructed Tatiana to deviate from the planned course to capture something of interest, and at first she did so without complaint, her mind obviously elsewhere. But as they neared their destination she became more herself and refused his requests because they had fallen behind schedule.

The ship came to a stop.

"I have never seen anything like it," Tatiana said.

Satomura, who was occupied with the surface directly beneath, looked up in surprise.

"My," was all he could manage to utter.

Before them loomed a wall with thick maroon stripes stretched horizontal across its length. The wall towered over five kilometers into the Martian sky and was scarred by ridges and gullies. At the foot of the gully before them, Satomura could see the remnants of a massive landslide, which he judged to be relatively young—a few hundred thousand years. To the east was the great divide between Ophir and Candor Chasma. A long, thin hill with a flat top and finely fluted slopes was situated inside the divide. The slopes formed such a regular pattern that they looked as if they had been tilled. These were the layered deposits. He swung the camera in the direction of the deposits and panned back and forth across their length.

"Fascinating," he said at last. "They have every appearance of having been created by a large body of standing water."

"How's that?" Tatiana asked.

"Notice the regularity of the layers. Such regularity would not be evident if they had been created by mass wasting or a catastrophic event. A lake, on the other hand, probably could have produced that pattern."

"It must have been a rather large lake," she said as she scanned her surroundings.

"Large, indeed."

"Where to?" Tatiana asked.

Satomura extended a gnarled finger, held it stiffly upright as he contemplated the alternatives, then pointed toward a spot at the base of the layered deposits. "We should land there."

Tatiana surveyed the proposed site and, seeing that it was reasonably flat and clear of rocks, accepted his suggestion.

"Hurry," Satomura said.

The giant dirigible descended slowly toward the site. At three hundred meters, Satomura abandoned the cameras and pressed his helmet against the window so that he could see all of the approaching floor. His eye caught a bright reflection, and before the image had fully registered in his mind, he was shouting new instructions to Tatiana. As the ship turned the reflection disappeared. Satomura searched the surface, his fingers gripping the sill of the window. It could have been light reflected from ice, he thought to himself.

"Did you see it?" he demanded.

"See what?"

"The light," he shouted. "The light."

A full two minutes passed before a second flash exploded into view.

"Over there," he shouted, twisting to his right.

"I saw it this time," she said. Tatiana found herself caught up in his excitement. She had no idea what it was she had seen, but whatever it was she felt it must be important. In all her time with Satomura, she had never seen him so excited.

The flash flickered rapidly several times, then stopped. She eyed a clearing where they could land the dirigible and headed directly for it.

"It is ice!" Satomura exclaimed.

"I believe you're right," Tatiana said.

"This may very well be what I was looking for." His voice shook as he spoke. He tore his eyes away from the ice to glance at her and saw that she seemed excited. He smiled, pleased to have someone to share his discovery with, and placed his hand on hers. Her eyes opened wide in surprise. He continued to hold her hand as he gazed down at the pool below.

The descent passed swiftly. Moments after the ship had landed, Satomura jumped onto the surface and strode hastily toward the ice. He twirled his head back over his shoulder and shouted at the diminishing Tatiana, "Quickly."

"No need to shout," Tatiana retorted. "My headset works just fine."

Rocks of pinkish ice were scattered across the surface. Satomura walked past them, and upon reaching what he assumed to be their source, a pool of ice nearly five meters in diameter, he fell to his knees and began examining the surface of the pool. He was crawling on all fours around the outer edges of the pool when Tatiana arrived several minutes later. Loaded down with equipment, she sat upon a rock to catch her breath and watch.

"This must be recent," he said without looking up. "Water ice is unstable at this latitude."

"So where did all this ice come from?" she asked.

"From this geyser, of course," Satomura said. "It must have reached at least fifty meters, judging from the scattering of the ice. A similar phenomenon has been observed on Neptune's moon Triton. I can show you photographs of active geysers spewing frozen nitrogen several kilometers into the sky." He paused to consider the implications of the discovery. "Water at this latitude would have to reside nearly a kilometer beneath the surface for it not to freeze. What a spectacular sight the eruption must have made." He stood up and brushed the red dirt from his space suit.

"I must film this," he said.

The pool of ice was frosty white with a slight pink tinge. Wisps of smoke floated over its surface like a miniature fog. Strewn around its perimeter were small blocks of ice, no larger than a fist, each with its own little cloud. With a slow, sweeping motion, he filmed the pool and its surrounding area. He then walked around the pool and filmed it from the opposite side. Touching a control on his chest plate, Satomura displayed the outside temperature on his visor. It read negative fifty-three degrees Celsius. He considered this for a while, his eyes affixed to the light mist that hovered above the ice.

"I believe the ice may be serving as a cap." He stepped up to the edge to get a better look.

"When did it last erupt?" Tatiana asked.

"It must have been fairly recent. Last night, perhaps."

"Are you saying this thing is active?" she asked wide-eyed.

"Oh, there's no doubt about that."

Komarov, who had been listening from the *Gagarin*, suddenly grew interested. "When will it explode again?"

"Difficult to say," Satomura responded. "It will erupt whenever the pressure inside the geyser is great enough to blow off the cap."

"I want you out of there," Komarov demanded.

"Yes, of course," Satomura responded, sounding somewhat annoyed. "That was my intention all along. But first, I must set up the equipment and gather some samples. With the geophones in place we should be able to predict an eruption well before it happens."

"How much time do you need?"

"No more than an hour."

"You've got thirty minutes, and at the slightest sign of a disturbance I want you out of there."

Satomura smiled because thirty minutes was actually all he needed. Folding his arms, he surveyed his surroundings, walked to the north side of the geyser, then motioned for Tatiana to approach. "Deploy a geophone at this spot here and position the other in the center of that depression." He pointed a thickly gloved finger at a clearing north of their position. "We'll set up the camera on the way out."

Satomura bent down at the base of the ice and, waving aside the gases, touched it with his glove. It was pockmarked with ragged holes. He selected the chisel from his utility belt and struck the outer edge of the ice. After he had knocked loose several large chunks, he looked up to note Tatiana's progress. She would require the full thirty minutes. He scooped up several handfuls of ice and placed the cubes in the Teflon-coated sample-collection bag. He sealed the airtight bag, and then double-checked the seal for leaks.

Once he had filled several bags, he took a moment to relax. Tatiana was heading north with a geophone in her hand. He reached down amongst the nuggets and picked out the clearest and largest he could find. He held the ice up to the pink sun. As he slowly turned it, rainbowlike colors appeared and disappeared upon its many facets. Filled with elation over the significance of his discovery, he marveled at the simple phenomenon. He now had strong proof that water flowed under the Martian surface.

"This is the stuff of life," he said, holding the ice up for Tatiana to see.

On their way out, they situated the remote camera upon a rock fifty meters from the geyser. The camera would be activated automatically by the geophones if they detected an eruption.

The Discovery

"She is lying," he hissed vehemently.

Dr. Endicott, approaching the monitor, noted with concern how thin Vladimir appeared. His eyes were bloodshot and sunken, and he was floating, half-naked, wrapped in a white blanket.

"You really should eat more," Endicott said.

"To hell with food," Vladimir retorted. "I find sustenance in vodka." With that he put a plastic container to his mouth and sucked for a long time upon the nipple. Endicott concealed his disapproval with an expression that seemed to say he understood.

"I've taken to growing a beard myself," Endicott said after a while.

Vladimir released the vial of vodka and ran his fingers through the tiny curled hairs of his beard. "Do you like it?" he asked. The hair was short and tangled and grew in patches.

Endicott nodded and permitted a slight smile to appear on his lips.

"Ah, you are lying. But no matter. I like you. Too bad you cannot share vodka with me. We could get drunk together. Yes?"

"I'm not entirely unprepared." Endicott produced a bottle of liquor from beneath the screen. "Medicinal purposes, of course."

"What is it you have there? I cannot make out the label."

"Cognac," Endicott replied.

"You are a resourceful man, Dr. Endicott," Vladimir said, grinning with approval. "I like that. To your health, then."

They raised their respective containers in the air—Vladimir tapped his against the monitor screen—and brought them to their lips. Endicott took a small sip but made certain not to withdraw his bottle before Vladimir.

"Now we can talk," Vladimir announced. There was a moment of silence as he contemplated his next words. His left hand was rubbing the short hairs of his beard. "They should have never put her on the same ship as him."

Endicott nodded to indicate he understood.

"He has an insatiable appetite for women. They are like candy to him. He eats them one right after another, pop, pop, pop. I don't blame him. He is a great test pilot and cosmonaut, a national hero, he can take liberties not permitted other men. It's my misfortune that the only woman available is my wife. I should have known Tatiana would be his next victim. His reputation is well founded. My wife, you see, she could tempt the pope himself into sin. It's not him I blame. It is her. She is the guilty one. She is the one who has vowed to be faithful to me for as long as she lives. She has broken faith with me, not him. She has lied to me."

"You are certain, then, that she has broken faith?" Endicott asked. He was careful to use the same words Vladimir had used.

"I can see it in her eyes. I can see it in the way she talks to me. Yet she still loves me. She lies to protect me. Isn't that why we all lie? We lie because we love each other; it is the only way love can be sustained."

"I don't know if I can accept that."

"I am not asking you to. Perhaps I have generalized too much. Perhaps you are right. No matter, let us drink."

The hot liquid burned Endicott's throat, and despite his moderate sips he was already beginning to feel its effects. Rather than fight its influence, which was his initial reaction, he decided he would get further with Vladimir if he at least seemed drunk. With that thought he open his throat and allowed several ounces to drop down it. The liquid, which burned the moment it hit his tongue, somehow got itself trapped between his throat and stomach, and the muscles that normally sent everything to his stomach were caught in a spasm of indecision. His eyes widened and filled with tears. He started to choke. Not wanting to lose face in front of Vladimir, he clamped his teeth shut and fought his body's instinctive reaction to reject the liquid. Nearly a minute passed before he had regained his composure.

"Cognac, you say," Vladimir remarked. "It is not as easy to drink as vodka."

"It's been a while," Endicott offered in explanation.

"Where were we?"

"Faith."

"Ah, yes. She has broken faith. The question I keep asking myself is, what should I do?"

Endicott felt his pulse quicken as he considered how he should respond. He had been instructed to reassure Vladimir that Tatiana was not having an affair. But he knew doing so would only anger Vladimir and destroy the trust that he was attempting to establish.

"Perhaps you should not judge her so harshly," Endicott said.

An eternity passed while Endicott gazed down at the bottle in his hands. He wondered how much Vladimir would drink that night and when his seemingly endless source of vodka would run out.

"How do you mean?"

Endicott noticed that Vladimir's voice had lost some of its bitterness. He took it as a hopeful sign.

"Assuming there has been an affair . . . I'm not entirely convinced there has been, but, for the sake of argument, let's say there has been . . . then, clearly, Dmitri was the pursuer."

"She has been unfaithful."

"My point is that she did not bring it about."

"But she has been unfaithful all the same."

"Perhaps Dmitri is the one you should blame, not Tatiana."

"It does not matter. I am not married to Dmitri."

"Placed in a similar situation, alone with a woman as beautiful as your wife, would you not also be tempted?"

Endicott could see that the liquor was beginning to have an effect on Vladimir, and him, too. Although Vladimir was floating in zero g, he appeared to be swaying as if he were having some difficulty maintaining his balance. His features darkened, and in their shadowy lines an expression of guilt emerged.

"I was tempted," he said inaudibly.

It was only two months before the launch date. He had been sent to Japan to train with their computerized mock-up of the *Druzhba*. She was wrapped in a tight skirt that clung translucent to the contours of her buttocks. The skirt stopped high on her legs, revealing almost their entire length. They were youthful legs, firm, and sensuous, and were delicately colored the light shade with which oriental women were blessed. The legs held him transfixed, his cover the simulator, until she spoke, but he could not understand what she said because her words were in Japanese. But they did accomplish the task of diverting his attention upward. As his eyes traveled he noticed her hands on her hips, palms outward, and the inward slope of her waist. Conscious of her scrutiny, he lingered for only a fraction of a second, then continued his climb. At eye level, poking through the fabric of her blouse, two erect nipples peered back at him.

He went up her slim neck, past her delicate jaw, to her thin, red lips, which glistened with moisture. Finally, he reached her eyes.

"Major Pavlov?" she said in near perfect English.

They were nocturnal eyes. The slits were lined with long eyelashes that opened and closed like the wings of a black butterfly. Her pupils formed two large circles. Vladimir sensed that she was attracted to him.

"Yes, I am Major Vladimir Pavlov," he replied in English. "And you are?"

"You can call me Mariko," she said musically.

"Mariko," he repeated, hoping she would approve of his pronunciation.

She nodded slightly and smiled, then stepped forward and leaned over so that her eyes would be level with his. A layer of glass, less than one millimeter in thickness, separated them. Her blouse hung loose at the neck and through the narrow opening he could see her breasts. They hung pendulously, swaying with the slight motion of her shoulders as she propped herself against the simulator.

"Mariko," she corrected him, with a very pleasant smile.

They had dinner that evening, and made love that night, and made love every night for a week, at the end of which he had to leave. He did not feel guilty, nor did he feel guilty when he returned to Tatiana and made love to her. As long as Tatiana did not know, his conscience did not trouble him. Mariko, to whom he had not spoken or written since his return, had ceased to exist—that is, until Tatiana resurrected her. How she found out, Vladimir did not know, nor was he absolutely certain she had found out. But she dropped subtle hints, her manner changed, and she became less receptive to his advances. His doubts and her suspicions fueled each other. And he felt that all that had gone wrong could be traced back to that one week with Mariko. This troubled him more than anything else, so he did not like to think about it.

"What was that?" Endicott asked.

"Nothing," Vladimir replied.

"Most men would at the very least be tempted. It is human nature."

Vladimir did not respond.

"Tatiana loves you."

Vladimir turned away from the camera to keep Endicott from seeing the moisture gathering in his eyes. He reached for the container that was floating empty in front of him. "I must go now," he whispered. Without waiting for a reply, he shut down the comm link. He bounced off a wall, caught a handhold, and hurried down the corridor in search of more vodka.

―――――――――

S atomura held the rope with both hands as he took another step forward. The seesaw sound of his breathing was amplified by the microphone inside his helmet. Komarov was in front of him, testing the ground with the tip of his boot. They were following a path, at points no more than five meters wide, that ran down the northeast wall of Candor Mensa.

"How are you doing?" Komarov asked.

"I'm right behind you," Satomura replied.

"If you need to rest, speak up. There is no need to hurry."

"Don't slow down on my account."

The grade of the path was erratic and in places much steeper than they would have liked. They could barely make out the canyon floor through the morning mist. Upon reaching the upper layer of the stratification that had so interested him in the dirigible, Satomura ran up to the rock and rubbed his hand across its surface. There was a sharp line of division between the two layers.

"Where do we start?" Komarov asked.

"I will start here. Perhaps you should continue down the

path. Look for anything unusual. Speak up as soon as you find something, even it doesn't seem significant."

"Very well," Komarov replied, and headed in the designated direction.

Satomura stepped back to examine the division between the two layers in the rock. It was diffused, fluvial in appearance, similar to formations he had seen in dry riverbeds on Earth. He panned the area with the camera, then moved in closer. After a moment of reflection, he attached his camera to his suit and laid out his equipment. He selected a hammer and began to take samples. As he worked, his mind raced with theories. Dmitri and Vladimir had vanished completely from his thoughts. He had performed this type of work on Earth many times before, in preparation for the Mars trip and in actual fieldwork. The field-work had been during the years immediately following his first doctorate. He was still undecided about entering the National Space Development Agency, which, at the time, seemed to be in a state of perpetual collapse. He had fallen into a rhythm and was extracting the third sample when his work was interrupted by a sudden exclamation.

"What was that?" he said, standing upright.

"I have found something!" Komarov exclaimed.

Satomura looked down the path, attempting to locate the Russian cosmonaut. He could only see about forty meters of the path before it bent around the cliff. Komarov was nowhere to be seen.

"What have you found?" Satomura asked, partly annoyed at having been interrupted.

"It looks like some sort of fossil. It's big. A plant or some-thing. My God, this is incredible! You've got to get over here quick."

The announcement stopped Satomura from breathing. "Say again."

"I think I found a fossil. It's nearly a meter long."

Satomura reached out to steady himself. Komarov must be mistaken. A fossil nearly a meter long? Preposterous. Perhaps he is pulling some sort of practical joke. It would not be unlike him. Yes. That is it. He closed his eyes so that he could listen better.

"Oh my," exclaimed Tatiana.

"Stop moving," Vladimir said excitedly. "The image is jumping too much. I can't quite make it out."

"Oh my," Tatiana repeated.

"It looks like the leaf from a palm tree," said Vladimir.

"Congratulations." It was in English, Endicott's voice, then the other Americans; everyone was talking at once, their voices growing louder with each exclamation. Satomura opened his eyes and frantically searched the path for signs of Komarov. It occurred to him that he was perhaps the only one who had not yet seen whatever Komarov had found.

"I will be right there," Satomura shouted excitedly. "Do not touch anything." He bounded down the path without regard to his safety and realized, as he was rounding the bend, that he had left his equipment behind. He decided to retrieve it later. First he would assess the validity of the find.

"Where?" he demanded upon reaching Komarov, and took in several deep breaths.

Komarov stepped aside. What struck Satomura first was its sheer size. It was larger than Komarov had indicated, nearly a meter and a half in total length and perhaps twenty-five centimeters wide at its broadest point. He realized at once that it was a real fossil and not some freak formation carved by erosion. And it was, as Vladimir had suggested, similar to a palm leaf. The detail was stunning. He lifted his hands and traced an imaginary copy of the fossil in the air before him. He did this several times. He reached for a brush and discovered that it was missing. Suddenly, he realized they were waiting in silence for him to make some sort of pronouncement.

"*Aracales,*" he said.

"What?"

"On Earth it would belong to the order *Aracales,* the palm order." He paused while he considered the many ways his statement could be misinterpreted. "Vladimir, your observation is surprisingly accurate; the fossil does bear a resemblance to a palm leaf. Of course that does not mean this fossil belongs to the same order. I only make the statement for comparison purposes. I would imagine, Dmitri, that they will name this plant after you since you are the one who discovered it."

Komarov approached the fossil to take a closer look. "I should be photographed next to it," he said.

"Of course." Satomura stepped back and focused the camera upon Komarov and the fossil. After several minutes, he asked Komarov to step aside because he was blocking the light. He filmed the fossil for several more minutes, then reattached the camera to his suit and sat down upon a rock to consider the find. The impression of the leaf upon the cliff was flawless. He chose a vein and followed it until it diminished into the rock, then chose another. He imagined what the plant that bore the leaf must have looked like several hundred million years ago. He envisioned a tall stem with a single giant leaf emerging from the edge of a lake. Next to it was another leaf of similar height and dimensions and next to it another. They ringed the perimeter of the mesa. The first action he would take upon returning to the ship would be to date the material. Then he would search for fossilized organic particles. The remainder of their mission plan would have to undergo a drastic revision, and in his mind he was already beginning to formulate the new plan. Suddenly he remembered that they were scheduled to depart in two weeks. This was five days earlier than originally planned. It was to give them sufficient time to use the backup lander, if the *Gagarin* failed to launch. He would recommend pushing their liftoff to the original departure date.

"I will take an impression of it first, then we should extract it."

"Extract it?" Komarov asked doubtfully.

"Of course," Satomura replied. "We must take it back with us."

"But it's part of the cliff. Won't it break apart?"

"Not if we are careful." Satomura stood up and walked over to the fossil. He examined the surrounding rock. "We should get started. There are only so many hours in a day."

Vladimir had bathed for the first time in several days and had shaved off his beard. He was checking himself in the mirror. His hair shone from the gel that held it in place. He had used more than usual that morning because he wanted to make certain that it stayed in place. He opened his mouth to check his teeth. In exactly one minute and thirteen seconds, he was to initiate a private call with his wife. He kept glancing at the clock. He ran his finger across the bare skin of his cheeks and wondered what she would think. She had never said anything about the beard. He found that strange. His eyes were red, and that bothered him. But there was nothing he could do. He should not have drunk so much the night before. Seeing that it was time, he took a deep breath and opened the comm link.

"Hello," he said, his lips forming a forced smile. She was also smiling, and this made him feel better.

"Hello."

"How have you been?" he asked.

"Busy." He could tell that she was scrutinizing his appearance. He looked away from the camera, hoping that she would not notice the redness in his eyes. "With the discovery of the fossil, I've barely had time to breathe. Yourself?"

Vladimir wondered why she would ask such a question. She knew as well as he that he had fallen behind on his duties. But from the innocent manner in which she had asked the question and waited for his response, he realized she had not meant anything by it. He knew by the look in her eyes that she wanted the conversation to go well.

"Not so busy," he said. "Not as much to do up here." He looked nervously around as if to verify that there was not that much to do.

"You look much healthier," she said.

"I shaved," he said in explanation, and pointed at his bare chin. "It was beginning to itch. Tell me about the fossil."

"It is authentic," she said. "I am arranging the itinerary for another trip to the geyser. Takashi believes that if there is life to be found, it will be there. He wants to collect additional samples. I think he's right."

"Indeed," said Vladimir. He was surprised at how easily they had avoided the original purpose of the call. "But what about the samples he has already collected? I thought he had examined them for evidence of life."

"He didn't find anything," Tatiana said. "He believes the ice he had collected may have only been permafrost knocked loose by the geyser. He wants to drill for water. The geophones have detected a subsurface river. Although the river itself is too far beneath the surface for our drills to reach, there may be water near the mouth of the geyser. The pressure is so great that it should be able to maintain a liquid form."

"That sounds dangerous," Vladimir said.

"You're not the only one who thinks so, but he has managed to convince them to let him try. He's going to operate the drill remotely."

"Does he have the necessary equipment to do that?"

"I've helped him rig something up," she said.

"So he thinks he'll find life," Vladimir said, mostly to himself.

"To hear him talk it's almost a certainty."

"That would be incredible." He noticed that Tatiana was

stroking her forehead, which he interpreted to mean her mind was elsewhere. He grew uncomfortable. He had been preparing for this moment for the past several days, and now that it had arrived, he felt that everything he had planned to say seemed inappropriate.

"Vladimir," she said.

"Yes?"

"We are not here to discuss the fossil."

"Yes," he agreed hesitantly.

"We are here to discuss us."

"Yes."

"I think you should start."

"Yes," he said, then became silent as he wondered how he should start. He wanted to tell her that he blamed himself more than her, but then he wasn't sure that she really knew about Japan. To mention the affair if she did not already know about it would certainly make matters worse. She would be furious. He was growing confused as he tried to think of what he should say. He would tell her that he could forgive her if she just stopped seeing Komarov. That above all else, she had to stop seeing him. "I want us to work things out," he said.

"And so do I, Vladimir. I have been thinking of you so much lately and cannot bear to see you suffer so. I wish none of this had ever happened."

He studied her curiously, his face contorting with thought. "Do you really mean what you say?" he asked.

"Yes, every word." He noticed that there was some hesitancy in her voice.

"You will renounce him?"

"Yes."

"You admit sleeping with him, then?"

She paused before responding. He could tell that she was trying to make up her mind as to what she should say. If she were to lie, it would be now, he told himself. She almost appeared frightened. It was clear that she did not want to upset him.

"There wasn't really anything going on," she said. "He made several advances, yes. But I never gave in. We are good friends, that is all."

Vladimir's face underwent a terrible alteration. He raised his fist over his head and sent it crashing down onto the table before him.

"You are lying!" he exclaimed vehemently. "You can't fool me with your lies. You are sleeping with him. The American, Endicott, has as much as told me so. Admit it. Why can't you admit this?"

"Vladimir, I . . ." she began.

"Don't even bother. The guilt is written all over your face. What do you see in him? He doesn't care about you. He just wants you for sex. Can't you see that?"

"He doesn't mean anything to me." She was trying hard to remain calm.

"He doesn't mean anything to you," Vladimir repeated sarcastically. He knew that his anger was out of control and that he would regret what he said later, but he was unable to stop himself. He was pacing back and forth. "Then why the hell are you sleeping with him? How do you suppose that makes me feel? Answer me that."

"Vladimir, listen to me, I'm not sleeping with him," she said.

"Yes you are," he said. "Endicott wouldn't make something like that up."

"You must have misunderstood him."

"The deception is over, Tanya."

"I . . ." she faltered.

He watched her with a growing sense of distaste. She pulled her falling hair back behind her ears and with one hand held it there. Her lips quivered with half-formed words. He took this as a sign of her guilt, and at that instant he imagined Komarov having sex with her. By the time he spoke, his face was bright red with fury.

"You disgust me," he declared. "I thought you were different, but I was wrong. It's all over between us. I will not be married to a slut."

He spat upon the monitor and walked away, calling her names that he knew she must have heard. He went to get the vodka that he kept in his compartment. After he had time to calm down and had finished several drinks, he became upset with himself for having lost his temper. He did not know if she would forgive him. The thought filled him with despair, and he decided to drink until he passed out so that he wouldn't have to think about it anymore.

Within an hour after the cameras had captured the geyser spewing water fifty to sixty meters into the Martian sky, Satomura and Tatiana were aboard the blimp heading for the site. Satomura extracted a laptop from his backpack and plugged it into the main console. Looking over at Tatiana while his programs loaded, he could see that she was distracted.

"How did it go with Vladimir?" he asked.

She spoke for nearly fifteen minutes. Satomura listened as he typed, only once stopping her to ask for clarification on a seemingly trivial point. When she concluded, he closed the laptop and stared out at the red cliffs that dominated the western horizon. He appeared to be keenly interested in their shape.

"I had hoped it would've gone better," he finally said.

Tatiana waited as long as her patience would bear. "What can be done?" she asked.

"We must be careful not to upset him further," Satomura replied. His helmet hid almost his entire profile. The only portion of his face visible to her was the pockmarked tip of his long,

rounded nose. "His condition is delicate. You must stop sleeping with Dmitri, of course. Your husband seems to know when
you are lying."

Her immediate reaction was indignation. It was none of the
old man's business with whom she slept. But the firmness in his
voice, the certainty that left no doubt he was correct, prevented
her from protesting immediately. During all the time she had
spent with him, no matter how disagreeable or self-centered he
might have been, she had never known Satomura to be wrong.
His helmet remained perfectly still, waiting silently for her
response.

She did not care for Dmitri in the way she cared for
Vladimir. Dmitri was a very handsome man with a winning way
about him, but she did not love him. Ending the affair would
not cause her any great grief. What troubled her was how
Dmitri might react. His persistence in his lovemaking caused
Tatiana to think that he might truly love her. But even if he
didn't, he would still take offense. It was his nature. The very
thought of him angry with her concerned her greatly. He was a
powerful man, and he was her commander, and if he so wished
he could do considerable damage to her career. He might even
threaten her physically. Oddly enough, it was his power that she
found most attractive about him.

As if guessing her thoughts, Satomura said, "I have spoken
with Dmitri."

In her surprise, she did not know whether to be frightened
or relieved.

"What did he say?"

"He agreed, under the circumstances, that it would be best,"
Satomura said.

She wondered if he had agreed willingly, and made a mental
note to press Satomura for details later. For now, she was satisfied, and actually quite relieved.

"Of course," she said. "You are right."

"Good," he replied, and clapped his hands together.

Other than the tapping of Satomura's keyboard, the remainder of the flight passed mostly in silence. Tatiana brought the dirigible to a halt when it was two hundred meters out from the geyser. It was spewing water nearly sixty meters into the air, and the disturbance it produced in the atmosphere caused the dirigible to rock. Most of the water turned to ice before it struck the ground. They could hear a deep rumbling sound.

"Magnificent," Satomura muttered.

"I want you to land well outside the radius of the falling debris," Komarov interjected over the intercom.

"A distance of fifty meters . . ." Tatiana began.

"One hundred," Komarov countered.

"That should do nicely," Satomura said, pointing at a spot not quite one hundred meters out. Tatiana directed the dirigible toward the site.

Satomura jumped out of the dirigible and ran toward the geyser without waiting for Tatiana. He stopped at the edge of the geyser, a falling mixture of water and ice, and placed his arms akimbo. Some of the water that struck the ground bubbled up and boiled away before it could freeze. The ice had formed tiny spheres, inside of which the water was still liquid. A misty vapor rose from the ice. The water was actually boiling and freezing at the same time. Satomura was not surprised. The phenomenon resulted from the combination of low atmospheric pressure and subzero temperatures. He knew now that the ice they had collected on their first visit was not just permafrost. It, too, was from the subsurface river, which meant his chances of finding life had diminished, since he had already examined similar samples. He took a step backwards, not to move out of danger, but to obtain a better view of the entire geyser. Tatiana tapped him on the shoulder.

"The ship is secured," she said, annoyed that he had left her to do this by herself.

"Good," he responded. After a momentary pause, he swung both arms majestically over his head and held them there, his whole body trembling. "What do you think of it?"

Tatiana glanced up and rapidly took several steps backwards, her look of annoyance transforming to one of astonishment.

"Aren't you a little close?" she asked.

Upon hearing Tatiana's concern, Komarov ordered them to retreat to a safe distance. Satomura spun rapidly around, his eyes wild with excitement, and marched over to Tatiana, who had moved back another several meters.

"We must collect what we can," he blurted.

Tatiana watched with amazement as he disappeared into the mist and returned several minutes later with two collection bags full of samples. Water that had clung to his suit was bubbling, and a cloud of vapors surrounded him as if his suit were smoldering. He placated Komarov by telling him that the ice in the ejecta was too small to do any harm. Tatiana wasn't certain that the ice was harmless, but she did not say anything.

They worked continuously for several hours, Satomura running into the mist and back, while Tatiana carried the bags to the dirigible. The ice in the bags was murky, and when Tatiana pointed that out to Satomura, he said that it was a promising sign. She held a bag up to the sun, but did not see anything of interest. Since they were able to collect the water at the surface, there was no need to set up the drill. They both felt the drill wouldn't have been sturdy enough to withstand the pressure. The geyser had gained over ten meters in height by the time they had filled the last bag.

As they made their way back toward the dirigible, they were startled by how dark the sky in the distant horizon had become; neither had noticed the darkening before. It almost appeared as if a rainstorm were brewing in the distance, something they knew to be impossible; and after a few slow steps the possibility of a Martian dust storm occurred to them. They broke into a run.

Satomura shouted instructions in between gasps for air. "Dmitri, check the weather southeast of you!"

He was climbing into the dirigible when the response came back. "High winds," Komarov said excitedly. "One hundred and seventy-five kilometers per hour heading northwest. Temperatures are rising. The surface is completely obscured. It looks like a dust storm, and it's heading straight for us. Hold on." The sound of rapid typing could be heard in the background, then a momentary pause as they waited for Komarov to read the data displayed by the computer. "It will reach the lander in approximately one hour and forty-five minutes."

"Shut the hatch!" Tanya shouted. Satomura slammed his knee against the metal handle of the hatch and cursed out loud. His eyes watered with tears. With a groan and a curse he grabbed the handle. Through the open portal, he caught a glimpse of the geyser, reddish pink against the darkening sky, spurting as if it were a burst artery.

"We're going up in five seconds," Tatiana announced.

Pulling back with what strength he could muster, Satomura drew the hatch shut. He dropped limply into his chair, and as he rubbed his knee he considered the dangers of being caught in a dust storm. He knew that the force of the wind was not as great as it would have been on Earth. In fact, it was one-tenth as strong because the atmospheric pressure of Mars was less than that of Earth's. But there was still much to be concerned about. Dust entrained by the wind would be highly abrasive and could damage the hull of the dirigible. It would obscure the surface and might even interfere with the mechanics of the ship. But what troubled him the most was that the winds might increase in speed. They had been known to exceed four hundred kilometers per hour. This was the equivalent of a forty-kilometer-per-hour wind on Earth, which was too high for the dirigible to fly through safely. It was also too high for the lander. And since the dirigible would be flying against the wind, their progress would be slowed. He knew that the canyon might actually intensify the winds.

"We should be able to reach the lander with about ten minutes to spare," Tatiana said. "That won't give us enough time to deflate the dirigible."

"Nor will it give me enough time to prepare the *Gagarin* for departure," Komarov said. They were scheduled to leave the planet in two weeks. "I'd better alert the *Shepard*."

When Nelson came on-line several seconds later, Komarov instructed him to pull up the transmission he had just sent him.

"What am I looking at?"

"It is a satellite image of a dust storm, and it's heading northwest at approximately one hundred and seventy-five kilometers per hour," Komarov said.

"It probably won't get this far. Dust storms are normally confined to the southern hemisphere. But just in case, we'll batten down the hatches. It shouldn't last for more than a few days."

"It looks as if it's getting larger," Komarov said. "I am comparing the first photograph with one that has just come in. I estimate that its north–south axis has increased by five kilometers."

"You'd best get to work. Good luck, Dmitri."

During the interval prior to the storm's arrival, Komarov and Nelson performed emergency EVAs to secure equipment and tie down the protective tarps that covered the landers. Carter coordinated their activities from a laptop in his bunk, while Endicott reported on the storm's progress. They tried to reach Vladimir, but he did not respond to their call. The horizon grew more menacing with each passing second.

Tatiana could not get the dirigible to achieve its maximum speed and suggested to Satomura that he dump some of the samples to lighten their load. He sorted through the samples and threw two of the bags out. Upset but knowing that he would not part with more, she told him to throw out whatever else he could. Their speed increased slightly, but not enough to make her feel any more comfortable. Every time she glanced out the side window the storm appeared closer. By the time the dirigible was in sight of the camp, the winds had picked up another twenty kilometers per hour.

Tatiana pointed at a small figure, which she knew to be Komarov, standing next to the *Gagarin*. Komarov stepped forward and waved his arms over his head. The sky above him was a mixture of colors, a whirlpool of yellow, maroon, and dark gray.

"Get on the ground," Komarov shouted. "You only have a few minutes."

"I'm taking her down," Tatiana said.

"Take as many collection bags as you can," Satomura said.

"To hell with the collection bags," Komarov said. "Just get the hell off that thing."

When the ship touched ground, Tatiana kicked the door open and jumped out. Satomura was right behind her, with several bags in his arms. The dust was swirling at their feet. They took a few minutes to secure the dirigible and then walked quickly for the lander. Now that they were off the dirigible the winds posed less of a danger. They could stand upright in a two-hundred-kilometer-per-hour wind as if it were a mild zephyr. Komarov helped them into the airlock.

As they rested against the walls of the chamber to catch their breath, they heard the first sounds of the storm. It began with a low whistle. Gradually, the whistle grew louder and became high-pitched.

"Two hundred kilometers per hour and still increasing," came Endicott's voice over the intercom, and all eyes turned toward the monitor on which he appeared. "It is growing fast. I have several satellite photographs, each taken fifteen minutes apart. I'll display them on the monitor."

The Valles Marineris Canyon dominated the lower half of the picture, running horizontally, east to west. They recognized Candor Chasma, at the northwest tip of the Marineris system, and the mesa inside Candor upon which their lander was perched.

"This picture of the storm was taken just minutes before you first noticed it. If you look southeast of the landing site, at the very edge of Candor Chasma, you can see where the surface features are blurred. Dust from the winds is obscuring the surface."

The second picture depicted a storm system that had grown nearly twice in size from the first. The storm continued to grow in the third and the fourth, and by the sixth it had reached the edge of the mesa. The mesa was completely covered in the seventh.

"It looks as if it might be going global," Satomura said.

"The models I've run have the storm dissipating within a few days. But it does have sufficient force to lift the dust into the lower atmosphere. You might be right."

Endicott removed the photograph and replaced it with a mosaic of the western hemisphere. The small corner of the planet they occupied was blurred, as if someone had smudged it with an eraser. "This mosaic was generated just five minutes ago."

Satomura rudely stepped in between the two cosmonauts and placed himself directly in front of the screen. "Overlay wind and pressure patterns." Seconds later the photograph was covered with dotted lines, animated arrows, and neon numbers. Satomura traced the patterns with his fingers as he hummed a tune that no one recognized.

His lips twitched to form a brief smile before he spoke. "The local winds and the tidal winds appear to be augmenting each other. This could produce a runaway situation. Notice the tornadoes to the south. I suspect we will have the opportunity to observe the development of a global dust storm firsthand. We must make haste. There is much work to be done."

Komarov was not in any hurry. He instructed the crew to take their time and be thorough as they cleared the airlock of dust.

Carter opened the package of mixed Italian vegetables and poured its contents onto his plate. The vegetables sounded like balsa wood. Resisting the temptation to pluck an uncooked piece, he added water, stirred, and placed the tray inside the microwave. He turned the timer to three minutes and switched on the nearest monitor to view the latest news from Earth.

The newscaster was in her mid-forties and had grown more attractive with age. Her hair was dark and cut short in a style that had fallen out of fashion several years before, but she bore the style well, and Carter felt certain that no one, even her producer, would suggest a change. He stared unabashedly at her blouse and cursed when her image was replaced by a news clip. The planet Mars appeared on the screen, but much of its familiar markings were missing. They were replaced by dark swirls. The title GLOBAL DUST STORM appeared in black letters across the screen.

He could hear Nelson approaching, then felt a hand on his shoulder. Neither said anything.

A shot of Carter's cast appeared on the screen. The camera pulled back to show his entire body leaning upon a pair of makeshift crutches. Balancing most of his weight on the crutch farther from his broken leg, he lifted his free arm and waved at the camera. The shot switched to Nelson, who was studying the most recent weather map. He looked up briefly and smiled. A businesslike voice was commenting upon the crew being in good spirits. A brief shot of the Russian crew, then two still photos of Endicott and Vladimir, a photo of Brunnet, then Dr.

James D. Cain standing behind a podium, besieged by reporters and flashing bulbs.

Dr. Cain threw a switch on the panel built into the podium, and a satellite picture of Mars appeared behind him. As the lights dimmed, a laser beam sprang from the pointer in his hand. "This area, as you can see, has no visible surface features. They are blocked from our view by the beginnings of a global dust storm. It has formed a veil over the two landing sites and—"

Carter turned off the volume and glanced at his watch.

"What are you doing?" Nelson asked.

"Timing the broadcast."

Nelson considered this, but refrained from comment. They had just watched a similar broadcast a half hour earlier. The mosaic of Mars was replaced by a photograph of Amazonis Planitia; the entire photograph was a blur except for its northern edge. Nelson watched the silent screen for a while, then said, "It's not as bad as it looks."

"They say this thing could last nearly three months."

"The global storm, yes. But the winds are relatively light. Ten to thirty kilometers. The lander can handle that. We've got nineteen days before the launch window to Earth closes. That gives us plenty of time to pick a safe launch date."

"Not if we're caught in the same storm that struck the Russians," Carter said. "They're reporting winds over two hundred kilometers per hour."

"It should let up in a few days."

The news station flashed its logo on the screen. The picture switched to the Russian press room and Colonel Schebalin, who was fielding questions from reporters. A final shot of Mars, features obliterated, and the news anchor was beginning another story as if the first had never taken place. The buzzer for the food startled both men.

"Exactly three minutes," Carter observed wryly. "That's a minute and a half less than yesterday's report."

"You should take it as a positive sign," Colonel Nelson replied. "There is a direct relation between airtime and perceived danger."

Carter gazed at his food with disappointment. He switched the monitor to a view of the surface. The sky was overcast with what appeared to be yellow clouds of dust. Other than that there was no other evidence of a global dust storm. The sand on the ground did not move. A readout on the lower part of the screen showed that the wind speed was only eighteen kilometers per hour.

"Did you replace the CO_2-detector cartridges this morning?"

Carter nodded that he had. He did not like the way the sky looked. It had the eerie stillness of the calm before a storm. With his leg still healing there wasn't much they could do on the surface. The risk was too great to conduct an EVA with one astronaut. It seemed to him that they should just leave. But he knew that there were surface experiments that still needed to be collected, and that in a few days his leg would be strong enough for him to participate in their collection.

"How are you feeling?" Nelson asked.

"I'll survive." Carter swept up the remaining juices with his fingers as he stared out at the barren landscape. He was troubled that his immobility had resulted in the cancellation of several of the mission objectives and that it seemed now to be a factor in most of the decisions that were made.

Dust Storm

Propelled by the force of Komarov's fist pounding smartly against the table, an aluminum meal tray with two empty food containers jumped several centimeters into the air and flipped twice before landing upon the floor. The resulting clatter did not distract Tatiana from the monitor that displayed the tarp flapping loosely in the wind.

"Damn," Komarov cursed. The faintly foul smell of rehydrated eggs filled the compartment. He took a sip of his coffee and nearly burned his mouth. "I'll radio Kaliningrad and inform them we are going out for an emergency EVA to secure the tarp."

"Shouldn't we wait till the storm has passed?" Tatiana asked.

"I'm worried about dust buildup in the engine manifolds."

"We're not supposed to leave the lander during a local storm," she said. "It's a safety violation."

"Unless it is an emergency," Komarov replied. "And I consider this an emergency. The dust could interfere with the operation of the engines."

"I agree," Tatiana conceded. She still felt it would be better to wait. The storm was only supposed to last another twelve hours.

"Meet me in the airlock," Komarov said. "I'll inform Takashi."

Komarov found the scientist bent over a microscope in the laboratory, which was a multipurpose compartment, much too small, that also served as the crew quarters. Satomura often skipped meals or ate them without bothering to prepare them properly. He felt his time was better spent working. Komarov, who now stood directly behind the hunched back of the scientist, cleared his throat. His presence was acknowledged with a low grumble. Having relayed his intent to perform an EVA and the need for Satomura to monitor the activity, Komarov left, uncertain that he had been heard.

It was not until he and Tatiana completed their final cross-check that Satomura emerged from the lab and took his place at the command station.

"All systems check," he said. "You are clear for EVA."

"Opening airlock portal," Komarov replied.

They had tied blankets around their suits to protect them from the dust. A rope, thirty-five meters in length, was attached to a harness that crisscrossed the torso of each of their space suits. It was connected to a hook on the wall. Komarov tugged on the ropes to make certain they were secured, then keyed in the final sequence that opened the portal.

The tarp was billowing outward, and a faint reddish mist blew into the airlock. He could see through the tarp; it was made of a clear plastic. The sky was overcast, and a cloud of dust was heading toward the lander. The eastern edge of the tarpaulin had pulled free from the ground and had allowed an opening for the wind and the dust to enter. The dust came in bursts. He could vaguely make out the loose coils of rope where the dirigible had broken free from its moorings. A strong gust had sent it into the side of the canyon.

They could hear the howling of the storm through their helmets as they climbed down the ladder and made for the eastern edge of the tarpaulin. The wind was blowing at a speed of 150 kilometers per hour, but they could barely feel it. The dust streaked past them and made it difficult for them to see. Two of the stakes that held the covering to the ground had come loose. Tatiana held the tarp in place while Komarov pounded the stakes into the rocky surface. She looked through the plastic and when a wave of dust had passed saw that the surface appeared unchanged. The winds were not strong enough to lift the sand. When they had finished, they took a moment to look at each other and were surprised to see that the blankets, which had been white, had turned red from the dust.

They then noticed that the lower half of the lander was also red. That troubled Tatiana. She got down on her knees and examined a nozzle extension. She did not like what she saw. The interior was caked with dust. She told Komarov to get some brushes and began to clear what she could with her hand. She decided they would have to rig some sort of extension to the vacuum, but could wait to do so until after the storm. They had worked for two and half hours when Tatiana straightened her back and declared that she had done all she could. Komarov was exhausted and did not object. Tatiana had been avoiding him since the beginning of the storm, which he decided had been Satomura's doing. But it did not trouble him as much as he had thought it would. Now that they would be leaving the planet soon, he was growing more concerned about Vladimir. He did not want to push him over the edge.

Upon closing the portal, they dropped to the floor and listened to the howling of the wind. It took nearly an hour to clear the dust from the airlock. The blankets they had worn to protect their suits were impregnated with the fine particles. They had to store the blankets in plastic bags. They stretched their

arms and tested their legs, taking small steps as if to make certain they could still walk.

As they stepped into the main compartment of the lander,
they were grabbed by the shoulders and wrapped together in a
large hug. Utterly shocked, but too weak to resist, they stood in
place and waited for Satomura to release them. Satomura took a
step back, held them at arm's length, and was about to make
another joyful lunge for them when Komarov raised his hand in
protest. Tatiana retreated to the nearest chair.

"What has gotten into you?" Komarov demanded.

"Follow me," Satomura cried excitedly, and plunged down
the corridor.

Komarov and Tatiana exchanged curious glances. Tatiana
shrugged and stood up. It was clear to both they had no other
choice; neither had ever seen Satomura so excited, and they
knew he would hunt them down if they did not follow. Pausing
for a moment to gather their strength, they plodded after him.

They found Satomura in the laboratory, standing proudly
next to the microscope with his left hand extended, asking them
to take a look. Neither Komarov nor Tatiana had the slightest
clue as to the source of all the excitement, but when they saw
the microscope and the glee in Satomura's face, they both felt
chills run down their spines.

Komarov took a hesitant step forward.

"Go ahead," Satomura said, encouraging him.

The entire microscope, except for the eyepiece, was encased
in a small glass box that sat upon a table. Built into the side of
the box were two openings, attached to which, dangling limp,
were a pair of thin plastic gloves. The outside glass was spotted
with condensation. Komarov was familiar enough with the box
to notice with some surprise that it had been altered. The glass
had been tinted pink and an additional tube fed into a hole in
the rear of the box. This angered him since it was a violation of
safety regulations, but he did not say anything. He sat down

upon the stool and slid his hands into the gloves. Taking a deep breath, he cocked his head and placed an eye upon the lens.

It took him several seconds to adjust the image. He saw a colony of what he assumed to be single-celled creatures moving frantically about in a film of pink liquid. He was reminded of the amoebas he had studied in grade school. He heard Satomura talking excitedly in the background and could feel Tatiana nudging his shoulder. He did not want to relinquish the microscope. "One moment," he said. He watched with amazement as a cell divided in half. Two cells, slightly smaller than the original, otherwise identical, floated their separate ways. He pushed back his chair and stood up; his hands were wet with perspiration.

"What do you make of it?" he asked, not having heard a word Satomura had said.

The scientist shook his head at the interruption and allowed several seconds to pass before he continued. "Fission is the self-replication of a molecule. The whole process of evolution began with that primary function. The Drake equation predicted the inevitability of this moment. It calculates the probability of intelligent life on other planets." Tatiana pushed past her commander and sat down. She held her breath as she placed her right eye against the eyepiece of the microscope. "The equation is quite simple. Several factors, such as the number of stars and the number of planets around those stars and so on, are multiplied together to give a probability. There were six factors in the original equation. It has since been modified to determine the probability of life not only on other planets, but on all other possible habitats. Even space itself. Life need not exist on a planet." Komarov was more amazed by Satomura's manner than by the content of his speech. The permanent frown had been replaced by a genuine, untainted smile. "The probability calculated by Drake was fifty billion to one."

This last figure caught Komarov's attention, and Tatiana actually looked up from the microscope.

"Fifty billion?" Komarov questioned incredulously.

"Approximately, of course," Satomura responded with a laugh. "And that is for intelligent life. The probability of primitive life-forms is considerably higher. You are looking at samples that were collected during our first trip to the geyser. We had the evidence nearly a month ago. I simply did not recognize it."

"How can that be?" Tatiana asked.

"In certain respects the life-form is similar to the amoeba. When exposed to adverse conditions, it assumes a circular shape, ejects most of its liquid, and secretes a cyst membrane for protection. Not being a biologist, I mistook the damn thing for a grain of sand." This time he roared with laughter. "It will shed its shell when the environment is once again favorable. The temperature I started with was much too high, and, unknowingly, I fried the cells before they had a chance to revive. The breakthrough came while you were in the airlock." They waited as Satomura coughed and produced a handkerchief to wipe his mouth. Komarov glanced over at the altered enclosure with some uncertainty. Satomura returned the handkerchief to his pocket, then proudly pointed at the enclosure. "Thirty-three minutes ago I discovered life on Mars."

The two cosmonauts stared at the wild-eyed scientist, speechless. He stood there, waiting for them to congratulate him. Komarov clasped his hand and shook it heartily; Tatiana swung back to the microscope to make certain she had not been hallucinating.

"I must inform Endicott," Satomura announced, and left the compartment in a great hurry.

Overwhelmed by the event, Komarov sat down to collect his thoughts. He looked at Tatiana, who was bent intently over the microscope, then at the altered enclosure, then back at Tatiana. His gaze settled upon the enclosure.

"The old man did it," she said with a conviction that seemed to indicate she always knew he would.

"I don't think that thing is safe," Komarov said. His voice was low and serious and had a sobering effect.

She knew immediately what he meant. Would the altered enclosure safely contain the microscopic creatures within? She stood up to obtain a better view of the contraption and, after some thought, took a precautionary step backwards. Komarov brushed past her. They studied the joints, the rubber seals, the painted glass, and the black tube leading to a jar neither could recall ever seeing. The bottom half of the jar contained a reddish liquid that bubbled, and the top half a pinkish haze. After several minutes of circling, they decided the enclosure did not pose an immediate threat.

"Nonetheless," Komarov said, "it is in violation of safety regulations. He will have to dismantle it."

"He will not like that." Tatiana decided that she did not like Komarov's attitude. It was so like him to cite regulations to get his way. "He will challenge the decision. This is perhaps the most significant discovery in the history of mankind. RSA may back him."

"He can continue his research aboard the *Druzhba*," Komarov retaliated. He looked tired and irritated. "I will not permit him to endanger our lives like this."

The sky was overcast with yellow clouds of dust. Otherwise, the planet appeared normal. Carter steered around a rock that blocked the way of the rover and, looking out at the horizon, decided the term "dust storm" was inappropriate for the calm conditions that prevailed. His leg was still wrapped, but had healed enough for him to move about. The wrapping was underneath the liquid cooling garment. He and Nelson were en route to a lava tube, the entrance to which a miniature rover had found several days earlier. The vehicle had only explored the first forty meters because its radio signal wasn't strong enough to pass through the tube's ceiling. The tube was exceptionally large and was at the base of a geological formation that appeared to have been carved by water rather than lava. Carter doubted the tube's scientific value was the reason the EVA had been approved. Now that the Russians had discovered life on Mars, he figured the Americans were desperate to accomplish something of equal importance.

This was the first time Carter was out since he had broken his leg, and he found it difficult to concentrate on his driving as he thought of the tube. He had been inside several caves on Earth as a child, and his recollection of the experience invoked feelings of awe and wonder. The lava tube, at 50 kilometers in length and 250 meters in width, would dwarf the caves of his childhood. He had read that a lava tube would make a good location for the habitats of future explorers, since its ceiling provided protection against solar radiation. This thought intrigued him. He wondered what it would be like to live underground for an extended period of time, and decided that it couldn't be any worse than being cooped up in a spacecraft for nine months. Nelson was pointing out a detour on the map that took them around a smaller tube. The map was a seismic profile of the subsurface structures. It scrolled across the monitor as they moved so that they could see the structures immediately ahead of them.

Prior to their landing, and again just prior to the EVA, a rover from the supply ship had sounded for tubes and other structures that might pose a danger. A tube, which was formed by flowing lava that had crusted over, sometimes formed a mound at the surface, but not always; usually the only visible sign was a line of pits that marked its path. The pits were best seen from an aerial viewpoint. Since tubes were most often near the surface, their thin ceilings could collapse under the weight of whatever passed over them.

They caught a flash of light in the distance and knew it to be the miniature rover. He pointed out the location to Nelson. The tube could not be seen.

"OK, you should be all right if you head straight for it," Nelson said. "The entrance is just beyond the rover."

They stopped twenty meters short of the miniature rover, at a point where the map indicated the ground beneath them was still solid. Nelson slapped Carter on the back as he turned the engine off. They grabbed the halogen flashlights and, without bothering to gather the remainder of their gear, walked straight to the vehicle. They spotted what looked like a dried-up riverbed. It sank nearly forty meters beneath the surface and ended at an opening that was large enough for both of them to walk through. Nelson had to hold Carter back.

"We should collect our gear first." He opened the comm channel to the *Gagarin*. "Takashi, can you see it?"

"Yes, yes. Please make haste."

Satomura was to take the miniature rover into areas of the tube that the astronauts felt might not be safe. The rover was to be equipped with several comm relay units that it could drop off along the way in order to extend its range.

It took nearly fifteen minutes to prepare the equipment, which consisted of flashlights, ropes, aseptic samplers, scoops, tongs, picks, brushes, sample-collection bags, and the comm relay units. As Carter finished packing the last of the items, he saw the rover take off ahead of them.

They were careful as they descended into the riverbed. Although the decline of the bank was not so steep that it was difficult to negotiate, the surrounding basaltic rock was quite sharp. This troubled Nelson, but he did not say anything. Their instructions had been clear. They were not to take any unnecessary risks and were to limit their exploration to the first two hundred meters, unless they spotted something of unusual scientific value. Satomura was to assist them in that determination.

The miniature rover darted into the dark entrance of the tube. Carter turned on the halogen flashlight and waited for

Nelson to catch up with him. He attempted to look into the cave, but the dim sunlight outside was too bright for his eyes to adjust. They placed a comm relay unit at the entrance of the tube.

Colonel Nelson stepped inside with Carter immediately behind. They froze in astonishment at the sight that stretched out before them. The cavern was huge. To think that it had been formed by flowing lava was almost beyond comprehension. The halogen light barely reached the other end. It seemed to Carter that a fleet of ocean liners could fit inside of it. The rock was reddish black and porous. Light streamed from the cracks and pits in the ceiling and was diffused by thin vaporous clouds. They were about twenty meters from the floor of the tube, and after nearly a minute of scanning their surroundings with the narrow beams of their flashlights they commenced their descent.

"We need to find the source of that moisture," Satomura declared.

Carter looked around for the rover and saw that it was almost out of view. Upon reaching the floor of the tube, the two astronauts stood speechless as they scanned the walls of the cavern. The tube extended as far as the eye could see in either direction.

"We are to go northwest," Nelson said, and pointed the flashlight where they had last seen the rover. "Toward the volcano. It looks as if the temperature has risen a few degrees."

"Thermal activity," Satomura replied. "It was expected. But there is no need to be concerned. Olympus Mons has been dormant for several million years. An eruption would be a spectacular sight though. Don't you agree?"

The astronauts did not bother to reply.

The floor of the cavern was remarkably smooth, but littered with rocks that had evidently fallen from the walls and the ceiling. Carter bent down and picked up a rock that was the size of his fist. It looked much like the rocks he had seen on the surface, which he knew meant the rock was rich in iron. The orange tint was rust. He tossed it before him as if he were skipping a rock on a pond. Nelson looked at him disapprovingly.

They struck out in the direction that they had last seen the rover. The cavern seemed to go on forever. The occasional pit in the ceiling made Nelson uneasy, but Satomura assured him that there was nothing to be concerned about. They only stopped once to collect samples. They would fill their bags on the return trip in order to limit the length of time they would be carrying the additional weight. Upon reaching the two hundred meters, Carter suggested that they break to eat lunch, and plopped himself on a rock before Nelson had time to object. The miniature rover was nowhere in sight.

"I've never seen anything like it," Carter said after a while.

Nelson nodded in agreement. He was looking in the direction of the rover, wondering where Satomura had gotten off to. The meal of rehydrated mixed vegetables he sucked in through the tube was barely palatable. When he had finished eating, he stood up and shined the halogen light down the length of the cavern. "We're about to head back, Takashi."

"I may have found something of interest," Satomura said excitedly. "It is a passageway that is not part of the tube. Both temperature and barometric pressure have increased remarkably. Some sort of heat anomaly. Most likely volcanic in origin. Could be cryptovulcanism, which is subsurface magmatic intrusion. I may need you to check it out."

"How far are you from our position?" Nelson asked hesitantly.

"The entrance to the passageway is approximately three hundred meters from your current location."

"I'm not so sure we can do that," Nelson said.

"Give me a few more minutes. I suspect that I am near the source."

"We could collect some samples while we wait," Carter said. If Satomura was on to something, he wanted to see it. But he knew that Nelson wasn't keen on the idea. He also knew that whenever it suited Nelson's purpose the letter could very easily become the law. To his surprise, Nelson concurred.

They thought of the passage as they worked. It wasn't necessary for them to concentrate on what they were doing. They had collected many samples already, and knew instinctively which ones the scientists were most interested in. The actual selection of which rocks were to go back to Earth with them would take place at the lander. They had filled several bags when Satomura interrupted their work.

"I've found the source," he said, his voice trembling. "You may want to pull up the video feed from the rover."

They did as he requested, and in a window on their heads-up display there appeared the inside of a cave. There was a large body of water. Occasionally, a bubble appeared at the surface and burst, sending ripples outward. Steam was rising from the walls of the cave, and a heavy cloud hung over the water. Although they could not be certain, the walls seemed to be of different colors.

"Now watch this," Satomura said, as if he were a magician.

He turned the lights of the rover off and for a moment the image in the window went black. But then colored lights began to appear. The walls of the cave were glowing. Patches of red and green and blue and purple shone dimly from the walls. The water seemed to be flickering. A light would appear, then disappear.

"What on Earth is it?" Nelson asked.

"Not exactly an appropriate expression, is it?" Satomura replied. "What you are witnessing is not terrestrial."

"Spare me the lesson in semantics. I just want to know what it is."

"I suspect the walls of the cave are composed of phosphorescent rock. Although I must admit, I am a bit puzzled about the light in the lake. It is probably pebble-sized fragments of phosphorescent rock being brought to the surface by the bubbles. Although its movement seems to suggest something else."

"Something else?"

"If you watch closely, there is random horizontal movement. Since the movement is random, we have to eliminate current. It's almost as if the lights are moving by their own power."

"What are you suggesting?"

"Well, I am reluctant to say until I've had a better look." He paused for a moment. "However, if I were to speculate, I would say that the light is being produced by an aquatic life-form."

"There are fish in that lake?" Carter asked incredulously.

"Fish? Well, I suppose you could call them that," Satomura replied. "The only way to determine for certain is for you to go there."

"How far is the lake from our current position?" Nelson asked.

"Approximately six hundred meters."

There was a pause as Nelson considered this.

"That shouldn't be a problem," Carter said.

"Suppose it is a life-form?" Nelson said. "How do we know it's not dangerous?"

"For crissakes," Carter said. "What do you think we have here? Some kind of space monster?"

Nelson scowled at Carter. Their conversation would be heard back on Earth.

"Switching to voice channel nine," Nelson said. The channel allowed them to speak privately. "I don't know what we have here. What I do know is that I am responsible for our safety. I must evaluate the risk."

"It's a damn fish. Fish don't just jump out of the water and attack you."

"Takashi?"

"To speculate that it is a fish or any other form of life is premature. I suggest we take the rover to the edge of the water and see what happens. If whatever is in there doesn't attack the rover, then we can probably assume that it won't attack you." Satomura emphasized the word *attack* so that it was clear that he felt the measure was an unnecessary precaution.

Nelson considered Satomura's suggestion, attempting not to be annoyed by his tone.

"We'll observe the area for ten minutes and then decide."

The rover pulled up to the lake and stopped. They watched the occasional ripple and the flickering lights, and the more they watched the lights the more they convinced themselves that their source was something other than fragments of phosphorescent rock. The light was clear, unlike the colored rock on the cave wall. Sometimes it zigzagged, but it never lasted for more than a few seconds. They watched the water in anticipation of something breaking the surface. At the end of ten minutes, Carter motioned that he was switching back to voice channel nine.

"I say we check it out."

"We still don't know what it is. I think we should speak with mission control first."

"Jesus," Carter said. "That'll take at least forty-five minutes, and then there's no guarantee that they'll let us go. This may be our only chance. I say we take it."

"If the risk is yours," Satomura said, "so should be the decision."

Carter could see that this angered Nelson, who, when in doubt, usually did things by the book. Nelson walked up to a rock and placed his foot upon it. He looked down the cavern and estimated in his mind how long it would take to traverse the distance. Nearly a minute passed before he announced his decision.

"OK, we go, but we turn back the moment I feel it is not safe."

"I agree," Carter said, relieved.

They decided to leave the samples they had collected on top of a rock that could be easily seen from a distance. Carter dumped out the contents of one of the bags in hope of filling it with something of greater importance. Nelson noticed, but did not say anything. He was preoccupied, wondering how he would justify his decision to mission control. They had already gone as far as they were authorized, unless they discovered something of scientific value. This clearly qualified, but the nature of their discovery bothered him. He knew that they should probably observe the site for at least a day. But even then there was always the possibility, for whatever reason, that NASA might not let them go. Time was short. They were to launch in five days. He knew this might be their only chance, and he, like the others, was convinced the light in the lake was more than just phosphorescent rock.

They walked quickly in the direction of the cave, the beams of their flashlights swaying up and down with their footsteps. The mist above their heads seemed to grow thicker, but the change was not great enough for them to be certain. The occasional opening in the ceiling threw faint rays into the mist. The ground sloped downward, and Carter estimated that they were at least fifty meters beneath the surface. This struck Carter as odd since they were heading toward the volcano, but he could see in the distance that the ground sloped upward again. Carter was thinking of the cave that Satomura had found. It seemed to him that the lights could only be one thing. Martian life. A life-form that was far more substantial than what Satomura had discovered at the geyser. The very thought filled him with excitement and apprehension.

They were at the entrance of the cave within what seemed only a matter of minutes. The comm relay unit left by the rover was at their feet. Nelson took the lead. The entrance was only large enough for one person to pass through at a time. A white mist was blowing out from the entrance. It was clearly the source of at least some of the moisture. Carter had to keep an eye on the roof of the passage to keep from striking his helmet against it. He could touch the walls on either side of him. They were different from the walls of the lava tube. The rock was not porous and wasn't as dark. It reminded him of the rock he had seen in caves on Earth. He stayed several feet behind Nelson so as not to bump into him. They were descending deeper beneath the surface. After they had walked nearly two hundred meters, the ground began to rise. They paused to catch their breath. The outside temperature was getting warmer, and they adjusted their liquid cooling garments to compensate. Carter swung the flashlight beam from his feet to the roof. The passage was becoming narrower. Nelson came to an abrupt stop.

"What is it?" Carter asked.

"We're at the entrance," Nelson replied. He stepped forward, and Carter passed through after him.

The image presented by the rover had made the cave seem smaller than it actually was. Although there was a heavy mist in the air, they could see that the cave stretched several kilometers out from where they stood and that the roof was about fifty meters high. There were stalactites hanging from the roof. The rover was at the edge of the lake, about twenty meters away. The lake appeared to occupy the entire cave, except for the narrow shore that encircled it. They could see lights flickering in the water. The astronauts did not move. Instead they took their flashlights and scanned their surroundings. The ground at their feet was relatively smooth and seemed solid. There were patches of dim light on the wall.

"I suspect the cave is several hundred million years old," Satomura said. "Mars is not subject to the destructive force of plate tectonics, so structures like this can survive for quite some time."

Both Nelson and Carter were watching the lights in the water.

"The temperature of the lake," Satomura continued, "is three hundred and seven degrees Kelvin, which is remarkably high and, of course, above freezing. The temperature of the atmosphere is two hundred and seventy degrees."

Carter took a cautionary step forward, testing the ground with his foot. He thought that it might be slippery since it was glistening with moisture.

"Barometric pressure is two hundred millibars. The thick walls of the cave are containing the gases. The air is composed of carbon dioxide, nitrogen, water vapor, and some hydrogen sulfite. Not a pleasant environment, but much nicer than the surface."

Both Carter and Nelson were standing several feet from the edge of the lake. The water was clear, and they could see that the rocks beneath the water were covered by some sort of mossy substance. They waited for a light to appear. Several appeared in the distance, but none were close enough for them to make out their source. Satomura suggested that they turn their flashlights off. As their eyes adjusted, the lights around them became brighter and more colorful. Carter was tempted to go over to the walls for a closer look, but he held his position, waiting for another light in the lake. He did not have to wait long. Something was swimming toward them. They took a step back, even though whatever was swimming toward them was not much larger than a closed fist. It brightened suddenly, like a flashbulb, causing the astronauts to jump.

"Jesus," Carter said. "What the hell was that?"

It started to float away. They could see that it was gelatinous, and translucent, like a jellyfish, but it didn't look like any jellyfish they had ever seen. It possessed tentacles that snapped back and forth through the water, propelling the creature forward. Moments later it disappeared, and the water was calm.

"You must capture it," Satomura said.

"Jesus," Carter repeated. "What the hell was it?"

"It resembles a cephalopod. The light is probably a mating signal."

"Here comes something else," Nelson said.

Carter bent down for a closer look. The object was much smaller and looked something like a tadpole. A phosphorescent streak that resembled a lightning bolt marked its back. Two stalks protruded from its forehead; at the end of each was a dull-colored eyeball. It appeared to be grazing on the moss-covered rock. Carter flashed his light on it to obtain a better look, and the tadpolelike object darted away.

"It is afraid of the light," Satomura said. "It thinks you are a predator."

Carter scanned the surface of the lake with his flashlight. "How big do you think these creatures get?"

"Judging from the size of the lake, I doubt you'll find anything larger than a meter," Satomura said.

Carter took a step back and turned his flashlight to the luminous spots on the wall. There was something about the spots that troubled him. He could not be certain, but he thought that they pulsed. He was about to take a step toward them when Nelson grabbed his arm. Nelson was pointing at the center of the lake, where a geyserlike eruption had just broken the surface. The spouting water reached nearly ten meters high, then quickly subsided.

"The fish that produced that had to be hell of a lot bigger than one meter," Carter said.

"It wasn't a fish," Satomura replied. "I have observed the same phenomenon several times now. It seems to come in thirteen-minute intervals. I believe it's the primary source of the gases that fill the cave. It could be caused by the periodic release of gases built up from a hot vent. Such vents might have been where life first began on Earth."

Another cephalopod-like object came swimming toward them, and Carter shined his flashlight at it to scare it away. "I'm going to take a closer look at the wall," he said. Nelson nodded, but did not go with him. He bent down to examine the water.

Before Carter had even reached the wall, he was certain that the glowing spots were not phosphorescent rock. They were some sort of vegetation. It was similar in appearance to some of the lichen he had seen on Earth, with the notable exception that it glowed. He wondered why. And the spots were different colors, which seemed even stranger. The spots varied in size, from two to thirty centimeters in diameter, and were roughly circular. None of the spots actually touched each other. He then noticed some tiny movement. At first he thought it was just a trick of the light, but he approached the wall and saw that there were tiny insects crawling over the spots. These insects were no larger than aphids, and were the same white color as aphids, but they did not have any legs. They were pulling themselves along by some sort of pseudopod that extended outward from their body whenever they wanted to move forward. He had never seen anything quite like it. Then he noticed that the creatures were crawling between the spots, forming long lines, like ants do when they've found food.

"What do we have here?" Satomura said excitedly. He was watching the video from Carter's camera. "There appears to be a symbiotic relationship between those wormlike creatures and the vegetation."

"Why does it glow?" Carter asked.

"It could be a way to attract the worms. Or perhaps the colors signify different stages in the plant's development, which triggers certain behaviors in the worms. Or the plants could just be different species. Difficult to say without further examination."

Carter stepped closer to the rock. He felt like collecting several of the tiny worms in his hand, but did not want to contaminate his suit. He was amazed at how quickly they moved.

"We should bring back what we can," Nelson said.

"You'll need to return for additional samples," Satomura said. "The collection bags you have were not designed for transporting live specimens. A pressurized container is required."

"We may not have enough time. The next several days are filled with prelaunch activities."

"I'm certain they'll make an exception."

Nelson realized that Satomura was probably right, but he did not say anything to indicate that he agreed. He motioned for Carter to join him. "I'm going to need your help in catching one of these things."

Carter walked over and looked down into the water. He saw one of the jellyfishlike creatures approaching the edge of the lake. "Are you sure about this?"

"I'm going to hook him with the end of the pole and throw him up on the shore. I want you to use the tongs and place him inside a bag. I'll hold the bag open. Whatever you do, don't touch him. He might possess some sort of defense mechanism."

"Wouldn't it be easier if we came back with a net?"

"Yes, but there's no guarantee we'll be back. We need to collect what we can now."

Carter pulled out a collection bag and laid it out on the ground. He then produced the tongs, which were normally used to collect rock samples. "Ready," he said, taking several steps back so as to be out of the way.

Nelson carefully dipped the end of the pole into the water and rested it on a rock as he waited for another jellyfish to appear. His pulse quickened. He did not have to wait long. With a sudden swipe he caught the creature from behind and lifted it out of the water. It fell onto the rocks, glowing brightly and waving its tentacles around wildly.

"Jesus," Carter said.

Nelson picked up the bag and held it open.

"I think we should kill it first," Carter said. "I don't like the look of those tentacles."

"You might be right," Nelson said. He took the pole and thrust it into the creature. The tentacles wrapped tightly around the pole, then fell limp to the ground. Carter waited until he was certain it was dead before picking it up with the tongs. He placed the lifeless creature inside the bag. Nelson sealed the bag shut.

They looked at the bag and wondered about what they had just done. Nelson held the bag away from his body so that it would not touch him, even though he knew that there was no danger. The bag was designed to contain contaminants safely.

Carter did not feel good about killing the alien life-form. But he knew it had to be done. The creature had to be examined. This knowledge did not make him feel any better. He had followed halfheartedly the debate leading to the decision that they should bring back life-forms. There were those who felt any life found should be left undisturbed. And there were those who felt the life had to be studied. He had not paid much attention to the debate, but then he didn't really believe that they would find anything. Nor did the majority of the scientists, for that matter. But since the scientific value of such a discovery was so high, the outcome was never really in doubt. He watched as Nelson placed the bag on the ground.

"We need to collect a bag of that vegetation and some of those worms, or whatever they are," Nelson said.

They walked over to the wall where Carter had been standing and scraped the mosslike substance from the rock with a rake. It came off easily. They filled a bag with the substance and another with the worms. As he worked, Carter forgot about the guilt he had felt and began to wonder what the scientists on Earth would think about the samples they would bring back. He almost felt regret that he did not have children. He could see himself bouncing a grandchild on his knee, telling him about the time he had discovered life on Mars. He was careful not to touch the samples with his suit. They would have to undergo a thorough decontamination. When the bags were filled, he took one last look at the lake and watched as the geyser blew water into the air.

As the two astronauts walked back to the rover, mission control was talking excitedly about the cave. Because of the delay in the transmission, those on Earth had first seen it only moments ago. Carter chuckled to himself when mission control gave its belated recommendation to explore the cave.

They were preparing for the launch of the *Gagarin*, and each member of the crew was wondering if the engines would fire, although not one of them expressed this thought out loud. The prelaunch diagnostics had gone flawlessly, so they rationalized that this provided a good reason not to be concerned. The local storm had long since passed, and wind speed was thirteen kilometers per hour, which would not affect the liftoff. There was still dust from the global storm in the lower atmosphere, but that did not trouble them. The launch was to take place in fifteen minutes.

Vladimir appeared to be looking down upon his colleagues from the monitor above their heads. The strain of the past month had sucked the fullness from his cheeks and made him look much older. His condition had worsened after his last talk with Tatiana, but in the past several days he had shown some improvement. His eyes were clear, no longer streaked with red lines; he had apparently put aside the bottle. His hair was neatly trimmed. His voice did not tremble, although his speech was cautious, sometimes disjointed. He was wearing his uniform. The crew had noticed the changes and were grateful, for it was Vladimir who would rendezvous with the lander when it reached the appropriate altitude. The fuel in the main engines of the lander would be spent. The sixteen reaction-control-system rockets would still have several hundred pounds of thrust, but they were to be used for docking maneuvers. They had to rely upon Vladimir in order to make it safely back to the mother ship.

It was clear that Vladimir's rehabilitation had not been entirely successful. He found it difficult to maintain eye contact for any length of time. His eyes often shifted downward. Tatiana felt it was from shame for his outbursts. But perhaps more noticeable were some of the difficulties he still experienced with his speech. He would speak clearly for several minutes, then suddenly start stumbling over his words. It was as if he had forgotten why he was talking. To recover he would either change the subject or terminate the discussion altogether. He often felt uncomfortable during these episodes, and avoided them by keeping his conversations brief and to the point.

He was careful not to speak with Tatiana except when absolutely necessary, and then he would speak to her strictly as a professional. Tatiana responded in the same manner. She did not want to disturb what appeared to be an honest attempt toward recovery. Their differences could wait until she was safely off the planet. Satomura had recommended that she should avoid mentioning Komarov. He was afraid that the very sound of his name spoken from her lips might be disastrous. She suspected that he was right. Satomura had also advised Komarov to keep his communication with Vladimir at a strictly professional level. Komarov did as he was told. Endicott was the only one Satomura permitted to speak freely with Vladimir.

Satomura's tactics appeared to work. During the past week they had been in constant contact with Vladimir, and not once had there been a problem. Satomura knew that he could only control his end of the conversation and that the true danger lay at the other end. For reasons Satomura did not fully understand, which made him even more cautious, Vladimir appeared equally eager to avoid another breakdown.

What motivated Vladimir was an overwhelming fear that Tatiana might die. In the past couple of days it had become an obsession. He was plagued by nightmares that he failed in the docking maneuver and that the lander, running short of fuel, crashed back into the surface. He saw her face pressed against the cold glass of the small portal. The glass was wet from her tears. He knew that the dream was flawed, that the lander would not crash if the docking failed, at least not immediately. It would remain in orbit. The crew might even be able to do an emergency EVA from one ship to the other. But if they were not able to do the EVA, the crew aboard the lander would die when the life-support systems finally failed. This thought horrified him even more than his dream. He had begun to wonder if he was still capable of playing his part in the docking maneuver. He had stopped drinking, cut his hair, and put his uniform back on in an attempt to restore his self-confidence. But he was experiencing symptoms of withdrawal from the alcohol, and this frightened him. The symptoms were not severe, but they were sufficient to dull his reflexes.

Satomura glanced at Vladimir's image, then out the window at the yellow dust clouds that darkened the horizon. He looked at the launch clock. Three minutes and thirty-five seconds to ignition. There was nothing left for him to do but sit and wait and watch the seconds disappear. Tatiana was calling out items from the checklist, and Komarov responded each time with a positive acknowledgment. Satomura thought of the recognition that he would receive back on Earth for having discovered the first extraterrestrial life-form. He would have to isolate himself from the reporters, at least as much as his country would allow. The thought annoyed him. A low growl emanated from his throat, but no one heard the sound, and if they had, they would have simply dismissed it as just another one of his disgruntled moods. He glanced at the clock, then back up at Vladimir.

The young pilot appeared busy. He must be reviewing the burn times for the rendezvous, thought Satomura. He looked at

Vladimir's face more closely. There was something there that unsettled him. At first he could not place it. His appearance, for the most part, appeared normal; a casual observer would not give him a second thought, other, perhaps, than to think that this was a man bent on his work. That was it, thought Satomura. There was an intensity there that he had never seen in Vladimir before. As Satomura pondered its possible significance, he glanced out the window and suddenly realized that this would be his last glimpse of the Martian surface. With only a few seconds remaining, he attempted to take in every detail and stamp what he saw indelibly into his memory. A sense of sadness and regret came over him. He did not want to leave. He felt as if his work had just begun. He knew that he was too old ever to return to Mars and that even if he were not, the radiation he had received from the solar flare on the outbound leg had put an end to his career as an astronaut.

"Thirty seconds to ignition," Tatiana announced.

Komarov's attention was focused entirely on the instrument panel before him and the master arm that ignited the ascent engine. It only had two positions—ON and OFF—and it was his responsibility to make the go, no-go decision. The ascent engine was powered by a mixture of fluorine/oxygen and methane and produced thirty-five thousand pounds of thrust. To reduce the likelihood of a malfunction, the engineers had kept the engine simple. This, however, did not alleviate Komarov's concern, for he had seen firsthand the sand that had managed to work its way into the plug nozzle. They had removed what they could, and he hoped it was sufficient. The *Gagarin* would have to obtain a speed of 17,500 kilometers per hour to reach low-Mars orbit. If the engine fired, that wouldn't be a problem. It would then ignite again to put the lander in the same orbit as the *Druzhba*. These thoughts and their contingencies and the actions he would have to take raced through Komarov's mind as he prepared himself for the piloting of the *Gagarin*.

"Mode control auto," Tatiana said.

Komarov held his breath as he threw the switch.

"Master arm on." To a stranger's ear the tension in his voice would have gone unnoticed, but Satomura jerked around to examine his commander.

"Nine," Tatiana began, "eight . . . seven . . . six . . . five . . . engine arm ascent . . . go!"

They braced themselves for the initial g impact. When the launch clock reached zero seconds remaining, the only sound heard was that of the environmental-control system circulating oxygen. They did not feel any vibrations or hear any rumblings. The *Gagarin* remained deathly silent on the surface. Tatiana dropped her head into her hands.

"The engines have failed to ignite," Komarov said calmly.

Satomura unstrapped his safety harness and stood up, stretching his limbs as if they had been confined by iron shackles. He saw that Komarov was entering commands to shut down the launch sequence. Tatiana had her head cradled in her arms. There was nothing here for him to do.

"I will be in the lab if you require me," he said.

Komarov spun rapidly around and raised a hand as if he were going to order him to stay, but before he spoke his stern expression melted into gloom, and his hand dropped weakly to his side. The futility of his efforts had struck him. His head sank slowly into his shoulders as he nodded his acknowledgment.

———

Carter eased himself into the pilot's seat and gave Nelson a thumbs-up. Behind him and to his left was an empty chair. He gazed at it momentarily, then turned away to look out the small window. The sky was still dark with yellow clouds. The global dust storm had not yet passed. But he was not all that concerned, since the wind speed was well below the abort threshold. He scanned the instrument panel as he chewed a stick of gum, which he had placed in his mouth prior to locking down his helmet.

The launch checklist appeared on the monitor. He read each item out loud, and Nelson responded with a sharp: "Check." When they had finished fifteen minutes later, Carter instructed the computer to initiate the launch sequence. He allowed himself to relax. His remaining responsibility prior to the actual launch was to arm the engines. The computer would handle the rest.

He rested his head against the back of his helmet. He wondered what the Russians were doing and what he would do if he were in their situation. The ascent engine for the *Shepard* was of a different design. It used a different fuel mixture. Nitrogen tetroxide and hydrazine, which burned on contact, eliminating the need for an igniter. Diagnostics performed by the *Druzhba* computer had revealed it was the igniter that had failed. The Russian Space Agency believed that the hard landing might have cracked the insulation that protected the ignition system, and that dust from the local storm shorted the circuitry. The crew would have to dismantle the engine to know for certain, and they did not possess the proper tools or equipment to do that. It was not something that they could fix. Carter then thought of their second trip to the cave. They had managed to capture one of the cephalopod-like creatures in a pressurized container. Satomura had said that it probably would not live for more than a few days. The pressurized container was strapped down inside the airlock.

Carter was stirred from his thoughts by the computer as it announced the commencement of the final sequence. He sat up straight and strapped the safety belt across his waist. A quick glance out the window revealed that the weather conditions had not changed. He watched the monitor as the computer displayed the launch sequence activities.

"Verify rendezvous radar circuit breakers are pulled," Nelson requested.

"Radar rendezvous switch in APP," Carter replied. "The circuits are pulled."

"Abort to abort stage reset."

"Roger, push-button reset." Carter glanced out the window. The wind speed was holding steady at twenty-three kilometers per hour. "Switching to upper-stage batteries."

"Updating guidance telemetry."

"Guidance telemetry received. Mode control is computer-assist. Deadband minimum."

In bright blue characters the computer flashed ONE MINUTE REMAINING across the upper half of the launch screen. The NO-GO light was flashing at him from a bright red window. He closed the window.

"Master arm on," Carter said as he armed the engines for ignition.

"Ten . . . nine . . . eight . . . seven . . . six . . . five . . . engine arm ascent . . . go!"

Carter felt his seat shake as the ascent engine exploded. A smaller set of explosions simultaneously severed the nuts and bolts and hoses that connected the upper and lower stages of the Martian excursion module. The half g Carter felt as the lander started to leave the surface sent an exhilarating rush of adrenaline through his system.

"We have liftoff," he announced. He was watching the artificial horizon displayed by the attitude indicator. If something went wrong, he could assume manual control. He glanced over at the time. Thirty seconds. It took six minutes to reach low-Mars orbit. He could feel the lander shake as the powerful engines propelled them upward. At two minutes and ten seconds, he glanced out the window. They had already flown through the dust clouds, and the sky was a bright pink. He allowed himself to relax.

"The *Shepard* should be in low-Mars orbit in three minutes," he announced calmly.

"Congratulations, *Shepard*," Endicott said. "Now I know what to expect when my heart stops beating."

Carter looked out the window at the departing planet with relief. He was unable to make out the Tharsis volcanoes, or the Valles Marineris canyon, or even the formidable peak of Olympus Mons. The dust was much too thick. He wondered where under the turbulent shroud the Russians were, but the thought quickly strayed. He turned his eyes away from the surface, away from the Russians, and looked up at the thin pink sky. It was rapidly dissipating. It possessed the consistency of a light mist. One by one, stars poked through the mist and flickered like distant candles. Pink vapors faded into ebony, and a band of sparkling beacons appeared before him. It was the Milky Way. The sight sent a warm and pleasing shiver through his body. He was suddenly possessed with an overwhelming desire to return to Earth.

"You're three-point-seven meters off course," Endicott said. "Computer is calculating new trajectory."

"RCS engines at eighty-seven percent. Enough gas left over to do a couple spins around the block."

"Burn sequence coded. Primary burn in seven seconds. Twenty-six minutes to rendezvous."

"Roger," replied Carter. "Good to be back."

The Valley of Death

"**N**ot now," Komarov said tiredly. His thick eyebrows drooped over his eyes like the branches of an old willow tree. He was reviewing the output from the diagnostic tests of the backup lander. Vladimir had boarded the supply ship earlier that morning and had just finished executing the test. There appeared to be a problem with one of the computer chips that interfaced with the reaction-control system.

"I know they left it up to you," Tatiana said.

"I said, not now. We must make preparations."

"He is not fit to fly."

Komarov was staring fixedly at the terminal, and he was determined not to turn around. He did not respond to her remark.

"I said, he is not fit to fly."

"I think differently."

"Bullshit, you think differently. What the hell has gotten into you? Carter is the better pilot."

"How many times do we have to go over this?"

Tatiana could see that Komarov was getting angry and in a way it pleased her. She was finally getting a reaction out of him.

"Why must it be Vladimir?" she persisted.

"Vladimir is perfectly capable of flying the lander."

"He is half-mad with jealousy. There is no telling what he might do. They gave you a choice. You know what that means. They don't think he is up to it."

"I said I disagree."

"What is it? Are you afraid that Carter might actually rescue you? The great Dmitri Fyodorivich Komarov rescued by an American."

Komarov spun around to confront her, his face contorted with fury. He was ugly when he was angry, and as she looked at his expression she wondered what she had ever seen in him. She could tell that he hated her at that moment, and it did not bother her. Any love that she might have felt for him was gone. She blamed him for their predicament, and she wanted him to know that she blamed him. That it was his fault. If it hadn't been for his goddamned ego, they would be safely aboard the *Druzhba*. He should have aborted the landing as soon as the descent tanks had run dry.

"If we can't determine the problem with the lander," he said, "then it doesn't really matter who flies it, does it?"

"What is it that you are afraid of?"

"What are you talking about?"

"It's Carter, isn't it?"

"No it's not," he yelled, and stood up.

She took a step back, because she thought that he might hit her. He had never hit her before, and she had never heard that he had hit a woman, but she was scared for a moment because his muscles were tightening in such a way that he looked as if he were preparing to hit her. She did not say anything.

"The descent is controlled by the computer. It doesn't matter who flies the damn lander. A goddamn monkey could fly it."

"Yes, but Vladimir could decide to do something irrational. He could decide to commit suicide. He is not in his right mind. There is no telling what he might do."

"Don't you think I've considered that?"

"No I don't."

"Look, it's not that simple. There are many different factors that I must take into account. I wasn't given as much of a choice as you might think."

"What do you mean?" Tatiana said, calming down somewhat, seeing that he wasn't going to hit her and that he was about to tell her something that she had not been privy to.

"We must think of the New Republic. It is a matter of national prestige."

"I am not going to die for national prestige."

"No one is going to die. I told you a goddamn monkey could fly the thing."

"Yes, but a monkey is not going to do something stupid, like take control and crash the lander on purpose."

"You need to calm down."

"We're talking about our lives here. How can you stand there and pretend that this doesn't matter? I tell you, Vladimir is not right."

"I said, you need to calm down."

"And you need to come to your senses. I'm sure as hell not going to let your goddamn pride be the cause of our deaths."

"Look, if Carter flies the lander, the lander has to dock at two ships. That is an unnecessary complication. It introduces an additional risk. You've got to admit at least that."

"I've taken that into account," Tatiana replied indignantly. She gathered her breath and was about to continue, but Komarov held up his hand to stop her.

"Look, I've talked to Takashi. I think he may have a valid point. Vladimir is more likely to behave irrationally if we don't let him fly the lander. He is in the *Druzhba* all by himself. If we provoke him, he might do something that we'd all regret."

"Takashi said that?" Tatiana asked, wanting to consider every aspect. She told herself that her primary concern was their safety, and what Satomura had said did seem to make sense. She had seen how Vladimir reacted lately when they did things that disturbed him, and this would certainly disturb him. But she was not yet ready to accept that having Vladimir fly the lander was the safer course. It also annoyed her that Komarov might actually be right.

"Yes he did," Komarov replied.

"What did Takashi say he might do?"

"He didn't actually go into details. But the possibilities should be obvious. Vladimir could do a number of things. He could permanently disable the backup lander, which would leave us stranded on the surface. Or if he is feeling suicidal, he could just take the lander and fly her out into space. God knows where. He could even crash her into the planet."

It seemed to Tatiana that everything Komarov had just said was indeed possible; and that it had been Satomura's idea made it easier to accept. But she was still angry at Komarov. It had not been his idea. He had brought it up as a last resort. His motivation was still his pride. She was certain of that. But she did feel better about Vladimir flying the lander, although she wanted to think about it some more.

"Well, if Takashi thinks it would be more dangerous not to choose Vladimir, then I think I would have to agree with him." She fought back an urge to strike Komarov in the face. He was looking at her with a victorious glint in his eyes. "But you're an asshole, and all of this is still your fault."

"Fifteen seconds to primary burn," Vladimir announced as he scanned the lander's instrument panel. His mind was elsewhere. The diagnostic error with the computer chip that controlled the reaction-control system had turned out to be a false alarm. The error had been caused by a faulty line of code in the diagnostic program, not by the chip. But it had taken them several days to determine that for certain, and it made Vladimir wonder what other faulty lines might be buried within the programs.

Beyond the portal, the supply ship from which he had launched thirty minutes earlier had dwindled to a point and was impossible to distinguish from the many stars that filled the sky. He felt a jolt as the braking engines fired to commence the descent. Mars appeared momentarily, then disappeared as the ship tipped over backwards and plummeted toward the rocky surface. His body began to shake with the g forces. He dug his fingers into the fabric of his chair. A quick glance at the monitor revealed 3.2 g's. A red glow appeared outside the portal as the heat shield of the lander grew hotter. An ionized sheath of atmospheric gases enveloped the ship, severing his communications link. He stared at the fiery blaze for a few moments, then returned his attention to the instruments of the flight-control panel.

The initial stages of the descent were controlled by the computer; Vladimir's role was limited to the red abort button, which would fire the ascent engines and return the lander to low-Mars orbit. But he was determined not to push the abort button, and at one point had even considered dismantling the button altogether. He didn't do it because he was afraid that they might find out and decide he was unfit to fly the lander. He did not know how close they had come to choosing Carter. They had not consulted him, other than to ask a few questions that were not quite to the point, questions he suspected were intended to assay his competence as a pilot. This concerned him and caused him to question his own abilities, but he had managed to convince himself that his government would not subject itself to such an embarrassment unless it absolutely had to. His performance on the simulator was quite good, even though it was not as good as it had been. And he no longer suffered from the physical symptoms of alcohol withdrawal, a problem he had kept to himself but suspected might have been apparent to the others.

He looked at the abort button and thought of Tatiana. He still had the dream. He was terrified that she might die and feared that the dream might be prophetic. He knew that if he failed, she would remain stranded on the planet. Their life-support systems would only last for a few months. Their food would go first. They had pills they could take that would end their lives quickly and painlessly. But he tried not to think about that, even though his mind kept going back to it. He thought by saving her that he would be able to restore their relationship. He was hoping that she would see his actions as heroic. Right now he was her only chance. He wanted to be with her, to hold her in his arms, and to show Komarov that he was the better man, at least in Tatiana's eyes. He had convinced himself that she would never have been unfaithful had they not been separated. And because he himself had been unfaithful, he was able to forgive her. He still suspected that ultimately he was to blame, but he did not possess the courage to tell her about Mariko. His guilt troubled him, and he vaguely hoped that it would not be as great once he had rescued her.

A message indicating the comm link had been reestablished flashed across the screen. Behind Komarov's image, which filled most of the monitor, Vladimir detected movement he imagined to be Tatiana's.

Vladimir could feel his weight shifting toward the bottom of his seat as the lander righted itself. At approximately seven kilometers above the surface the computer deployed a drogue to open the parachutes. The drogue pulled the main chute from its housing. Vladimir felt the gentle tug of the drogue . . . but not the expected, more forceful tug of the main chute. He enlarged a window that displayed data from the exterior sensors. The compartment that had housed the parachutes was empty. The chutes had deployed—there was still a chance they would open. He then glanced at his airspeed. It had not decreased.

A recommendation to abort flashed before him. Komarov's head disappeared from the screen as it fell into his hands and revealed Tatiana grasping for a table. Her skin was pale white. Vladimir realized that this might be his last glimpse of her.

"Abort," Komarov ordered, lifting his head, blocking Tatiana from Vladimir's view.

"There seems to be a problem with the communications link," Vladimir responded. The bastard, he thought, wanting me to abort when he did not do so himself. He pointed a finger at his ear for emphasis.

The computer dropped the likelihood of a successful landing to 66 percent.

"Abort," Komarov repeated more forcefully.

Vladimir pretended not to hear the command.

"Abort, now!" Komarov shouted.

Vladimir did not point at his ear this time. He tried to put Komarov out of his mind as he considered his options. The chutes, he reasoned, were tangled. The computer had just come to the same conclusion and was flashing the message urgently on the screen. His only hope for reaching the surface was to pray the parachutes might miraculously untangle. Suddenly he was afraid he might die. He glanced at the abort button and tightened his grip on the arms of his chair. He could feel the ship shaking. He watched the digits decrease on the counter that now dominated the screen. It gave the seconds remaining in which the abort sequence could be successfully launched. The number fifteen appeared on the screen, then disappeared. If he delayed the abort past the final second, the lander's descent would be too unstable for the ascent engines to fire reliably. At ten seconds Komarov abruptly disappeared from the screen and was replaced by Tatiana.

"Save yourself," she pleaded.

He glanced at the timer. There were seven seconds left.

"Vladimir." Her eyes opened wide with concern as she realized he had not responded to her plea. Reaching out, she touched the screen with the tips of her fingers. "Vladimir," she repeated with a pained look. A watery mist filled her eyes, and she wiped a tear before it was able to roll down her cheek. "Please."

He felt her pain, and that more than anything else made him want to be with her. She seemed fragile. He glanced quickly at the timer. Two seconds.

There was one last desperate option available to him. During his preparation for the rescue, he had performed two simulations where the chutes had failed to open. In the first he aborted as the contingency plan dictated and returned to orbit. In the second, however, he chose to continue the descent. The main parachute finally opened seven seconds beyond the point an abort could be safely performed. He managed to land by using a longer burn on the retro-rockets. He had not sent the results of the second simulation to the Russian Space Agency because he knew that they would have disapproved.

"I must try," he said, pulling his eyes away from Tatiana. He did not know how much time he would have. He figured that it was not much more than seven seconds, since he had barely succeeded with the simulated landing. He punched the override button so the lander would not automatically abort. The event timer was displaying negative seconds. He watched the seconds pass, and when they reached negative seven, he knew that he was going to die. He waited another three seconds before firing the retro-rockets. The ship seemed to lurch backwards, but had only slowed down. He continued the burn until there was no more fuel. The monitor showed that he was still above the veil of dust shrouding the planet. Beads of sweat were rolling down his face and into the collar of his space suit. The ship started to pick up speed again. He looked over at Tatiana. They both knew he had failed.

"Vladimir . . ." she began, then faltered as her words were lost in short gasps for air, and for a moment he thought she was choking. Then she started to cry.

"Forgive me," he said apologetically, as if he had done something terribly wrong. He touched the screen with his fingers, and she did the same.

The ship began to shake more violently as its speed increased. Tatiana was wiping her cheeks with the back of her hands when her image flickered, then disappeared. The circuitry within the communications antenna had fused together. Seconds later the antenna itself was ripped from the outer hull of the lander. Vladimir was attempting to restore the comm link when the lander's primary fuel tank exploded. He was dead before his mind had time to register the blinding flash of light produced by the combustion. The few pieces of the lander that struck the surface formed a small crater nine kilometers from the *Gagarin*.

———

The once plump and rosy cheeks of Dr. Cain were pale white and pasty and resembled the damp flesh characteristic of a fresh corpse. He had requisitioned a cot for his office the night before, shortly after the lander had crashed, but had not managed to find the time to sleep. His hands were wrapped tightly around a steaming cup of black coffee. He was seated at the head of a conference room that contained NASA's elite and was watching the Russians, projected against a wall screen, present their recommendation for a rescue attempt. What bothered Cain was that since the attempt had been Carter's idea, there was no tactful way to back out.

Wearing the wrinkled remnants of a business suit, Emil Levchenko raised his body from his chair and cleared his throat. His face was dominated by large, dark semicircles that extended past the bridge of his nose. They filled the screen like the swirling coins of a hypnotist. The bodies behind Emil shifted out of focus.

"Jesus Christ," muttered Carter as he took another bite of his steak and washed it down with a pint of reconstituted skim milk.

"Please," Endicott admonished.

Nelson walked up behind the two and placed his hands on their shoulders. They were looking up at the monitor on the wall.

"It is my professional and personal opinion," Levchenko began, "that the rescue plan proposed by Lieutenant Colonel Carter presents an acceptable risk. The backup lander for the *Volnost* was designed to last ten years, in the hope that it might be used in future missions. Four years remain. I recommend that Lieutenant Colonel Carter restore power to the supply ship and run diagnostics on the lander. We are not concerned about the power failure for the simple reason that the lander does not require power when it's shut down. The decision to launch can be made once the diagnostics are completed." He paused to observe the reactions of his colleagues. They were nodding in concurrence. Glancing at the monitor, he could see that the Americans did not display the same enthusiasm. "I should probably add that the global dust storm is not a concern. Contrary to several stories that appeared in the press this morning, we are confident that the dust storm had nothing to do with the failure of Vladimir's attempt."

"Thank you." A commanding voice rumbled through the conference room. It belonged to Colonel Leonid Schebalin. He was dressed in a recently pressed uniform, a crisply starched shirt, a tie, also pressed, and a pair of black boots. He was staring fixedly at the camera. His eyes were bloodshot from lack of sleep, but they held a determination that said he would not accept anything less than full cooperation from the Americans.

"Dr. Cain," he said, "the launch window for Earth closes in six days. This gives us more than sufficient time to conduct the rescue. I recommend that we proceed."

Cain wiped his brow with the back of his hand. He knew

that he could not object without good cause. As long as the lander passed diagnostics, it should be capable of the attempt. The reason the lander had been excluded from the backup plan for the joint mission was not the loss of power, but the loss of communications. They could not rely on hardware that they were uncertain about. All the same, Cain was uncomfortable about sending Carter on a lander that had been on ice for six years. It was still dangerous, and everyone knew it, but it seemed he had no other choice. If he did not agree, the three people on the surface would die.

"We here at NASA concur," Dr. Cain said. He had to clear his throat before continuing. "Lieutenant Colonel Carter, you are authorized to proceed with the rescue. An updated contingency plan and a new set of simulations will be appended to this transmission. Good luck."

"Good luck, gentlemen," Schebalin said, and both screens went blank. A message appeared indicating the *Liberty* had received an executable transmission.

Carter turned to face the other two astronauts. He could see that they were looking at him to see how he would react. They appeared uneasy about the decision. This amused him. He was actually excited at the prospect of flying the lander, and having flown many times under circumstances he deemed less favorable, was not all that concerned.

"It looks like we're on," Carter said as he patted his pockets for a stick of gum.

"Docking maneuver complete," Colonel Nelson announced from the monitor on the airlock wall. "Initiating airlock-pressure adjustment."

Carter had always disliked the hardsuit, and his dislike had been significantly reinforced after suffering its discomforts for the past hour. NASA had not allowed him to wear the softsuit because of the loose ice in the supply ship. He released a painful groan as he stretched and banged his limbs against the hard interior of the outfit. He had only managed to get a couple of hours' sleep. He glanced at the toolbox at his feet. His first task was to isolate the fault and restore power to the Russian supply ship. He had spent only a portion of the evening studying the schematics of the electrical subsystem. The greater portion had been spent familiarizing himself with the operation and flight characteristics of the Russian lander. The light above the airlock portal turned from red to green.

"Pressure adjustment complete."

He typed in the command to open the outer hatch. The hatch slid back to reveal the metallic exterior of the hatch to the Russian supply ship. It was pitted with small craters created by micrometeoroids. Cyrillic letters were painted above and below the long red lever. The words were meaningless to Carter. But he knew how the lever worked and pulled down on it as he had done several times before in the simulation. He was surprised at how easily the hatch opened.

He turned on his flashlight and peered into the Russian airlock. It was slightly smaller than the one he was currently standing in. It was also very empty. He had a vivid memory of Vladimir calling out if anyone was home. He shuddered. Having gathered his equipment, he announced his intention to step inside. He proceeded with caution. At the opposite end of the compartment was another hatch, which he knew opened into the central corridor of the supply ship.

He pushed himself in the direction of the hatch. He had viewed Vladimir's video of the ship that morning. Floating, with arms outstretched, he saw the rack upon which Vladimir had hung his MMU. It had made Carter uncomfortable watching Vladimir's film so soon after his death—the perspective from the camera mounted on the cosmonaut's space suit had given Carter the eerie sense of being inside his body. He could hear Vladimir saying that he was going to stow his MMU.

He forced Vladimir and all other ghostly thoughts from his mind. He had to concentrate. When the pressure gauge reached one hundred kilopascals, he grabbed the hatch lever with both hands and pulled it to the open position. It gave easily. The hatch pivoted back on its hinges. He swung the beam of his flashlight into the dark opening and was astonished by what he saw. The long, white corridor was littered with floating objects. Many of them were flashing lights at him. The simulator had not prepared him for that, and he was momentarily confused. He stood his ground as he studied the lights. Several seconds passed before he realized that they were shards of ice from the hydroponic garden. He managed to contain a burst of laughter.

Carter stepped into the corridor. The walls were lined with black Cyrillic letters that gave the corridor a mythical appearance. He could only make out what fell within the circular beam of his flashlight. He directed the beam to the nearest set of letters. The scribble was meaningless to him, but he knew it described the contents of the container. Resisting the temptation to open the drawer, he allowed the beam slowly to travel the length of the corridor. There was no up or down. Each wall was exactly the same. There were several rows of containers, the lines of which converged at the far end. It seemed to Carter that the corridor resembled a mausoleum. He could hear the dull sound of ice striking his suit as he stepped cautiously toward the garden. He stopped and peered into an open drawer that he knew should not be open. It contained small plastic vials. He reached down to touch one. It squished under his finger. He picked up the vial, examined it, and to confirm his suspicions held it out in front of his camera for the others to view.

"What is this?" he asked.

"Vodka," Komarov replied without having to read the label. "You have found Vladimir's hoard."

Carter quietly pocketed several vials. No one questioned him or tried to stop him. He walked to the end of the corridor and looked in upon the hydroponic garden. Inside hung suspended sheets of ice that looked like broken glass. Some of it was glass.

"Holy shit, what a mess. You see this?"

"Be careful, Al."

"In this suit of armor. What, are you crazy? You could take a chain saw to this stuff."

"Just be cautious."

"You may want to use the drawers," suggested Komarov. "But don't—"

"I know," Carter replied, thinking of the maelstrom Vladimir had created. "I just reviewed the tape."

Carter went back to the drawers and pulled one out, dumping its contents into the corridor. Plastic packages joined the floating particles of ice and glass. Carter returned to the portal and examined the ice. He carved a path by slowly waving the drawer back and forth. It took several minutes to reach the far end of the room. He glanced over his shoulder and saw that the path he had cleared was already closing. Before him was a broken container, with a fountain of ice emerging from a hole. He walked past the container and to the wall behind it. The ice was thickest there. A thump sounded inside his helmet.

"What was that?" Nelson demanded.

"Ice, I think," Carter replied.

He pushed aside several clumps of ice and saw the panel to the electrical-control box. It was encased in ice. His first task was to remove the ice from the box. He could feel sweat forming on his forehead, and wanted to wipe it clear. He knew that the box might be live with current from the solar panels that fed it. He checked the metal casing with a voltmeter and the reading was zero. But still the box made him nervous. As a child, he had raced a friend to the top of a telephone pole. His friend had found him unconscious fifty meters from the pole with wisps of smoke rising from his clothes. A block of ice struck the back of his space suit.

He extracted a hammer and a small pick from the toolbox at his feet and began to chip away at the ice. He was careful not to strike so hard that he might damage the box. When he was finished, nearly an hour later, he collected what small chips he could and stored them in a bag so that they would be out of the way.

"Tatiana?" he said.

"Shut down all systems." Her voice was hoarse.

The panel contained a series of breaker switches, each neatly marked in Cyrillic. The primary breaker and several of the other switches were already in the off position. He flipped the remaining switches.

"All systems have been shut down."

"OK, let's take a look behind the panel and see what sort of damage was done."

He pried open the panel with a screwdriver. There was some ice behind the panel, but not nearly as much as there had been on the other side. It would not take long to clear it. He could see that several of the wires had been blackened by the sparks of an electrical short.

"I was expecting worse," Tatiana said. "You should check the incoming circuit from the solar panels for current. It is the thick white cord connected to the top of the box."

"I see it." Carter retrieved the voltmeter and checked the circuit. "I'm getting a reading."

"Good," Tatiana replied. "I want you to remove the ice and repair the damaged wires."

He cautiously followed Tatiana's instructions as he worked, and was watchful of the thick white cord. Removing the ice was not that difficult, since there was not that much of it, but he still had to be careful as it was a good conductor of electricity. In its liquid form it had been the cause of the short. He closed the panel and stared at the main breaker for a moment, wondering if it would actually restore power to the ship. The lives of those on the surface depended upon it. Holding his breath, he threw the breaker and a series of yellow lights lit up. Everything else remained dark. He reached for the switch that controlled the power for the garden and flipped it to the on position. The compartment was suddenly bathed in light from the recessed bulbs in the ceiling. A pair of hands clapped in the background.

"Restoring power," he said, and flipped on the remaining switches. The lights came on in other parts of the ship. He adjusted the thermostat to a couple of degrees below freezing so that the ice would not melt.

"Congratulations, Al," Nelson said. "Let's check out the lander."

Carter lifted the drawer and made for a portal opposite the one he had just entered. He touched the upper of two buttons against the wall next to the portal, and watched the hatch unlock and swing back. He stepped into the small compartment on the other side. To his right there was an antiquated console with a computer display that covered nearly the entire wall, and to his left, a series of drawers similar in color and design to the drawers that lined the main corridor. Directly in front of him was the portal that led to the lander. He walked over to the console. A horizontal row of switches marked in Cyrillic were beneath the display.

"You will want," Komarov said, "to flip the switch on the far left."

Carter did so. Almost immediately the screen above the keyboard flickered, then expanded. Cyrillic appeared, a message of some sort, then an array of icons. He slipped his boots into the foot restraints. Komarov told him what to type. When Komarov said that they were finished, he turned around to verify that the portal to the lander was open. He stepped up to the opening and looked inside. The first thing he noticed was the lighted panels on the ceiling, which meant the lander's electrical subsystem was functioning.

"I'm goin' in."

He rotated his body ninety degrees to orient himself with the lander's floor, then entered the small airlock, which was nearly half the size of its American counterpart. The lander was intended only as a backup: it was to launch in the event of an emergency. Three decapitated space suits hung side by side against the wall. They were red except for the chest plates, which were yellow and bore the Russian flag.

"I'm inside the lander," Carter announced.

"Open the interior hatch," Komarov said, "and proceed to the flight station."

Carter made for the portal at the other end of the airlock and opened it by pressing the upper button. Before him was a man-sized tunnel with a ladder. He grabbed a rung and pulled his weightless body upward. Moments later he emerged inside the flight station. The quarters were cramped. He had to maneuver around a chair and a control panel before he could find room to stand. The equipment that surrounded him was less sophisticated than that of the American lander: the flight console with its control stick and its vast array of switches more closely resembled the consoles he had seen in museums. The keyboard was a late-Japanese model. He plumped himself into the pilot's chair and fingered the knobs and gauges.

"We will start with Checklist Alpha," Komarov said.

Fifteen minutes into Alpha, the growing euphoria abruptly vanished. Carter reset the reluctant switch and flipped it again. The light still did not appear.

"It could be the bulb," he offered hopefully, not fully realizing what system had just failed.

"Check the computer," Komarov urged.

Carter looked desperately at the foreign keyboard. Several

seconds passed in awkward silence before Komarov provided the necessary instructions.

"What does it mean?" Endicott asked.

"One moment please," Komarov said.

A schematic of the plug nozzle appeared on the screen, and even for someone who did not understand Cyrillic the red flashing lines in the small section at the top of the diagram clearly indicated something was wrong with the main fuel line.

"The purge-line check valve," Komarov finally replied. "The valve bleeds excess gas from the main line."

"Could be a malfunction in the sensor?" Carter offered.

"Usually it is," Komarov replied, "but you can't take that chance. You must check it out."

"That may take several days," Carter objected.

"We've got the time," Nelson said.

"OK. But I want to finish the diagnostics first." Carter flipped the switch several more times before moving on to the next test. They would probably have him check the bulb first, he thought. It was the most likely component to fail. He scanned the control panel as he continued his testing and decided that it would only require a screwdriver to dismantle.

"They have named the crater Pavlov," Komarov said to no one in particular. He made the announcement with a false enthusiasm. It stirred little notice.

Satomura was absorbed with a series of calculations he had asked the computer to perform, and the only sign he had heard the remark was a brief pause in his keystrokes. He was thinner than usual, having lost several pounds in the past few days. He leaned forward and placed his head in his hands. Tatiana stopped pacing, and Komarov turned to look at him. They waited for him to speak.

It was two days ago that the purge-line check valve had failed to pass the diagnostic test, and Carter was still unable to determine the cause. They had conducted several tests that seemed to indicate that the valve was fine. The error was believed to be the result of a faulty sensor. But the only way to know for certain was to ignite the engines. The valve itself was inaccessible. The Russian Space Agency and NASA were discussing whether or not the rescue should be attempted and had given themselves a deadline of twelve hours to make the decision.

Lifting his head, Satomura turned to meet their anxious eyes. "At quarter rations, the food will last twenty days," he began bluntly. "We can stretch it to thirty, but we would have to keep physical activity to a minimum. Oxygen and water are not a concern. One hundred and eighty days if we continue to consume at the present rate. The power supply should last one, maybe two years. A shutdown of certain systems could extend that." He stopped to consider how best to proceed without sounding too callous, because what he had to say next was something they would not at first understand. "Certain measures could extend the life of any one individual."

Komarov could feel his heartbeat quicken as he tried to think of measures other than the only one that had occurred to him. He turned to see if Tatiana was having the same thought.

"Certain measures?" she asked slowly.

"A significant discovery has been made," Satomura continued. "Considerable research remains to be conducted. This research would be of the highest scientific value. It could perhaps change man's understanding of life forever."

"Certain measures?" Tatiana repeated, her voice rising to a dangerous pitch.

"It would be painless, of course."

"What would be painless?"

Komarov was rising from his chair as he looked nervously at Tatiana. She was standing absolutely straight, her arms rigid at her side.

"Euthanasia," Satomura said.

"For what purpose?"

"Nutrition—so to speak."

Tatiana's reaction was immediate. She pounced upon Satomura and struck him several times in the face before Komarov wrapped his arms around her. She was pleased to see that she had drawn blood. As Komarov dragged her away, she kicked Satomura squarely in the groin. The scientist fell to the ground, his hands between his legs, his face pale white.

At that awkward moment a high-pitched whistle sounded from the intercoms overhead and a monitor lit up indicating someone on the *Liberty* wanted to open a comm link. The struggle came to an instant halt, and the three forms became rigid. Their eyes were fixed upon the monitor. For several seconds they remained as still as statues, uncertain what to do.

"Release me," Tatiana demanded forcefully.

"First, you must promise not to strike him," Komarov replied.

The whistle sounded again, and once again they turned their heads toward the intruding noise. As before, the request message blinked persistently at them.

"Please, let me go," said Tatiana. Her muscles had relaxed, and she was making an attempt to sound under control.

Komarov looked down at Satomura, who managed to sit up but was still visibly in great pain. "Are you hurt?" he asked, without releasing her. Satomura replied hoarsely that he thought he would survive.

Tightening his grip, Komarov returned his attention to Tatiana. The whistle sounded, but this time they ignored it. Satomura dragged himself outside the range of the camera.

"I'll leave him alone," she assured him.

"You must give me your word."

"You have it."

Although uncertain he could trust her, Komarov relaxed his grip because he did not seem to have any other choice. He could not hold her captive forever. Besides, the Americans would wonder what was wrong. She turned her back with an exaggerated air of defiance and marched out of the cabin. Komarov was concerned about how she was handling Vladimir's death. He could tell that her pain was greater than she let on. It was as if she blamed herself. He brushed the wrinkles from his shirt as he sat down to initiate communications with the *Liberty*. Before opening the link, he glanced at Satomura, who was now against the far wall, curled into an upright fetal position.

"*Gagarin* here," Komarov said, opening the link.

"What the hell happened to you," Carter blurted, then grinned as he divined the embarrassing truth. "Looks like you came out the wrong side of a catfight."

"Never mind what happened to me," Komarov replied sternly. "What is it that you want?"

The screen split in two and Dr. Endicott, with an apologetic nod, appeared on the other half. He appeared nervous and greatly irritated and did not greet Komarov upon seeing him. The Russian was so struck by the unusual behavior that he motioned Satomura to watch from another monitor. With a feeble finger, Satomura reached up to open a window on the screen that still held his earlier calculations. Exhausted by the effort, he leaned back against the wall.

"I have been watching the weather," Endicott said.

"Yes?"

"And there appears to be another dust storm heading your way."

"We are in the midst of a global dust storm," Komarov

replied, even though he already knew what Endicott was about to say. "The entire planet is engulfed in dust. What do you mean another storm is heading our way?"

"Another local storm."

"A local storm?" Komarov repeated with disbelief. "How can that be?"

"The barometric conditions are such that—"

"Never mind. How soon will it arrive?"

"Three hours and forty-seven minutes."

"I see." Komarov paused to consider what this might mean. "Can you land before then?"

"Not enough time," Carter replied. "It will take at least that long to prepare the lander. And then I'd have to wait until the next launch window. I need at least six hours."

"We'll have to wait until the storm passes, then."

"I'm afraid so," Carter replied.

"And how long will that be?"

"Difficult to say," Endicott said. "It could be several days."

"We only have three."

"I know," Carter replied. "I think they'll go for a rescue on the final day, regardless of conditions."

"What makes you so sure?"

"I'm not sure. But what other choice do they have?"

"They could minimize their losses. It is what I would do."

"Nonsense. You'd do the same damn thing that I'd do, and you know it."

"Let us hope the storm subsides."

"Yes," Endicott responded, "that would be best."

Komarov shut down the comm link and turned to say something to Satomura, but hesitated when he saw that Satomura was still crumpled in the corner.

"What do you think?" Komarov said after a while.

"I would not worry," Satomura replied. "He appears determined to rescue you."

Komarov laughed out loud at this, even though he was terribly annoyed at Satomura's smug remark. "Yes, I think you're right," he said.

————————

"Average wind speed?" Carter asked.

"Two hundred and fifty," Satomura replied.

"I can't land in that," Carter said. "How much time?"

"Fifteen minutes are left in the window," Komarov replied.

"Any chance it might calm down?" Carter asked.

"There's always a chance," Satomura said doubtfully.

"Can you upload the map?"

"I'm not sure the software is compatible."

"Give it a try," Carter said. He flipped several of the switches on the panel before him. "I'm going to initiate the launch sequence."

"I cannot permit a launch under these conditions," Nelson said.

"There may be a clearing." Carter waited for Nelson to object, but the radio remained silent. The storm had maintained high winds for three days, and it gave no sign of weakening. "Separation in twenty seconds." A launch clock appeared on the upper half of the computer screen. "L minus thirteen minutes and forty-five seconds."

"I can't permit this," Nelson said.

"Tom, goddamn it, this is our last chance. If I don't pull them off the planet in the next eight hours, they're going to die."

The distant sound of a keyboard was followed by a message on Carter's heads-up display indicating the supply ship had initiated the separation sequence. Carter returned his attention to the Russian lander.

"Two seconds to separation," he announced.

Several small springs gently pushed the lander away from

the supply ship. Carter rotated the lander with small bursts of hydrazine from the reaction-control system.

"You should have the map," Komarov said.

A window appeared on the console to Carter's left. He bent forward, as close to the map as his safety belt would stretch. The map was shaded with different contours that represented different wind speeds, and almost at once Carter spotted what he was looking for.

"I see a possibility," he said. "Take a look at six degrees south, seventy-four degrees west. Winds speeds are less than fifty klicks per hour."

"It's too far," Komarov replied.

"Seventy kilometers max," Carter replied. The contour crossed the tip of a peninsula at the northernmost point of the mesa. The peninsula was long and narrow and looked like a bent index finger.

"There is not enough room to land," Komarov said.

"That's my problem," Carter replied.

"It is less than ten kilometers across at that point."

"I said that's my problem."

"Can the rover make it?" Tatiana asked doubtfully.

There was a pause. "It should be able to. The storm may pose a problem, however. Visibility is less than a few meters."

"For crissakes," Carter interrupted, "this is our last chance. As long as the purge valve checks out, I'm coming down." He looked at the monitor and clicked upon the button that said descent in Russian. He knew the button by its position on the screen. "Initiating descent sequence. L minus nine minutes and counting."

Komarov ordered his crew to prepare for EVA, and several minutes later Nelson broke his silence and wished Carter good luck.

"Ten seconds." Carter kept one eye fixed on the sensors for the main line, his hand hovering over the abort switch. "Five seconds. Four. Three." The sensors indicated the purge valve was operating as it should, and Carter's hand withdrew and wrapped around the controls as he braced himself for the ignition of the main engine. "One."

"I have ignition."

The main engine fired, and the lander began its short descent into the Martian atmosphere. From the monitor on his left, Carter saw a shroud of swirling red dust, then a pink glow that turned red as the gases outside the ship reached several thousand degrees Fahrenheit. The computer displayed a message indicating that the comm link had dropped.

Komarov gripped the outer edges of the monitor as he waited for the link to be reestablished. Over his shoulders peered Tatiana, hardly breathing, her eyes fixed on the screen. A dotted line circling a three-dimensional, rotating globe displayed the path of the lander as it dropped into the Martian atmosphere. It was converging with another, much smaller line that extended to the planet's surface. They could hear the tapping of Nelson's fingers over the intercom.

"Contact in nine seconds," Komarov whispered.

It was a long nine seconds, during which the only motion within the *Gagarin* was from the light of the monitors and a bead of sweat that had formed on Komarov's brow. The monitor flashed brightly.

"How you folks doin' down there?" came the Southern drawl.

"Contact reestablished," Komarov said, not certain how he should reply to Carter's remark. It annoyed him that Carter spoke so casually. "Your trajectory looks good."

"Roger," Carter confirmed. "Eight-point-five kilometers above the surface. Releasing the drogue in four seconds."

Komarov could feel Tatiana's nails dig into his flesh. This was the point at which Vladimir's descent had gone horribly wrong. He reached back to touch her hand.

"Drogue successfully released . . . all three chutes are open . . . I'm coming in."

"Winds holding steady at forty-seven kilometers per hour," Komarov said.

"She's a little bumpy. I can't make out the surface. Will come in using instruments. As long as I don't land on a damn boulder, I should be all right. Extending landing legs."

"Your trajectory looks good."

"Visibility six meters max. Jettisoning chutes in five seconds."

They watched as the speed of the lander increased after the parachutes had been disengaged.

"Experiencing a problem."

"What sort of problem?" Nelson asked over the intercom. There was an eerie silence. The monitor provided no insight. It displayed the same trajectory and the same settings. A frantic shout burst from the intercom. It took several seconds to realize it was Endicott. Finally, Carter's voice, short of breath.

"Ran into some turbulence. Almost lost control."

"Wind speeds holding at forty-seven klicks."

"One-point-nine kilometers from the surface. Firing retrorockets."

Komarov enlarged the window containing the view from Carter's outside cameras. He saw nothing but a red blur. He glanced at a monitor that displayed the conditions outside his own ship. The view was similar, only darker.

"Initiating burn."

A message appeared indicating the lander's rockets had fired, but Komarov waited for Carter to confirm the event before he squeezed Tatiana's hand.

"Thirty seconds to touchdown. The ship is handling well. Still don't see the surface."

"You won't," Komarov said flatly. "Take her down quickly."

The monitor that displayed the view outside the lander went reddish black from the sand kicked up by the retro-rockets. A moment later, the lander's altimeter stopped decreasing. Komarov released Tatiana's hand to point this out.

"I have landed." Carter was unable to fully contain his excitement and spoke in bursts. "A perfect three-point. Thank God she found level ground." They heard the sound of his safety belt being unbuckled, followed by a groan as he lifted himself, the rustling of his softsuit, and then a long silence. "Can't see a damn thing out the window."

"Welcome back," Komarov said.

"Let's hope we can get off this planet," Carter replied. He had dropped his usual cockiness. "What's the latest forecast?"

"The storm is heading your direction," Satomura said. "Gusts are peaking at four hundred kilometers per hour."

"Jesus." For nearly a minute the only sound was that of Carter's heavy breathing. They heard him suck in a large quantity of air and hold it. A full ten seconds passed before he spoke. "How long will it take to get you and your crew over here?"

"Including detours . . . nearly three hours at top speed. But we won't be able to push top speed under these conditions. Six or seven if we're lucky. The rover carries enough fuel to run ten hours at full power."

"That's cutting it pretty damn close."

"We'll be there in six," Komarov replied.

The Final Challenge

A stiff gust of 350 kilometers per hour tugged at Komarov as he descended the ladder. He was wrapped in a sheet cut from the tarpaulin that had protected the *Gagarin*. A rope joined him to Tatiana. When she touched the ground he guided her to the closest leg of the lander, where she instinctively wrapped her arms around the metallic limb. Several minutes later Satomura was at her side.

"Stand upright." Komarov's natural impulse was to shout, but with the sophisticated acoustics of the headset there was only a hint of the fierce howling outside his helmet. He could feel the sand striking the lower half of his softsuit. He took a last look at the *Gagarin*. The undercarriage was barely visible. It was the same reddish color as the surface. He tightened the tarp around his suit.

"Thirty-seven meters northwest," he said, pointing into the cloud of dust. The rover could not be seen. He motioned with his hand, thrusting a finger emphatically forward. "Over there."

Komarov stepped into the cloud and disappeared. Tatiana

and Satomura tightened their grips on the rope and followed quickly behind him. Their eyes were on the ground before their feet, with Komarov glancing upward every few meters to see if the rover had materialized. Seeing mostly dust and sand, they were grateful to find solid ground after each step. At ten meters, a rover-sized mound appeared slightly to their left, and Komarov, correcting his course, made straight for it. A gray tarp covered the rover. They grabbed hold of the ropes that bound the tarp and planted their feet.

"Cut it free!"

They slashed at the ropes with their utility knives. A liberated edge snapped at them. Watchful of the rope, they circled the rover and cut the remaining ties. The tarp lifted into the air, causing them to shrink back. It hovered above their heads, then flapped like a giant manta ray before disappearing into the storm.

"Takashi, I want you in back," Komarov said. The rover, an open-air buggy, was designed to seat two, and in their space suits it was impossible to squeeze three up front. Satomura was to sit upon the aft chassis, where they normally stored equipment and supplies and which was now vacant since they had not planned on using the rover during the final week of their stay. With Tatiana's aid, Satomura lifted himself onto the back of the rover.

"Tie me in," he said, and retracted his helmet turtlelike into the safety of his tarp.

Komarov grinned as the control console lit up, and a green bar extending its full length indicated the batteries were fully charged. He initiated the self-test. Tatiana strapped herself in next to him. To Komarov's relief, all systems were operational. He knew, however, that this would at best be short-lived. The high-gain antenna, Tatiana had predicted, would probably be the first to go, for it was shaped like an inverted umbrella. In these winds she gave it less than ten minutes, which was five minutes longer than Satomura's dire prediction.

They were both wrong. A strong gust snapped off the antenna less than thirty seconds after Komarov had sent the signal to open it. With sinking hearts they watched the antenna tumble across the surface. When it disappeared they glanced at the low-gain, a tin can-like contraption fixed to a short rod. It appeared unaffected by the wind.

"Are you there, Al?" Komarov asked

"Can hear you loud and clear."

"We lost the high-gain."

"Are you surprised?"

Carter's flippant response annoyed Komarov. "We're going to have to reduce navigational traffic."

"Just point that thing northwest and step on it."

They both knew it was not that simple. Because of the low visibility, Komarov would have to rely on computer-generated topographicals to avoid the pits and crevices that lay between him and the backup lander. The onboard computer did not have sufficient storage to hold the data. If the low-gain failed, he would have to reduce his speed to a crawl, which meant they would never make the window. He touched the switch to activate the navigational systems. A top-down view of a three-dimensional map appeared. It contained the entire mesa. He keyed in the coordinates of the lander and requested the optimal path after altering the parameters to favor speed over safety. By the change in Tatiana's breathing, he knew that she was not fully behind this move, but she said nothing.

A tortuous and jagged path appeared between the two landers. He frowned. They would have to travel farther east than he had anticipated. He reduced the safety parameter, and the neon line snapped to a much straighter path. He was pleased with the output, and Tatiana was still quiet. They would arrive with nearly two hours to spare, which was the cushion he figured they needed.

He glanced up at the cones in the dust formed by the rover's headlights. The visibility was ten meters at best. He increased the magnification until only the first fifty meters of the path was displayed on the screen. The rover leapt forward as he pressed down on the accelerator, then bounced seconds later as it hit its first rock.

"Easy," Tatiana cautioned.

"I didn't see it," Komarov explained, as the force of the rover turning pressed her next to him. She grabbed on to the control panel to maintain her balance. "Time is of the essence," he offered in explanation. "You still back there, Takashi?"

"A warning would be appreciated."

He ignored the reply and pressed forward full speed into the storm. The ground was barely visible, and it took his entire concentration to miss the rocks that appeared suddenly before him. Tatiana was watching the navigational screen and gave instructions whenever he veered off course. After a while he slowed down a bit, his nerves on edge. The wind was blowing hard, with gusts as high as four hundred kilometers per hour, which raised the sand and made it even more difficult for him to see.

The rover bounced over a small crevice, and a shrill, pained yelp sounded inside their helmets. Komarov brought the rover to a stop. "What happened?" he inquired, attempting to look back at Satomura.

The impact had driven a collection bag sharply into Satomura's lower back. He had not been allowed to carry the many bags of samples he had adamantly declared were indispensable to his research. His collection had been reduced to the three bags he had secured to his suit and the one he had slipped surreptitiously through its neck, which was now lodged painfully against his lower lumbar.

"Something struck me in the back. You could be more careful."

"How are we doing on time?" Komarov demanded of Tatiana.

"We're ten minutes ahead of schedule."

Komarov surveyed his surroundings, but he was immediately disappointed, for all he could see was swirling dust. The wall of a mountain or the steep drop of a precipice could be less than a meter away, and he would not see it. He decided to proceed at a slower pace. The navigational screen showed that they had traveled thirty kilometers. Clouds of dust blew past him, and, occasionally, as the storm waned, he could make out a boulder in the distance.

"Get the hell out of there!" Carter ordered sharply. "You've got tornadoes forming east of you."

Komarov did not wait to ask questions. He slammed his foot on the accelerator. Tatiana was thrust back into her chair, and Satomura would have flown off the back had he not been tied to the chassis. He yelped in pain.

"Hold on," Komarov shouted belatedly. "How far east?"

"Six hundred meters." They looked to the east, but the dust was too thick for them to see the tornadoes.

"We're never going to make it." Tatiana's voice was filled with despair.

"Shut up," Komarov demanded. "Drop the safety factor to one. I want the fastest route to the lander."

Tatiana punched in the necessary commands. The neon path snapped almost to a straight line, and Komarov turned sharply to follow the new course. The rover was pushing its maximum speed of thirty-nine kilometers per hour. Komarov could feel sweat building on his brow.

"Watch out!" Tatiana shouted.

It was a large boulder, nearly the size of the rover, and it was less than two meters in front of them. Komarov realized that he could not stop in time so he turned the wheel sharply. The front end of the rover swerved past, but the back end lost traction and slammed hard into the rock. Komarov regained control of the rover and continued onward at the same speed, not willing to slow down with the tornadoes so near.

"That was close," he said.

His comment was followed by an unexpected silence. Fearful, he slowed the vehicle and turned to look at Tatiana. To his relief she was still there. But she was not moving, and her head was cocked slightly back, and for a moment he feared she was dead. He was about to stop the rover when he heard her voice.

"Takashi," she whispered.

They both waited, but there was no reply.

"Takashi," she repeated with growing panic, this time much louder.

"Yes?" It was Takashi, and he sounded irritated.

"You frightened me," she said.

"I find that hard to believe. Dmitri is the one driving."

"You better keep moving," Carter warned.

"Where are they now?" Komarov asked, increasing his speed.

"Four hundred meters and heading straight for you," Carter replied. "If you can maintain your present speed, they may just miss you. Whatever you do, don't stop."

"Keep a close lookout," Komarov said tensely.

"I can't see a fucking thing," Tatiana replied.

Komarov drove as quickly as he could. Carter announced that one of the tornadoes had dissipated, but that the other two were still on a direct collision course. It was Satomura who saw them first. The winds had died down somewhat, and for the first time since they emerged from their lander the sky was almost visible. The relative calm was more frightening than the storm itself. At the edge of the storm, visibility now nearly half a kilometer, a swirling tower danced into view. Its path was erratic, but by its increasing size, he knew it was getting closer. Nearly a minute passed before he said anything.

"It is in view," he finally uttered.

Tatiana, who was no longer needed for guidance, turned in her seat to see the tornado. The sight left her speechless.

"How far is it?" Komarov asked.

"Three hundred meters, maybe less," Satomura replied.

"The rover won't go any faster."

Tatiana, pointing in the direction of the tornado, finally managed to speak after several false starts.

"I see the other one," she gasped.

Satomura saw it, too. It was faint, behind the first, but rapidly approaching. The tornadoes grew larger with each passing second. The first tornado was now only two hundred meters away and dominated the sky. "Faster," Tatiana pleaded. It towered over their heads, and had become so large it blocked the other tornado from view. It twisted and twirled and roared, and they could barely hear Carter shouting at them to keep moving. Frozen in place, the tarp at his shoulders, Satomura stared with mouth agape. The tornado closed to fifty meters.

"Oh no," Tatiana said with disbelief.

The second tornado emerged from behind the first and was heading for a point directly in front of them.

"Stop!" she shrieked. She closed her eyes and pressed her head between her knees.

Komarov obeyed the command and turned to see what had provoked Tatiana's outburst. He stopped breathing. His throat went dry. The tips of the tornadoes were twisting madly across the planet's surface, sucking up sand and rock. He witnessed a boulder half the size of the rover disappear and several others being ejected like cannon shot. Instinctively, he wrapped his arms around Tatiana in an attempt to protect her.

The tornado at the rear of the rover turned sharply and headed southward. Satomura felt his bowels loosen as it disappeared into the storm. But the second tornado held its course. At its closest point Komarov closed his eyes and wondered if this was how he was going to die. The tornado passed within fifteen meters of the rover, then continued westward. Carter was asking for their status. Several minutes passed before Komarov replied.

"Any more of those?" he asked apprehensively.

"Nothing on the maps."

"I certainly hope not." He stood up to survey the rover and his surroundings while the winds were weak. Tatiana still had her head in her knees. He placed a comforting hand on her back, but she did not react. He noticed that the low-gain antenna was still attached. "It'll be all right," he said. "Takashi, any damage?"

"None that I can see."

"You holding up all right?" he asked. She did not reply. It sounded as if she were having trouble breathing. "Why don't you switch positions with Takashi."

Her body stiffened, and for a moment he was fearful of what she might do. She lifted her head. Her face was drained of color, her eyes red and filled with tears, her lips trembling.

"Yes," she said. "I could use the rest."

The winds were picking up, and Komarov encouraged them to move quickly. But they had to untie the rope that bound Satomura to the rover, and retie it for Tatiana. By the time Satomura finally managed to sit down next to Komarov, the storm was in full fury.

"Only thirty more kilometers," Komarov informed his new copilot.

Satomura was staring wide-eyed into the storm, wondering how Tatiana had managed to see anything beyond the tips of her fingers.

Satomura's directions were quick and accurate, and were the only words spoken as they made their way across the mesa. Small crevices posed the greatest danger—they were more difficult to make out—and occasionally the rover would strike one and sink unexpectedly with a crash that jarred their spines.

They were approximately four kilometers from the lander when the rover broke down. The diagnostic program was unable to identify the cause. They clambered off to see if they could locate the problem, but did so without much hope. The gears were caked in sand. In many places the sand was so densely packed that they were able to scrape only a small bit away. After fifteen minutes, Komarov declared the effort futile.

"We'll have to go it on foot," he said. The three were huddled in a tight circle, their backs braced against the wind. "It should take us about an hour. Tatiana, I want you in the middle. Any questions?"

They shook their heads. To make for the lander was their only option. Komarov examined them through their darkened helmets. Tatiana's hair was damp and matted against her forehead. Her eyes met his. They were tired, but determined. He could see though that she still blamed him for their predicament. Satomura appeared not to care, and Komarov wondered if he was still upset about his rocks. It took several minutes to secure the rope between them.

"Are you ready?" he asked.

"Yes, of course," Satomura replied.

A silver arrow on Komarov's heads-up display indicated the direction he was to take, and a number under the arrow gave the distance in meters. It was not as informative as the navigational console on the rover, but it was sufficient. He kept his eyes on the ground just before his feet. He moved quickly. The wind, with the exception of the more forceful gusts, was not strong enough to hinder his movement. The danger lay mostly in his inability to make out his surroundings. Occasionally, the rope tied around his waist would pull him back, and he would turn to investigate and would find Tatiana off to one side attempting to regain her balance. She was growing tired. Komarov was the

only one who spoke as they walked, and he did so only to warn
them of a hazard he had spotted. He was glad they were not
heading directly into the wind and wondered how far they
would have made it without the tarps. After two and a half kilometers Tatiana requested that they stop to rest, but Komarov
convinced her to go farther. He was concerned about the time
they had lost.

They walked for another kilometer before he pointed out a
boulder that they could sit behind. They huddled close together
and listened to the sound of their breathing as they considered
the remaining distance. Komarov kept a close eye on the time;
he was going to allow five minutes, no more. He did not like
being on the surface during the storm. He wondered if everyone
would make it to the lander alive. Now that they only had four
hundred meters left, he felt reasonably certain that they would.
He inspected his suit for damage. There was none that he could
see. Then he got up and inspected Tatiana's and Satomura's
suits. They sat exhausted as he scanned their visors for damage.
The two suits appeared to be in good condition. He told them
to keep their tarps tightly wrapped, then sat back down and
watched the time. The sooner they were inside the lander, the
better. He wondered how long they would have to wait for the
winds to die down so that they could launch. He almost wished
that Carter had not made the attempt. At five minutes precisely,
he stood back up.

They had traveled less than fifty meters when Komarov felt
a sharp tug against the rope that was tied around his waist. The
tug pulled him back several steps. He turned around to investigate what had happened, and saw only Satomura. He looked
down at his feet and found Tatiana lying on the surface, her
limbs flung outward.

"Help me," Komarov said.

They bent down and picked her up. She offered some assistance but not enough for them to step back and let her stand on

her own. Komarov pressed up against her visor. Her eyes were glassy. Her head rolled forward and snapped back.

"I lost my footing," she said.

"We'll have to hold up until she recovers."

They guided her to a boulder and sat her down in the shelter behind it. Komarov cursed his luck. He realized he was pushing them too hard. They were only a few hundred meters away. He could ease the pace. He studied her closely as he talked to her. She seemed more angry with herself than anything else, and kept insisting that she was fine. Ten minutes passed before Komarov decided that they could continue. He shortened the rope between them.

"Hold on to me if you have to," Komarov said.

They had regained much of their strength and were eager to continue. Visibility had improved considerably. They could see nearly forty meters, and the sky, still dark, had lightened. This filled them with hope. They made their way across the broken surface at a hurried pace, pressed by the knowledge that the lull in the storm was only temporary. With each step they felt their chances of reaching the lander improved. They engaged in light bantering as they walked. At ninety meters from the lander, they came to an abrupt halt. At their feet there was a crevice that sank into the planet's surface and stretched as far as they could see in either direction. They could barely make out the rocky surface at the far end. The winds were picking up strength.

"What is this?" Komarov demanded.

"A runoff channel," said Satomura, stepping perilously close to the edge to look down into its interior. It was only twenty meters deep, but the descent appeared too dangerous to attempt. He scanned the near wall.

"What are we to do?" Tatiana asked. There was a hint of panic in her voice, and this concerned Komarov because he already had enough to worry about.

"The rover was to go around," Carter broke in.

"And where was the rover to go around?" Komarov asked.

"About two and a half klicks up the north side."

"That would take too long," Komarov said, and stepped closer to the edge. "We'll have to cross here."

"Another location farther—" Satomura was interrupted by a powerful gust. The two men retreated several steps, their tarps flapping hard against the wind.

"Twenty meters north," Satomura said, pointing. "It did not look as steep."

"Are you sure?" Komarov asked. He stared into the storm, but saw only waves of red sand. A gust struck him from the rear and shoved him with unexpected force toward the gully. He managed to regain his footing within inches of the edge. He took several steps back and motioned the others to do the same.

"Twenty meters." Without waiting for Komarov's instruction, Satomura headed in the direction he had pointed. He leapt over a rock and disappeared into the storm. As the rope grew taut, Tatiana realized that she would have to follow. Surprised by Satomura's impulsive act, she looked back at Komarov for guidance. He motioned for her to go.

They found Satomura on all fours looking over the edge of the gully.

"The channel may actually increase the velocity of the wind," he said, glancing up at them.

Komarov peered over the edge and saw that the grade was indeed less steep, but he could only make out the first few meters. The rest was obscured by dust. "I'll go first." He dropped to his hands and knees and motioned Tatiana to do the same. He gripped the edge and lowered himself into the gully. The winds tugged at him, making the descent more difficult than it would have otherwise been. Twice he lost his grip and almost fell. His hands grew tired as he climbed down, and he wondered if Tatiana would be able to make it. When he reached the bottom he called for Tatiana to descend. The wind was much stronger, and he found that it helped to hold on to the rock wall to maintain his balance. He instructed Satomura to keep the rope taut. Several minutes later Tatiana was standing next to him. She appeared worn and tired, but eager. He assisted her to a low, flat boulder, where she lowered herself with a grateful sigh.

"We're almost there," he reassured her. She nodded to indicate she understood, but he had missed the gesture, for his flashlight was already pointing upward at the murky ceiling formed by the storm. "Any time you're ready, Takashi."

Moments later a pair of disembodied boots poked through the ceiling. Satomura proceeded down the gully wall at a quick, almost reckless pace. Breathing hard, he spotted the rock upon which Tatiana was sitting and made directly for it. He sat down next to her. The gully was obscured by fallout from the storm above.

Komarov tightened his grip on his tarp and stepped carefully to the far wall. His pace slackened with disbelief. The wall was nearly vertical, and as far as he could determine, it provided little in footholds or handholds. It would be impossible to scale without the proper climbing gear. He touched the wall as if to make certain it was real. It was smooth and flat, like a rock burnished by the sea. He stepped back from the wall and searched for a place to ascend. Certainly, he thought, there must be a way up. I will send Takashi north and myself south and leave Tatiana here. One of us will find a way. He turned to announce his plan to the others, but hesitated, surprised at how faint they appeared. The dust made it difficult to see anything beyond a meter.

"We will not be able to ascend here," he said.

"Why not?" Tatiana demanded.

"The wall is too steep. There should be a place nearby. Al, anything on the maps?"

"Sorry, but the detail is not that good." They could hear him tapping at the keyboard. "Hold on. There is a spot approximately four hundred meters north of you, but . . ."

"Yes?"

"To get there you'll have to descend into some rather deep terrain."

"How deep?"

"Forty-plus meters."

"Impossible," Komarov replied impatiently. "Anything else?"

Several long seconds passed before Carter responded. "I think you're boxed in."

"What do you mean, boxed in?"

"It sinks rather deep on the south side also. You've got about sixty meters in either direction. After that it's more or less impassable."

"Takashi, I want you to go north. If you find a way up, announce your position and remain there. We'll come to you. I'll go south and do the same. Tanya, you stay here."

"Certainly," Takashi said, rising to his feet.

Komarov looked at Tatiana and with his eyes silently queried if she would be all right. She was grateful for the rest and waved him to go, smiling in case he misunderstood. He pressed her hand in his, then turned southward and disappeared.

The surface, to Komarov's surprise, was relatively free of loose rocks. He supposed they had been washed away by the water that must have once flowed through the channel. He was able to concentrate on the wall, without having to look at the ground every few seconds, and managed to maintain a good pace. The wall, he noted, was uniformly steep and grew higher with nearly every step. The circles his flashlight formed became larger and less distinct. At approximately sixty meters, the point at which Carter had said he would be boxed in, the ground fell away completely. With the red dust drifting into the drop, he could not see more than a dozen meters beyond his feet. He took a step back, fearful that he might fall in. It looked as if it might lead to the molten core of the planet. He had traversed the entire passable length and had not found a point at which they could ascend. For a while he remained silent, waiting, listening for Satomura. Five minutes passed, and he knew Satomura must have reached the end of the northern stretch.

"Takashi, have you found anything?"

"Perhaps," Satomura replied. "If only we had the proper gear."

"Yes?" Komarov prompted him.

"I found a point where we could possibly ascend, approximately thirty meters north of Tatiana. Stripped of my space suit, I could reach the top by hand. The wall, from what I can make out, appears to stand about fifteen meters high. I'm not sure it can be scaled without gear. Have you found anything?"

"Nothing. It only gets worse."

"This will have to do."

"But you said—" Tatiana began.

"We'll need assistance from above, of course," Satomura interrupted. "Al, I assume, that would be you."

"Ah, roger," came the startled response. After several seconds had passed in silence, Carter asked Satomura to confirm his position.

———

With a rope wound around his shoulder and several spikes tucked into his utility bag, Carter cursed lightly as a gust of wind struck him at the portal opening. He turned his back to the wind and descended the ladder. Upon reaching the rocky surface, a neon arrow appeared on his heads-up display, pointing in the direction of the stranded explorers. Visibility was less than a few meters. He could feel the sand striking the bottom half of his tarp. He surveyed what he could of his surroundings, then turned to secure the rope to the ladder.

The digits "87" were suspended just underneath the neon arrow. They represented the number of meters between him and the gully. He wanted to switch his visor to virtual mode, but the computer did not possess sufficient data to build a simulation. He walked at a quick pace, avoiding the boulders as they materialized in front of him. The wind felt like a light breeze, except for the occasional gusts, which pushed at him but did not cause him to lose his footing. When the numeral underneath the arrow reached "5," he dropped to his hands and knees and crawled the remaining distance. He kept the rope taut as he poked his head over the edge. Through a thick haze of dust he saw three beams of light crisscrossing at the bottom of the gully.

"I have visual contact," he said.

The beams lifted in unison and became bright circles. The light caused him to flinch.

"Can you point those damn lights somewhere else."

"Of course," Komarov replied, and the beams quickly turned away. "Have you secured the rope?"

"It is tied to the lander."

"Good. Throw the other end down."

Carter unwrapped the rope and tossed it out toward the center of the gully and watched as the wind caught it and threw it back against the wall, where it slid snakelike toward the three explorers. He fed more rope out and saw the lights converge upon a point, then felt a tug.

"I've got it," Komarov said. "Tanya first."

The lights became frantic. Carter assumed they were preparing Tatiana for the ascent. A moment later the rope grew taut. A light approached the gully wall as Tatiana announced that she was about to begin her climb. After a few minutes her space suit became more distinct. They could all hear her breathing as she struggled upward. At the halfway mark Komarov asked how she was doing. She stopped, gasped something in reply, then resumed her climb. Her helmet was less than a meter away when Carter reached out to grab her raised arm. She was kicking her legs as if the gully were filled with water. For a brief moment he thought that she might fall back in and kept pulling until she was on the ground next to him.

Carter was startled by Tatiana's appearance. Her skin was damp and sallow, and her black hair was plastered to her face. He pointed in the direction of the lander, then at the rope that lay at her feet. She understood immediately and, picking up the rope, vanished behind a wave of dust. When Carter returned to the edge of the gully, Satomura was already making his ascent. A moment later they were shaking hands, and Carter, looking into Satomura's visor, saw that he was exhausted, but grateful. They both reached down to pull Komarov up.

Carter extended his hand, but the cosmonaut knocked it aside and wrapped Carter in a large bear hug. The storm was howling around them. They would have stayed embraced longer had not Satomura broke in to remind them that they were not out of danger yet. As they pulled apart Carter saw a tear on Komarov's cheek. The cosmonaut attempted to say thank you, but he was too choked up to speak. Carter could feel his emotions building. He had not expected this. It was almost over. They held each other at shoulder's length.

"Let's get the hell out of here," Carter said.

The three Martian explorers grabbed the rope and made quickly for the lander.

The launch window grew irretrievably shorter as the seconds flickered briefly and disappeared. The thirty-minute mark had just passed. Their eyes returned to the weather map. The forecast module brought to life the dust that formed the local

storm and moved it east to west across the chasma. The dust
was divided by contoured lines, and in between the lines was a
number that gave the wind speed. One hundred and two was
the smallest number on the map, and that was well south of
their position. They were inside a contour that indicated winds
in excess of two hundred kilometers per hours, with gusts as
high as four hundred. It was the gusts that concerned Carter.
The lander was represented by a small yellow dot, and a dotted
line extending in an arc from the lander plotted the intended
trajectory. Carter was becoming more and more convinced that
the storm was not going to relent.

"Projection for most favorable launch time," Carter demanded.

"Seventeen minutes and thirty-three seconds," Tatiana
replied. "But the wind speed is well out—"

"Disable launch shutdown parameters," Carter interrupted.

The command was received with an uncertain silence as
Tatiana hesitated. She looked to Komarov, but he was absorbed
with the details of the map, and Satomura did not appear to be
listening. Disabling the shutdown parameters meant the lander's computer could not abort the launch without confirmation from the pilot. She looked down at the keys she had to
strike, and was about to enter the instructions when Komarov
finally spoke.

"What will the wind speed be?" he asked.

"Gusts as high as three hundred and sixty kilometers per
hour." The reply was almost instantaneous, the words having
been perched on Tatiana's lips ever since the figure had
appeared on the screen before her. The cabin fell into silence as
Komarov considered the information.

Carter pretended to watch the contours of the storm as they
slid across the monitor. The simulation was deceptively peace-
ful.

Several seconds passed before Komarov turned to Tatiana.

With a stern, taut look he nodded for her to proceed, and, without waiting to see if she would carry out the command, he returned his attention to the map. Tatiana held her breath as she typed the instructions.

"Shutdown parameters have been disabled."

"Starting launch clock," Carter said. "T plus fourteen minutes and fifty-five seconds."

There had been a brief quarrel when Komarov and Carter had entered the command station of the lander. Despite the Russian Space Agency's decision otherwise, Komarov had made for the pilot's chair with the half-formed notion of assuming control. He was seated and reviewing the panels when Carter had appeared on one side of him. Komarov had glanced up to find a gigantic good ol' boy grin. He'd smiled briefly, then returned his attention to the control panels. He was annoyed that Carter had been chosen to fly the lander, particularly since it was a Russian ship. But he could not think of how he could take command, other than by force, which he wasn't prepared to do. Komarov glanced up again and feigned surprise at finding Carter still there.

"Yes?"

The grin grew larger until it was the only feature Komarov could make out.

"She's a fine piece of machinery," Carter said with an unbearable Southern accent. "As soon as you're done admiring her, I'll need to take that seat."

"This is a Russian ship," Komarov declared.

Carter considered the remark as he placed a hand on the back of Komarov's chair. The hand bothered the cosmonaut, but he pretended not to notice in order to conceal his annoyance.

"That she is," Carter agreed amiably. "But she's mine for the time being."

"I am capable of flying her."

"So am I," Carter replied. "And it's my job to get her off this godforsaken planet."

"I am the senior officer here," Komarov said, regretting the remark even as he spoke. He continued with forced authority. "I should be the one flying this ship."

Carter's grin disappeared. "Under any other circumstances I would be happy to step aside. But with all due respect, you're in no shape to fly." Komarov noticed that Carter was not talking directly to his face, but to his outstretched hand.

Komarov looked at his hand and to his horror saw that it was shaking. He tried to stop it, but could not. He placed his hand on his leg and held it there.

"It's the adrenaline," he'd finally said.

"Of course," Carter had agreed as he offered an arm for support.

"Five minutes and counting," Komarov said from the chair he now occupied.

"Propellant tanks are pressurized," Carter announced.

"The wind speeds are dropping," Nelson broke in. "They are down to a hundred and fifty klicks, with gusts around three hundred and forty."

"Actuating valves pressurized," Carter continued. He enlarged the prelaunch screen and proceeded systematically down the list. He glanced at the launch clock. Two minutes remaining. Nelson interrupted to announce that the winds were holding steady.

"Master arm on," Carter said as he armed the engines for ignition. "Commencing final countdown." He scanned the instrument panel to make certain that all systems were go. "Nine . . . eight . . . seven . . . six . . . five . . . engine arm ascent . . . We have liftoff."

The lander was caught immediately by a gust of wind, causing several alarms to sound simultaneously. The interior of the cabin was pulsating red from the light of flashing warning messages. Carter tightened his grip on the controls and provided, mostly from instinct, the slight adjustments permitted him by the computer. At first he feared the lander was not responding. His eyes darted across the cluttered array of readouts and the three active-matrix displays. The displays were arranged in an upside-down triangle at the very center of the flight-deck console. An artificial horizon was bouncing in the lower screen. He glanced up at the narrow window above the console to confirm the horizon was indeed where the display placed it. All he could see was a red blanket of dust. He heard Komarov relaying flight statistics over the roar of the engines. His voice sounded distant. He felt the lander shifting. The simulator had been unable to duplicate the actual movement of the ship. He checked the console to make sure they were still on course.

The ship shuddered as it struggled to correct its trajectory. His grip tightened. He forced the muscles in his hand to relax. He concentrated upon the controls, which were jumping erratically in front of him.

Nearly five minutes had passed, and the pink sky was disintegrating into a black field of stars before Carter realized that Tatiana was congratulating him and that the ship was safely above the storm. But he did not relax his grip until he reached orbit. He wanted to remove his space suit. They still had to rendezvous with the Russian supply ship. He wouldn't be able to remove the suit until they were inside the *Liberty*'s airlock. He glanced at the launch clock. The rendezvous would occur in seventeen minutes. Komarov was out of his chair and slapping him on the back. A pair of arms wrapped around his neck. He decided they belonged to Tatiana, and his suspicion was confirmed moments later when her helmet came crashing against his in what he assumed was meant to be a kiss. Her thick lips opened and closed and Carter was temporarily mesmerized. Everyone was talking at once. He twisted his head, and from the

corner of his eye he saw Satomura, who bowed deeply, then protruded his thumb upward as he had seen the Americans do so
many times before on television. Carter managed to break one
arm free from Tatiana's grip to return the gesture. Satomura
bowed again.

As he was unbuckling his safety belt, Carter noticed the
planet Mars through the narrow window. He stood up and
leaned over the console to look out. The room fell silent as the
others turned their gazes upon the planet. They stared with
wonder and horror at the dust that obscured the surface. The
entire planet was shrouded in dust. Not a single surface feature
could be seen. Carter fell back into his chair and, closing his
eyes, breathed a long sigh of relief.

———————

They were crowded inside the *Liberty*'s airlock, jovial and
exhausted. Trans-Earth injection was not scheduled for another
five hours. Komarov and Carter were bumping into each other
in their efforts to release Tatiana from her space suit. The inner
portal opened, and Nelson and Endicott appeared behind massive grins. There was loud, joyous talk as Nelson grabbed the
new arrivals by the shoulders and shook them as if to make sure
they were real and not just figments of his imagination.
Endicott mentioned the specimen to Satomura and moments
later the two disappeared. The others barely noticed their
departure. Carter sat down on a helmet and rested his head
against the wall behind him.

"Well, I never thought I'd see the day," Komarov blurted in
Carter's direction, "when I'd be thankful for your skills as a
pilot."

"More luck than skill, my friend. I should never have
returned to the surface. It was too friggin' dangerous."

"Well, then, we are fortunate that you were so brave."

"Foolish would be closer to the mark."

"Perhaps. Perhaps not. You, of course, would be the better judge." Komarov laughed at this.

"So why did you do it?" Tatiana asked.

At first Carter did not know what to say. It had been over a year since he had been in the same room with a woman, and her presence excited him. The return flight would take nine months. They were to return together in the *Liberty*, since it would take too long to prepare the *Druzhba* for the inbound leg. Carter tried to remember how many women he had conquered in the time it took to order a drink. He noticed Komarov eyeing him suspiciously, and he understood why Vladimir had been so insanely jealous.

"To aid a lady in distress," Carter said, then grinned broadly as he leaned back.

Tatiana smiled at first, but then her face went pale, and she turned her head away. Carter wondered what was wrong. He looked over at Komarov, who silently mouthed her husband's name, Vladimir. Carter wished that he had responded differently. How could he have forgotten? But he wasn't sure why Tatiana was upset. He figured that it was either because he had invoked Vladimir's memory or because he had been too forward. The latter made him feel like a louse. It was then, for the first time, that he took a close look at the two cosmonauts. Despite their elation at being alive, they did not look all that well. Tatiana's hair was wet and flat and clung in strings against her skin. Her eyes were drawn, and she had lost weight. Komarov did not look much better.

"Is there anything I can get you?" Nelson asked. He, too, had noticed their condition.

"Vodka," roared Komarov.

"I'm afraid we don't have any. As you know, regulations—"

"Actually," Carter interrupted, "there is some aboard the Russian lander."

Nelson hesitated a moment before responding. He then nodded for Carter to get it.

Carter groaned as he stood up, his muscles sore from the past several days. He knew that Nelson could not object to the vodka on any other grounds than the restriction imposed by NASA. The ship had already been prepared for trans-Earth injection, and there was little left for the crew to do. He wondered what he could say to Tatiana to express his condolences at her loss. When he returned, the three explorers were talking about the rescue.

"Courtesy of the *Volnost*," Carter said, extending the two vials. He recalled the cosmonauts who had died on the first attempt, particularly Titov and his last transmission to his wife Valentina. He felt like proposing a toast to the cosmonauts, but decided against it.

"One ounce each," Nelson said. "No more."

"Give me that," Komarov said, taking a vial. He took several gulps, then handed it to Tatiana. She took a sip and smiled. The warm liquor felt good. Carter filled his mouth, swallowed, and almost choked, not having had a drink in over a year. This brought a smirk to Komarov's lips. Nelson took the two vials and placed them inside his shirt so that they would be out of reach. The drinking of the alcohol lifted their spirits.

Komarov began talking about their trek across the mesa. To the mild amusement of the others, Komarov was already embellishing upon the story. Tatiana interrupted several times to give her version of the events. The rover had just broken down when they heard a shout from inside the ship, and for a moment they froze convinced something terrible had happened. They listened, but there was no second cry, and this seemed to confirm their suspicions. Nelson shouted in reply.

"Come quickly to the laboratory," Satomura's voice boomed over the intercom.

"Is anything wrong?" Nelson asked.

"No, no. But hurry. It's the cephalopod."

They moved awkwardly as if they were drunk, colliding with each other while attempting to find solid ground. The corridor that led to the laboratory was only large enough to allow one person to pass at a time. Komarov was in the lead. He realized that this was the first time in several months that he was able to run without a space suit. The largest compartment aboard the lander was three meters in length, and most of that was obstructed. He felt a sense of freedom, and his thoughts turned to Earth. As he slowed down, he noticed that the sounds were different. He did not hear the howling of the storm or the more obtrusive subsystems of the smaller craft. Instead he heard the quiet, steady hum of the oxygen-regeneration system as it gathered carbon dioxide for recycling.

They entered the laboratory and found Satomura sitting with his feet up. He was motioning for them to come forward. Endicott was pacing the room with a thoughtful gait. He stopped when he noticed Komarov and the others behind him. The room was flashing brightly, and the source of the light was the plastic container in the center of the room.

Komarov walked up to the container. He could make out the jellyfish-like creature inside of it. The sight of the creature excited him, and he felt a chill run down his spine.

"What is it doing?" he asked.

"I am surprised that it is still alive," Satomura said. "This is most extraordinary."

"But why is it flashing like that?" Komarov asked.

"It must sense our presence. I suspect that the bright light is to temporarily blind its predators."

"Is it afraid of us, then?" Tatiana asked.

"I'm afraid so," Satomura replied.

Komarov placed his hand on the container, moving slowly so as not to alarm the creature. The presence of his hand seemed to have a calming effect. It was flashing in irregular intervals, and for a moment Komarov actually believed that it was attempting to communicate with him.

Earth

"Control, this is *Explorer*. We have acquired autoland guidance. Glideslope twenty-two degrees." The shuttle commander tightened his grip on the rotational hand controller as he switched to full manual control.

"Roger, out," replied ground control. The voice came in clearly over the intercom.

Carter strained against the restraint straps as he tried to lift himself so that he could look at the heads-up display, which was just beyond the shoulder of the pilot, who was seated directly in front of him. He saw that they were seven and a half miles from the landing field at Edwards Air Force Base, and that they would be landing in eighty-seven seconds. After the zero-g environment of the space station quarantine facility, his body felt as if it were filled with lead. He relaxed back into the chair. It annoyed him that he was not flying the shuttle, but that had never been part of the mission profile. He had to admit that the shuttle commander and the pilot, neither of whom he had met before, appeared to be doing an adequate job. He could see the blue sky of Earth through the shuttle window, and he thought how good it was to be back.

He had not enjoyed the time spent in quarantine. Their exposure to Martian life-forms and to the creature, which had died shortly after they left Mars, had induced the space agencies to quadruple the isolation period. It was feared that the returning crew members might have been carriers of an alien virus. Endicott came down with the flu, which only made matters worse and prolonged their stay. It took three months before the medics finally agreed that the Martian explorers were not harboring anything that might pose a threat to Earth.

"I can't wait to get my feet on solid ground," Carter said.

Nelson looked over at him and grinned. "It has been a long trip."

"The last one for me. I'm sticking to aircraft. Something you can actually fly."

"The last one for all of us, I'm afraid," Endicott said from behind them. "The radiation, you know. We have surpassed the career limit."

"I'll tell them to increase the limit," Komarov bellowed. "They'll let me back up."

"Like hell," Carter said. What bothered Carter was that the Russians might just let the old son of a bitch back up. Ever since the rescue, Komarov had been getting on his nerves. The cosmonaut kept trying to prove that he was the better man, and it seemed to Carter that no matter what they did, it turned into some sort of contest.

Carter strained against the straps again. They were 600 meters from the surface, their airspeed 576 kilometers per hour. The long, flowing plains of the Mojave Desert appeared in the window, and they did not look that much different from those of Mars, except for the occasional cactus bush. Even the sand was red. He was pushed forward, away from his seat, as the commander activated the speed brake.

"Control, this is *Explorer*. Preflare initiated. Over."

"Roger."

"Adjusting glideslope to one-point-five degrees. Over."

The front end of the shuttle lifted, and the Mojave disappeared beneath the panel. The sky was bright blue with tufts of white cirrus, and to Carter it seemed as if he had never seen anything as beautiful. It had been two years, but it seemed like ages.

"Preflare complete. Lowering landing gear. Over."

"Roger, *Explorer*. We confirm that your gear is down."

"Roger. Gear down and locked. Out."

"*Explorer*, main gear at ten meters . . . four meters . . . three meters . . . two . . . one . . . contact."

The shuttle jumped slightly as it struck the ground at 346 kilometers per hour.

"Nosewheel at two meters . . . one . . . contact."

"Roger, out."

The Mojave reappeared, and Carter watched as the commander pushed the speed brake to 100 percent. They were 689 meters from the end of the runway. The commander pumped the pedal for the wheel brakes. The runway did not seem long enough, and the shuttle shook and roared as if it were about to break apart. It came to a stop with nearly sixty meters to spare.

"Wheels stop. Over."

"Roger."

"Control, this is *Explorer*. We are ready for egress."

"Roger, *Explorer*. Proceed with egress."

"Roger, out."

The commander undid his restraint strap and turned around to look at the crew.

"Welcome back to Earth," he said.

The passengers smiled and undid their straps. Carter pushed up front to look out the window. The runway was crowded with people, and there was a podium one hundred meters from the shuttle. A fence held back the people, and FBI and Secret Service Agents, dressed in dark blue suits and sunglasses, were standing on the other side. A long, black limousine, with the presidential insignia on the door and American flags on the hood, was parked near the podium. Several limousines were parked behind it, and he could make out the Russian flag on one of the limousines. A press helicopter was hovering overhead. Scaffolds with cameramen on them were scattered throughout the crowd.

"My, oh, my," said Carter as pulled a stick of gum from his shirt pocket and placed it in his mouth. "We've got one helluva welcoming committee."

Nelson stepped up beside him, and so did Tatiana. He could smell her scent, and he turned to smile, but she did not look at him. She had avoided him the entire trip back, but then she had also avoided Komarov. Carter felt bad now that he had tried to approach her, and that he had been so persistent, and he felt bad that he had not been able to control his desires better. He was certain she blamed herself for Vladimir's death. He could feel someone tapping him on the shoulder. It was Komarov.

"I would like to see," he said.

"Sure."

Carter's legs felt wobbly as he walked between the seats, and he grabbed a seat to support himself. One g would take some getting used to, he thought. Endicott and Satomura were at the back of the shuttle, still seated, engaged in conversation. Carter walked toward them, testing his strength with each step.

"Gentlemen, we have landed," Carter said.

"So we have," Endicott replied. "I was just telling Takashi here that the cellular structure of the life-form was remarkably similar to that of creatures found on Earth."

"Yes," Satomura said, "I suspect some sort of cross-pollination between the planets took place."

"It would explain the similarity," Endicott said. "But I would venture, rather than cross-pollination, that they were seeded, if you will, by an extrasolar source. A shower of comets from another solar system."

"That's all very interesting," Carter interrupted. "But, I believe, we are expected to leave the shuttle."

Endicott looked at Carter in surprise. "Yes, yes, of course." He then continued his discussion with Satomura, as if Carter wasn't standing there. The suggestion of an extrasolar source did not seem congenial to Satomura, for his face was twisted in a scowl, and he was shaking his head.

Carter turned in time to see Komarov place his hand on Tatiana's, and he watched with amusement as she pulled her hand away. She did not look at Komarov, and he did not look at her. A moment later, she turned around and was walking down the aisle toward Carter. But she did not see Carter, even though she was looking directly at him. She was smiling contentedly, and it occurred to Carter that she must be happy about being back home.

The shuttle commander cleared his throat to get the attention of the passengers. "We are to exit in a specific order," he said, and he looked apologetic and slightly embarrassed for having to enforce the formality. "Commander Nelson, you are to go first, followed by Commander Komarov, then Carter, Satomura, Pavlova, and Endicott. A reception vehicle will transport you to the podium."

Carter made his way to the front of the craft. When they were all standing in the proper order, the commander opened the shuttle door, and bright rays of sunlight came shining through. As Carter stepped forward, he held his hands up to his eyes to block the light. The hot Mojave air struck him hard. He took in a breath and nearly gagged. He had been in a temperature-controlled environment for two years, and the sudden, natural, dry, scorching hot air that came blasting through the portal was an unexpected shock to his system. His first instinct was to turn back, but he could feel Satomura pressing against him, and he saw that Komarov was already several feet ahead. He stepped out onto the mobile stairs, and as he did, he heard the cheering of nearly half a million people gathered in the desert around him, and he waved a hand overhead as he held on to a railing.

About the Author

Chris Anderson was born in 1957. Since attending the University of Virginia, he has been employed at a high-tech consulting firm. He currently resides in Leesburg, Virginia, with his wife and two children, where he is at work on a novel about an international hacker organization.

The author can be reached at CKAnderson@sff.net. He maintains a Mars site at http://www.sff.net/people/ckanderson/.